THE COMING WRATH

John K. Reed

MABBUL
Publishing

THE COMING WRATH

This is a work of fiction. Though based on people and events recorded in the book of Genesis, most characters, as well as the places and details of the incidents of this book are products of the author's imagination, are used fictitiously, and not to be construed as real. The reader is invited to compare the contents to the book of Genesis and decide which parts are historical and which are not.

Copyright © 2005 John K. Reed

All rights reserved. No part of this book may be used or reproduced or transmitted in any form or by any means whatsoever without written permission, except in the case of brief quotations in critical articles and reviews. For permission contact Mabbul Publishing at <books@mabbul.com>.

A Mabbul Publishing original book

Mabbul Publishing
Word Ministries
P.O. Box 2717
Evans, GA 30809
www.wordmin.org

ISBN 0-9762860-1-7

Library of Congress Control Number: 2004116820

Cover modified from photograph "Blue Water" © Paul Topp
Song "White Lace" used by permission from Rod & Staff Music ®

Scripture quotations are from The Holy Bible, English Standard Version, copyright © 2001 by Crossway Bibles, a division of Good News Publishers. Used by permission. All rights reserved.

For more information, visit
www.thecomingwrath.com

Acknowledgements

Thanks to the many people who helped in the development and publication of this book. Special thanks go to all the "in-progress" readers and critics. Their valuable comments improved each draft. Special thanks to Chris, Jill, Roger, Virginia, Clark, and Mom. My family provided support, encouragement, and most importantly, lots of love during many long months. Thanks, Rod, for the music and the creative and technical assistance. I am grateful for the support of the board of Word Ministries. Finally, I would like to express my appreciation to John Woodmorappe, whose book *Noah's Ark: A Feasibility Study* lit the fuse which led to this project.

...whatever you do, do all to the glory of God. I Corinthians 10:31

Thanks Diana
for a scenic view of love

THE COMING WRATH

Five and a half centuries had not dimmed her eyes. Light from the westering sun glittered off the ice and snow that mantled the mountains from lofty peaks to the base of the foothills. Rainbows flared as facets of ice caught the shifting afternoon rays. Today, the clouds that usually obscured the mountains had withdrawn and their opaque whiteness had momentarily yielded to a dazzling vista of color and light. Rare slivers of contrasting blackness were scattered among the icy slopes; a reminder that the great stone roots would remain long after snow and ice vanished.

Bare rock had been there first. In the early days of this new age, there had been no ice or snow—only stark grays, blacks, and dark greens, unrelieved by even rich brown soil. Closing her eyes, she could see again the survivors pick their way down the treacherous paths of the mountains and across the bare, dank face of the valley. Again and again they had traveled those paths during those first dark days to salvage what they could for a new life. She shook her head to dispel the remembered fear—the ways were steep and when the ground shook, loose walls of rock had been ever ready to crush the unwary. Many times they had to find new paths up the ever-changing mountain.

But it was not tremors that had ultimately closed the mountain paths. Even in that first year, clouds rode the northwest winds and gathered among the peaks. Storms in the heights raged for days, even weeks. Snow on the mountaintops drove all life down before it. She shivered, remembering her first surprise at its icy touch: so beautiful, yet so lethal. Snow had persisted unmelted in the dim sun after the first winter, and within a few years it had been impossible to ascend the higher peaks. The men tried. But year after year their best efforts marked a steady retreat into the lowlands.

During the second year, the sun had defeated the gloom. But there were other seasons when the sky became dark again; sometimes for a few months, once for four seasons—a time of sickness and death. They learned from bitter experience to store grain against the dark times. For when darkness came, endless cold storms followed and crops would not grow. Snow dusted the lowlands and fell relentlessly in the heights, drifting to incredible depths.

The mountain snow pack grew each year, hardening under its own weight into heavy ice. Then it began to move. Foot by foot, down the steep slopes, into the high valleys, inexorably it carved its way through rock and debris with equal ease. Sometimes cascading in an avalanche of new snow; sometimes slowed by a low ridge; it never ceased to advance. After almost five centuries, it had swallowed the peaks, filled and overflowed the hanging valleys, and forced its way to the very foot of the mountains. There it still hung, its face an ugly unbroken wall, forming the northern scarp of the great valley that paralleled the northwest run of the mountains, looming ever on the boundary of her world with its implied threat of further conquest.

She frowned at that barrier, illuminated by the sun but unlike the clean ice above reflecting no rainbow brilliance. Dirt stained its pitted face and fractures rent its imposing height. There the glacial conquest had finally been thwarted. In spite of an illusion of stillness, the ice kept moving, but the river had held against it. At times, an abrupt, sharp cracking would announce the fall of some great block into the water, commonly when the earth shook. Although the shakings had diminished with the passing years, blocks still cracked and fell, thanks to the relentless work of the sun. Its heat was more destructive to the ice than quakings. Ice melted on the surface, then trickled through hidden crevices to join small streams that emerged from cracks where stone met ice, continually eroding the great glacier. Each trickle of pale green water that escaped from the base of the ice wall and ran down the steep bank of rock and gravel debris ate away at the heart of the ice.

Her eyes tracked the river's course. It ran along the base of the ice wall from far to the northwest, rushing in alternating reaches of rippling green and churning white. It flowed past rocky bars as the current twisted along its rocky bed. In summer it could carry pebbles and boulders with equal ease, but in winter the flow lessened, and water hid beneath a veneer of ice in gentle pools. Spring brought new melt water and once again the water surged to the lowlands. Above the water's edge, long bars of rounded rocks gave way to tangles of green vegetation; thick on the south side, but sparse on the steep north bank below the ice cliffs. Away to the east the river bent south, slowed, widened, and then meandered into the hazy distance. The river was the boundary of her world, separating the ice from the wide green valley—a giant rolling meadow with long grass and thick groves of trees that sloped gently down to the riverbank along small streams.

Looking across the rippling green grass, she felt again her first unexpected joy of long ago at the rapid change from dank rock and sediment to this green paradise. Grass, herb, and tree transformed the waste, and animals soon swarmed the new fields. In only ten seasons she had seen her valley full of birds and small plant-eaters. The larger grass eaters were slower to reproduce, and happily the predators were even slower—the long-legged wolves, large bears, and long-tooth cats. Men drove most of them away, and to everyone's relief the great lizards had quickly migrated south, seeking warm lands.

Now her old eyes caught motion under the trees to her left. Her valley attracted many kinds of animals, and they stayed in strangely mixed company. Herds of deer, sheep, bison, and elk grazed the meadows, and joined the innumerable small animals in avoiding those that preyed upon them. The largest had little fear—an occasional musk ox or solitary mammoth tramped wherever they wished, shy only with men. Although winters brought icy winds from the heights, the mild summers usually provided sufficient forage for all of the animals in the valley and it was only a short journey to the warmer south for those that could not survive the cold.

On the other hand, animals that would have preferred colder climes were trapped, baffled by the impenetrable barriers of mountain and ice. But food was plentiful and there was no reason to try. Some of the animals would soon begin their annual migration south, but today was still summer. The sky was clear above the highest peaks and the sun a welcome sight in the face of the coming winter.

To the circling eagle above her, the westering sun reflected a smaller gleam from a knoll in the green hills on the south side of the valley. Too dull for ice, the light reflected from the white stones of a large square house set on the very edge of a low hill at the south end of the valley. Its walls were thick stone: its steep roofs, mud-covered thatch. A covered portico on the north side of the house was set on the edge of a steep slope, offering a vista across the valley to the river and the mountains beyond. Outbuildings were scattered about and stone walls defined the geometric fields and orchards, mostly to the south of the house. Eagle eyes saw sheep in their fields, but they were well guarded and the great bird was looking for easy prey. It drifted on the high airs over into the edge of sight from the north porch.

She sat at a wooden table by the railing of the porch, an old woman facing memories beyond vision to the north. Before her lay three scrolls of the finest lambskin, and a narrow brush beside a narrow-necked jar of black ink. Two were closed and tied, but the third lay partially unrolled. The hand that lifted the brush was seamed with blue veins, but the delicate structure of the fingers preserved the memory of a well-formed body that now lay well back down the trail of years. White hair was covered by the green hood of a cloak that matched the still-intense eyes, for even the evenings of summer brought a chill wind off the ice. Snow, clouds, and cold would return soon and replace the view with gray gloom, but this day showed the best of summer—warm, mild sunshine on the grassy meadows and groves of the valley, with clear air bringing even the far mountain peaks into sharp focus. Her hand held the brush immobile for a minute hovering over the clean parchment.

A spasm of pain flashed across her face, settling into its familiar sadness. So many lost, but one pair of bright blue eyes remained clear in her mind. The realization, the regret, the myriad of unspoken words contained in those eyes—she saw it all again. Even after so many years and so many lives, those few minutes remained as clear as the air in the heights. What other words might have been said? Her mind had tried them all many times and always to no end but renewed sadness. A tear trickled down the wrinkled cheek. Then she paused, drew a deep breath, set down the brush, and grasped the bottom of the scroll. As she rolled the rods with the ease of long practice, the unstained whiteness gave way to a blur of dry words that sped by until she reached the beginning.

Her hands stopped and gently laid the scroll down upon the table. Under the warm rays of the sun a finger began to trace the story that would be committed to generations that might—no, would—forget as time stretched ahead of them. They ignored the past to their own peril, and too few were willing to stop and consider its vistas in the activity of today and anticipation of tomorrow. Men had scattered into the rich plains to the south centuries ago, and thanks to their lesser lives they considered their settlements, cities, and kingdoms already ancient. As their years shortened, their histories lengthened into grandiose nonsense. Suppressing the truth stranded on the high peaks under the ice, they clung to any alternative, no matter how outrageous. If one were to take their dynastic claims at face value, their ancient kings would have been ruling before the world began! But she had seen many of them born and many more die.

She was the last of the first; a few other elders clung to these northern highlands, but even they were from later generations, and most of them would soon pass into history, too. Shunned by the short-lived southerners, they clung to a past lost in the heights, equally reluctant to intrude into the rapidly changing world in which they were now aliens. Modern men were of a different mind and pushed forward with their eyes south and east. Whether from an attraction of new lands or from revulsion at the truth buried on the peaks, none could say.

Either way, old memories would be lost unless some record was passed down. There were rumors of good men in the south, men of her own line. She hoped that some would preserve her stories, and with them the truth, but truth was so easily lost. She clung to a hope that there must be a few who would remember and heed. She searched back down the corridors of her mind and events came rushing back almost of their own accord. Her beloved husband was dead these two years and she knew that she would soon follow. She was ready—but not today. His death had brought a new clarity to the ancient events in her mind, and for the sake of children not yet born she had labored daily to record them faithfully before they were lost in the dust of her own passage. She had her memories, she had still a few old writings, and she had her gift. What would endure?

Now as the shadow of a passing cloud fell across the scroll, she looked at the first words that she had so carefully scribed long months ago. The lines blurred as ink flowed into memory and she was carried back to a night more than five hundred years before.

Chapter 1
NIGHTMARE

The young woman stood rooted to the beach. The moon's light had grown harsh, revealing her nakedness against the backdrop of pale sand, but terror left no room for shame. Shivering, she saw silver grains of sand jump and roll across her bare feet seeking escape. She trembled, as much from the ground's vibration as from fright, thinking the inanimate sand fortunate to feel no fear. She could not run or even look away, so she watched doom gather on the horizon.

Only moments before she had been at peace, enjoying a salt breeze off silver water. Summer stars shone bright around a full moon and light from heaven rippled in the gentle ruffles of the night swell. Lost in reflection, lulled by the regular rhythm of waves lapping on the shingle, she missed the instant when the surface of the sea imperceptibly began to slip towards the horizon until some hidden sense disturbed her reverie, raising chill bumps on her skin. Only then did she see that the tide had changed, but the water withdrew beyond any ebb she had ever seen. Slowly at first, then with gathering speed it swept out to the edge of sight, the once-silver surface as black and solid as iron. In its path, dark patches of seaweed and grass lay limply against exposed sand that had moments before been seafloor.

Vertigo paralyzed her muscles, but her senses remained aware. She was frozen in time and space, naked and afraid, while the world around her tilted and water spilled out and away with gathering speed. Rather than disappear over the far horizon, it began to mound into a towering wall, a range of liquid mountains at the limit of her sight. Higher and higher it rose, until the sand was laid bare to the foot of that monstrous wall. The stars on the horizon blinked out, swallowed by the rising sea. She distinctly heard each beat of her heart; every throb consumed hours. *How foolish men are to be deceived by the sea; we usually stand above it and are content in that superior position. Yet let it rise above us and we see its awful potential for destruction—its true nature.* She saw it and trembled.

Her chest ached, she remembered to draw breath. Sweat beaded and ran down her face as she struggled to pull air into her chest. But there was none in the deadly stillness around her; it had retreated with the waters. The random motions of a few stranded fish caught the corner of her sight. They glimmered in the gloom, like her unable to move or breathe on the bare sand. With sight that caught every moment, her eyes saw drops of water slowly flying into the air off their silvery scales as they arched their bodies against the night.

Underneath her terror, the cold rationality that usually ruled her knew that the water would fall, swallowing her with all else. Fear screamed to run; the rational coldly noted that it would do no good, even if she could. And the immense, towering sea was hypnotic; her legs refused to move or even to buckle and allow the respite of hiding her face in the sand. So she stood, watched, and saw sea and sky merge, hovering with malignant purpose to bury her in the bowels of the earth. She was nothing before the coming chaos.

As the moment lingered, the rising mass slowed, impossibly high on the horizon, blotting out part of the moon and all the stars below. It stopped and hung there for a lifetime and all was very still. Then the tableau was broken by a gentle wind. It chilled the sweat on her face, gave her one breath, and heralded her last. Just as it had risen, the mountain began to slowly fall. The wind grew in violence, but the roar of the thundering water quickly overwhelmed it.

The black wall rolled forward and down. Whatever giant hand had tilted the earth to create this mountain of destruction now released it to obliterate life and land. But her vision was wrenched from the onrushing wall, for now the seafloor itself was disappearing. The very sands were shaking and slipping down. She could see nothing but a yawning abyss, open at the base of the wave, and rending the ground apart as it rushed towards her even faster than the water. In grotesque symmetry, the sandy floor vanished into the black maw that mirrored the descending water above.

As the rift sped to her, she saw a dull red tinge from some deep fire imparting its bloody light to the oncoming wall. She tensed herself for the fall as the sands beneath her feet joined in the rush into nothingness, just another insignificant speck falling with the sand down into the fire. Her body twisted as she fell and she saw the black waters above crashing down. Drops seemed to slow, stop, and hover just before her vision, as clear and hard as anything she had ever seen, just before blackness blotted out all sensation.

But her mind remained, screaming that she was buried forever under earth, fire, and water in the endless void. Her previous fear was nothing to the claustrophobic panic that now surged through her soul. However, a small corner remained rational. She would not submit. Stubbornly she fought for the use of her limbs, and flailing arms beat at the mountain of water. But they were caught and tangled in the tangible darkness. Despair left her weak, but anger triumphed and she continued to fight. Lifting her head against the weight of the world, she felt air rush into aching lungs as her face pulled away from the pillow. Tangled coverings wrapped around her legs and pinned her left arm against a shuddering body.

Panting and dripping with sweat, familiar shapes in her room swam into focus and the salt air off the ocean brought only its scent. She repressed a gathering scream, but tears were as inevitable as the waters of her dream. She sat up abruptly, simply to prove that she could and wept quietly at the return of the dark vision that had haunted her youth. She had been free for many years, but to what end? The spirit who sent it had desisted just long enough for her youthful terror to evaporate, making its return even more devastating. She hated him and she hated his physical manifestation—the sea.

Though she hated the ocean, she was bound to it. It was the basis of her family's wealth and her father's happiness. From the first, the vision had left her with an enduring dread of the deep. Even when the terror dwindled, a suspicion of the sea and of ships remained firmly implanted, and she sailed with her father as little as possible, persisting only because she loved him. Her involvement in other aspects of his business had come easily, having an aptitude for numbers, reading the heavens, and a mind for detail. Even though her utility demanded a minimal commitment to the sea and its terrors, she gave it grudgingly.

A crescent moon was visible through her open window; the night was only half done. She climbed off her bed and forced herself to examine the contents of the room in its dim light, touching each familiar surface. *They are real, it is not. They are real, it is not.* But in the moonlight, it was difficult to be fully convinced. What was real? The shadowy room or the vivid image seared into her mind? Was the sea still within its bounds? Shaking, she forced herself to the balcony, grimaced, and looked out over the beach. All looked as it had for the past fifty years. The veil that separated what she saw with her eyes from what she had seen in her mind had been drawn.

Ironically, the haunting vision was rooted in past happiness. When she was but fifteen years her great-grandfather, Methuselah, had come to her home for several months. Although a young child, he treated her with an affable deference, and within a few days she knew that she had found a friend. She was too young to see the value of those days, the beginning of what would be one of her great loves, but he did not seem to mind. As the days passed, her childish affection deepened. He encouraged it, giving her time and attention even at the expense her parents and brothers. By the end of the first week, she had worked up the courage to tell him that he was her best friend. Expecting rejection or condescension, he had instead smiled and asked her a curious question. "Do you trust me, Madrazi?"

"Of course, Granpapa!"

"Good! Do not forget. Best friends hold trust even when apart."

She had assured him that she would remain true and, nodding in his knowing way, he just smiled. Her young heart was full. He had not rejected her nor had he laughed; he had treated her as a peer, not a child. Her excitement continued all during his visit with the added spice of her brothers' jealousy. Instead of hours spent with the men in the shipyard or shops, he stayed with her, just walking on the beach or in the hills, telling amazing stories about people he had known over the span of his life.

He even spoke of the original parents, now long dead. They seemed quite distant to her, but the old man had known them and claimed their friendship. "I wish you could have seen his face, Madrazi," he sighed as they sat watching the waves. "Even in his last years, it was unlike any other. He did not seem old to me; the lines of age were subtle. To look into his eyes was to see joy, sadness, wisdom, and regret. He knew perfection and its loss, and lived patiently with guilt, ruin, and naught but a vague promise... But a sure promise," he murmured. "A sure promise."

He was quiet for a moment, and Madrazi, without understanding, but with a friend's empathy, remained still. He turned back to her and sighed. "But there was about him something else that I have seen only in one other man. At times you could see a light that seemed to well up in his eyes. Maybe I imagined it, but I found it easy to understand—what other man can say that he has looked on the face of the Creator?"

During those days, Madrazi had learned much that was new. She had been well schooled by her parents and knew many ancient stories and songs, but he opened doors that she had never suspected. His stories were anchored to a theme; war between the lines of Cain and Seth, her own ancestor. Madrazi said nothing. She preferred her father's wisdom in this; he accepted all men as they were, some good, all flawed, and each defined on his own terms. Where her new friend saw antipathy between two lines that transcended individual lives, her father would have shrugged his broad shoulders and said that there were many ways to measure a man. "What a man does with his life counts for more than his ancestors," he always said. Was he not living proof of this?

Sitting one day on the crown of one of the green hills behind the house, she asked her great-grandfather of his present life. She drew back as he stood suddenly tall and proud and spread his arms to the sea. "My girl, I am a lord of a great city, built with the strength of my own hands." She stared at him, catching her first adult glimpse of the man who stood before her. After a moment, he seemed to shrink again into her beloved Granpapa, and burst out laughing. "No one is ever as important as they think, Madrazi. But I live in the city that I worked hard to raise from the ground, and I called it after the name of my first-born son, Lamech. It is a growing, prosperous town, but men are inclined to forget the past during times of ease and wealth. I am old, and there are many who probably wish that I was already in the halls of my fathers. But I remain."

At her urging, he told her of that city, for she had always lived in this lonely seaside fastness. Her travels with her father prepared her to picture the high stone walls overlooking the sea and guarding the great buildings within. She was eager to hear more, until he mentioned his present home outside of the town. It was a large farm on the edge of the Great Forest. Once he began to talk of the dim depths beneath giant trees, hidden meadows of flowers beside bubbling streams of clear fresh water, and the soft sounds of unseen life, Madrazi forgot her desire of the town. His descriptions of the forest touched something deep inside her and she suddenly found a great desire to walk those woods and hear the songs of its birds.

Her great-grandfather's favorite tale had been about his own father, Enoch, who mysteriously disappeared long years ago. It was a story that she did not like, finding it disquieting. He claimed that Enoch had been taken to the dwellings of the Creator without seeing death. Madrazi had never been sure where that was, whether it was on the sun, moon, some far-off star, or whether he chose to inhabit some far corner of the Earth, but she did not want to show ignorance, so she said little and listened. She asked him instead what Enoch was like.

"He was a good man who hated evil, and thus made himself hateful to evil men. So he pursued the company of the Creator over the company of men. In his last days he began to manifest the light I saw in Adam. Finally, he went out one morning and did not return. No one could find him, though we searched for many days. Some years later, in a dream, I saw him standing in the midst of his fathers." Madrazi stared at him uncomfortably, but the old man eyes were lost in the distant horizon and he did not notice.

But he was her friend and even when he told it again, Madrazi hid her skepticism and listened politely. She had heard her father and brothers talking about Enoch before. He was the topic of many unusual family stories, the most common speculating that he had been struck in the prime of life by some disease, or had wandered off into the wilderness to an unfortunate death. She would never hurt her new friend, so she said nothing. She loved him too much. She realized that the only cloud hovering over their friendship was her inability to understand his enthusiasm for the Creator. He always spoke of Him as being present, like a specter at his shoulder. But Madrazi thought Him far away and unconcerned with the ways of ordinary men. She could not understand how Enoch or any other man could actually talk with Him. The Creator was certainly not concerned with her life, and even if He was, He could not be displeased as long as she conformed to the customs of proper society, was honest, and showed proper respect for others.

But one small story could not dim their growing friendship. Many pleasant days passed but the hour came almost as a surprise when her Granpapa bade her farewell. She held her tears until his party vanished out of sight, and then wandered off to keep them from the others. Though her tears only lasted an hour, her heart was heavy long after they were exhausted. It had taken his absence to discover her loneliness, and she intensely missed his companionship, his stories, and his love. There had been an indefinable joy in his presence that departed with him.

That short period of happiness cost her dearly for many years. Perhaps it was the sadness of his leaving that had brought the dream, or perhaps it was stirred by his tales. But whatever the reason, the very night he departed she first saw the destroying sea and endless abyss. She awoke screaming and could not be comforted by her servant, Jahaz. Though only a hint of more vivid visitations to come, she knew deep within that it was more than a dream; it was a certain premonition of death, and in the dark, wakeful hours before dawn, she knew the exodus of childhood innocence.

The next morning, her father and brothers laughed away her fevered descriptions. Their mirth roused her anger, but even that could not overcome fear. That day and the next she ate little and avoided the beach. Finally her mother took her hand, led her to the shore, and walked up and down by her side. Seeing her daughter cringe at each crash of the surf, she spoke soothing words and eventually drove away the fear.

Once again the dream returned. Once again Madrazi was cast into the depths of despair. Once again her mother defeated the terror of the vision. So began a battle; one that drew mother and daughter together over those months. Madrazi even began to believe that her mother would prevail. But battle had just been joined. Her nightmare returned a seventh time, vivid and interminable. Madrazi awoke and then finally fell back into a troubled sleep that lasted until she was awakened by a commotion outside her window. Hearing screams of women and men's agitated voices, she raced down the stairs and out the door.

She was confronted by chaos; a scene that remained indelibly imprinted on her mind. A knot of shouting men and wailing women were gathered at the top of the shingle. She stumbled forward, and amid the babble, she heard the sobbed out words of her mother's maid. Disaster had befallen. Before anyone could catch her, Madrazi felt her legs give way as she finally understood; the sea had taken her mother. Her father's booming voice cut through the commotion. He silenced everyone, ordered a servant to see to his daughter, and forced the story out of the wailing maid. Madrazi remained slumped on the sand, but heard the fragments of words come together into a coherent story. Her mother had been swimming that morning in the surf. The maid had dozed on the sand and later woke to the unbroken surface of the water. Several men frantically ran to the water and dove beneath the waves while others raced away to bring boats around the headland to search beyond the breakers, but nothing was found. Several of the more practical women stifled their tears and helped the young girl up to her bed, where she lay tasting despair in the evil vision's triumph, magnified in stealing her only defense—her mother's love.

How easily sorrow is multiplied and magnified by fear! Over the blur of the following days the young girl thought it best to end her own life and cheat the victor of her haunted nights. How could she? She would not give herself to the sea as her mother had. She began to see the sea itself as her vital enemy. After all, it possessed motion, change, and power—and behind the vision was malevolent personality. What more was needed to be called living?

Morbid and weak thinking could only go so far with Madrazi. Her mind rebelled at both, rescued by the iron-willed stubbornness that was a legacy of her father. Love, innocence, and happiness had been ripped from her life, but she could still hate. A curtain of cold passion descended over her heart, shaping it for years to come. Certainly she had an antagonist worthy of her animosity. She would live unconquered and so conquer herself. She clung to that and found that hate focused her mind away from fear and weakness. She resumed the routine of her life, filling each activity with new purpose and seeing each sunrise as a new victory.

It was a lonely fight. She knew her brothers would not understand. Kindly enough, they were caught up in their own lives imbued with their father's spirit of adventure and eager to make their own mark. Once, and only once, she tried to convince her father of a nexus between her vision and her mother's death. He listened politely to the practiced speech but in the end rejected it. "You are all I have left of her," he had said as he held her, "and I do not want to lose you to such foolishness. Your mother drowned, and the sea has taken hundreds before her. If you insist on trying to find some hidden meaning in your grief, it will lead to a bad end. Put it aside and live your own life. That is what you mother would want. What will you do when the sea takes me? It will not be from any omen. I will perish on the sea because it is perilous and I will continue to brave it as long as I am able. I would sooner die at sea seeking new lands than to live forever holed up here."

Afterwards, he never discussed his wife's death, only rarely the good times they had shared. He was a man who looked forward, not back, and it seemed such a practical way to live that Madrazi found herself becoming more like him and less like her mother as the years went by. A happy childhood, a loving mother; that road had been left behind. She had found courage in hatred, but also found that it could not be sustained. As if sensing that its work was complete for a time, the vision came less frequently and her memory of its fear was clouded.

As the conflict faded, Madrazi found new direction for her life in her father's business. Even as a child she had shown a ready mind for numbers and an eye for detail. Those were the twin pillars of success in trade, and the passage from child to woman went unnoticed as she immersed herself in work. There came a day when she knew her father's business almost as well as he did. Of course she could not deal directly with any of his partners or contacts, but out of their sight she wrote many letters and contracts to be signed by Pomorolac's hand. In time, he ceased to offer corrections, confident in her expanding ability.

Always desiring more of his life, she haunted the warehouses, docks, and shipyard, and discovered ready talents for ship design and in reading the heavens. Many an evening was spent arguing with her father about how to use the signs of the day and night skies to navigate the uncharted vastness of the oceans. Had she been a man, she would have been captain of her own ship despite her youth.

Time and work covered the pain of her loss and the fearful child hardened into a cold woman whose passion was reserved for her father's happiness and success. His approval was all and the memory of her mother faded. It was enough that her father was happy. She truly became his daughter, displaying more each day of his strength and a will. She even forced herself to travel upon the sea, hiding her remaining fear behind an aloof exterior. Her father's men admired her, but the women shook their heads behind her back, seeing everything that was her mother vanish like fog in the sunlight. She knew their hidden mutterings and disdained them.

Until this night, she had thought herself free and strong; the vision had been absent for almost twenty years. But a few minutes of sleep had proven her wrong. Bitterly she realized that time and activity had dimmed the terror. Her vaunted strength had proven nothing more than a fragile forgetfulness, and fear was multiplied by its return. She recoiled from the vividness with which it had so easily violated the deepest recesses of her adult mind and for the first time in years, searched within for the comforting memory of her mother. Surprisingly, she found that door unlocked; she remembered much that had been shut away for years.

As she lay back cautiously on top of her blankets, she wondered aloud, "Why tonight?" That very day had been her fiftieth birthday, and she was now of an acceptable age to marry. Her wedding had been arranged ten years earlier, probably, she thought, at the instigation of her great-grandfather. The invitation and betrothal gift had come from Noah on behalf of his son, Shem, but the offer had also borne the seal and stamp of Methuselah. Madrazi was sure that they had been added for her benefit. It was easy, therefore, to give eager assent.

Her father had been convinced for other reasons. Even for a man of his wealth, the betrothal gift had been princely. There was gold molded into intricate shapes with inlaid agate and jasper, or woven as fine wire into cunning designs of animals and birds. Intricate carvings decorated small casks of teak and cedar, set with golden hinges and filled with rare herbs and spices. They admired the beautifully preserved animal skins and feathers of birds found only in the Great Forest.

But her father had sailed far upon the seas and dealt with wealthy men in a score of cities. He was not easily impressed and always one to want certainty in his dealings. For several months he entertained the servants of Noah, while quietly seeking recent knowledge of the family. Through his many contacts, he gathered information and sifted through the various accounts.

He confided his news to his daughter, as was his habit. "Lamech has grown into a large town, ruled by a council of five elders. The three leading men of the council are Methuselah, Lamech, and Noah. Although he still judges, Noah no longer lives in the town. As it grew in prosperity, he evidently became restless, and started a settlement in the wilderness at the edge of the Great Forest. This settlement is not yet a town, but is reputed to be a strange and wonderful place where Noah seeks to understand plants and animals. He is well known among those people for his knowledge and it is rumored that he is adept at some of the lost gifts."

He paused to let her absorb the information and then continued, "There are rumors, too, that he has alienated some of the people of Lamech."

Pomorolac laughed sardonically. "Are not all men who pursue their own way considered strange by others?" It was certainly true of him, and yet Madrazi had enjoyed a better life with him than she would have in a city. Her father clearly admired Noah's independence, and it was this last report that assured him that she would be happy in that family and garnered his consent.

"I will be sorry to lose you, Madrazi," he had sighed. "Your brothers are good sailors, but you already understand the business of trade better than they ever will. I will have to work twice as hard now. But if you are happy with young Shem, then I suppose that the prize is worth the price."

Madrazi had already made up her mind. Were not wealth and position two strong foundations for building a good life? Was not her favorite relative, her avowed friend, a cause of the proposal? Now she understood his insight into trust between friends in spite of time and distance. She had greater confidence in Methuselah's love than in rumors from her father's associates. She was young. She knew that she possessed beauty, and though many thought she lacked warmth or passion, she knew better. She was a woman, but one who earned respect from her father and his men by a shell of cold competence.

So Pomorolac had sent a proper reply along with gifts of garnet, ruby, and sapphire found in the nearby hills and spices that he knew were not available in Lamech. In his reply he specified the day of their arrival during the first week of the month following Madrazi's fiftieth birthday, a subtle boast of his competence. He then sent the servants of Noah back to Lamech in one of his ships, a gift of many weeks from the overland journey.

Madrazi was pleased by these arrangements until she discovered that he had successfully hidden his own. For when the proper documents had been exchanged and ratified by the council of Lamech (for her husband was one who would be considered for the council), her father had taken a new wife. She was a woman from the city of Nin, Peniah, the widow of one of his trading partners. A strong woman, she was determined to exercise her will in Madrazi's house and over Madrazi's father.

Almost as soon as she arrived, she took over much of the work and proved able in her involvement in the accounts, the ventures of the ships, and the profits. The two women were natural adversaries, both selfish for one man's affection and both skilled in winning it. They sparred for a year before Madrazi grew tired of the game, only to discover that it was no game to Peniah, and she learned what the jealousy and bitterness of another woman could mean. But both were ruled by the will of Pomorolac and observed rigid rules of courtesy that kept their animosity from disrupting the household. It was hard to determine which woman was happier that Madrazi's years in the seaside home were numbered.

Madrazi soon perceived that Peniah loved the profits, not the adventure of earning them, and that she avoided the men and the ships. So Madrazi spent many of her hours at the shipyard arguing with the builders about the number or shape of sails, ratios between the heights of masts and the lengths of hulls, or the shape of the hulls under water and above. When not at the shipyard, she could be found mapping the cycles of the heavens, spending many evenings upon the high hill behind the house recording the mysterious passages of the stars. During those solitary times, she often wondered about Shem. Would he be like her father? Would he let her stand beside him and use her strength with his, or would he want an ornament to keep his house and keep her silence?

Between work, dreams of a new life, and her efforts to avoid Peniah, the last ten years had passed in relative peace. The nightmare of her youth and her mother's death both became distant memories. It was the unexpected assault of the dream after so many years that shook her so now. How could it be that an omen of death and destruction should haunt her on this night when the anticipation of happiness should prevent any sadness? Was it a sign for her? For her father? Her brothers? Or for them all? Or was it a warning against tomorrow's journey? Madrazi breathed a sigh of relief that they were taking the overland route to her new home. After all, how could the sea destroy her if she was nowhere near it?

Besides, she had to go. Tomorrow was the beginning of many journeys. Travel to a new home was only the beginning. She would soon be a woman with her own house, no longer the dependent daughter in a home that now belonged to another. Her husband was a stranger, but many women took husbands in this fashion and made good homes. Besides, he was of the line of her fathers. They were both great-grandchildren of her favorite relative. Noah was wealthy and Shem enjoyed standing—his father, grandfather, and great-grandfather were the leading elders of his city. She was strong, intelligent, and could manage wealth. How could their union fail to bring happiness? But now? Was the vision's return a sign that some lurking doom? She did not know. Questions raced around her head while shadows crawled around the room. Some time later, the thoughts and shadows merged into an uneasy sleep.

Madrazi woke to a pounding in her head. The pounding continued. It stopped, started again, and as the haze of sleep cleared, she realized that it was coming from her door. "What do you want, Jahaz?" Only her servant would be beating on the door at this time of day.

Her voice came clearly through the wood, "Madrazi, the hour is late, and the morning meal is prepared. Your father is waiting for you."

Madrazi came fully awake, stretched herself upon the bed and replied, "I am up, Jahaz. Go and tell Father that I will be down as soon as I dress."

She rose to her feet, glad that the shadowy illusion of the night was gone, replaced by sharp edges and hard surfaces. Morning had scattered the ethereal moon shadows and their fears. The sun was already above the horizon as she walked to the window and its rising brought a gift of light across the quiet waters, taming the sea. Fear shrunk before light and was always easier to lock away in the morning. Quickly she washed, not wanting to keep her father waiting. They had all learned at a young age that he measured part of his wealth in time and did not take kindly to its waste.

Pleasing her father sprang easily from her love and admiration. He believed that a man was what he made of himself, and thus valued skill and persistence in work, independence in thought and action, courage to search out knowledge of far-flung places, and the ability to use that knowledge for profit. Those very traits that shaped her youth had marked his as well. His restless spirit had led him away from his father's home many years ago. She knew little of his family, and suspected that his father, the third son of Methuselah, had disowned him after he left, for there was no communication with his family except for Methuselah's visit years ago. Madrazi's scant knowledge of those days had come from her mother's stories—stories she remembered clearly.

As a young man, Pomorolac grew restless; the regular cycles of growing crops or tending sheep and cattle held little appeal. Instead, he yearned for travel. Against his father's will, he left home, finding work in the caravans. It was no life for a well-born young man, but he endured and learned the business of trade from its masters. They taught him where cities had been built, what people in those cities wanted, and how to make a profit from them. He learned that trade could be a highly competitive venture when a ship moved the same goods to their destination ahead of his caravan. A man of quick decision, he left the caravan and begged a position on the ship. A natural leader, he was soon its captain. Ambitious, he soon was the owner of his own. Madrazi had heard stories of his early voyages from his oldest crewmen and remained amazed at his early travels. He had spent months at sea in boats ill suited for the open ocean.

As men spread across the face of the earth, Pomorolac and a very few others discovered that they could venture farther and faster in a ship than overland competitors, and found the profits worth the risk. Many of the most prosperous towns had been founded beside the sea. Men were eager to take advantage of its bounty, but ever cautious to tread its unknown paths. Where others saw only waves on every horizon and trembled in fear, Pomorolac saw beyond the horizon and trembled with the anticipation of yet another discovery. The ability to build and sail ships was still new and even rarer was the skill to make a vessel that could survive for weeks upon the open ocean. Few wanted to risk their lives to try, but there were always the few bold ones who did, and some even settled lands that could only be reached by ship.

Among those few, Pomorolac set himself apart by discovering that the winds and water formed paths that would carry a ship predictably from one place to another. He had experienced that flash of insight that comes to few men and then directs their lives. He had reasoned that as the caravans traveled over well-defined paths on land, ships could do the same by sea. Caravan travel depended partly on the ability to read the heavens; sea travel did too, but with less room for error. His inspiration matured until, after many voyages, he possessed maps that showed his secret paths across many waters and the corresponding positions of the stars. Madrazi was one of the privileged few that had ever glimpsed them.

Over time, her father had attracted others who knew the sea and ships. A master of shipbuilding and sailing, he was renowned as a great captain and trader who voyaged far in search of metal ores, exotic fabrics, woods, and spices. His secrets were safe with his crews; he treated them well, and traded wealth and adventure for loyalty. As a result he now had a band of almost four hundred subordinates increasing his wealth as they did their own. Before Madrazi had been born, they had moved to this seaside fastness. The harbor was small, but it sat at the confluence of his major trade routes. Like a spider in a web, her father sat in the center of his business and directed its growing success. He had established trade between many cities and his eight ships were now sent out under the command of her two brothers and a few trusted men.

Most of the men with families lived a few hours to the south in a small town that had grown up around another small harbor. Those without families lived in quarters next to the shipyard at the main harbor below the family house. However, there were seldom many about; the ships were kept at sea amassing wealth. Although Madrazi and her mother had yearned at times for the society of the towns, they both admitted that their freedom in this remote home was better than town life and its restrictions.

As she stared out upon the morning, Madrazi wondered if her father had achieved happiness. He seemed satisfied, but was that an illusion? "People always value that which they do not have, and despise the familiar," he said. "Moving things from an area where they are despised to another where they are precious is the secret of all success in trade." Was that statement an insight into his inner life? How else to explain his continuing desire to risk his life to sail the remote stretches of the ocean where none had gone before? Was that desire evidence of some present discontent or was the anticipation of discovery the source of greater happiness? Or was it simply the resulting wealth and fame?

She did not know, but she knew that she was her father's daughter. Would she always chase happiness, even in her new life? She was happy imagining her life with Shem, but would it survive the upcoming reality? Or would it open even greater vistas to happiness that they could explore together? Was her anticipation of marriage and a new home merely the desire for something unfamiliar—and would unhappiness and evil omens follow her no matter where she went?

She shook her head as she heard Jahaz outside the door, and walked over to open it. Turning aside, she saw her image in the polished copper sheet mounted on the wall. Its warm glow reflected a challenging stare. The light brown hair was thick and long, with lighter streaks from the sun's rays. Clear green eyes stared at high cheekbones; her father's straight, thin nose; and her mother's well-formed, generous mouth completed the picture. Behind the copper glow, smooth, clear skin covered the features that melded into an image that others frequently told her was one of beauty. Their opinion was confirmed by Peniah's poorly concealed jealousy. Madrazi stared for a moment and wondered yet again what Shem might think of this reflection? Would his eyes and hands enjoy what she now saw? The face staring back at her blushed at the thought. Quickly she pulled on the clothes Jahaz laid out, her favorite pale green silk pants—tight at the waist and ankles, but loose in between, and the matching tunic that slid down the tall, well-formed body almost to the knees. Sliding her feet into comfortable sandals, she only then opened the door to her servant.

Jahaz followed patiently as always. She was older, shorter, and heavier than Madrazi, with a plain, honest face under her dark hair. She had been Madrazi's nurse and companion all of her life, but the childhood friendship had not blossomed, primarily because Jahaz did not share her mistress' interests in trade, shipbuilding, or the stars, though she still served faithfully. Their differences prevented the bridge between faithful servant and friend from ever being crossed, and Madrazi at times felt a twinge of guilt over the one-sided nature of their relationship. In the absence of her mother or any other suitable woman, Jahaz was her only female friend, even though they were not close in the ways that Madrazi knew women could be.

Walking down the stairs and through the hall towards the great room, she realized that she would miss this home. It was large and comfortable. Many years and much work had gone into its construction. Its heart was a great eight-sided room with thick stone walls. It had been built to shelter many defenders for many days, with a hidden well in one corner and food carefully stored. It had not been needed as a fortress, but they were remote from the larger towns and had taken no chances. "Just the appearance of strength was sufficient to avoid much trouble," her father had said when asked. Later, as his crews and their success multiplied, their reputation as fighting men became a much stronger shield against bandits or jealous competitors.

The great hall remained unchanged. A pillar formed of a single massive tree trunk rested in the center of the hall. Large wooden beams spiraled up and out from the pillar, supporting the walls and roof. Squared stones lay neatly on the floor, fitted closely into pleasing patterns. Behind her was the north wing, and others faced south and east. They had been built later, after the growing strength of the settlement deterred any attack. The east wing was the oldest, away from the sea. It contained kitchens, workshops, servants quarters, and stores of food. The others overlooked the ocean, north and south. She lived in the northern wing on the second floor, while her two brothers, Ithiel and Ucal, shared the first level. The southern wing housed her father and Peniah, and looked down upon the harbor, shipyard, and low buildings that housed his crews and less valuable trade goods. His most precious possessions, his maps and records of his voyages, were hidden in his rooms.

Slowly Madrazi walked across the immense stone flags, trying to recommit every detail to memory. Her father sat at the table with Peniah near the servants' door. She thrilled anew to the sight of him, for he was still a man of striking appearance in spite of his age. His hair was still dark and his face unlined. Shorter than some men, he was broad in the shoulders and his arms retained the great strength of his youth. But the gray eyes were experienced and showed only what he wanted them to, with a subtle hint of the wild independence of his younger life. An appearance of contentment had settled upon him as a mantle through the years, broken only during the time around his first wife's death.

Madrazi walked quietly up to the table. The high ceiling of the great hall had windows open to the sky, and sunlight brightened the room. Her father and Peniah were talking and gave no sign of seeing her. Food was on the table, but they had refrained from eating, awaiting her arrival. Apologizing for the delay, she sat beside her father. Out of the side of her eye she saw Peniah glancing at her, as if measuring something, but Madrazi could not read her face. Nor did she want to try. Today was the last day in this home and absence from Peniah, at least, would be a vast improvement. All sat silent with their own thoughts as they began to enjoy the cool fruits, breads, and hot, sweet tea.

Madrazi discerned that her father wanted to speak, yet he was hesitant, and his eyes were tense. She stiffened inside, for she had seen that look before and it always boded bad news. Surely they were not delayed! She had heard nothing and her packing had been completed without comment. But she would not make it easy for him, eating quietly and pretending not to notice anything amiss.

Peniah relieved him of the telling, with obvious relish. With an ill-concealed smirk, she said, "You will travel with your father and brothers to Lamech on board Hakkem. Unfortunately, I cannot accompany you since someone must stay here and direct the house and trading."

Although Hakkem was the newest and finest of her father's ships, the words reawakened the horror of the previous night. Madrazi tried to keep her face still, but was betrayed by a trembling in her hands before she could hide them under the table. She saw again, faintly in the shadows of the hall, the devouring sea of last night—and knew in that moment that its omen was directed against her. There would be no new life, only a death long foreseen, but not yet experienced. Her father knew her feelings about the sea, but was unaware that the previous night had scraped them raw. She said nothing, but he knew her and had seen her hands.

He sought to explain. "My dear, change is upon us. The wind is fair to Lamech and it will be a short voyage. You will be on the water less than a fortnight. But other changes make me fear the longer road. I have received bad news from Bosheth, one of the traders of the guild. Roads that were safe even a few years ago are so no longer. Since the roads grow ever more dangerous, I have decided to forsake all overland trading and only travel only by sea."

"Are the bandits that bold? What of your men? They are all good fighters."

He sighed, "The bandits could be dealt with in the past. My men are well armed, skilled fighters. A few undisciplined outlaws can be defeated easily. We have done so before, and can do so on any road. But it is no longer the bandits. Many cities have now forsaken the old ways of peace and wisdom, and the new rulers revel in war. Traders are no longer safe—the new rulers are bold to attack even the caravans of the guild. Bosheth's caravan was attacked two months ago. When he passed near the city of Chalech, its ruler was not content with the customary tariff, but demanded all his goods. When refused, the ruler attacked the camp, slaughtering even those who threw down their weapons. Bosheth alone escaped to warn us. He said that the men of Chalech took more pleasure in shedding blood than in stealing the riches of his caravan."

He shook his head at the waste of life and goods and continued, "I cannot risk one of these foolish young rulers destroying all that I have built over the last five hundred years. These Nephil are mighty warriors, but they know no law but their own strength. There was a time when humanity pushed outward to far lands. Perhaps they pushed too far. Tales return of some who have lost their humanity: I have even heard that some outlanders are not satisfied with eating animals, but have even begun to eat men. They have no laws and no barriers to perversion. These Nephilim return to more settled lands supposedly to escape the outlanders, but they have become a scourge to civilized men.

"So even though I abandon your presence, I cannot escape your problems." Madrazi tried to speak lightly, but her bitterness was evident, and he replied bluntly. "We will sail two weeks from tomorrow at the high tide. Your dowry and belongings that were packed are already aboard. After we provision and refit, we sail. You must load the last of your trunks for the voyage by then."

He hesitated, and his voice softened a little for the next blow. "We also must send you to Shem without any servants, even Jahaz. She may accompany you on the voyage, but must return with me. Peniah will need all of them here. But your husband comes from a wealthy family and I am sure that you will be well provided for."

Madrazi started to speak, but refrained when she saw the determination in Peniah's face. This was a fight that she could not win. But Jahaz had been her servant and companion all her life, and although they no longer enjoyed the easy friendship of her younger days, she was a faithful companion and servant. It rankled her to give anything to Peniah, much less Jahaz. She could not even console herself with the thought that Jahaz would remain safe here. But she would never give Peniah the satisfaction of tears.

Although her father's word was the law in the house, he did not rule her feelings. Nudging as close to rebellion as she could, she rose abruptly, turned her back rudely on them both, and left before her face revealed anything. Glancing back, she saw that Peniah had not even the grace to disguise her satisfaction. She had won whatever battle she imagined she had been fighting and was exulting in it. There would be only one woman ruling this household and it would not be Madrazi's dead mother, or her exiled daughter.

Storming up to her room, Madrazi was distracted by the sight of her trunks awaiting her traveling clothes. Jahaz fluttered about the room, but there was little left to do, and now there remained two interminable weeks of waiting. Wanting time to think through the return of her vision and the disturbing news that would place her at the sea's mercy, she found her feet carrying her up the path to her hill. The familiar path had been carefully built to be smooth, for it was often traveled in the dark. It led to the flat hilltop, now a grassy knoll that marked her initiation into the mysteries of the heavens. She paused upon its threshold and thought back to her first days here. She could not stay angry with her father. How could he understand that he was delivering her into the hand of her worst enemy? The sea was his friend, his mistress.

Madrazi shook off her morbid thoughts. Death was the fate of all men, and she could not let its fear rule her days, even if those remaining were few. She looked around at the wooden posts forming the circle on the perimeter of the smooth grass with the standing stone in the center. She had lived a good life, enriched by many gifts. One of the most precious was her father's gift of the stars, a knowledge that would outlast her present distress. It was on this hill that the heavens had been unfolded to her. It had required many patient nights, but those lessons remained.

On the night of her twenty-second birthday, Pomorolac had taken Madrazi outside and stood with her on the beach watching the stars for some time before he spoke. "You wish to help me, Madrazi, in my work, do you not?" he asked gently.

"Yes, father. You know that I love you."

"Then my gift to you this night is a promise," he said, waving his hands at the skies, "I will give you the knowledge that is the foundation of my success—knowledge of the heavens."

Madrazi experienced one of the great thrills of her young life. She loved knowledge and that of the heavens was both rare and sublime. Perhaps heaven would reveal some secret that might protect her from her dark enemy. The stars would speak to her, she was certain.

The next morning, he had shown her the hill that would be her classroom. Not content to wait, she had helped with the hard work of clearing and leveling its top, resulting in an elevated platform for her observations. Madrazi took pride as new grass formed a smooth lawn in the rough circle almost fifty cubits across. At the center, they carefully dug a deep hole. Then a smooth, straight stone pillar was fixed immovable and perfectly upright. With the gnomon in place, she had ascended the hill three times each day to mark the ends of its shadows at sunrise, noon, and sunset with small stakes. The noon shadow showed her the way north. She then supervised the erection of four wooden posts around the perimeter of her hilltop to define the cardinal directions.

Over time the noon shadow moved in a line away from the gnomon and then back towards it. Its farthest point from the gnomon marked the winter solstice and its nearest point that of summer. Posts were again planted at the edge of the circle marking sunrise and sunset of these important days. Midway between these posts, she marked the sunrise and sunset shadows of both the spring and fall equinox. These taught her the beginnings of the solar calendar.

Her education soon progressed to timing the phases and motions of the moon. She observed that the new moon came 30 days after the last. After a few months, she realized to her surprise that the new moon appeared early. After some months of charting the phases, she realized that alternating counts of 29 and 30 days kept her in phase with the moon. However, at the end of a year, the lunar year of 12 months was only 354 days, while the solar return to the midsummer solstice took 365 days. When struck with this discrepancy, she immediately complained to her father that he had set her to an impossible task.

His laughter had been long and loud. Finally, he took her by the shoulders and looked affectionately into her eyes. As her anger evaporated, he said, "My daughter, you have learned two valuable lessons. First, plotting the seasons and days is not an easy task, and the sun and moon do not lead you down the best path, even though it appears to be the easiest. You must learn the stars. Second, and more importantly, you have learned that many things are not as simple as they appear and to be careful in your judgments."

He gave her an afternoon to consider his words before taking her back up the hill that night. Pointing beyond the wooden marker for due north, he asked, "Do you see the North Star?"

Madrazi nodded.

"Good," he replied. "Mark it in your memory. There is a dark point just beside it that defines the fixed point around which all the heavens move. Even that reference is not perfect, but the change is minute; you must observe carefully for more than ten years to see any discrepancy. So for all practical purposes, I use the North Star to fix my northerly position at sea."

As the years followed the stars, her father taught her the names of stars and constellations, the making of star maps, and the skill of plotting the motions of the sun and moon against the fixed stars. She came to understand how the zodiac was developed and how it could be used with the solar calendar to plot planting and harvesting. She had begun to see the cyclical order in the night skies, and the knowledge gave her feelings of both pleasure and power. She listened eagerly as her father supplemented her nightly lessons over the years.

Two weeks dragged by. The sun was crossing the sky over her classroom for the last time. It was hurrying, but she was loath to leave, knowing it was the final descent down the familiar path. Doubts and fears could not alter the course of events or the passage of time. Reluctantly Madrazi turned her feet down the path and went to her room to complete packing. Jahaz was waiting, still subdued, but Madrazi's mind was on her own misfortunes. So two silent women packed the remainder of the clothes and personal treasures and men came to carry them aboard. Madrazi smiled to herself as they left, for she had one consolation. She had packed her mother's wedding robes privately at the bottom of one trunk. They had been intended for her use long ago, but were of a rare and precious weave. When she had first learned of her father's marriage, Madrazi had moved them to her quarters. Peniah might have her home, her father, and her servant, but she would not rob her of her mother's memory.

By midday preparations were complete and Madrazi's belongings were stowed aboard, her two traveling chests lashed to the wall of her cabin. If the voyage was to be her death, she would meet it with courage. She stood bravely on the raised afterdeck of Hakkem near the tiller. It was not the largest of her father's fleet, but it was the newest, the easiest sailing, and by far the fastest.

It was more than a new ship: Hakkem was a new design that her father had contemplated for many years. Madrazi knew it well; much of her work in the shipyard over the past ten years had contributed to this magnificent ship. Centuries of experience and months of trial and correction had been poured lovingly into Hakkem. Everything about this ship was different. Instead of assembling the planking first, they had created a heavy skeleton, a frame of solid timbers set into a thick keel. The design was broader and deeper than the other ships relative to its length, and could carry more cargo with greater stability than the others. After much argument among his captains, her father had decided that the Hakkem would be a daughter of the wind, and no provision was made in the design for oars. There were some stored below decks, but only for emergencies.

Since wind alone powered the ship, its two masts each carried two sails, a smaller square sail atop the larger main sails. Another mast angled up at the bow, and its small sails helped turn the ship quickly. They had found that adding sails at the bow and upper sails on the masts dramatically increased the ship's maneuverability, even at a sharp angle to contrary winds. Hakkem also boasted her father's newest innovation; a single rudder mounted at the center of the stern that could be raised or lowered slightly to limit drift toward dangerous shores. His other ships used steering oars mounted to the side just in front of the high peaked sterns. In any condition other than a dead calm, Hakkem could outsail any other ship on the sea.

It needed a crew of only forty men, and as Madrazi watched, several of them expertly cast off the lines from the stone pier. Others strained at ropes and hauled the sails into position, singing together the familiar songs that her father had composed to maintain the correct timing and sequence of each task. The early beginnings of a land breeze bore them toward the mouth of the harbor. Although she hated the sea, she loved the beauty and harmony of wood, rope, and canvas harnessing the wind to defeat it. The water protested, gently at first, slapping the timbers of the ship as they began to move ahead.

As the ship slipped away from her mooring, the disparity between Madrazi and the men swarming to their work struck her like a blow. They were oblivious to the menace that engulfed her mind, and for them, a short voyage along a known route was akin to a holiday. Madrazi alone saw the imminent threat, but she had decided over the past days that it was a necessary gamble with her life. She would not stay in this house any longer and despite the looming darkness of the voyage, she irrationally clung to the hope that there was light beyond. It was feeble, but she held it with all of her stubbornness. Her mother had once been that light and Madrazi yearned for her comfort and love. Methuselah, Shem, and a new future beckoned, but would she ever see it? This voyage would either be the end of her life or a new beginning and there was no going back.

Her thoughts were interrupted by the deep-voiced orders of the ship's captain, Jakeh. As she shook her head, she felt pain in her fingers and saw them white against the dark wood railing. With some effort, she forced them to open and relax, then clasped them together to hide any lingering tremor.

Slowly, the shore began to recede. Light reflected off the stone walls of the great house. It sat on a low bluff of dark, hard stone that gradually sank to form a ridge that was the northern breakwater of the harbor. From the front door, a path bent right to the harbor and another left to the footpath that led to the open sea above. Thirty-five years ago, her mother had walked down that path never to return. Now, her daughter had taken the other—would both lead to the same watery grave? Her eyes blurred. She wiped them on her robe and continued to look back.

Sunlight reflected off of the house and down the stone pier. In that instant she saw with a clarity that merged memory and sight. Although no longer the welcoming haven of her childhood, it was the only home she had known. Memories of happiness lay scattered between the beach and hills. Then her tears obscured the view. Unwilling to let anyone see such an emotional display, she fled across the deck and down the ladder to her cabin as quickly as dignity and motion of the ship would allow. Throwing herself upon her cot, she let the tears out. All that had been was now gone; she no longer had a home, and in that moment of black despair, she was now certain that her life was forfeit to her enemy.

Chapter 3
VOYAGE

Haunting shadows swirled and faded into nothingness as another night swallowed up the last light dancing around the cabin from the open hatch above. Madrazi now welcomed the dark, for it hid her misery from concerned eyes trying too hard not to notice. As the living reminder of her mother, she was the favorite of all her father's men, especially on Hakkem, whose crew included only men who had long proven their loyalty and skill. So they knew how she despised any show of weakness. In another mood she might have been amused at the obvious attempts to hide sympathy and concern. As it was, the only emotions that she could still stir besides self-pity were anger and the shreds of pride.

That first rush of seasickness had not been unexpected; the transition from the relatively calm waters of the harbor to a pronounced roll was sudden, as the wind pushed the ship south. Its motion, parallel to the ocean swell, brought on that all too familiar light-headed, stomach-churning sensation. Whether it killed her or not, it was well that Jahaz accompanied her—the older woman was not affected in the least by any motion aboard a ship and someone would have to attend her needs for several days. Madrazi always hoped that the next voyage would be the one in which sickness did not strike, but this one only brought it with increased severity. Within a few hours of leaving the harbor, her emotional turmoil was swamped by that of her body.

Every time she ventured on the hateful sea, it had toyed with her by flooding her body with weakness and misery. Always before she had possessed the strength to fight it off after a few days. Would she have such strength again? At first, she thought so. After a few days in her cabin, hiding her wretchedness, she began to reassert control of her body. On the third morning, the familiar feeling of clear-headed hunger and thirst that signaled the end of the sickness granted her some relief, and she braved the deck. Turning aft, she saw her father and Captain Jakeh in deep discussion. Her spirit lifted and a hope of survival pierced her heart. It was a bright day and she desperately longed for the end of their journey.

The two men glanced her way and resumed talking as she walked closer. Curiosity overcame pique and as she walked closer she heard Captain Jakeh rumble, "...the sun does not lie."

"What is the matter?" she interrupted.

Her father replied shortly. "The westerly winds that will take us to Lamech have come, but we are not yet far enough south."

Madrazi immediately understood. Her father followed the paths of the sea. Winds and currents were always in the same place. His books of charts with his personal observations and maps were his most closely guarded possessions. Any change in the predictable winds or currents would have serious consequences indeed, for he trusted his life and those of his men to the accuracy of those charts. The sea was unforgiving—uncounted bones littering its floor was proof of that.

To know where one was going, one must know where one was—a difficult task when surrounded by endless waves. Close inshore, men who knew the local winds and currents found their way easily enough. But the open sea was different. So her father was unceasingly cautious: the ship's position was determined each day and noted in the ship's book to be compared to the appropriate charts. North and south were easy, east and west, difficult. When possible, journeys tended to follow straight lines north and south and then east and west.

"Last night was clear and the stars and sun agree, but the winds do not," continued Pomorolac. "What kind of omen is this?" he muttered. "I would as soon think the earth could be destroyed as the sea and winds change."

He shook his head and stared out over the endless waters. Jakeh and Madrazi exchanged glances. It was a measure of Pomorolac's concern that he would even consider assigning any phenomenon to some inexplicable, unseen work of god.

"In time, you will find an answer," returned Jakeh, confidently. "The sea saves her best tricks for those who have already mastered her, so take heart! Our turn east will take us to Lamech whether here or two more days south. I will sail the ship and you decide what these strange winds mean."

Madrazi nodded her assent, smiling her approval at the prospect of finishing the voyage early. She was intensely interested too in the problem itself, for this was one of the aspects of sailing that she enjoyed. She understood the art of finding your way at sea better than most sailors and was already calculating the meaning of this discrepancy. If she could decipher it before her father, it would be something to be proud of for the rest of her life. But even as she began to consider it, she realized that while the men might interpret such a change as just another trick of the impersonal ocean, it might be a sign from her malignant enemy. She shivered.

Pomorolac hesitated, then nodded his approval, and Jakeh swung the tiller around. Hakkem swung smoothly towards the east, pushed by a steady southwesterly wind. Jakeh continued to make light of the puzzle. "This is worth at least two days if the winds hold true," he gloated. "It is a shame that you will not have your best artist to redraw the map," he said, winking at Madrazi. "I will have to accustom my old eyes to your scratch, master." His laugh brought a weak smile from Madrazi, but her humor did not last, for her worst fears soon came to pass.

Watching the sun shift around with the new course, her body felt misgivings at the new motion. Instead of a simple roll or pitch, Hakkem combined the two in a manner that brought new twinges to her stomach. Within a few minutes, Madrazi was back down in her cabin, delivered into a bout of sickness even worse than the first. The prospect of a shorter voyage was no comfort; each minute was a year. She moaned, facedown on her cot, as Jahaz shook her head and began to clean the cabin floor.

This attack was more stubborn than its predecessor. Each day brought new misery. The premonition of death became a certainty in her mind, and Madrazi could not sleep. Day merged with night and her courage failed. Death would be preferable to this misery. She regretted not taking the overland route or even the minor mercy of travel in one of the older, larger ships which would have been slower and steadier. She cursed Hakkem, the winds and waves, and her weakness. She cursed Jahaz too, which only increased the already unpleasant burden of her ministrations. But in her present state, she was determined to inflict her misery on all around her.

On the sixth night, Madrazi, no longer even sure of the days, lay listening to Jahaz sleeping soundly across the cabin. Madrazi could not face sleep and she drifted in and out of awareness, fear of her night vision battling exhaustion and sickness. Her mind wandered down dark paths, and every roll of the ship triggered the memory of the dark, destroying wave. Sleep was the doorway into a terrifying reality, but she had discovered that extended sleeplessness carried her to the same place; it merely drew the curtain aside more slowly.

Madrazi was ready to surrender to the darkness, half in and half out of sleep, when the memory of her mother flooded back with a startling clarity. There was no warning—she was simply present. Not just in the cold dimension of memory, but in the blackness of her heart, that forgotten sense of gentle love and care suddenly rose and overcame all darkness. In that moment, the girl sensed a peaceful presence in the cabin. Awake or dreaming, she saw her mother's face clearly outlined in soft light. As she reached out a weak hand, her own arm seemed dim and ethereal, but her mother's was clear and hard, and its brightness hurt her eyes. Familiar sounds of the ship and the sea faded away, and within the cocoon of silence, she heard echoes of forgotten words of comfort. Time had no meaning, then suddenly her mother vanished from her life—again. Tears flooded her eyes, washing the remaining darkness away. Though not physically present, the essence of her mother lived: maybe only in memory, but perhaps much more if her great grandfather's stories were true. But if only in memory, it remained clear in spite of the years, and she took comfort from that clarity. Her inner turmoil ceased. She would live, she told herself, and so she slept.

Late the next morning, Madrazi awoke to the sunlight streaming into the cabin from an open hatch. Her head was clear and her body refreshed. She was hungry and thirsty—feelings that had not been known for many days. She felt weak; having eaten little for a number of days except the hot tea prepared each evening before the galley fire was put out. Madrazi let her body sag back into her bed, staring at the beams overhead and watching the sunlight move back and forth across the grain of the wood.

Soon, her observant eye noticed the pattern of light. It had changed, and within a few moments she had worked out their new direction. The sea was calmer, too, and her northerly course had calmed Hakkem's motion to a gentle roll. Perhaps that change had settled Madrazi's head and stomach, but she believed instead it was a gift from her mother. Still weak in body, her mind found its old strength, and it commanded her body to move.

Rising cautiously, she stretched her limbs and found that in spite of their weakness, her feet were able to negotiate the floor of the cabin. "Good morning," grinned Jahaz, awake and watching. "I believe young Shem may get married after all. I feared that he would be a widower before ever he saw your white robes."

Madrazi smiled in response, and then the same thought struck both women at the same time—that the new life with Shem would not include Jahaz. Madrazi forced herself to be cheerful to help atone for the last week. The return of her confidence brought with it guilt over her behavior. "It would take more than a great storm at sea, even were it to last for a year, to keep me from the destiny of my new life. Now, let's find something dry to wear and see to some breakfast." Jahaz was happiest when busy serving her mistress.

"Lie still and rest for a bit while I fetch some water for washing."

Madrazi wrinkled her nose and had to agree. Jahaz had already cleaned and aired the cabin and Madrazi was suddenly eager to be clean, too. After several buckets of the precious fresh water and some scented oil, Jahaz was content to let her wander onto the decks.

Although Madrazi's gait was not yet steady, the women were soon enjoying the new day together. Jahaz was visibly relieved at Madrazi's recovery and in high spirits. Nature cooperated with bright sunshine reflecting off the water. The gentle roll of the ship was easy for Madrazi, even in her weakness, and she forced herself to accept the motion with confidence, knowing that soon she would not even notice it. They made their way aft and carefully climbed the steep steps to the steering deck, where Jakeh held the tiller. He smiled at their approach. "Ah, beautiful weather brings beauty on deck."

Jakeh was Madrazi's favorite captain, a good sailor and prudent trader. He was unfailingly kind, respecting her knowledge of trade, and spoke freely with her. But his eye was on Jahaz as he spoke. Madrazi hoped that they would find happiness together after they returned from this journey and deliver Jahaz from the petty tyranny of Peniah. The weather was beautiful as the sun glinted off the white arrow of the wake. The wind ruffled her hair and pressed the cloth of her tunic against bare skin.

"Beautiful weather!" Madrazi exclaimed, "I thought that the sailing had finally been given over to a real seaman, and not the captain."

Captain Jakeh grinned broadly in return at this weak jest. "None of the crew can take credit, young lady. We have made good time these last few days, have cleared the great reef, and now have turned north. If the wind holds, we will see the harbor of Lamech in three or four days. I hope that we shall enjoy your company on deck." Madrazi's reply was interrupted by a voice behind her.

"So it is true that the dead live again." Her father had come up behind them silently. "Are you well enough to join me for a morning meal?"

"A small one, perhaps," she replied. "The food and company will both be welcome." They turned and left Jahaz and Jakeh talking together quietly.

Her father waved his hand to a couple of idle crewmen. "Ho, men," he called, "rig the deck table and two chairs on the weather side of the main deck. Then tell the cook to bring a light breakfast."

Old Bozeth waved back. He had sailed with the family for many years, and had been a friend to Madrazi all her life, the source of many strange tales of the sea. Unambitious, he had been content to remain a common sailor, although he could easily have been a captain. He preferred a life with little responsibility and her father was content to let him remain as he was, for he was a willing worker. Winking at Madrazi as he walked by to fetch the table, he asked, "Are you sure about the morning meal, master Pomorolac?" While her father smothered a smile, Bozeth slid away with a sly grin. But she refused to let anything spoil her mood this morning, and surprised both men by laughing and flinging an order after Bozeth, "Bring the best wine with the food, sailor!"

After the table and chairs were fastened to a shaded patch of deck, her father politely waved her to a seat and served her bread and wine. The bread was still fresh enough and the wine smooth. The air was warm as the sun began to climb through the sky, and the steady wind felt delicious in the shade. The men seemed to understand and kept a discreet distance as they moved about deck performing their work. A steady rasp and occasional splash told her ears that the men were scrubbing the decks. Captain Jakeh always kept his ships spotless and the men were further motivated by the master's presence. The men in the forepeak were singing as they polished the woodwork.

Her father leaned back and sipped wine from his silver goblet. "Your mother used to eat with me on deck in the early days when she accompanied me on almost every voyage. It was a smaller ship and poorer fare, but we were happy! Her smile put every problem in its proper perspective. She was strong, like you, and insisted on being a part of my trading as well as making a home. Most women did not like her, and that is one reason that we built our home away from existing towns. We found everything that we needed in our own lives, and together we built a good home and a good business."

Madrazi looked up at him carefully. He never talked about her mother and she wondered whether this change was coincidence. He was usually reticent about the past, particularly his first wife, unless there was some lesson in his story. "Always look to the future, not the past," he told his children again and again. "That way your life will always be a challenge, an adventure. Many men have died young because they just became tired of their existence after a few hundred years and could not find new directions for their lives. When one has lost his zest for life, death lurks upon the porch."

She seldom opened her heart to her father, but his words brought back the feelings of the night. She spoke where she would have been otherwise silent. "I saw her last night," she began, faltering and unwilling to look at his face, but finding strength in the thought of the vision. "I was sick and exhausted. I saw only darkness and death ahead. She came and spoke comfort to me. You may say that it could not be," she paused and lifted her eyes to his, "but she was there... more than I was." She stopped, realizing how ridiculous she must sound, but was again struck by the force of the memory. "It was the first night that I have slept since we left home, and it was because she was there. I miss her."

Madrazi paused, expecting his laughter. But she saw amazement in his eyes, not the expected cynicism masked by affection. So she continued. "I am sorry to leave you, but last night was a good omen. I will walk this path content."

They sat silent for a moment, watching the waves pass alongside. Her father recovered first. "I have my own memories," he said abruptly, "and it is enough. In you, I had the extra gift of a living reminder. For that alone I will miss you. You will do well with young Shem. You will have to bend, but Methuselah is a wise and farsighted man, and I believe that he came to us before with this very thing in mind. He loved your mother and always treated me with respect."

She nodded, also suspecting her Granpapa's part in this wedding.

After a moment, Pomorolac looked directly into her eyes and asked, "Do you understand why I married Peniah?"

He saw the answer in her eyes before she answered. "Who am I to question your life?"

He snorted. "You have done it for many years and often to my face. You did it with Peniah, only you kept it to yourself." He paused. "Madrazi, my daughter, it is important to me that you know. You have my gifts. You proved to me that a woman could enlarge my trade and wealth. I had a true partner as well as a living reminder of my happiest years. Often I have wished that you were a son: you would have been a true heir and the oceans of the world would have been ours."

Madrazi stared openly at him. Her father was parsimonious with praise, and she never expected those words from him.

He continued in a softer voice. "A man cannot make a home without a woman. I would have been content to stay as I was, with you as the woman of my house for many years, but it would have cheated you of your own destiny. While I hoped that you would refuse Noah, I knew that such an opportunity must be seized. How I was torn!"

Madrazi did not know what to say. If she had known...

Pomorolac saw her mind. "Do not regret your decision, my dear. As I sit before you now, I know in my bones that it was right." He looked down and shook his head slowly. "You still do not see. You are the reason that I married her, Madrazi. I knew her husband's trade far exceeded his talents. She had the ability, the drive, and the knowledge to take your place. My error was my blindness to the ways of women; I thought that she would work with you. Her mind is sharp, but her vision, limited. Her petty jealousy surprised me, but a man must stand by his vow."

Affection and guilt welled up together in Madrazi. How she loved him! Would she have refused Shem had she only known? Perhaps. Her face burned with shame at the cool aloofness with which she had treated him over the past few years: he had needed her to rise above Peniah's standards and she had failed. "I'm sorry, Father," she said with a trembling voice. She had not the words to explain her tangled emotions.

"I know," he returned softly, and looking at him, she realized that he understood what she could not say. "It is done," he finished, closing the discussion.

They sat for a moment, wrapped in their thoughts. Pomorolac was never one to wallow in emotion. Smoothly he began to talk about her new family. "I have not seen Lamech for many years, but he was a strong, forceful man even as a youth. He has probably had more to do than either Methuselah or Noah in shaping the city that bears his name. I don't know Noah at all, although I like what I hear. Everyone acknowledges him as an honest and good man. They say that he shares Methuselah's enthusiasm for a religious life, but that does not have to be a bad thing. In these days, most men have lost all respect for religious tradition and worship, and I prefer Methuselah's extreme to theirs. True submission to god is usually joined to honesty and integrity, although there are many who use the appearance of religion to mask their own greed. But those who lose all sight of god usually lose touch with their own souls to the detriment of all."

Madrazi agreed silently. Religious expression, like so many other things in life, required a delicate balance. Too much or too little could both bring trouble.

Her father continued, "Men have done so much that is great and noble, but also much evil. We may be destined to walk in the dust, but we all choose where to fix our eyes—on the ground or on the stars. My lamp will be extinguished someday, but I am content to know that it will burn on in your brothers and in you. I have kept a good name for all these years, and have done good to many. Perhaps that and your mother's prayers are enough. The world is wide and the sea leads to many hidden corners. I am a wanderer and a seeker, Madrazi. I have always been so, and expect that I will remain curious about all that I don't know and have not yet seen until the day that I die. I have spent more than four hundred years sailing the ocean as my own master, and have seen what few men have. But it is never enough. Perhaps that is the secret to my happiness—always seeking and never finding.... I expect that the sea will claim my life in return for all that I have taken from it, but I am satisfied."

Madrazi shuddered at the thought. Her father paused and smiled as she remembered from her childhood. "I hope that your dream last night was an omen for your future. I have always thought that your were as hardheaded and practical as me, but your mother's blood cannot be denied. Perhaps this marriage contract has awakened it, bringing a connection to the unseen world. Your mother talked of the Creator and felt things that I could not. Perhaps that is her gift to you. You will carry the life of your mother in you. I only hope there is room for mine, too."

She was not sure what to say to this, but knew she must try. It should have been easy. For many years he had been her life and she thrilled to think that she was as much like him as a woman could be. But something long dormant had been awakened in the night, and she paused before speaking. "Perhaps I have some small part of Mother inside. But it has been many years, and your strength, your wisdom, and your determination are mine, too. I have enjoyed a good life with you. I will keep you in my heart and my children will know your wisdom."

"It is enough, daughter. Let us enjoy the days ahead as they are given to us. We have shared your mother's love, some good years, and regard for each other. With that, when we part, we will not be separated completely. Come, let us watch the birds guide Hakkem along the swiftest winds to our destination—an end that will be a new beginning for us both."

They rose and went to the very front of the ship, and spent a time of companionable silence watching the birds, the sea, and the passing land now just visible off to the right. They both took comfort from the morning, and Madrazi wanted to keep a part of it always. So she concentrated on sights, sounds, and the touch of wind and spray on her face, and the play of her father's shadow on the gently rolling deck. The water was clear and shallow; a brilliant green mantling the vast stretches of reefs and banks of limestone that fringed the coast.

The following day, the outline of the coast that loomed to their right began to converge with the ship on Lamech. The morning sun was to the right, and a westerly sea breeze pushed them on to her new life, now only three days away. The latest change in course had been a blessing to her condition. Able to eat and walk the deck, to sleep all night and during the heat of midday, Madrazi felt her strength return by the hour. With a clear head and a light heart, she came on deck in the middle of the afternoon watch, and stood with her father and Captain Jakeh. They were closer to the shore now, and could see the dull gleam of stone from a city on a plateau overlooking the ocean. "The city of Y'tor," her father explained. "A good place to avoid these days, even if they had a decent harbor. That young upstart Torech seized control of the army, then of the town. The place might as well be a military camp, from what my friends tell me."

"Aye," answered Jakeh. "I wonder if he has any designs on Lamech?" Madrazi saw with discerning eyes that he immediately regretted his speech, as though it might spoil her day. Her father evidently thought so, too and he spoke a little too quickly.

"He would overreach himself if he did. Only a fool would deliberately provoke Delonias of Taspar. And since Lamech's army is now closely allied with Taspar.... If Torech attempts Taspar's might, his city will end up a smoldering ruin before he has time to plot his second battle."

As Jahaz and Madrazi turned to go down to the main deck, her sharp ears heard him continue softly. "But one never knows, Jakeh. The world is changing, and even centuries of wisdom and experience of the elders is little respected by young Nephil like Torech. I fear sometimes for the future."

Leaving the men to their talk of politics and trade, the two women wandered to the front of the ship, and watched the seabirds soar. In harmony with their graceful flight, Madrazi's spirits continued to lift. Jahaz returned to their cabin after a short time, but Madrazi remained, eager to be done with the voyage. A new spirit had infused her. Her mother had led her through the darkness and new days of happiness beckoned. Only a few more days in the bosom of her enemy, the sea, and then she would be free. She spent a pleasant afternoon daydreaming; her mind wandering from serious consideration of what kind of man was Shem, to more frivolous topics of what kind of clothes the women of Lamech wore. Her reverie was interrupted by the shout of the lookout. "Smoke ahead," he cried, and with everyone else, she turned to look.

Ahead to the right, rays of the late afternoon sun were caught and distorted by a great column of dark smoke that curled up to the sky. "Must be quite a distance inland," muttered a sailor nearby.

"Aye, and quite a burning to put out that much smoke," replied his companion.

As Madrazi stared at the rising cloud, her sunny mood evaporated and she felt a chill cover her skin. She shivered involuntarily for she knew with the certainty of premonition that beneath the majestic column of smoke lay death.

****

A tang of burning cedar wafted down onto the porch as an errant breeze pulled it across the roof and down toward the valley. Although the sun was fading, light off the face of the ice kept the late afternoon strangely bright. Soon darkness would come, heralded by the evening wind rushing down the icy slopes and bending the trees on the plain before its chill blast washed over the white stone house.

A soft voice spoke her name again and the old woman was translated back from her mental meandering. Her body was stiff from sitting and she rose slowly, pulling the robe around her frail frame and shuffling across the dark wood floor. With an affectionate hint of a smile, the younger woman carefully bound the opened scroll, caught up all three, and followed. Sunlight gave way to firelight as they passed into a broad room. Long years lay heavily upon the room and its furnishings, but the old woman was comforted by the memories it brought and now spent her evenings staring into the endless motion of the flames. The young woman fancied that the fire was a curtain through which her mistress saw hidden things.

A low couch faced the fire. A table snug against one end held old scrolls and curiously bound papers. None but the old woman could understand their strange writing. Her interest in them had been reborn after the master's death; she had spent many evenings rereading them and then staring into the flames. The young woman helped the old onto the couch and arranged a thick blanket across the thin legs and soft pillows behind her head. Then she left to heat wine that would ease the aches of old age and food that would prolong the waning spark that remained.

Alone, but now more comfortable, the old woman glanced over to the table. Two books caught her eye this evening; they were bound in hard leather, flaking with age, but still showing a workmanship beyond anything men could now match. She reached out to one and felt again the story inside—of the old days, of a man and his dream, both long dead and forgotten. But she remembered. She remembered him whose bones now lay perhaps at the root of the very mountains across the valley. She trembled at the merging of memory and the words of the books, now virtually a part of her own memory. Books, memories, dreams; all feeding her mind with knowledge and pain. She felt the cleansing tears and holding the old leather, she peered into the shimmering embers before her, and saw it as though she were there.

Chapter 4
FIRST VICTORY

The pillar of smoke ascended over gouts of red and orange flame that leapt among the dozens of bodies stacked on a pyramid of burning logs. Flesh shriveled from bone and exuded a black, malodorous smoke as the defeated received their final insult. No soil would cover these bones. After desecration by fire, they would be left for the scavenging birds; a message to the enemies of Lamech. The smoke curled into a clear afternoon sky above the blazing pyre and drifted high into the west towards the ocean. Weary soldiers stood talking in clusters reliving the glory of victory while gloating over the destruction of the bodies of the men of Y'tor—enemies they had ambushed and killed earlier that day.

More attentive men lined the hilltop to their south. There was little risk of the enemy returning and attempting a surprise attack, but little risk was still risk. The commander knew better than to tempt any unneeded chance—there were enough necessary ones in battle. So the unlucky few kept watch while the overhead sun flared from their bronze spearheads and the wind waved through the green plumes of their helmets as they faced the empty land to the south. Ordinarily they would be cursing the boring duty, but like their comrades below, the celebratory mood was too strong. Grumbling and complaining were no part of this day.

Battle Commander Jared stood alone scanning the field; taking in the pyre, the watchmen, and scattered groups of soldiers. Most were busy burying their own dead, tending the wounded, gathering weapons and armor, and packing horses and mules for the return trek to Lamech. Despite a night of forced marching and a bitter fight following the ambush at dawn, even the men laboring under the hot sun reflected the jubilant attitude that permeated the entire army. But their pride and satisfaction could not equal his. They knew victory in the field, but he knew what had really been achieved. The sun tomorrow would rise on a changed world.

He should have been tired, but Jared's emotions continued to buoy his weary body. In one morning, decades of effort had borne fruit. Lamech's men had outfought a superior force and he had outfoxed a notorious warrior—the savage general Torech. That battle merely foreshadowed a more important victory that would take place in the public vindication of his brilliant young protégé, now Jared's superior by Jared's choice. Sechiall would receive the acclaim for Torech's defeat, but that was as it should be. The soldiers knew Jared's role, and he prized their respect more than the adulation of the crowds or the nods of the council.

Jared did not have to look hard for the Supreme Commander. He was in the middle of the largest group; men were swirling around him like bees in springtime around a large blossom. He was reveling in their adulation as much as he had in the battle itself. As the group parted momentarily, their eyes met across the field and Jared grinned in spite of himself. Though only a youth, Sechiall had a unique gift to stir men's blood and his charisma forced a smile even from the hardened Jared. Never had he seen the troops so excited, and there had been many years when he believed that he never would.

Things had been so different decades ago, when Jared had entered service. It was expected of him. His father had been a commander in the army of Lamech for hundreds of years, and would soon assume the mantle of Supreme Commander. For as long as the city had existed, Lamech's army had been a small, part-time force—more of a volunteer guard than a real army. Strong stone walls, a relatively isolated location, and the barrier of the sea had been deemed sufficient protection from occasional raiders and bandits.

So on his fiftieth birthday, with nothing more than a desire to please his father, Jared had undergone the ritual of enlistment and been duly approved for service by the council. Duty in the army was usually light and service had become a byword for laziness in Lamech. Thanks to his father's position, Jared could have pursued a course of ease and privilege. There was little effort required, and little work apart from weapons training—a matter of individual pride more than professional resolve. But in his first decade in service, Jared discovered that his skill with weapons—one of the few pleasures of his youth—was superior to that of the older, more experienced men. It arose seemingly without effort from his great strength and uncanny coordination. In spite of his youth, he soon earned the reputation as the finest swordsman in Lamech and the surrounding area. His ability with the bow and spear were little less.

By his sixtieth year, he had reached the decision to make the army his life—for himself, not his father. Unlike many of Lamech's soldiers, Jared was no sluggard. With his decision came a single-minded commitment that pleased his father and discomfited his peers. His passion for his own warrior skills and those of his comrades consumed him. Although Lamech enjoyed peace and prosperity, reports were beginning to be heard from merchants and traders of increasing lawlessness and banditry. Towns were expanding and consolidating surrounding regions into city-states, with a strong prince or general equal to the traditional council of elders. Some cities in troubled regions had even instituted military rule. Lamech's only choice was their own strong, well-organized army, and Jared saw the possibilities for growth. After all, Lamech and its surrounding villages boasted more than 15,000 citizens of military age and a degree of wealth to tempt any would-be conqueror. Unfortunately, few soldiers and, more importantly, fewer elders shared Jared's vision.

His vague dreams crystallized during a trip to Taspar during his sixty-sixth year. Although he and his father were both uncomfortable at the open and brazen display of shrine prostitutes outside the great city's gates, Jared's interest was captured by the alertly guarded outposts, well-drilled mounted patrols outside the city, and the splendor of the military display inside the walls. Why should not Lamech enjoy the same? Their small party had received a warm welcome from Delonias himself, the famed commander of Taspar's army. Taspar's influence was growing, and the port of Lamech would be a useful ally. Jared and his father, Zered, did not initially perceive their city's importance to their host and were thus surprised by the honor lavished upon them.

After a public welcome fit for an elder or wealthy merchant, father and son found themselves that very night at a feast hosted by Delonias and his commanders. Jared felt out of place, but the visitors from Lamech were seated at the head table next to the great man himself. In marked contrast to Lamech's forces, the professional dedication and camaraderie of Taspar's military leaders were clear to both. As the feast progressed and the wine flowed, Zered told Delonias of his son's desire to be a warrior and bragged on his skill with the sword.

Jared's embarrassment at his father's boasts became acute when the great man turned and looked him over appraisingly. "So you would be a leader of warriors?" queried Delonias.

Jared sensed something important behind the question and took a few moments to frame his reply, thankful that he had been sparing of wine. "I have become a man and still aspire to be a warrior. To be a leader of warriors demands more, for leading great men demands a great gift."

"That is true," replied Delonias, acknowledging the skillful compliment with a smile. "Perhaps in the morning you will join other men who aspire to become warriors. They conduct their exercises with the sword at the fourth hour. I will send my aide for you then."

Delonias left unsaid that the "exercise" was in fact that of one of Taspar's elite companies. When he arrived at the yard near the fortress, Jared's instincts lifted the hair on his neck. These men were special. Their bearing proclaimed it and their eyes told stories that few could comprehend and fewer could share. Jared understood that much, but even then he could not suspect that this particular company included more master swordsmen than any other in Taspar. The invitation to participate as an honored guest of Lamech's army made Jared uncomfortable, for he knew that Zered's opinion of his skill had been formed in comparison to the army of Lamech, not that of Taspar.

As he waited, he saw Delonias gesture to one of the men and then speak to him softly for a moment. Jared bowed his appreciation when the man graciously invited him to participate, but he feared that he would embarrass himself, his father, and his city. He sensed an importance to the hour that he could not understand, but the uncertainty sped the blood through his body, and he found the challenge bringing out his best. As he donned armor he glanced at the man appraisingly, and was glad that he had an advantage in height at least. His opponent looked thinner, too; tough and wiry perhaps, but his arm could not be nearly as strong as Jared's.

Jared learned the first of that day's many lessons in the man's first steps. Compared to the skilled grace of his opponent, Jared's feet were heavy and clumsy. Only quickness and instinct allowed him to fend off the initial attack. He wondered if he belonged here at all. Then the man hesitated, deliberately inviting attack. Jared complied, but was met with an easy skill and strength that seemed impossible in such stringy arms. As they traded blows, Jared could see that his opponent was clearly holding back. If he could see it, then all could. The perceived contempt spurred Jared to new strength. But his shrewdest strokes were turned aside with a polished ease. As they circled, Jared realized that his best was not enough. Although fractionally quicker, he had not the skill to use it to his advantage. The man's sword told a story that Jared should have seen in his eyes.

But the challenge was exhilarating. Jared had never fought such an opponent. As the exercise continued, he began to feel his blade in a new way. He no longer was conscious of his sword and arm, only of his opponent. For a few precious minutes, he felt his skill ascend to a new level, boosted in some fashion by the superiority of his opponent. His mind felt rather than thought and his combinations were now pushing the man closer to his full ability. It was as if a hundred lessons passed in a few heartbeats.

But even with this newfound insight and skill, his opponent's blade was always exactly where it needed to be—just ahead of Jared's. The master drew out the exercise, and finally terminated it with a curious twist of his wrist that seemed to wrap his blade around Jared's and pull irresistibly. The spell broke, and Jared watched his sword fly through the air and land at the feet of the men who had gathered around to watch. Jared feared their ridicule, so easily had he been disarmed, and was surprised when instead, they surged forward and congratulated him. Their obvious acceptance of him as a peer was the proudest moment of Jared's short life.

Only then did one of the others laughingly inform him that Pohtile was the best blade in their company, and one of the five best in the city. Jared relaxed and then basked in the acceptance of Taspar's warriors. It was then that he glanced over and saw Delonias standing aside with Zered with a knowing smile on his face. At that instant, Jared's eyes met those of Delonias, and a bond was recognized by both. Only later would Jared realize that moment marked Delonias' decision to make the young soldier the linchpin of his desired alliance.

Delonias, true to his reputation, took decisive action. Instead of a few months of leisure, Jared found his time filled with what amounted to the best military education possible during his stay. When Jared was not exercising with Taspar's weapon-masters, he was close by the side of Delonias. As their visit dragged out to six months, he learned techniques for sword, spear, and bow from the elite of Taspar's army—the best in the world. Delonias himself taught him the art of maneuver, modes of attack and defense, the moving of supplies, and leadership. Jared absorbed all he was taught and gained many new friends along with his new mentor. By the end of their stay, Jared could glance at any terrain and visualize a battlefield; where to attack and where to defend. The lessons culminated when he was honored as the aide to Delonias during their annual games. Jared saw for the first time the disciplined maneuver of a large army in the field, imprinting on his mind every move that Delonias made during those three days.

The skillful movements of yesterday's battle had been born in those lessons, and Jared's mastery of them had been evident in the success of the ambush he had set for Torech's forces. The army group of Y'tor had been deliberately made aware of their approach and had formed a predictable battle line in a shallow east-west valley between two low ridges. Their backs to the southern hill, they waited confidently for the small army of Lamech to arrive, line up, and be slaughtered, like so many other small armies.

"Never fight on your opponent's terms," Delonias had stressed. Jared knew he would be proud of the long forced march after sunset, looping around the valley and hiding behind the rim of the southern hill as the sun started to rise. As Torech's men were eating, one group attacked over the hill to the rear of the surprised enemy force.

After an initial push deep into the camp, the army of Y'tor began to rally around the giant figure of Torech, whose fearsome temper and great strength halted the charge where he stood. Then, superior numbers allowed Y'tor's troops to fully engage the attackers and stop the impetus of that first charge. For a brief moment, Torech must have thought another victory was at hand, for he was a mighty warrior and no man of Lamech was able to stand against him.

But as Y'tor's attention turned to the first thrust, Jared and Sechiall had led the remainder of Lamech's men hard into their flank, the rising sun to their backs. Sechiall was the larger man and more dominating presence, but he fought focused on the few men in front of him that would soon fall to his long spear. Jared accounted for his men quickly with his sword, but kept an eye on the battle as well. Side by side, the two opened a lane into the army of Y'tor that was quickly exploited by the following men.

Torech was no fool. What might have been a costly battle for both sides was cut short when he saw that his disadvantage was too great, and he led a fighting retreat to the west and then south. The blood lust was hot in Sechiall, and he screamed for men to follow hard after Torech. It took an effort for Jared to calm him and convince him that the victory was already theirs. "Supreme Commander," he called sharply, using the formal title to arrest Sechiall's attention. "We have won. Do not give Torech a chance to gain some small victory from the day. You have slain many men and led the army of Lamech to glory! It is enough!"

With obvious effort, Sechiall fought down his anger at the hard words, and curbed his blood lust. Although the fighting retreat had left Torech and many of his men alive and fleeing, Jared had wisely settled for the victory, remembering that Delonias taught him to value patience. Sechiall knew it was true, and knew that Jared was his superior in fighting a battle, regardless of titles. Suddenly he relaxed, grinned at Jared, and roared, "Very well, Battle Commander. But my spear has not slaked its thirst for Y'torian blood. Today is only a token payment."

Jared nodded, understanding the conflicting emotions seething in Sechiall's blood. Not really a full scale battle, the skirmish would serve notice to Torech to limit the expansion of Y'tor's boundaries in the direction of Lamech. Jared knew in his bones that Torech would have to be defeated again. Only death would still his ambition. But Jared was confident that his forces could repeat the day's victory. The death of many fighting men would rein in Torech's ambition for a few decades, no matter what he wanted to do. That would give Jared additional time to continue to build his own army.

But duplicating the might of Taspar, even on a smaller scale, faced an obstacle more formidable than Torech. During his training there, Jared had seen that the foundation of Taspar's army was the enthusiastic support from the leading citizens and elders. Their army had become a source of civic pride. Merchants supported the army in the councils and with rich gifts, for it had eradicated bandits in the surrounding countryside, making Taspar a hive of rich trade. As a result, Delonias had won a place on Taspar's council, and many considered him a leader among even the elders. Lamech's elders and leading merchants did not share that vision.

Jared returned to Lamech determined to spend his life transforming his city's inefficient and inadequate military into a replica of Taspar's. During the trip home, he realized that Lamech's army must be changed from its very foundations. No basis for respect was possible unless he could create a fighting force that could earn it. Once those changes were made, the men of Lamech would realize the value of the army and Zered could take his rightful place on the council of elders.

Jared's hot ambition was quickly cooled by intransigence in the decrepit organization that was Lamech's army. Its current leaders were old, comfortable, and had no stomach for change. For them, the army was little more than a source of easy income. In spite of his father's position and his own hard work, Jared had little to show after twenty years of effort; he was commander of one of the three battle groups, which together were less than a third of the army. His post was the least desired among the officers; hope of advancement was found in the ceremonial posts that included frequent contact with leading merchants and elders.

But Jared clung to his vision with a stubbornness that had older men shaking their beards. He knew that the ultimate purpose of an army was to fight. Delonias had taught him patience, and Jared remembered, in spite of chafing under the restrictions it imposed. During those years he became a man of iron will and self-discipline. When the time for fighting came, he would be ready. So he ruthlessly prepared for his moment, training his battle group in weapons skills and battle tactics that he learned in Taspar, spending more time out of town in the surrounding countryside. Although many of the older men became disgusted and transferred or quit when their term of service was finished, Jared found more willing men among the youth. They were open to his leadership, and eager for any path to adventure and glory. There were many ambitious young men who found in the young commander a like mind, but one who tempered their raw ambitions with discipline and professional pride.

Jared's command soon became a magnet to the young men of the city, and the material gratitude of Taspar following their first battle as allies won some much-needed support from their fathers. The first step from obscurity had been taken, and the men of the city easily agreed to pay to expand the size of his command. It had won honor and wealth for the city and the older men soon realized that it provided an outlet for impatient sons that were not ready to fully participate in the trades of their family.

Over the next fifty years, the other battle groups dwindled, and their commanders conveniently found other duties in policing the harbor and accompanying trading caravans. Jared commanded a consolidated battle group, which fought using the fast-moving and hard-striking tactics of Taspar. Those years provided invaluable experience. Six times Jared had been called upon to march with Delonias of Taspar. None of the battles had seriously tasked the great army of Taspar, but they taught Jared and his small command the difference between training and combat, and won him the further gratitude of Delonias, who continued to gain power in Taspar.

Torech had erred in assuming a lack of experience in Lamech's army and he knew very little about Jared. He assumed that even if Lamech would enforce its borders so far south, that its unprofessional, untested, and small army would be merely a light field exercise for his vicious horde. Sechiall had proven his mettle as the new Supreme Commander by leaving the details of the battle to Jared, and Torech had become another victim of an underestimated general and force. Jared only regretted that his father Zered had not lived long enough to see their success.

For Zered's early death had forced a change in Jared's plans. His father had been well liked and popular with merchants and members of the council. He had assumed the role of Supreme Commander on the strength of the alliance with Taspar, and Jared knew that a place on the council was within reach. Jared's military skills flourished under the bright sun of his growing maturity, and his lack of the political skills needed to sit on the council was of no consequence. His ambition was for Zered to sit in the gate. Jared did not want that honor.

But with Zered's demise the dream of integrating the army into the council died, too. Jared knew that he would never acquire the necessary polish and sophistication to speak and act as an equal to the elders, and he had the character to admit it to himself. He was certain to succeed to Supreme Commander of the army, and he was just as certain that he would advance no higher. Even his role in the Taspar alliance and success on the battlefield could not overcome his political shortcomings.

Even before Zered's death, his ill health had forced Jared to conclude that if he were to pursue his vision, he would have to be content as merely a battlefield general. His ultimate ambition required a solider who, like Zered, could also be a political leader and could stir the merchants and leading men. Being practical above all else, Jared began to search for a protégé who could complete his vision. He decided that he would train such a man and guide him, but in the end he would serve him. If he could find the right kind of young man or boy, he would be content.

But it was a fight against great odds. The council had a long memory and Jared still remembered that cursed afternoon following their first battle alongside the forces of Taspar. Zered had brought him before the full council to be recognized for his part, his best armor polished and shining in the sun. Lamech had read aloud the letter from Delonias, and had added to it his praise for the hard work of the young men of the army. He praised Zered for his wise delegation of authority, and the benefits in trade to the city. He then conferred a great honor on Jared by asking him to speak to the assembly.

Had Jared just held his tongue, perhaps events would have turned in another direction. Still flush with the confidence won by playing an important part in a decisive victory, he believed that his time was at hand. Had he been older by a few hundred years, he would have known better. He still remembered that final part of his speech—the only part of it that had any real meaning—but which had been so ill advised at the time.

"Fathers and elders of Lamech. You have acknowledged the success of Lamech's army in battle and in protecting and even promoting trade. We have proven ourselves able to deter bandits and thieves from our own territory. We have proven a match for most other towns, and through our wise alliance, we can even enhance commerce and trade and enrich the men of our fair city.

"Fathers and elders of Lamech. The world marches on. Evil and ambitious men pursue their sordid ends without regard for man or god. The Nephilim are spreading and even hardened warriors avoid combat with them. For Lamech to prosper, she must increase in her strength and defense. As the future brings uncertainty, should not the army's voice be heard in the closest councils of the elders? Consider well, fathers and elders, our civic role in preserving the future of our city."

If the council had been willing to ignore Jared's speech or if it had dealt with his impertinence though his father, things might still have turned out differently. But Noah had responded, with gracious voice, but in a public rebuke, nonetheless. The words struck Jared's heart and embittered it.

"*Young Jared has rightly won honor for himself, his father, and our town in his courageous conduct on the field of battle. However, the future does not lie in the counsel of any warrior, or of any group of warriors. It lies in the mind and will of the Almighty Creator of the Earth, and His favor and beneficence toward His children. Peace and prosperity are in His hand for the righteous, and judgment and retribution for the wicked. Let us not add to the wickedness of this generation by heeding the call to arms as a substitute for wisdom and righteousness. Let us all submit our hearts to the Judge of the World, and pray for His patience and mercy to us who offend Him daily.*"

Noah's words were to be long resented by Jared and the men of his battle group. The council had shown that the army might be a useful servant, but no more. These words plunged Jared into a valley of despair, but there are always hills on the other side of valleys, and Jared soon climbed two that restored fire and vigor to his dreams.

Chapter 5

BATTLE PLANS

Jared shook his head to clear his thoughts as he heard his name called by Juloch. The son of a servant of Zered, Juloch had grown up with Jared and was fiercely loyal. He could have been a notable warrior, but had insisted on serving Jared instead. His rugged smile lifted Jared's spirits, erasing the memory of Noah's words.

"All is in readiness, Commander," he reported. "The men want to know how far they will have to march before we camp."

"Not too far," replied Jared, confident that Juloch would spread the news quickly. "We only need to leave this valley and find a site that can be defended. It would be a pity to ruin a great victory by allowing Torech to come upon us unawares during the night. Even a small band could do enough killing to tarnish what we accomplished today."

"Do you think that Torech will attempt it?"

"No," Jared paused, "I think Torech will take his men back to Y'tor, start them drinking, and try to convince them that they won a great victory by slipping away, but it would be better not to take any chances. Besides," he added raising his voice so that those around would hear, "soldiers that can defeat Torech's army should be able to march into the cool of the evening."

Soon the column was winding back into the hills, its scouts probing the land all around for signs of life. Jared sank back into thought of what that fateful day before the council had wrought. After all these years, he still resented the words of Noah, but later events of that day had started him on a path to thwart the will of Noah. Jared smiled as he considered just how far down that path this day's victory had brought him.

Even as Noah was speaking, Jared had forced himself to maintain a calm face and resume his place among his own men. But after the council adjourned, he sought to leave immediately. He imagined that the leading men of the city were concealing their amusement at the events of the council, and he had no desire to remain for their entertainment. However, Zered had placed a heavy hand on his arm and restrained him. So Jared stood stolidly by his father as the crowd dispersed. Noah, Lamech, and Methuselah left together, and

Jared's father dismissed the troops.

Then without a word, he led Jared to the large public building at the far side of the square. It was deserted and dim inside with the coming evening. Through the shadows the father and son walked unerringly across the tiled floor to stairs that led to the privacy of the roof. Jared was surprised to see the elders Dajus and Subtur waiting for them. He had not noticed them entering the building, and he stiffened behind his father at the sight of them, and wondered what further misfortune would attend him this day. Whatever it was, he would face it like a man and a warrior.

"Hail, good Zered! Hail, young Jared," greeted Dajus. "Our thanks for your willingness to grant us your time. May the blessings of the city rest upon you both! Wise Subtur and I wished some private words with you, apart from the distraction of the crowd and the streets. We trust your discretion as we speak of important things as friends."

Jared could hardly hide his surprise at these words. They were not a prelude to further rebuke, but were spoken with a sincerity and familiarity that warmed his heart.

Dajus spoke on. "As you are aware, Lamech grows in numbers and prosperity. It is not difficult to foresee that it shall take its rightful place among the great cities of the earth. And yet such a thing will not happen apart from the best efforts of us all. A measure of wisdom, a measure of strength, a measure of wealth, and a measure of civic pride in the hearts of our men will be needed to lead Lamech to her obvious destiny."

"Strength must come from the young and wisdom from the old," interjected Subtur. "Civic virtue may be found in both and provide a meeting place for might and mind. Your sentiments expressed so directly today, young Jared, are not altogether unwelcome by all on the council. Dajus and I are men of the world—we live, trade, and legislate with an eye to the ultimate happiness of all men of Lamech. Our fellow elders at times allow a slightly excessive religious affection to misdirect their words and actions. Most commendable is their zeal, but a fine balance of more worldly wisdom is often required, and Dajus and I attempt to supply it with an eye to the future of Lamech."

"Thank you for your words, elder," returned Jared cautiously. "Your private kindness has helped to remove the sting from the public speech of your peer. But as you said, the wisdom of the old must meet the strength of the young in civic virtue. Please explain to me more plainly what you wish."

"Son," cautioned Zered, "patience is learned with experience. Allow our gracious leaders to express themselves in their own manner."

"Peace, Zered," interjected Subtur with a wave of his hand. "Young Jared is a noteworthy warrior with a warrior's direct manner. To answer your question, young man, we wish to encourage you to continue in your admirable work with the army. Perhaps Noah sees the future with the eyes of his god, as he boasted long ago, but it is a future that bodes ill. We see with the eyes of men, but cannot men see with wisdom? In that wisdom, we read the future as do you: strength will be needed and its very necessity will earn it a place among the councils of the wise.

"You desire to see the might of Lamech with a voice, currently enjoyed only by the wisdom, wealth, and piety of Lamech. This goal of investing the defense of the city with an appropriate aura of civic pride is noble and shared by some of the council. Methuselah, Lamech, and Noah are great men and their piety is a model for all, but perhaps in time the city will move beyond them. Keep patience, young friend, and allow the subtle application of our wisdom to come to your aid."

"My friend speaks as always with great wisdom," added Dajus. "But I would add a small word. The glorious future of Lamech must include the security of commerce and its resulting wealth. Poverty is the enemy of all men. We are not unaware of the economic advantages of our alliance with Taspar, an alliance that owes much to both father and son in its creation and maintenance. My own fortunes have benefited in a modest fashion in recent years, as have those of many of our leading merchants. Such things ultimately lead to their own reward."

Jared was unsure what to say, and was afraid to allow the words of these two great men to spark too much hope in his heart. He was glad when his father spoke instead, "We submit to your wisdom and advice, peerless in our city, and we bow to the honor that you pour out on us both. However, we know that there are many men of short sight in Lamech. Please accept our humble thanks and our word that no tale of our speech together today will be made known."

With that, Jared and Zered bowed and withdrew quietly down the stairs and out of the building. Dajus and Subtur stayed behind for a few minutes, walking to the coaming of the roof and looking down on the busy life on the streets below them.

Dajus broke the companionable silence. "I believe, my friend, that we have taken a sure step in a direction that will see great good come to us and to our city. Zered should outlive Methuselah by some years. He will be a compliant partner on the council. With the weight of the entire council against them, perhaps Noah and Lamech will come to their senses. If not, maybe they would withdraw to their settlement and start another town, leaving us to increase the wealth, security, and glory of Lamech as our wisdom directs us."

Subtur nodded as Dajus turned to leave. He left the building with a friendly smile and kind word for the merchants who were closing their stalls in the marketplace as he strolled to his home. Subtur remained on the parapet, looking down on his city and reflecting upon events. Methuselah and Lamech were his mentors. They had recognized early on a depth of understanding and an immense civic pride flowing throughout Subtur's life. Long years of friendship and service had culminated in his elevation to the council of elders, and Subtur knew that he owed his present position to those two men. Yet, as time went by, he found himself disagreeing with them more and more. Much of the time, he kept it to himself, but an open break seemed inevitable. They seemed to lack a vision of the future that would mine the noble parts of the human spirit beyond a simple god-man emphasis. After all, god had placed Earth under the rule of man. Adam's supposed sin had not really changed that. Not everyone was Adam.

Chapter 6
PROTÉGÉ

Jared's hope was thus reborn the same day that Noah had dashed it. As his father directed, he spoke no word about their meeting with the two elders, and to make certain that he guarded his tongue he also kept his silence about the entire day's events and especially the words of Noah. When several of his officers came to him to express their anger at the elders on his behalf, he merely replied, "We serve the council and people of Lamech, not ourselves. I will hear no insults against them." His men wondered at his restraint, and admired him all the more for his ability to put aside such a slight.

Jared's self discipline had always been a source of respect among his men. Although they cursed him tonight for forcing a march past sundown, they knew that he was as tired as any of them, and they did no more than curse as soldiers will. How could they resent a commander who personally inspected each unit's camp before seeing to his own comfort? Despite his body's complaints, Jared had a ready smile and warm words for each of the men, and they admired him all the more for showing none of the weakness that they all shared.

When finally he returned to his own fire, he found the Supreme Commander waiting for him with Juloch hovering over wine and food. Jared saluted the Commander, but was interrupted before he could speak. "Sit and eat, Jared! Consider that the order of your Supreme Commander. Then you will retire for the night. That is another order!"

The ready smile that accompanied these words robbed them of force. Jared sat and replied, "Let it not be said that anyone would dare disobey the Supreme Commander of the armies of Lamech!"

Sechiall grinned and began to talk while Jared ate and drank. Every detail of their successful charge evidently remained clear in Sechiall's mind, and he relished the retelling of every thrust of his spear and every wound that he had inflicted during those frantic minutes. Jared nodded while he ate and drank, and saw before him the instrument by which he would force the army into the circle of power of the council. It had been just thirty short years since Sechiall had strode into his tent—unafraid and even then exuding a confidence and power that belied his status as little more than a slave. Jared remembered that first meeting well.

In the summer following his humiliation at the hands of Noah, the army was camped outside of town, the season's training almost complete. Men were busy preparing to shed their swords and begin work at the harvest. The sun was setting on a tired camp and Jared was removing his armor in his tent when Juloch entered. "Your pardon, commander," he interrupted, "but there is a messenger from Delonias outside."

"Send him to me immediately," Jared replied, wrapping his cloak about him. He wondered if Delonias had heard about his encounter with the council. Considering the vast network of Taspar's spies in both allied and enemy towns, he probably had.

The man who entered wore the livery of Taspar's army, and Jared recognized him as Menelos, a personal aide to Delonias. He and Jared were on good terms, and Menelos was aware of the regard Delonias had for the young officer of Lamech. Jared was glad to see him; others associated with Delonias were jealous of the preference given to the 'outsider.'

"Please enter and welcome," said Jared, and gestured to a carpeted annex of the tent. "Bring us wine and food, Juloch," Jared continued, and waited for his guest to be seated. After exchanging greetings, they ate and drank after the manner of hungry soldiers, finally turning to more serious conversation.

"What news, Menelos?" Jared finally asked his guest. "Is Delonias well?"

"Yes, Commander. He has won another victory—he defeated a savage band from the Nephil town of Hasell. They were few in numbers, but it was a hard fight. You remember the battle at Babaresh?"

"Yes," replied Jared, "we had a bitter fight that day. What was it—twenty-five years ago? Their army was small and inadequate, but the Nephilim mercenaries were quite another tale. What warriors! They fought hard, and would not surrender." Jared unconsciously fingered the scar on his forearm, a relic of that day from which he had learned another painful lesson about warfare.

"Delonias is willing to use any weapon," Menelos continued. "He has seen that few men can match a Nephil warrior. He considered recruiting a Nephil battle group into the army, but decided instead to integrate individual warriors into companies to increase their overall effectiveness.

"He believes that a small leavening of such warriors in our best battle groups would be a prudent policy, and would increase the fighting efficiency of both Taspar and its allies. Group efficiency would remain consistent, but each group would have a strong core of irresistible fighting men to lead a charge or anchor a stand. In his most recent battle, Delonias refused to destroy Hasell. Instead, he entered the city and was able to capture a number of young boys, who he has scattered among the battle groups of Taspar."

Jared waited, wondering what this news had to do with him. Menelos satisfied his curiosity with a compliment. "There is not a commander in the Taspar army who does not respect and praise the forces of Lamech and its Battle Commander, and most are amazed at what you have accomplished in your short years and without the enthusiasm of your council. When Delonias decided to send one of the boys to Lamech in preference of some of our own battle groups, those commanders did not begrudge it, and all acknowledged the wisdom of Delonias. He often speaks of you when he insists that fighting is for the very young, and Taspar has decided to lower the recruiting age to thirty years because of what you have accomplished here."

Jared winced inwardly at the oblique reference to his recent rebuke by Noah and its knowledge in Taspar, but kept his face indifferent.

"And," continued the aide with a smile, "Delonias would rather you defeat Y'tor than do it himself. Keep your eyes on them. Our spies tell us that a young Nephil named Torech became commander of their army fifteen years ago, and now he is virtually the ruler of the entire city. We can no longer maintain a presence there but trust Lamech to keep an eye on the upstart."

Jared laughed. "Trust Delonias to grasp an advantage from even his kindness. You flatter me and honor Lamech with your words. Although it is true that our council may not see the honor as clearly, they have seen that our traders and merchants receive preference in Taspar, and perhaps in time they will see more. But Methuselah, Lamech, and Noah fear that our young men may move beyond their commitment to the defense of our city and come to love war for itself."

"A grave temptation," returned Menelos with a knowing smile. Both men laughed suddenly in the shared pride and professionalism that old fools on town councils could never appreciate. Jared was glad to see an expression of sympathy from a respected fellow.

Menelos continued, "Even if Delonias cannot convince the old men of Lamech's council of your importance, we believe that Torech will. But, back to business." He paused and assumed a more formal tone. "In recognition of your loyalty and skill, Delonias sends a gift of one of the captives to you. He is confident that if anyone can harness the young warrior's fire, you can. Make what use of the boy that you can, and report back to Delonias."

"Your master is too kind," Jared replied, not yet sure what to make of the news. However, it was clear that if he had bothered to send his trusted aide all the way to Lamech to deliver one captive, that at the very least, it was an important move to Delonias.

"Please grant us the privilege of your companionship tonight, and I will prepare a message to Delonias for your return." Jared motioned to his orderly, standing quietly in the corner. "Take Menelos to my other tent, and see to his men and animals."

"If it would not inconvenience you, commander," Menelos returned, "please allow me to bring you the boy before I refresh myself."

"Very well. Juloch, bring the boy to me."

The man returned almost immediately. Behind him followed a young lad of no more than thirteen or fourteen years. As they walked into the main room of the tent, Jared was most immediately struck by his mien. There was an absence of both fear and anger. Curiosity shown in the boy's eyes as they took in the tent, the small table with its maps, and then lingered over the stand of weapons and armor behind it, before coming to rest on Jared. Those eyes met Jared's squarely and did not waver. They were a peculiar intense blue, with flecks of color that gave them fire and passion. Although clearly a young boy, he was already as large as many men and his stature and yellow hair clearly set him apart as one of the Nephilim.

"What is your name, boy?" asked Jared quietly.

"Sechiall, Commander," he answered with a strong and steady voice, "your servant by the will of Delonias, victor over my people."

"What of your own will?" asked Jared, voicing the first thought that came to him.

"Does it matter?" returned the boy quickly. Juloch moved forward to strike the boy for his impertinence, but Jared halted him with a motion of his hand.

"To you, I'm sure it does—to me, it might," replied Jared. It seemed to him that he and the boy were the only two people in the tent.

"Then my will is to be served, not to serve," the boy said in a level voice, "but I will be content to learn from you until that time comes. Delonias told me that I was the most likely of his captives, and that you were the best commander that he knew. He said that you would be a good teacher. I would like to learn."

"What would you learn?"

"First, to be a man. Then a warrior. These will fulfill the debts that I owe to my fathers. Then I would reach further. I would be a leader of warriors."

"If you can be a man, then perhaps you can be trained as a warrior. If you can be a warrior, perhaps you can be taught the rudiments of leadership. But to be a true leader will take something else—a gift of god."

"Do not the leaders of Lamech say that there is only one god, the creator; and do not the people of Lamech follow this god? My people say that there are many gods, and we follow the god of war."

"Maybe I do also," mused Jared, almost to himself. He turned to his servant.

"Juloch," he commanded, "take Sechiall into your tent. He may learn your duties for the present—then we will see."

That night, the young boy lay awake on his rug and watched the shadow of the moon rise past the roof of the tent. Slow, regular breathing proclaimed the sleep of the man on the other rug. Perhaps he was a slave for now, but men in their weakness had opened a door for him; his own people would have slain everyone in the town had the situation been reversed. For the Nephilim had no such weaknesses. From his earliest memories he had known that his was a special race destined to achieve and hold power over lesser men. Let them keep their leash on the cub for the present. He would be patient. The cub must grow before it could roar and rend, but one day he would seize that leash and drag those on the end of it within the reach of his teeth. He would satisfy their wishes because they were steps that he must take to his own mark. In the end, through his own strength and cunning, he would have a kingdom and a place for his people. Those who did not submit would die. The thought was pleasant, and with it, he fell asleep.

To all appearances, Delonias' wisdom was vindicated in Sechiall. He grew, he learned, and he became immensely popular with the men of the army. The townsfolk overcame their initial fear of a wolf inside their walls after observing his dignified and humble behavior, and all respected Jared, who they saw as the boy's father, although no formal adoption was performed. Despite his behavior, Sechiall could not help but stand out. There was an aura about him. All were drawn to him and desired his friendship. To all appearances he gave it freely, but for Jared alone there was sincere respect, and that came from the lessons that Jared alone gave in weapons skills.

Before he reached thirty summers, Sechiall stood a head taller than any other man in the army. Already powerful, under Jared's tutelage his strength was harnessed to a warrior's skill. No one could throw a spear with the same force and only Jared remained the superior swordsman—though Jared was the first to admit that his own skill had been improved by constant practice with

Sechiall. A few of the wiser and older men felt a tinge of fear with their respect, but the younger men vied openly for his affection and favor. No one doubted that he did possess the special gift of leading men. Only Jared commanded more love among the men. But among those warriors who most exulted in battle itself for blood and death, Sechiall stood second to none. Jared honored him on his thirtieth birthday by giving him command of a small unit, and was surprised when some of his best fighters, including Oman, Gatar, and Kenah, volunteered to serve under Sechiall.

It was that year when Jared was first forced to reconsider his plans. Zered had taken ill with a severe fever, and was sick in bed for several weeks. Although he recovered, and began to regain his strength, the event caused Jared to ponder the consequences of Zered dying before Methuselah. Zered's death might elevate Jared to Supreme Commander, but it would doom any possibility of the Supreme Commander being elevated to the council. He cast about for alternatives. He considered man after man, but some inner voice kept leading him back to Sechiall. He knew that was foolish; it would be decades before Sechiall would be ready for even high command in the army. But no one else had that inner fire that so attracted both warriors and the people of the city. Would Lamech even accept an outsider for high office? Sechiall might need hundreds of years to attain the necessary experience and wisdom required of an elder, but logic forced his consideration. Sechiall would have the support of all of the fighting men, who being young themselves, had no qualms in elevating a younger man. Other leaders of the army would support him for guarantees of their present lucrative positions. Sechiall was popular with the prominent young men of Lamech, and their fathers might be drawn along.

Jared never made a decision in haste and spent several years considering his alternatives. But he could find no other and so he decided to take action. First, he took the younger man into his confidence. He shared his dream of a powerful army with a seat on the council, and Zered's potential elevation. But he admitted that if his father died before Methuselah, there was little possibility of the council accepting the son. The future of the army must be realized through another; through Sechiall. After much discussion they agreed that if events so demanded, Jared would decline the position of Supreme Commander in favor of Sechiall, and remain Battle Commander. Sechiall argued that he could not become Jared's superior, but Jared assuaged his fears. "You and I will not change with circumstance or title. We are men. We are warriors. We are leaders." Sechiall shrugged and grinned, "You will always be a father to me, regardless of what title men give. That is enough for me."

They both knew that Jared's support, backed by the enthusiasm of the entire army, should be sufficient to force consideration by the council of such a dramatic move, but Jared knew that more would be required. What would his father think? He needed his support. Overcoming his repugnance at discussing his father's demise, Jared rode into town and opened his heart to his father. Zered laughed for many minutes when he finished. "Your appetite for intrigue is growing, my son. No," he waved away Jared's frown, "it is a skill that you must cultivate to succeed. You need the support of our friends on the council. I will invite them to inspect your camp next week, but will say nothing about our discussion here. I leave that to you. Consider it another lesson."

So Jared found himself a nervous host of Dajus and Subtur within a few days. He arranged extended displays of martial skill that required them to stay overnight, and they were lavishly entertained that night by Jared and Sechiall. After the meal, Jared served more wine and after a period of polite discussion of the events of the day, he broached his proposal. "Esteemed elders, I am grateful for your presence here at this time. The troops are highly motivated by your presence and I hope that the rigors of camp life tonight will not discourage you from granting them your personal attention in days ahead. But there is another reason that I have requested your presence here today—it provides an opportunity for private speech."

Dajus expressed mild curiosity and said, "We are more than willing to endure discomfort for the good of our army and city. Your men are obviously well trained and appear to be quite happy with your leadership. They are a credit to your hard work these past years."

Subtur nodded, then interrupted his friend. "But what need is there for private speech, young commander?" He looked meaningfully at Sechiall and continued, "What needs to be said that cannot be said before all?"

Jared hesitated, and admitted, "Sechiall is privy to my deepest desires regarding the army and not only will support them with his right arm, but can play a significant part in fulfilling them." He saw concern on the faces of both men and felt his entire dream slipping away. Faced with a battle on an unfamiliar field, he struggled on.

"Please hear me, elders. I know that if what is said or done here displeases you, that our previous plans will come to naught, and that I can expect nothing from you in the future. But before you withdraw your kindness from me, please listen to what I have to say."

At their tight-lipped nods, he continued, "The recent illness of Zered, my beloved father, fills me with dread that he may not remain among us for as many years as we desire. Methuselah has walked the earth for many centuries and is still accounted a strong man. If Zered fails to outlive him, then

Lamech's army would never gain its voice amid the seats of power. My elevation to Supreme Commander would please the army, but it would also ensure that the Supreme Commander of the army of Lamech will not be elevated to the council. Therefore, for the good of the city and the army, another man is needed to take the place of Zered—a man who could win the hearts of the men of the city."

Dajus stirred briefly, "What you say may be true, young man, but your father is an unusual man. He is remarkable for his skill with both scroll and spear. Who is there that would be acceptable to both soldiers and elders? Speaking as an elder, I know of none."

Jared looked him directly in his eye and replied softly, "I know of such a man, elder. Sechiall has the hearts of every man in the army. He is well-liked in town and has the gifts of speech and manner to win those who are not soldiers."

Subtur was unable to control his face or voice. With evident heat, he replied sharply. "You have lost what sense I thought that you had, Jared! We have only to wait three or four hundred years until he is of age to serve. He is but a child, and an outsider at that!" He spluttered and tried visibly to calm his voice, but failed. Before he could continue, Dajus gripped his arm and silenced him. Unlike Subtur, he retained control of his voice, but the tightness around his eyes revealed his own agreement with Subtur.

He spoke calmly. "Jared, Jared. My friend is excited, but correct. How can the men of the city turn authority over to a stripling and an outsider? Even if what you say about his support among the army is true, the men of Lamech will resist him for this reason alone." He turned to Sechiall. "What have you to say to this, boy?"

Sechiall bowed his eyes before both men and sat silent in respect for several long minutes. "I am aware of the drawbacks of my age and experience, and we must bow to the wisdom of men such as yourselves," he stated quietly. "I understand that if such a miracle were to occur, my own lack of wisdom would force a certain dependence on the wise already serving. I must be the man that I am——and that is a warrior and leader of warriors. I could never hope to aspire to serve in the same capacity as either of you."

He paused for a moment, and Jared noted with relief that the two men had understood the intended message of subservience. Sechiall continued, "But times are changing and we must change with them. War is coming to Lamech, elders. Torech will attack this city and will not stop until he is dead or we are defeated. Wisdom will not defeat him, only a strong spear and a skillful arm. The task of our army must be that of making sure of his death. The specter of

Torech at our gates with thousands of his raging demons should be enough to create a modicum of appreciation for we who serve. Perhaps it is sufficient to justify a seat for the army. After all, a man who has proven himself against Torech might persuade many that expanding our understanding of qualifications is itself a wise decision."

Dajus stirred again, leaning slightly forward. Jared noticed with interest that Sechiall's magnetism that so attracted rough soldiers had an effect on the elders, too. Dàjus shot a warning glance at Subtur, and spoke. "What you propose would indeed be a mighty shift in our council. But have we not all considered that as Lamech grows into its rightful place in the world that changes may become necessary? A man who could defeat Torech would be worthy of great honor. A man who could also deliver the riches of Y'tor into the hands of Lamech would be a friend of the merchants as well. I remain dubious, but will not close my mind to the changing winds of the future. We will consider what you say. But be warned, Jared," he continued with authority, "let us not continue to share our private discussions with anyone else."

Jared bowed his head humbly and replied, "Truly, sir, I lack the subtlety of mind to engage in governance. I spoke to Sechiall because of my trust in his heart and his role in our future. No others will hear these words."

"Very well," warned Subtur, "but two keys will be needed to even unlock this door. The first is the unqualified support of all the army. The second is a decisive victory over Torech. You and I may recognize the threat, but many merchants assume that our relationship with Taspar will deter him. They must be convinced. I cannot guarantee my support even with these things. For that I need more thought."

Dajus nodded. "Of course that is known by both of these young men. And who knows? Life is uncertain. If Methuselah fails and Zered thrives, then all of this discussion is vain. But if it proves otherwise, then you are right to think of alternatives. You should expect your destination to require several steps. It will be difficult enough to convince the council that Sechiall could be Supreme Commander. It may be wise to have reliable men begin to speak of his qualities and exploits among the men of Lamech. For only if Jared insists, and all the army demands it, can Sechiall be considered.

"Truly your wisdom and understanding are beyond my reach, elder," returned Jared. "What you have said will be acceptable to us, and I will guarantee that the necessary steps are taken." The elders turned to Sechiall, who humbly bowed before them and left the tent.

Eventually, the plans hatched that night in Jared's tent had proven necessary. For Zered had died, the same day that news arrived of the capture of a wealthy caravan by Torech, and his massacre of the merchants. The town was thrown into an uproar, and the loss of Zered was felt all the more keenly in their hour of need. Most men assumed that his position would go to Jared. In spite of his youth, his stature as a warrior was undisputed, and all knew that he enjoyed the favor of the great Delonias. When he announced his preference for Sechiall, the square erupted into uncontrolled shouts for many minutes.

But Jared had used the time well, assiduously following the advice of Dajus and preparing the way. Indeed, enough men spoke so well of "the outsider" now that his youth or origin were of little consequence. He had been firmly adopted into the family of Lamech. The warriors knew his prowess; the merchants his ready smile and unfailing help; and most women were drawn to him in ways that embarrassed and thrilled them at the same time. When order had been restored, Jared spoke with a passion that swayed many. The good of the army and the city must come before his own ambition. Only one issue was at stake; who could best command and lead the city's warriors. With one voice, the carefully prepared army made it clear that the man they wanted was Sechiall. The merchants were so frightened by Torech's attack that they would not oppose the will of a unified army, and their voices also supported Sechiall.

In spite of the uproar, Noah, Lamech, and Methuselah still questioned the wisdom of the appointment, but Dajus and Subtur placated Lamech with the idea of a provisional command, and once he agreed, Noah and Methuselah were silent.

Jared pulled himself away from his reverie. Night was passing and he was bone weary. There was no possibility of Torech returning and catching them close to the battlefield in a surprise attack. He glanced at Sechiall who nodded in understanding, and allowed Juloch to lead him off to his tent, where he wearily removed his armor and sought his blankets. But sleep did not come easily. No man could now deny that the army of Lamech was a legitimate force, not just an appendage of Taspar. Behind the natural fire and charisma of Sechiall, the army would now be a powerful force in the city—a force to shape and direct, not just a tool to be used or not at the whim of a few elders. Even if it took another hundred years, Sechiall would sit on the council and Jared would be his right arm and sword.

In the next tent another commander smiled to himself as the pale light of the moon filtered into his tent. The cub had grown. Soon he would be ready to reveal himself. The fools would hand Lamech to him without a fight. Torech's head would be needed for a seat on the council, but once there, the council would find itself overcome from the inside. Y'tor might be a start—after all, Torech was king, and if he was dead, then who better to rule than one who had proven himself Torech's master? King of two cities... It was a pleasant thought.

****

Hearing the soft voice call again, the old woman slowly withdrew her gaze from the dancing embers and looked up. The young woman picked up the book, fallen unnoticed from her clenched hand, and placed it back on the table. Food and wine had already been laid out without the old woman's awareness. The young woman had learned to recognize the vacant stare and rigid stillness that denoted the old one's journeys. When she went to that other place, the young woman moved silently and smoothly, unnoticed.

The old woman mechanically picked up the carved wooden cup and sighed as the wine warmed her mouth and seemed to relax her stiff body. Her mind might travel, but it had not lost its acuity. She appreciated the quiet and efficient service. This one did not distract her. Thus, she was able to apply her mind to her writing. Occasionally she dipped into the old documents, more to trigger thought than to assist her recall. These past few years had seen a greater facility of memory, but it was becoming harder for her mind to return, for she caught shadows of the future now mingled with the past. She was ready, but willing to finish her task first. She smiled briefly to herself. She had always looked ahead with mixed feelings and worried more about the future than was good for her.

With warm wine inside her and a few bites of bread and honey, she relaxed back into the couch, letting her body sag into its comfortable contours. Moments stood out; the birth of her first child, her husband's face in the firelight, sunlight off the seas...

Chapter 7

LAMECH

The early afternoon sun permeated the ruffled surface of the water and opened its green depths to human vision. Madrazi stood at her accustomed place at the front of the ship, swaying unconsciously now to its easy motion and watching the shallow schools of fish wheel and dive in unison, then scatter before the attack of the ship's shadow. Far ahead, a dark smudge of land was now visible: Cape Lemuel, which formed the only good harbor for many days sailing up or down the coast. A white flash marked the light tower atop the steep cliffs. She was on the verge of a long anticipated future, but a sense of concealed danger touched her mind as she watched the white sentinel and suddenly, irrationally, she wanted Hakkem to turn about. But a glance down at the green depths reminded her of a deeper desire for the freedom of dry land.

"We will be free of you soon," interrupted a voice, mostly in jest but tinged with sincerity. It was Ithiel, her oldest brother, most like her father in body as she was most like him in mind. Growing up, her brothers had spoiled her, then avoided her during the emotional swings following their mother's death. As she grew, they were often gone, but their pride in her was tempered by jealousy of her emerging value to their father's trade. Eventually, they grew used to her role, and settled for adventurous voyages while Madrazi tended to the dull details, and on the whole, the siblings came to an equitable understanding, though the affections of early years had been irrevocably lost. Even mutual dislike for Peniah and pride in the quality of her upcoming marriage had not restored the deeper feelings of their youth.

He ran a keen eye over her face. "You certainly look better," he noted gruffly. "The easy waters inside the great barrier reefs are just what a woman needs. We need only pilot you a few more days."

Madrazi kept one hand lightly on the great bow mast, envying her brother's easy balance. "I thought that you and Ucal were grateful for the holiday," she returned pertly, directing the conversation away from her weakness. "If it were not for this wedding, you both would be rowing rocks to Ramsheed and returning with a load of goats."

Ithiel laughed unexpectedly. "I am sure that you would have written it so and had Father seal it without even reading it. I wonder if Shem is braced for the surprise coming to him on the wind? I hope that he is either a very adventurous or a very accommodating soul."

"You need not worry about me, brother. Just keep both your eyes on Peniah when you get back. Her mind is quick, but her heart cold."

Hakkem continued north, parallel to a flat, sandy shore to the east. Its barren topography was relieved only by small dunes, climbing steadily but smoothly inland to cultivated lands or sparse woods. A line of distant hills had interrupted the flat lands just north of Y'tor, but since then they had seen only a low, rolling plain. As the afternoon wind drew them closer to Lamech, Madrazi saw the land change, as the shoreline jogged sharply west ahead. The flat sands ended at that point and the rocky shoreline of the cape began, tilting upward to the west as the cape shouldered its way out into the sea. It ended in a headland where steep cliffs rose a hundred cubits above the crashing surf.

At the zenith of the western cliffs the dazzling white tower was now clearly visible in the sun. All mariners knew of the light tower of Lamech, but the tales did not prepare Madrazi for its magnificence. She could not believe that any structure built by humans could rise to such a height. Its base was easily a hundred cubits above the face of the sea and the tower itself reared easily another hundred above that. Even during the day it was impossible to miss the shining whiteness of its stone in the sun.

From the seaside cliffs, a rugged tentacle of rock ran south, forming a large bay, and a smaller parallel line of rock split the bay into two harbors. On the rugged western side Madrazi could see small boats and small hovels clustered along the steeper shores. She decided that it must be a fishing community, since the ground there was clearly unfit for cultivation. It seemed that nature had taken a hand to segregate the poorer, unfit citizens from the prosperity of the city.

As Hakkem sailed north into the bay, the westering sun drew her eyes to the walls of her new home. The city grew larger and more distinct as the ship glided across the bay and provided an impressive contrast to the small fishing village. White walls rose high above the bay, the ground between the walls and the water sloping quickly down to a narrow ledge at the water's edge. From the inner harbor, the city marched upward with the cape to the north and west. Hakkem was not alone; four other sea-going ships, two flying the bright red and yellow banner of Taspar, rode the quiet waters. Ahead, a large stone quay ran a short way out into the water. Stone warehouses and wooden sheds clustered along the narrow bench below the walls and its strong gate.

They glided down the channel towards the shore as the men took in the last bit of canvas. Pomorolac's clear voice rose over the sounds of the sea as he took charge of maneuvering the ship. He soon ordered the anchors over the sides at the front and rear of the ship and brought Hakkem to a smooth stop still some distance away from the quay, just out of the main channel. Within minutes, Madrazi's attention was drawn to a small boat rowing straight at them. A green and black banner flew from the stern and a man waved from the front. It passed to her left and around the back of Hakkem, where the man in the boat hailed the ship.

Madrazi walked towards the stern and heard her father's clear voice, "This is the trading ship, Hakkem, sailing under the flag of the guild, bearing the bride of the son of Noah." With a laugh, she realized that she was just so much cargo on a trading ship, and stopped at the mainmast to hear the men speak.

"Welcome with many blessings from our fair city of Lamech," she heard. "I am Pekod, the master of the harbor, and must certify your ship and crew to be free from sickness. May I come aboard?"

"Come with our welcome," replied her father, correctly. "I am Pomorolac, master of the ship. We are all in good health as you will see, but come and do your duty." He impatiently waved Madrazi away forward, but she merely stepped behind the mast and kept listening.

"Your great reputation precedes you, master of trade," replied the man after he had adroitly slipped up the side of the Hakkem onto the deck. His nimbleness revealed that he had been a sailor, who would of course be familiar with the name and reputation of Pomorolac. He bowed low and continued to speak. "Even were you not a kinsman of elders on our council and bearing such a precious cargo for our fair city, you would certainly enjoy the welcome and blessing of the elders. All the merchants would count it an honor to do trade with one of your honesty, and that honor would console them as they counted their narrow profits after tasting your skills. What ocean have you not traveled? What cargo have you not carried?"

Madrazi relished the words and tone of the city official. Even if they did not reveal the mind of Pekod, at least they indicated that her future would include respect from such as he. Her promised husband's family was prominent. She had every reason to believe that in leaving Hakkem behind, she would be turning to a promising new life. If only she could leave now! However, she guessed that her father, who had not been to Lamech in many years, would choose to stay aboard until morning. Her fears proved correct, and the disappointment was no less for being so. After he had seen the harbormaster courteously off the ship, he came forward.

"We stay aboard tonight, daughter. I do not know this town well, and with all the changes that are occurring elsewhere I do not trust what I do not know.

Although Methuselah, his son Lamech, and his son, Noah, are powerful men on the council of elders, only Lamech lives in town these days according to the master, and he is presently away at his son's house." Madrazi's face fell.

"Do not blame your new family," he laughed. "That strange shift of the winds brought us here four days early. You may have to wait, but men will now think the Hakkem faster than the sea eagles."

"They may, if the best they have seen are those scows," she returned lightly, waving at the other ships.

Pomorolac laughed with her. "There is other news," he continued, his smile disappearing. "Pekod told me that the army of Lamech has marched south to deal with Torech. He attacked and looted a caravan a few months ago and the council finally unleashed their army. I imagine that we saw the smoke of battle a few days past." He tried unsuccessfully to hide his worry from his daughter, and she wisely said nothing.

Changing the subject smoothly, he continued, "Noah is at his settlement a day's march from town on the edge of the Great Forest. This Pekod expressed regard for him and his sons, but there was something in his tone while discussing our kinsmen that made me uncomfortable. We will see in the morning."

Madrazi considered those words as she ate and prepared for sleep. No one could blame her preoccupation, and her mind stayed active even as her ears ignored Jahaz' conversation. Pomorolac had become a successful trader in part by an uncanny ability to understand men and read much in the shading of their expressions and voices. Madrazi knew his skill, and his overtones of concern gave her something new to ponder. Had Noah abandoned the city? Would Shem hold any hope of power or prestige if he had?

Lying in the dark, she suddenly realized that she had never considered the distance from Lamech to Noah's home. Methuselah had described it fully, but she had listened to only what she wanted to hear. She excoriated her stupidity. She had always assumed that she would be a short walk from the walls of the town and surrounded by other settlements. Did Shem live with his father in the wild? Would she? She had looked forward to being a woman respected by others, but how could that be if there were only animals and birds to bow down to her? While not averse to living outside of town, she did not desire isolation. She had lived that way long enough. But just as she was working herself into a temper, she remembered her Granpapa's tales of the forest and felt once again that deep stirring of inexplicable desire. Pictures from his tales came rushing back and she felt a strange thrill at being only a day's walk from that place. What would it be like to roam among those trees with a strong man who was her husband?

Morning surprised Madrazi. She had imagined that she would not sleep, but the gentle waters of the harbor had rocked her to sleep early and she awoke refreshed and excited about what lay ahead. Pomorolac saw to the order of the ship while she ate and prepared herself for town. His instructions to her came in the same tone as his orders to the crew.

"My daughter, we will enter the town and pay our respects to the elders at the gate. Then we will find lodging and await the pleasure of Master Noah. We do not know their plans for your wedding and their customs may seem strange to you. Be patient! Remember, inside the walls you must stay with me at all times outside your room. Wear a veil in public! We must make a good appearance for the townsfolk."

Madrazi nodded acquiescence. Such were the customs of the day. She did not care. Everyone would know who she was, regardless of her veil, but making a proper initial impression was important. Any lack of regard that she possessed for custom must remain hidden for the present. Quickly she dressed in her richest clothes, and let Jahaz drape her with heavy strings of pearls and gold. Seated in the ship's boat, she considered how quickly she would end up on the harbor bottom if she fell overboard. But the boat moved smoothly but rapidly, propelled by the powerful strokes of eight of the strongest crewmembers. Pomorolac had dressed them all alike, and their colors matched the trim painted on the boat. They reached the great pier and saw steps carved into a landing at the water's edge. Pomorolac slipped adroitly along the slippery rocks and carefully guided his daughter up to the quay as the men tied the boat to one of the posts. Madrazi felt a thrill course through her with her first step on this new shore, but stood quietly by her father until the men had gathered behind them. Already the confining veil and heavy cloth was making her hot, but she knew better than to complain. Her appearance today would help define both Pomorolac and Shem for years to come.

As they left the pier and climbed the broad steps to the city gate, she forgot her discomfort in the detail of the walls. They were constructed of close-fitting large white blocks; the smallest must have been four cubits across. The wall itself was at least fifteen cubits high. Two large towers jutted upwards another ten cubits protecting the great gate. People began to gather behind them as they climbed the stone stairs: rich traders were common in Lamech's harbor, but the name of Pomorolac had begun to circulate around the waterfront and everyone from captains to sailors wanted a glimpse of the great man.

Approaching the top stair, Madrazi saw that the white stone of the steps continued as a road to the wall. The gate was wide, its two heavy wooden doors banded with iron. They opened outward, and the road ran under a stone arch to a square just inside. As she walked under the dim recess of the arch, she could see sunshine illuminating the scene ahead. Eager to step into the bright future awaiting her, she stepped boldly forward.

In spite of her excitement, her eyes were still observant. On two sides of the square warriors in bronze armor and bronze helmets stood in rigid lines. Long green feathers formed bright plumes on the tops of their helmets, and decorated the long spears held beside them. Behind them were large buildings of the same white stone as the walls and a glimpse of roads branching in many directions into the town. Immediately on their right were five chairs set on a broad dais of green and white serpentine. The chairs were intricately carved out of a black stone that Madrazi had not seen before and inlaid with gold designs. The dark stone belied its first appearance: Madrazi caught blue flashes as the sun's rays sparkled across it. A rich awning of green cloth stretched over the dais, but was arranged to allow the pleasant morning sun to warm the chairs. Only the two nearest the gate were occupied.

Madrazi stood still amidst the crew and her brothers as Pomorolac stepped forward. He stopped and bowed before the two men. "I am Pomorolac, a humble seafarer in the guild. I come to Lamech with peace in my hands," he said, holding out both hands with his palms up in the ancient gesture. "I bring my most valued possession, not in trade but as a gift to the son of Noah."

The two men inclined their heads slightly while still sitting. The one in the second chair rose and advanced slowly. He was short and showed every sign of a comfortable and prosperous life. His voice was smooth, with only a hint of the condescending tone developed over long years of power. "Welcome, O master of the secrets of the seas. Who has not heard of the voyages of Pomorolac? In the name of the city of Lamech, we bid you peace and prosperity! I am Dajus of the Council of Elders of the city. My peer is Subtur."

Subtur rose, a taller dark-haired man with a strong face. He bowed, and stood slightly behind Dajus, who continued, "We deeply regret the absence of our brothers to welcome such an illustrious guest, but the greatness of your fame was still insufficient to account for the speed of your voyage. We did not expect to see you for several days and were not sure whether to expect you from sea or land. However, since they are all your kinsmen, perhaps your forgiveness will flow freely."

"O noble and wise Dajus," returned Pomorolac, "to be greeted in such a manner by any of the elders of the great city of Lamech would be considered an honor beyond this humble merchant. To be met by two takes my speech.

Were all my kinsmen here, the honor would be too great. We will see them as their valued time allows and thank god for the meeting. It has been many long years since I have beheld their faces, and we will rejoice at their arrival, whenever it comes."

"Your kinsmen will doubtless also rejoice in seeing you after such a long absence," replied Dajus. "Those years have earned you fame; your exploits are well known in Lamech. Our city is blessed by your presence, and even more by the gift of your daughter to our community. Messengers were sent at first light to the home of Noah to tell them of your coming and while we await his pleasure, we beg you to accept the hospitality of our town. You would honor me personally if you would consent to abide in the inn of my brother, Eldad. He can assure you rest and food to refresh you after your long journey. Perhaps later today you would consent to join Subtur and me in the evening meal. We would enjoy hearing the news of the world."

Pomorolac bowed his assent. Dajus did not pause, unable to imagine any brooking of his will. "Guard," he commanded, turning to one of the young soldiers, "escort our guests to the inn of Eldad."

The guard saluted and with a polite gesture, led the way toward the city center. Madrazi was intensely curious about the town that would be her new home and strove to remember every building and street. All her life she had lived in the rocky fastness beside the ocean. True, she had traveled to several prominent cities and knew how to judge the quality of the town. Were the roads paved with stone or simply dirt? Were they straight, level, and wide or merely large pathways? Was the city clean or did the refuse gather inside the walls? How much stone was used in building? Was there a liberal use of decoration, or were the buildings small and functional? As they walked, the streets of Lamech quickly satisfied her critical eye that this was indeed a great city and a fit home for her future life.

Immediately out of the square, they passed through a teeming marketplace of colorful tents and stalls that reflected the volume of trade through the city. Madrazi and her father both had to suppress the impulse to calculate opportunity and they smiled together as they each read the other's thoughts in their eyes. Then the straight road led them to a larger one that wound into the city. On the left was a magnificent building that reared on great pillars many cubits into the clear morning sky. The guard followed their gaze and commented, "This is the great temple of Lamech where sacrifice is made on the altar of the Creator. It was the first great stone building that was completed, and its beauty set a standard that has been upheld in all our construction ever since."

They followed the winding street—obviously a main thoroughfare. Another great building rose on their right, diagonally across from the temple. Four great columns, at least five cubits across supported the intricate carved stone beams above the portico. Encouraged by their obvious interest, the guard continued. "This is the hall of the merchants. All matters of trade and commerce are decided there by the local members of the guild."

Before he could continue, Pomorolac interrupted gently. "We are aware of the workings of the guild."

"Of course, master Pomorolac," returned the embarrassed soldier. "Who would know them better?"

The guard stayed silent for a while. Walking along, Madrazi noted that the intersecting streets were wide and straight and most were paved with dark stone. Most of the houses were set well back from the road and some were shaded by large trees. Bright flowers bordered many strips in front of the beautiful buildings. She decided that it was older than the other streets, for it wound through the city while the other roadways were straight. When she asked the soldier about it, he replied, "Lady, this way is called Methuselah's Path, and is the way that he followed from his first house to the sea. It has been preserved as he walked it." He turned his attention to the front, and Pomorolac warned his daughter to keep silent with a hard glance.

After some time of walking, the large stone buildings gave way to older wooden structures. They were spread farther apart and set back from the street. Trees were more common in this quarter and flowers were abundant, planted in beds in front of the dwellings and along the street. Everywhere there was evidence of prosperity. Soon, the guard was talking again, having taken upon himself the duty of familiarizing them with the city.

"This is the oldest part of the town, built before the walls were completed. Even then the town was well planned, and Methuselah insisted on wide streets and areas for trees and flowers. My grandfather came early to Lamech, and he has told me that the trees and fields here before the city were beautiful. We have tried to maintain some of that beauty both within and without our walls."

"It is also said that broad lawns make good neighbors," observed Pomorolac sardonically.

They passed into a newer section, with stone structures set closer together. Many of these were places of trade and the noises of work drifted from behind some of the larger buildings. The guard continued to speak, "The seaward side of the older town is the public area; the square of the elders and buildings for worship and civic assembly. There are warehouses outside the walls, but most of the riches of the merchants are kept within, behind the public buildings.

This side of the old town is where most of the work takes place. The old market is shrinking and more trade takes place behind the closed doors of the new town. The more prosperous have also built homes outside of town, north of the fields among the hills."

The guard droned on, and Madrazi heard less and saw more as she walked. Her head ached from the attempt to take in all the sights. They seemed to call to her, to offer a life of ease and comfort, with the social intercourse that she had been denied for so many years. She imagined herself as one of the great ladies of the town, one to whom all would incline their heads in respect and follow in fashion. Could she convince Shem to live in the city, or would she be forced to stay in the wild, just close enough to taste all that she would miss?

After an hour, the soldier turned into a side street. The great wall loomed ahead, rearing above the buildings, and Madrazi saw the distant opening of another large gate. She realized that they had walked entirely through Lamech. Facing them was a large wooden building with brightly-colored awnings shading the large front windows and two large trees shading the courtyard between the building and the street. A sign was visible above the front door. It showed a ship, highlighted with silver, sailing above large letters that read, 'The Trader's Rest.' In the corner of the sign was the mark of the guild—an honor not lightly bestowed.

A portly man with a red tinge to his beard was standing under the sign. He bowed low to Pomorolac. "You honor my humble house, master of the sea. I am Eldad. Welcome to my inn. I have prepared my best rooms for your party, and food is being made ready. Please enter with my blessing."

Madrazi smiled to herself at the cleverness of the guard. He had managed to lead them far enough out of a direct path to allow a runner from the council to reach the inn first.

"The honor is ours, master Eldad," returned Pomorolac gravely. "Thank you for your welcome and hospitality. Please show us to our rooms, and my men will refresh themselves with a drink in the great room before the noon meal."

Eldad led them into the inn, through a large great room and up a finely carved wooden stairway beside the stone fireplace in the back corner. At the top of the stair, halls branched to the right and left lit by skylights in the roof. The host led them down the left-hand hall and politely bowed towards open doors. "All of these rooms are at your disposal, master Pomorolac," he said, waving his hand at the open doors. "Please pull this cord"–he gestured to a red silk cord before the first door–"if you need anything. If you will permit, my daughter will host yours at the noon meal in a private room nearby."

"That would be quite suitable," returned Pomorolac, with a warning look that stopped Madrazi's protest. "After all, the rough talk of men in the great room might assault her delicate sensibilities." He winked at her as Eldad bowed low, and she didn't know whether to laugh or demonstrate her delicacy with a familiar sailor's oath. She contented herself with a nod that smothered a half snort of derision, turned, and flounced her way through the door indicated by Eldad.

Chapter 8
JERIAH

Pomorolac had arranged for their baggage to follow them off the ship and it was quickly brought to the inn—a testimony to the efficiency of the crew. Madrazi quickly changed into comfortable clothes and carefully packed away the more fragile silks and jewels, replacing the pearls and gold with her favorite beryl pendant. Growing tired of waiting, she opened another trunk, dug to the bottom, and carefully brought out the linen-wrapped robe that had been her mother's. It was white silk of dense weave, and much of its unusual beauty came from thin strands of gold wire woven into the cloth in patterns that caught and reflected the light with startling brightness. Jahaz became visibly nervous as her mistress fingered the robe, but Madrazi was too busy recalling her mother's face to notice. Mother and daughter would start new lives in the same robes.

She glanced up and saw Jahaz trembling. "What would your father say if he knew that you had this? You have stolen it from your home!"

Madrazi laughed. "Don't be foolish, Jahaz. Do you really think that Father does not know? Nothing in our house escapes his notice. In this, as in other things, he must pretend ignorance because of Peniah, but he knows that Mother intended it for me."

The explanation did not soothe Jahaz, which Madrazi thought silly, until she suddenly realized that her servant would have to answer to Peniah in the future. She was too hungry to find sympathy, for it was well past the noon hour, but with a twinge of conscience, she carefully repacked the robe, out of Jahaz' sight.

The knock on their door came just as she was closing the lid of the trunk. "My daughter," Madrazi heard, "come and dine. Our host has prepared a meal for us. You are invited to dine with his daughter."

She opened the door, glad that the required veil masked her impatience. She was even close to making some remark about not wanting to be bored by the drivel of an innkeeper's daughter, but kept her tongue. As Jahaz slipped away to dine with the servants, Pomorolac led her down the hall. Instead of going down the wooden steps that led to the main hall, they turned aside down another stairway and into another hall. The door at the end was open, and

Eldad was standing beside the open doorway. Smiling broadly, he beckoned Madrazi inside and went out, closing the door behind him.

Her first impression was the room. Although small, it was not what she expected from an inn. It was comfortably and tastefully furnished with rich couches and cloth hangings. Her eyes caught ceramic pottery with artistic designs and intricate wooden carvings. The tiled fireplace on the opposite wall was not needed on this day; light was provided through large windows in two walls of the room. Her eyes followed the light to the recumbent form of a woman. The table next caught her eye, for it was spread with a variety of foods and a bottle of pale yellow wine.

As soon as the door closed, the woman rose and began to unpin her veil. Madrazi thankfully imitated her, encouraged by this first favorable impression of her hostess. After laying the veil on a nearby table, she turned back to the woman and met her eyes. In that instant, the woman's appearance blurred and Madrazi saw only a pair of intense blue eyes. She stared, unashamed, for something within them called out to her, to the very depths of her soul.

The thought that she did not even know the woman's name flashed through Madrazi's mind, but it did not seem to matter; feelings surfaced, long hidden away and only experienced in the presence of her mother. Staggered by the unexpected wave of emotion, she strove for her customary self-control. It was not the woman's appearance; her features as they came into focus were not those of her mother, but the feelings were undeniable. They threatened to draw tears, and Madrazi was instantly embarrassed, feeling the heat rise up her face, but unable to look away.

Instantly, her mind was taken back to the vision of her mother on Hakkem and its memory seemed to bring an awareness that transcended ordinary perception. It was always afterward awkward to describe, and she never found words that were adequate. Her best effort, much later in her life, was the statement that in that brief instant the souls of the two women fled their bodies and embraced warmly in the middle of the room. Madrazi had heard of such meetings, usually between men and women, but had never felt anything like it before. She had always scoffed at such tales, but could not deny her feelings any more than she could deny herself and amazingly, the face before her told her that those feelings were mutual. Madrazi suddenly knew without doubt that they would be friends as long as they lived.

In the embarrassed silence that followed, the woman spoke first. Holding out her hands, she said, "I am Jeriah, the daughter of Eldad. Welcome to my home." Her voice was soft and clear, and it seemed to fit her face. She was almost as tall as Madrazi, with dark red hair that emphasized her bright blue eyes and light skin. Under her loose clothes, was a slim figure that matched the regular features of her face.

Quickly remembering her manners, her guest advanced in like fashion and returned, "And I am Madrazi, the daughter of Pomorolac, promised to the son of Noah. Thank you for your hospitality."

The woman laughed sweetly, "You are well known in Lamech by reputation though not by sight. Many of the daughters of the town are already jealous for the honor of marriage into the eldest family of our city. There will be even more resentment behind the pretty smiles that you receive when they see that in addition to great honor, you have been blessed with great beauty."

"I have been told of the honor of this marriage, but I am a stranger to this town, to my betrothed, and to his family. I have never in my short days met any of my people, except for my great-grandfather. He visited our home some years ago, and I was saddened at his leaving. I know that he is a man of repute here, but to me he was a wonderful companion, and the best friend that I have ever had apart from my mother, who is no more."

"You loved your mother very much." It was a statement, not a question, and there was certainty in her voice.

Madrazi was not sure why it seemed so normal to talk about her deepest feelings with this stranger. "Yes, very much. She was a better part of my life than I knew until she was gone. Since her death, my heart has grown cold. I hope that my new life here restores its warmth."

"I understand. I too loved my mother, and she departed this life ten years ago. I love my father, but a woman cannot share her heart with her father."

"You can share it with me," returned Madrazi impulsively, and then immediately blushed.

Jeriah took no offense. "We do not know each other," she said kindly, "but my heart agrees with yours. I would like to be your friend."

"I would like that, also," returned Madrazi, still wondering if the encounter was truly happening. Jeriah held out her hand and Madrazi took it and again their eyes met, the bargain sealed.

There was a short embarrassing silence, which Madrazi broke. "Tell me about the town and its people. I cannot live in ignorance of my new home."

Jeriah quickly regained her composure. "I will tell you all that you wish to know," she said, "but first, allow me to pour you a glass of wine and ask that you honor my father's house by taking some food."

"That will be easy, for it is well past the usual time for my noon meal." Jeriah poured two glasses of wine as Madrazi reclined on the pillow before the table. Jeriah waved her hand at the dishes as she sat, and as Madrazi began to sample the food, her hostess began to speak. "First I will tell you how our town came to be, then about its present life."

"Lamech was founded almost 700 years ago by Methuselah. He migrated from the north, stopping when he saw the harbor. He found abundant springs of fresh water and plentiful wood and stone for building. The bay was sheltered and full of fish. The soil was rich and as he stayed, he saw that it would grow good crops of grain and fruit. The Great Forest is only a day's march from the harbor, and it was even closer then. There are rare woods and spices to be found there, as well as unusual animals. As the years passed, he and the men of his household built homes of wood, then stone, on the bluff overlooking the harbor, and sowed fields and grazed their flocks. First a few, then more men began to gather from all around to live here."

"As word of disquiet grew in the south, the men of Lamech began to build walls in the second century and they have been extended and enlarged twice as the town has grown. Once they realized the value of the woods and spices of the Great Forest, and the advantages of our harbor, traders began to come with their ships and the town grew prosperous and strong. We were troubled for many years by the rise of bandits and warlords, but a hundred years ago the council agreed to an alliance with Taspar. With the exception of Torech of Y'tor, no city has since dared to attack our merchants for they rightly fear the army of Taspar. But that has not been the only benefit. Our merchants receive preference in Taspar, and our own army has grown and become strong by their help. In return, Taspar has the use of the harbor for her own trade for only a token payment.

You have met my uncle, Dajus, and the elder, Subtur. They both sit on the council along with Methuselah, Lamech, and Noah. The council governs all the affairs of the city, sets the laws and judges disputes. Lamech has prospered under their leadership, and most people are satisfied. Lamech is a city of strong traditions, and our fealty to custom does much to keep peace.

But times are changing. Young men are less patient than their fathers, and expect a full life at younger ages. Methuselah, Lamech, and Noah are not held in the same high esteem by many of the younger men, especially in their rigid worship of the Creator. Although a few of the wilder youths whisper allegiance to other gods, most agree with the council edict forbidding the worship of any save El Shaddai. But they think that there is room for innovation in worship and thought. Tradition is strong, but how long does it take to make a practice a tradition? Eldad is like many. He worships the Creator, but allows that men may worship him as they see fit. It is not as if we wanted to worship the stars with shrines for male and female prostitutes.

Madrazi nodded as she sipped the sweet wine and reached for a rich burgundy plum. Jeriah refilled her own cup and began again.

"Recently, the Supreme Commander of the army died. Zered had great respect for the elders and was their servant. There were rumors that he would ascend to the council in due time. He was a man comfortable with the powerful, and Jared, his son, was to have become Supreme Commander. Jared is a good man, but had not the rapport with the merchants that his father enjoyed, and so would never have gained a seat of power, although all thought he would take his father's place in the army. He is a great general and has the friendship of Delonias of Taspar." Madrazi stopped eating for a moment. She detected a hint of feeling in Jeriah's voice that had not been there before. But her hostess continued before she could say anything.

"But everyone was surprised when he stepped aside and recommended Sechiall as Supreme Commander. For Sechiall was Jared's subordinate. He is very young, but is a strong warrior, fearless in battle. He is loved by the warriors, and has a power to inflame men's hearts, while Jared is colder and not always comfortable with men who are not soldiers. In spite of his youth, Sechiall won the support of Dajus and Subtur, and will be confirmed as Supreme Commander if the army gains victory over Torech of Y'tor. I believe that when Methuselah dies, he may win power in the council, but it is unclear at present."

Madrazi was both pleased and surprised at Jeriah's recitation. Instead of gossip about clothes, jewels, and local personalities, Madrazi had received a succinct review worthy of a visiting dignitary or merchant. In this too, the women were very alike. Madrazi sensed that Jeriah wielded considerable influence in the inn of Eldad, though she was probably careful about flaunting it. Jeriah was a shrewd and observant woman, and her heart warmed all the more for the ability to discern and respond to her own temperament so easily. Jeriah smiled, seeing recognition of her insight, and binding the two yet closer in understanding.

"Now to your more immediate curiosity," she smiled. "For many years Noah and his fathers ruled the affairs of our city in peace and plenty. Noah spent many of his best years working for the city's good and did not take a wife until his middle years. Then, a hundred years ago, he claimed a vision of judgment from God. When he began to relate it to the people of the town, they did not receive it, for the wise of this town with the exception of Lamech and Methuselah rejected the vision. They claimed that whatever Noah had seen was not a true vision from the Creator, since it foretold death and destruction. However, Noah persisted, and for a short while, some argued that he should be removed from the council. Whether it was because of this opposition, or some other motivation that only he could explain, Noah moved his family to a new settlement on the edge of the Great Forest. Few but his own men went with him, and although he does a rich trade in forest products, many in town see the move as a failure because he has not developed his settlement into a new town."

"There is some murmuring that he is away from the city too much to serve on the council, but Methuselah and Lamech are founders of this city and none would openly insult them by insisting on Noah's removal. And in truth the older men remember his efforts for the town for many hundreds of years—he sacrificed much for the prosperity of Lamech. So he sits in the seat of judgment every month and comes into town when summoned. Certainly his wisdom in most affairs of law and justice is respected."

"I am only seventy years, but even I have seen many changes in my short life. Our alliance with Taspar has brought new wealth and power, but these things bring their own burdens. Eldad grumbles that men are less courteous and there are parts of town where a woman should no longer walk alone. Methuselah spends more of his time at Noah's settlement, and with two of our leading elders distracted by outside activities, the city suffers."

However, Lamech remains in the city and spends himself freely in its service. If more would follow his example, many of our problems would be solved. There is no official head of the council, but all recognize Lamech as the leading elder. He is practical and stronger in body and mind than his father or son."

Madrazi interrupted her hostess. "So Noah left the city of his own volition? Do any know his reasons?" Apprehension seized her as she felt the life she had envisioned slip away with Jeriah's words.

"Some say he was offended by the growing impiety of the city. Some say that he loves the forest. Others note that he has grown wealthier there. He is a good man, but Father thinks that he expects too much of people. He and his grandfather speak much of doing good and loving the Creator, but most men wish to pursue happiness, profit, and peace, without excess religious restraint."

Madrazi interrupted again. "My father is of their family, yet he left to pursue his own life. He has taught us that we must do what is right, but that men often profess a love of gods as an excuse to do wrong to others. We believe that it is important to judge a man by what he makes of his life. Those who profess ignorance of what is right and wrong do so with a lie, for everyone knows that truth, honor, and integrity are right for all men."

"Yes," Jeriah agreed, "older men tell me that when Lamech was young and unsettled, religion provided a strong bond among the people. But as the town grew and prospered, people found binds in years of civic tradition and family relationships. In these days, some claim that piety is an impediment to progress. Methuselah opposed our alliance with Taspar because the men of that city do not acknowledge the Creator, and worship other gods. He was overruled, and his opponents now claim that the Creator must approve of our association with Taspar, for it has brought us great prosperity."

Madrazi smiled. Religious differences could easily separate friends, but Jeriah's outlook was similar to her own. It did not strike her until later that those views were dissimilar to those of the house she had committed to join. Jeriah smiled and went on, "Few have visited the new house of Noah, but those who have say that he has built a beautiful home at the very edge of the woods. He knows much of crops, trees, and animals. He is even reputed to possess the old gifts; crops grow at his command and the trees and birds listen to his voice."

Madrazi's disbelief in the old fables must have been apparent on her face, for Jeriah smoothly changed the subject. "He has three sons, and both Japheth and the youngest, Ham, are but recently married. All of them live together in the house of Noah, and none of his sons has shown any interest in the army or trade here in town. They say that Japheth, like his father, is a cultivator of crops, vines, and trees. Ham is a craftsman in wood and stone. Shem is a hunter. He is said to be drawn to the forest and knows its ways better than even Noah."

"Tell me of him," asked Madrazi, trying not to sound overeager.

"Your Shem has been to town many times, and I have met him through my uncle's relationship with his father. He is quite handsome. He has dark curly hair, piercing dark eyes, and a friendly smile. He is a little above normal height and is not heavy, but compact and stronger than he first appears. He is also reputed to be one of the fastest runners in the city, but refused to compete in any races. In public, he is quiet and reserved and so is not well known by anyone in town."

Madrazi's heart sank. Jeriah had confirmed her worst fear. She would be dragged out into another wilderness settlement, tantalizingly within sight of her dreams, but beyond their reach. What kind of life would she have?

Jeriah caught the discordant emotion and tried to cheer her guest. "I think he will be a good husband; he talks little but thinks much. He has no time for the army, but is brave and skilled with the bow, and has slain many dangerous animals. He seems to have inherited Lamech's strength of will and mind, although Ham is more like Lamech in body. Many women in this town would have been glad to overlook the oddities of Noah's family to have their daughters become the wife of Shem, but Noah looked abroad."

Madrazi and Jeriah continued talking for many hours, about everything from the affairs of the council to the various shops in town. Madrazi, who had guarded both heart and tongue all her life, now found an inexplicable desire to unburden that pent up reservoir on Jeriah, who seemed to welcome the flood of words with equal enthusiasm. The afternoon slid by unnoticed. Servants interrupted some time during the evening and quietly set another meal. They both laughed, for neither had been aware of the passage of time.

Madrazi still felt a dream-like quality to the day. Her fears of living in the wilderness were tempered by the wonder of finding a friend like Jeriah on her first day in Lamech. Was it not proof that her mother's appearance during the voyage had overcome the evil omen of her nightmare? An inexplicable joy welled up inside and told her that these first steps in her new life marked a wonderful future. She marveled at the easy intimacy after all the lonely years by the sea. In these few short hours Jeriah was already closer to her heart than her own family.

T he next morning, Madrazi woke to her father's voice booming through her door. Quickly, she rose and pulled on a robe. Opening the door, she asked him in. He entered and turned back to her with a rare tender expression in his eyes. He put his hands on her shoulders and looked intently at her face. "It has finally come. After today you will belong to Shem, and Noah will be your father. I have lost your mother and now I am losing you."

Without a word, Madrazi threw her arms around his neck. Moments of affection were infrequent for both of them, but she was glad that one would start this day. Even in the midst of his embrace, she could not help a shiver of excitement in thinking of the hours ahead—a new day, another step on this new path. She would miss Pomorolac, but in that moment she was looking ahead eagerly felt no room for regrets. She tried to share that feeling with him as he stepped back. "We have had a good life together, Father, and you know that a part of you will always live in me, wherever we are."

He smiled at that and nodded. He understood letting go of the past. "You must prepare yourself, daughter. Noah and his family have come faster than expected. They have arrived in town and we are summoned before the council for your public betrothal later this morning. We must be ready at the fourth hour in the council square. Shem must be impatient, but I can't blame him."

Madrazi froze in place. She had not expected a public appearance and certainly not that very morning. Her heart beat faster and feelings overwhelmed clear thought. Pomorolac seemed to read her mood and explained, "Shem is the most likely of Noah's sons to become an elder. Therefore, his betrothal is important to the entire town, and provides an opportunity for you to be seen by all. The message that came to me this morning stated that the wedding itself would be at the house of Noah, so a public betrothal is all the more important."

Madrazi nodded, but wanted support. "Please ask our host if I may take a morning meal with his daughter before we go. I will be ready to eat as soon as she is prepared." He nodded and left, and in a few minutes a servant was leading the excited girl to her new friend. Madrazi was distracted and her emotions ran high. Had yesterday's time with Jeriah been real? Would they feel the same today? Walking down the hall, she managed to aggravate anxiety in doubt, but when she met Jeriah's eyes, all she felt was profound relief. The woman before her was the same intimate friend she had left the evening before. Relieved, Madrazi ran across the floor to meet Jeriah with a warm embrace.

"How happy I am for you," Jeriah said, and her face reflected her joy. "You will be honored before all the leaders of the town today, and tomorrow or the next day you will meet Shem."

In the grip of her emotion, Madrazi's joy turned instantly to consternation. Before Jeriah could even question which of her words had caused it, Madrazi blurted out, "Do you mean that he does not care enough to come into town to meet me?"

Jeriah laughed away her tone and ignorance, "No, no, I'm sure that he cares very much. But it is not the custom in Lamech for the bride and bridegroom to be together between the public betrothal and the marriage ceremony. I have heard that you will be joined at the house of Noah, and I shall miss seeing it, but I will be in the square today!"

"Will my great-grandfather come?" Madrazi asked eagerly, grateful for the explanation, but a little ashamed of her mercurial display.

"All the council will be present to honor you," soothed Jeriah. "Come, sit yourself and eat while you are able."

Jahaz had already laid out proper clothes for the public meeting. After she dressed, Madrazi submitted to Jeriah's attentions to her hair. The women laughed together over many small things and in a short time Madrazi was dressed in her best clothes. She wore her favorite jade green color, and Jeriah commented that it was a good omen—it was the color of the symbols of the town. After Jahaz weighed her down again with her gold and pearls, Jeriah fastened Madrazi's cloak and pinned her veil. She stood with Jahaz and the two women proclaimed their satisfaction with the result.

Hurrying through the inn, they met the men outside. Before they could leave, Eldad came to them with words of regret at their parting. Pomorolac brought out his purse, but Eldad held up his hand. "Please, master Pomorolac, I requested your presence at my inn as guests, and I would prefer the memory of your presence to your gold."

His guest protested politely, but then thanked Eldad for his hospitality and praised the inn. It appeared a generous gesture, but Madrazi understood the minds of traders, and knew that her father would be obligated to return to Eldad's inn were he back in Lamech. Eldad had also arranged for the hire of four animals to carry the baggage to Noah's settlement.

Before they could start, a group of soldiers arrived. Their captain bowed to them and said, "The elders of Lamech have decreed a guard of honor for Pomorolac and his daughter to escort them to the council." Pomorolac nodded and thanked the officer.

The soldiers formed two columns on either side of the road and marched in slow but regular time alongside the honored visitors. Keeping pace with the soldiers, Madrazi remembered her father's warnings, and kept her head down and did not talk. But she could not totally repress her curiosity, and thanked the shelter of the veil that allowed her eyes to take in the sights. Many people were already on the street and were directing their steps behind the procession. Before many minutes had passed, there was a large crowd following at a respectful distance.

The people made Madrazi nervous; she felt as if she was being forced along the road. The thought of Jeriah being among them was a comfort, but each step seemed to increase the beat of her heart and her hands fairly shook. At length, they turned the final corner and walked out into the already crowded council square. People moved politely aside, opening a path. As they stepped into the square, the morning sun shone in Madrazi's eyes and the shadow of the city wall obscured the black chairs. But she unfastened her cloak and handed it to Jahaz before moving forward. The light shifted, and the elders emerged and took definition.

Her quick eye and quicker mind were able to see much in the short walk across the stones of the square. Dajus and Subtur occupied the same chairs as yesterday; evidently each chair was reserved for its elder. Madrazi quickly scanned the other three as they walked between the soldiers towards the dais. In the first chair was her beloved Granpapa, and his familiar smile told her that he knew that her eyes were upon him behind the gossamer curtain that protected her from those less perceptive.

Next to Methuselah sat a large man with a strong face. She guessed him to be Lamech, for whom the city was named. He looked remarkably like Pomorolac, with dark hair and gray eyes poised above a thin nose and sharp face. His shoulders were broad and his hands large. It did not require insight to see strength of body in his powerful frame, but she sensed a similar strength of mind and will in those gray eyes. Wisdom was present, too, but subordinated to power. Madrazi felt that he would be a powerful enemy or staunch friend, and wondered which she would come to know.

Between Lamech and Dajus sat the man who would become her father. Noah reminded her immediately of Methuselah rather than Lamech, both in appearance and demeanor. His eyes were brown and his hair not as dark as Lamech, and his stature was less, although he was obviously a powerful man in the prime of life. But while the face of Lamech proclaimed his strength, Noah's was veiled, and her first impression was that he lacked the force clearly present in Lamech. It would be many years before she came to understand the hidden depths of Noah's power. He had an open and friendly face, and the same grace that she had seen in Methuselah's eyes was visible in his. She was drawn to him, and for some inexplicable reason was glad to be marrying his son, and not Lamech's.

Her impressions took only the space of a few steps across the square. The columns of soldiers widened as they approached the dais and with perfect precision came simultaneously into their places where they assumed their positions around the perimeter. The crowd respected those limits, but pushed as close as they could. The people were excited, and Madrazi, seeing a lathered horse and dirty soldier behind the elders, realized that not all of it was due to her presence.

Pomorolac, who knew the protocol of a hundred cities, stood forward and bowed low to each elder in turn. "Greetings, great leaders of Lamech, twice kinsmen. May the blessings of the god of our father Adam be upon you and this town! May peace and prosperity spring up anew each year in a bountiful crop to feed your children and your children's children! May the light of wisdom and understanding shine as the sun at noon upon each elder!" He continued on for many minutes as was the custom, extolling the virtues of the city and its people.

Finally, he paused to gather his breath, and completed his oration. "In accord with the promise made years ago, sealed by an exchange of gifts and ratified by the seal of the council of Lamech, I come before you at the appointed time and bring now my greatest treasure. I freely offer her to the son of my close kinsman, Noah, before the witnessing eyes of the elders of Lamech. Who will now receive my daughter?"

Methuselah nodded to Noah, who stood forward for the council. "Welcome to you, Pomorolac, kinsman. We are honored at your presence, borne upon the wings of the sea, and by the gift that you bring. May the blessings of God shine upon you and yours, and may His hand uphold you across the paths of the sea." He continued on for a polite interval with words very similar to his cousin's.

Finally, he concluded, "We are truly overwhelmed with gratitude for your consent to join your daughter to our city. Truly as God said, they will leave their parents and become one—a new family that cannot help but bring greater peace to our world and glory to the next. In the name of the council I agree that you have met all of your pledged obligations, and as the father of Shem, I pledge his troth publicly before these witnesses and swear to you that your daughter shall be my daughter. She shall enjoy the benefits of my household as long as life shall endure in me, my sons, and their sons after them."

As Noah finished he held his hands high and blessed the vows sworn and blessed the city in the name of God. At the finish, the crowd in the square erupted into loud cheers and shouts of joy. Pomorolac took his daughter's hand and led her to the dais. He placed it in the hand of Noah and said quietly, "Guard well your oath, cousin, and guard well my daughter whom I love. May she bear you strong grandchildren and be a comfort to your old age."

Noah bowed again and Pomorolac stepped away. Madrazi felt naked and alone in front of all the people. Noah sensed her tension and gently smiled at her before stepping back to his seat. Then slow, deep music sounded from behind the square. At its sound the elders formed a line before the lone woman and each passed by, laying their hands upon her head and uttering a short blessing. As they resumed their places in front of their seats, the crowd erupted into a spontaneous cheering.

Methuselah then stood forth and quieted the crowd with upraised hands. "Brothers of Lamech," he began, "today marks a double portion of God's blessings on our town. We have received a noble daughter of men as a sister into our fellowship, and we have seen the evidence of God's care of our city in the news of the morning. Let us each return to his own home with thanksgiving for the blessings of this day."

It was done. Madrazi felt the first stirrings of some unforeseen inner conflict at the passage from one father to another. Her future was with Noah, but she was suddenly uneasy at leaving Pomorolac. She wondered if it was fitting to be happy in the face of such a parting. Noah interrupted her thoughts as he spoke to Pomorolac. "It is indeed a good day for Lamech. Our army has won a great victory over Torech in the south, and the news has come after many days of silence. But for our family, this will be a day of rejoicing for a new daughter before any thought is given to deliverance from the evil to the south." Pomorolac nodded his relief as he heard the news, recognizing that it boded well for the city and alleviated his fears of any problems that might be caused by Torech.

Noah continued, "I have made preparations for us to travel this very afternoon to my home. We will stay along the road tonight, as this is our practice: we have a permanent camp established and will make you quite comfortable. Who will accompany us?"

Her father was visibly pleased to go at once. He thanked Noah and replied, "My sons and I, Captain Jakeh, the servant Jahaz, and eight of my men.

I have hired four donkeys to transport our baggage, and they await us in the stable of Eldad."

Noah smiled. "I have taken the liberty of having your belongings moved to our house for your convenience."

He then led them outside the square, following a broad street that led to the gate of a large house. Methuselah was beside Madrazi, and explained, "This was my home. It now belongs to my son, Lamech. You may refresh yourself and prepare for travel inside."

Inside the great front hall, they were shown to their rooms. Jahaz followed Madrazi, and the women selected traveling clothes from their trunks. Jahaz shook her head, "This is all too fast for me, mistress. I cannot keep up with you or your clothes!"

In a short time the party was striding through the quiet streets of Lamech toward the east gate. Away from town, Madrazi quickly removed her veil and sighed in appreciation as the breeze blew her hair away from her face. The men set an easy pace, and as the road wound on into the afternoon, Lamech settled into place ahead with Pomorolac and his sons, trading news from their respective regions. Noah and Methuselah walked on either side of her, and her step was light as the import of her transformation from the girl of her past into the woman of her future washed over her. She was full of anticipation of a future of happiness and was humbled by the sudden thought that this wonderful future rested upon the choices of these two men. How much of her happiness was really due to her own choices, she mused to herself?

Noah and Methuselah seemed to understand Madrazi's fears and took turns diverting her with stories. As she regained her composure, she told them in turn of her education and work of the past thirty five years. Noah asked her many questions about her knowledge of the stars and her answers obviously impressed him. Methuselah waved his arm back up the road and added, "The men of Lamech built a similar circle on the edge of the high cliffs below the light tower. They use it more to discern crop cycles from the sun and the moon, but a few have attempted to understand the night skies. The wise of the city would be jealous of your knowledge, daughter."

Noah agreed, but then frowned. "It is useful, even though I think it is becoming a shrine for those fools that see their lives in the motions of the heavens." He seemed to remember suddenly the girl's presence, and smoothly began to talk of the harvest at his settlement. But Madrazi remembered Jeriah's mention of his intolerance in matters of worship. She wondered for the first time what he would think of her own convictions, though she shared his disdain for fools who thought that the stars decreed their fates. For a time she walked in silence until the gleam of the walls of Lamech was lost in the distance.

An hour before sunset, they came over a small rise and Madrazi saw a shallow valley spread before her. A dark line on the horizon marked the Great Forest. The small valley before them was cloaked in shadow, but Madrazi could see a stream at the bottom of the hill and a stone bridge crossing it. To the left of the road, beside the stream, she saw a clearing with tents and people moving about, realizing that servants had accompanied Noah this far and prepared the camp for their return. As the travelers turned off the road, they saw fires already burning against the coming darkness. The visitors were directed to richly brocaded tents in the middle of the encampment.

Madrazi and Jahaz entered theirs while Pomorolac saw to his men. The tent was lit by hanging lamps and the floor was spread with rugs. A bronze brazier was set beneath an opening in the ceiling. Charcoal was laid, but not lit. Curtains hid two partitions of the tent for sleeping, and around the fire were low chairs covered with soft sheepskin.

Hearing her father, Madrazi returned to the entrance. He followed her in with her trunk. Swinging its weight easily down to the floor with one hand, he stood up. "Noah knows how to build a camp," he admitted, glancing around the tent. "We will eat in a short time. Rest now and someone will call you when it is time."

Later, as the women followed Pomorolac back through the camp, Madrazi instantly sensed an easy informality that contrasted sharply with the city. No one mentioned her lack of a veil, and everyone ate together under a large wooden structure that was no more than a roof and eight stout pillars that upheld it. Servants were treated as a part of the family, performing their duties cheerfully. Pomorolac led his daughter to a seat at the nearest table. Jakeh came forward and escorted Jahaz with a smile to the other. Madrazi was seated with her brothers near the head of the first table, which they shared with Methuselah, Lamech, and Noah. When all were seated, Methuselah stood, raised his arms, and said, "We bless you, Oh mighty God, maker of heaven and earth and provider of its fruit for your children! Accept our humble thanks for this and all your blessings."

The food was plain, but plentiful. Everyone ate to satisfaction and then lingered at the table listening to tales of the old days and talk of the present. As it turned to trade, cities, and their attendant problems, the two women quietly excused themselves and returned to their tent. Madrazi lay awake into the night considering the events of this day and the ones to follow and trying to remember Jeriah's every word about Shem.

The next day saw them off with the sun. It was an early start after a long day, but Noah said that they were expected back before noon. Madrazi woke tired; the rush of events made the past days seem like years. After a quick breakfast, they started off, but as they walked, Madrazi lagged behind. Soon all were more than a few minutes ahead. Methuselah glanced back, met her eyes, and stopped to wait while the others walked on. He seemed to sense that her hesitation was not a desire for solitude, but did not speak for the first mile. Madrazi walked beside him, gathering her thoughts.

Finally her apprehension caused her to ask, "What will happen today, Great-grandfather?" She was afraid to reveal ignorance, but feared more the possibility of embarrassment that might easily arise from that ignorance.

The old man seemed to hear the question behind the words. "Many good things, Madrazi. My heart will be glad tonight after many years of waiting. This very afternoon we will join you and Shem together before God. Tonight there will be a great feast, and we will celebrate for three days. After that, I hope that your father and brothers will stay for more days and enjoy the hospitality of our home before they return to Lamech."

She had not realized that events would move so quickly, but after the tension of waiting so many years, she found it quite appealing; much more so than more weeks of useless waiting. He watched her absorb this information and gently asked, "How do you feel?"

She answered as honestly as she could. "A little fear, a little excitement, much joy, some anticipation, and great uncertainty. I always thought of myself as a woman of great self-control, but I do not know myself today."

He chuckled. "You are feeling what anyone would who is trading all that she has known and held dear for the promise of something better. You cannot trust your own knowledge and you doubt your choices. But remember this: others have made good choices for you in this union with Shem. Be patient with him and with the household. It will become yours in time, even if many things seem strange at first. Remember that he is feeling many of the same things that you are, and that such common ground is a place to begin your marriage. Love is a seed that we plant and nurture that in good time brings us much fruit. The harvest depends on our decisions while the plant is still young."

Instead of calming her doubts and fears, her great-grandfather's words added new ones. She wondered if he was hinting at a cold reception into the household. Or did he simply mean that such would be the case with a few of the family? Was Shem really eager for this marriage, or was he also being led by the choices of others and perhaps resenting it? Her doubts threatened to overwhelm her happiness. But she realized with a start that she was happy, today, right now, and that the future would have to answer for itself. She had faith in the wisdom of Noah and love of Methuselah. There would be good and bad mixed in each person and situation, but her strength and ability would see her through.

As they continued walking across the low hills, the edge of the Great Forest gained resolution and was transformed from a green shimmer on the horizon to a sea of individual trees. The road did not go straight into the forest, but wound around its southern edge. Then, the trees retreated from the road to reveal a natural cove of green fields surrounding the buildings of a settlement. Barns and smaller outbuildings were visible among the scattered trees beyond the fields and beyond them along the road was a large building that was certainly the family dwelling. Madrazi noted with approval the pleasant patterns and orderly beauty of the gardens, fields, and orchards.

But her attention was drawn beyond the ordered symmetry of the fields to the dark green of the forest. The effort and resulting wealth visible in the works of man were but a fringe that existed before its overpowering vastness. Madrazi had always lived by the sea and the hills of her home were covered by no more than grass and a few small trees. She had never seen such a forest, with so many giant trees ruling over so wide a land. She was surprised at her reaction; she hated the dark shadows of the ocean depths, but longed to wander beneath the green waves of the forest roof. It called to her—there was something waiting there, but she did not know what. Far beyond the trees a blue haze marked a line of low mountains. What was beyond them? Perhaps this indescribable attraction was what her father saw in the sea. She vowed to explore those paths and follow those shadows, and learn the secrets of the woods.

"Madrazi!" Methuselah's voice brought her back.

"I'm sorry. My mind wandered."

"There is much to distract it," he said with a smile. "We are almost there."

His gentle warning was timely. They had drawn nearer their goal, but were still some distance behind the others. Methuselah had slowed his pace to accommodate Madrazi's dilatory steps, but now they both hurried to catch up. Madrazi found that it was not the increased pace alone that caused her heart to beat faster. Her new family was a few short minutes away. What would happen? Would the women be bitter and jealous, like Peniah? Would Shem be disappointed in her appearance or manner? Panic rose at the thought of existing unloved in a house of strangers. She felt her palms grow damp with fear and her breath grew short. But at the moment when fear had almost mastered her mind, Methuselah took her hand with a gentle squeeze and said, "I love you, Madrazi. Do not be afraid."

She took a deep breath. Somehow she knew that as long as she had her Granpapa, she would not be alone or unloved. He was and would remain her best friend. She had trusted him all these years, and it was foolish to stop now. Looking up into those soft brown eyes, she said, "I love you, too, Granpapa. I cannot fear while you are near."

"That is as it should be, my daughter," he replied. "Love and fear cannot live under the same roof."

****

Heat seeped into the burning log. Ice inside a small crack in the wood turned to water, and as the heat increased, to steam. Expanding in its wooden walls, it forced an exit with a loud snap. The old woman registered the sound, not sure what it was at first. The room swam back into focus and flames danced before her. She looked around. Darkness had fallen outside, and the moaning of the wind was now audible. The young woman was sitting in the corner, pulling interminable stitches through fine green cloth. The tray of food had been cleared away and in its place was a bowl of raisins and a cup. Steam rose from it, carrying the aroma of tea. The room was quiet; only the sound of the wood settling in the fireplace interrupted the whistle of the wind across the flue.

As she sipped her tea, her gaze fell upon the wooden mantle of the fireplace. It was old, so old, the dark wood worn smooth over many winters, but still dense and hard. She had rescued it as a memorial. Perfectly square and plane, it had been made to serve as a shelf, but words had been engraved into the face with care. They were worn, and in the dim light, hard to read. But she knew each letter, each indentation. The hand that had fashioned them had no equal now. "Yesterday dies, tomorrow lives," it read. She did not know why he had put those words there, nor could he have known what hope they had brought to her, later. It was for that hope that she had insisted on keeping it to honor the one who made it.

Chapter 10
MASTER BUILDER

Meshur swung the hammer in a short, controlled arc and the shaft of an iron nail vanished into the wood. His callused hand wiped the sweat from his face as he smiled, satisfied that he could so easily drive a nail with one blow at the end of a long day. The final plank was secured to the beam and the wall was complete. Stepping back, he examined the line of the boards with a critical eye. All were straight, smooth, square, and even; the overlap precise—exactly a finger's length across the entire wall. Nodding to himself, he placed the hammer carefully in the toolbox and automatically checked the floor around him for loose nails.

Seeing none, he picked up his tunic, threw it over his broad shoulder, and walked the length of the completed twelve sections of the upper deck. There it abruptly ended, and he stepped down a ladder to the middle deck below. His lonely footsteps echoed through the cavernous interior of that deck until he reached its end, three sections short of the front of the vessel. There he climbed down another ladder to the lower deck and then down the sturdy ramp that ran between the immense beams of the incomplete face, out into the face of the late afternoon sun, glaring over the hill before him. A large, silent man, Meshur was bound to this work with all the pride of a master craftsman.

The clearing was strangely silent in the lingering daylight until a cheerful voice called to him. "Cousin, hurry! I have prepared some food, but my hunger is telling me that it will not last much longer."

Meshur walked toward the line of buildings to the workers' quarters. His cousin Pashtur was standing in the doorway waving him on with a broad smile. The opposite of Meshur in many ways, his cousin was a small man, quick of foot, wit, and speech. He was friendly with all and quick to smile, but with few true friends. The two had been close since boyhood, and the threat of Meshur's strength was sufficient to protect the smaller man from those he annoyed. There was only one man in the clearing whose arm matched that of Meshur, but Meshur would never have sought a test of strength with him, for that man was Meshur's mentor and master—the youngest son of Noah.

"Wash the dirt of the day off your face and hands cousin," said Pashtur waving to the pan of water and clean towel that he had set out on the porch.

Meshur grunted and turned his steps to the end of the porch. His cousin had thoughtfully placed a cool pitcher of water beside the pan and Meshur drank half of it before he began to clean away the residue of the day's labor. As he washed, he thought back to the day when Pashtur had opened the door to his dreams. For that alone he would remain true to his cousin for the rest of his life.

Even as a young boy, Meshur lived to shape wood, metal, and stone into beautiful and useful things. His father was the headman of a large farm outside the city, and often away in the fields. Meshur had no brothers and quickly learned to spurn the company of his two sisters. He spent much of his time with his uncle, a carpenter and builder who kept a workshop nearby. His uncle realized early on that the boy had a gift with wood and stone, and he began to talk to his brother about it. Consequently, when Meshur turned twelve, he began to work for his uncle instead of in the fields with his father.

His uncle taught him many skills over the next thirteen years, but the love of the work that was the mark of a future master craftsman came from deep inside the young man. As he grew in skill, he also grew in strength, and hard work came easily to his broad shoulders and strong arms. The six years that he spent helping his uncle in the erection of the large stone sentinels of the heavenly circle had ended with Meshur fully as tall as his uncle, with broad shoulders and heavy arms and hands. But Meshur's size and strength was deceptive; he had the eye and touch of a latent master, and a burning desire to enhance his skills with wood, stone, and metal.

It was that aspiration that led him to accept Pashtur's invitation to the home of Lamech, a leading elder in the city. Pashtur had begun working in the Great Forest for Lamech's son, and liked the wages even though the work was hard. But knowing Meshur, the little man realized that the work would beckon regardless of the wages. The money would serve to placate his uncle and father, but one sight of the activity in the great clearing would keep Meshur there even if no wages were paid.

Lamech proved to be a gracious host and offered both of the young men a glass of wine as they talked. He asked Meshur about his work and appeared to be pleased when he spoke of the buildings that he had helped his uncle erect. Lamech then offered him work in the Great Forest at ten pieces of silver each month. Until he heard the words from the elder's own lips, he had not believed his cousin. Meshur could say nothing, and the offer seemed even better when Lamech told them that the job provided a place to sleep and food at no cost.

He had ventured to speak. "Master Lamech, the wage that you offer is more than a young man such as myself is worthy of, and I am sure that my father will approve."

Pashtur spoke next, answering Meshur's unspoken questions. "Master Lamech, if it meets your approval, I will take my cousin with me in three days."

Lamech nodded and Meshur and Pashtur bowed and were escorted out by a waiting servant. They met three days later at the city gate and began the journey to the forest. Meshur finally had the opportunity to ask his cousin, "What is the work, cousin?"

Pashtur smiled and replied, "Noah is building a wooden ship, three hundred cubits long."

Meshur stopped and stared in amazement at his cousin. "Is the man mad?"

Pashtur laughed. "Most of us think so, but for ten pieces of silver each month, all the workers pretend that it is the most sensible thing in the world to build a giant ship in the middle of a forest. But you love to work with wood and you will love the work here. Noah's son Ham is the headman at the site and he is a master of wood and metal. He has many innovative ideas, but he is not afraid to work with his own hands. He is probably the only man I know who is stronger than you."

Shaking away the memory and the water, Meshur finished washing away the dirt and sweat of the day, ready for a large meal. He and Pashtur were the only men here today. The others had taken the offer of a paid week in town, and the servants had gone back to Noah's house to prepare for the wedding of his son. But Meshur refused to leave until he had finished the room he had started. His cousin had argued to no avail, but had agreed to stay with him, even though he had not been much help. Now the work was finished, and four days remained in the week. They could leave in the morning and still have two full days at home.

Meshur turned and rubbed the coarse cloth over his head. The sight of the ark bathed in the late afternoon sun was one that never failed to thrill him. He remembered first walking over that rise; he had stopped at the top and stared down into the large open plain. The buildings around the edge of the vast clearing were well constructed and well sited. But it was the work in the middle of the field that drew and held his attention. The smooth green meadow was disturbed by a long, straight, level series of giant timbers, half buried in the ground. They were at least fifty cubits long, and beyond their flat, smooth tops, Meshur could see men working, setting another in place with the help of a large

A-framed lifter. Even at this distance, Meshur could estimate the weight of the smoothed tree trunk that hung from it, and he decided that he would like to know the man who had designed it.

Pashtur had pulled at him impatiently, and led him down to the first building where he met a serious young man with shrewd dark eyes who wrote his name on a scroll and welcomed him with a few well-chosen words. "You do not have to accept the reason for what we do here. But you are being paid a good wage and you are expected to work hard. You will have a trial for one month. If you work hard and cause no trouble, you may stay for as long as you desire. My name is Shem. If you need anything, ask me or one of my brothers, Japheth and Ham. You will come to know us as you work."

With those few words Meshur was thrown into the work. He cared little. Hard work was something that he knew well, and even though his first job was cutting and hauling timber from the forest, he did all that was asked of him, hiding his impatience at not being chosen for more skilled work. His strength often obscured his creative and capable mind, but he was satisfied to prove himself first, and with his customary curiosity, he saw an opportunity to learn how to fell large trees. He had always worked with rough cut timbers in town and absorbed this new knowledge quickly. He soon was proficient in judging the proper depth and angle of the cuts needed to fell a tree exactly where he wanted it, and his skill with ax and saw increased.

His hard work soon brought other benefits. After a year in the forest Meshur was moved to a group of men that would begin the actual construction of the ship. The foundation had been finished during that year and the thirty one giant trunks were perfectly square and level in the ground, a feat that cemented his growing respect for Ham. A trough had been cut down the middle of each trunk and a massive keel laid down in it.

There were five groups of twelve men who would begin the construction. Ham called them apart and spent three days showing them drawings and models and explaining how the ark would be built—as a series of identical sections. He even had a pile of small pieces of wood—the parts of a scale model of one of the sections. He showed them one by one how to join the timbers with intricate dovetail joints and how to build strength into the planking as well as the skeleton.

Once a group mastered the process of building one section, the next would be much easier. Meshur had nodded approval—with few men, this was an intelligent way to do the job. If it took long enough, a few men might even reach *tant-ror*, that state where their bodies, independent of conscious thought, could perform intricate tasks automatically and perfectly. It usually took a skilled craftsman many years to attain that state, but the skills required to build the ark's sections were not intrinsically difficult and repetition would be exaggerated. Each section would have the same number of identical timbers.

Meshur's group was the first to start work the next day. Although he was initially chosen for his great strength, it soon became apparent that he understood Ham's instructions better than any other in his group, and his quiet suggestions to the foreman enabled the framework of the first section to begin to take shape over the next few days. The foreman was a fair man, and mentioned Meshur's aptitude to Ham at the close of the week. The young worker put all of his efforts into the work, and though he took pride that his group was ahead of the others, he did not notice that he had been singled out or that Ham began to spend much of his time with them.

After two weeks of hard work, Ham pulled the young man aside. Wondering what he might have done wrong, Meshur braced himself and followed Ham some distance away from the others. But the expected criticism did not materialize; instead, Ham began questioning him about his experience. After getting over the initial awkwardness, Meshur soon discovered that Noah's son shared his passion for creating perfection in form and function, and his words came more freely.

Ham, likewise, soon recognized the bond between them. Despite their different backgrounds and stations, both were young, strong, and driven to seek perfection in making the wood and metal conform to that ideal picture that each could see so easily in his mind, but was seemingly denied to other men. After a short pause, Ham spoke. "Would you like to work with me, Meshur? It would mean a better wage, and together we can find ways to solve the problems that we both know will arise."

"I would be honored to work alongside you, sir. Were it not for my family I would ask no wage other than the knowledge." He could not believe his fortune. Here was a master far more worthy than his uncle of his complete devotion and effort and he could not hide his pleasure at being asked.

Ham nodded, with a rare smile that transformed his countenance. He too, felt the excitement of discovering a man with the same spirit and drive as his own. He threw an arm across Meshur's broad shoulder and said, "We must go to my father's house and you must learn more of our task. Will your family miss you if you do not return at the end of this week?"

He found it difficult to answer. Just when the day could hold no more for him, he was being asked to take a favored place that he would never have dared to dream possible. "My cousin can inform my family of my absence. How could they resent an invitation to the house of an elder of the city?"

And so, at the end of that week's labor, Meshur did not follow his usual way home. Instead he walked a new path to the house of Noah. Not a man of words, he found little difficulty carrying on an extended conversation with Ham as they walked. Oblivious to the forest around them, both men thought the journey a short one. If they noticed any trees as they walked, it was only for what the wood might yield to some cunning design.

The next few days had been spent in the house of Noah. He lacked for nothing to eat or drink. He saw the conveniences built into the house by Ham and his respect increased even more for the man he now saw as his master. Noah, too, spent many hours with him. He spoke of the prophecy and the need to build the ark. Meshur and his family were invited to join them in the ark. Meshur knew that his father would never consent and found it difficult himself to believe that the world could be destroyed. But he mumbled his thanks; he would never openly question an elder.

The prophecy mattered little; Meshur was consumed with the building. It was a challenge to his skills, nothing more, but what a challenge it was. When he saw the drawings for each of the decks, he was amazed: so many cages, bins, pipes, tanks, and enclosures. Storage space for food and water. Ingenious ways to feed and water the animals and dispose of their waste. In those few days, Meshur saw the ark as only Noah and Ham had envisioned it so far. His reputation would be built with this vessel. It was a magnificent task—a worthy challenge to a man of his strength and desire.

****

She sipped the tea, now barely warm. So much had been lost. Many were trying to recapture it, but too many of the arts of both body and mind required too long to master, and men counted their years now in decades instead of centuries. Quantity produced by the frenzied activity of many could not supplant the craftsmanship of the truly gifted, nurtured over hundreds of years. But the elders had been shunned since the fourth generation, and had been disgusted enough to embrace their alienation.

She stared into the dying fire, wondering anew at the mystery of certain moments—those times of great significance. Why were some so while others just marked the passage of time? Such moments were scattered across her own life, though sometimes it took many years to see their significance. Again and again she marveled at the circumstances that had led her from her small, but comfortable corner of her childhood to this place. She had been so unaware in the confusion of those days.

Chapter 11
FIRST STEP

Methuselah and Madrazi were silent during the stretch before the settlement, each enjoying the other's quiet company. In the face of her coming meeting with her new family, Madrazi found calm in the old man's companionship. As they hurried to catch the others, they passed by orchards, fields, and vineyards. Madrazi saw apple, plum, fig, and pear trees in the orchards, and barley, wheat, spelt, flax, and corn in the fields. The vineyards were closer to the main buildings and were rich and well tended. She was pleasantly surprised at the size of the fields and the variety of crops grown. She wondered how many servants were kept to tend such fields and estimated their profits. It was not a calculation of avarice; merely a reflex of her upbringing. No servants were visible in the fields as they walked toward the house.

Nearing the house, the two laggards were almost up to the rest of their party. The others were just passing through an arbor gate in a low stone wall that wound around the main buildings. Small trees surrounded the gate, creating the illusion of a much larger wall between the house and road. As Madrazi passed under the arbor, she saw a small crowd gathered along the paved walkway, enthusiastically greeting the wedding party. They caught sight of Madrazi and Methuselah at the back of the party and, much to Madrazi's embarrassment, cheers broke out as men, women, and children closed in behind them and followed them towards the great house.

As was her nature, Madrazi noticed the construction of the house before the people; she noted with approval the use of heavy timbers, and the clever way in which a wide shaded porch extended along the front of the house. But before she lost herself in that line of thought, her common sense rescued her. This was no time for woodworking. She saw the people gathered on the stone steps of the porch, and realized with a suddenly racing heart that she was looking at her new family. Methuselah squeezed her hand one last time to reassure her, but her heart beat quickly all the same as she strove to keep her face still and follow the men toward the gathering.

In the front of the group stood an older woman with dark hair, dressed in a beautiful indigo blue robe. Madrazi guessed at once that she was Noah's wife, and to her right stood two young couples. She inwardly thanked Jeriah for her detailed descriptions of Noah's family, and was confident that the shorter man with light brown hair and Noah's brown eyes was Japheth. His wife was shorter than Madrazi, with olive skin, dark eyes and hair, and full lips. Beside her was a much larger man with an aura of great strength. Even under his loose robe she could see that he was unusually broad across the shoulders, and his wrists and hands were large. His black hair and gray eyes reminded her immediately of Lamech and her father. His wife looked tiny next to him, though she was in truth less than a span shorter than Madrazi. Their glances met, and the newcomer saw shrewd, appraising eyes measuring her. For a moment, Madrazi thought she saw something of Peniah in those eyes, but whatever she saw was quickly replaced by the appearance of warmth.

Noah's wife immediately came to meet the men and embraced her husband. She then bowed to Pomorolac, Lamech and Methuselah. The moment broken, Ham, Japheth, and their wives moved up to join her. They were gracious, devoid of the discomfort often seen when people meet strangers who are also family. Then all three women pushed through the men and approached Madrazi. She stilled her heart and made sure that a smile lit her face.

Noah's wife led the way with hands outstretched. As she stopped before her, Madrazi was able to meet her warm blue eyes. "Welcome, daughter to our home. I am Wen-Tehrom. These are your sisters, Debseda, wife of Ham, and Yaran, wife of Japheth. Madrazi murmured words of greeting, and was led to Ham and Japheth. They broke away from her brothers with quick smiles and warm words. As the rest of the men gathered around, Wen-Tehrom stopped them with a word. "The day is upon us. Go and care for our guests. The women will take Madrazi into the house and help her prepare. See that all are made welcome."

With a confidence in instant obedience, she briskly led Madrazi into the house, while Jahaz crowded close behind. They walked around several corners before Madrazi's eyes could adjust to the dim hall, and she realized that she was already lost. The house was larger than it appeared from the front, but the inside was comfortable and contrary to the rough appearance of the exterior. Walls, floors, and ceilings were smooth, polished wood, with rugs softening the floors, and tapestries, the walls. Madrazi loved fine woodwork and believed that she could easily be comfortable in this house. She followed along, trying to see everything at once until at last they passed down one last passage and through a door back into a large, sunlit room decorated in a distinctively feminine fashion. The polished wooden floor was covered with soft rugs, and comfortable couches and chairs were scattered across the center of the room.

To the right were five doors in the wall across from the windows.

Wen-Tehrom turned to Madrazi and gestured about her. "This wing of the house is reserved for the women; a retreat from the men when we wish it. They do not come here."

Yaran and Debseda had followed behind, and now laughed with her, as if their domain had been won in some great battle of the past. The older woman pointed to the doors. "The middle door leads to a room for bathing. We discovered a spring of hot water when we first settled here. Ham designed the means to capture the water and divert it here for our use. Now we have hot baths whenever we wish. You will find that Ham is responsible for most of the clever devices around our home."

Debseda smiled at the compliment, and Wen-Tehrom continued. "Each of these other doors leads to a small room. Everyone needs a place to be alone, and these rooms offer that solitude for each of us. We ask that when the doors are closed that you do not disturb the peace of that person without good cause. Yours will be the door on the end yonder." She waved down the length of the great room. "It is currently furnished only for comfort, but over time you can change it as you see fit to suit your own taste."

Madrazi was still admiring the furnishings of the large room and trying to listen at the same time. Wen-Tehrom noticed her confusion, and took her hands, "I know that all is strange now, my dear, and you are surrounded by strangers. But we are a family and soon we will all be good friends. Be patient with us and learn of our home and our ways. We will be patient too, and God will bless us all. Come now," she said in a more practical voice, "we will have the servants bring your things in while you bathe away the dust of the road and prepare yourself."

Madrazi thanked her haltingly, overcome for a moment by the jumble of new information. "Jahaz," she waved her hand to her servant, "can assist me now, but she must return with my father when he leaves." In the midst of such a grand house, she was discomfited to admit that she could not even keep her cherished servant. In spite of the wealth of her dowry, Madrazi felt that this simple admission lowered her worth in their eyes.

But instead it became her first opportunity to see the generous and practical spirit that enabled Wen-Tehrom to direct such a large household. The older woman saw much behind the words. "Do not worry, my daughter," she said without the hint of condescension Madrazi feared. "I am sorry that you must lose your friend, but we have three women who have begged leave to serve you here. You may choose one or all of them as you wish. We are one family, and you are entering it as an honored relative and beloved daughter and wife. Noah rules this house in peace, and God provides us with all that we need. In you, our prayers for Shem are finally answered."

While they were talking, servants had carried in Madrazi's belongings and stacked the boxes and trunks on the floor. Debseda and Yaran excused themselves and left. Wen-Tehrom waved to the small mountain in the middle of the floor. "We will sort all of that out later," she said, waving away the servants.

"Excuse me," Madrazi interrupted hesitantly, "could Jahaz point out to them those that I will need today?"

"Of course," she replied, and then speaking to one of the servants, "Ramat, help Madrazi's servant with what she needs."

They searched through the stack and found her two traveling trunks in the back. Ramat carried them both over to the women, and looked at Wen-Tehrom inquiringly.

"Place them on the table here," she pointed, "and be excused." He set them down gently, bowed, and left.

Jahaz began to open them, but Wen-Tehrom stopped her with a gesture. "Please. I know that it has been a long road, and there is much to be done today. But nothing is done well on an empty stomach. First, let us have some bread and drink. It would not do to have you faint during the middle of your wedding, although it might fan the pride of the bridegroom if you did it at the right moment," she said with an open smile.

She pulled a cord dangling from the wall, and soon servants knocked on the door and brought in food and drink. In spite of her nervousness, Madrazi found an appetite, knowing that it would be some hours before she could eat again. During that time, Wen-Tehrom began to explain some of the ways of their house. Neither thought that Madrazi would remember, but it was a distraction that fit well with Madrazi's ordered intellect.

After they finished, Jahaz opened the trunk that contained Madrazi's wedding robe, and laid it out on one of the couches. Wen-Tehrom stared at it in wonder, and Madrazi explained. "It was my mother's. She wore it when she married my father, and now I would extend her legacy by wearing it today." Suddenly it struck Madrazi that Wen-Tehrom might have made other plans. "Is it appropriate?" she asked, wondering if she was unwittingly insulting her new mother.

"Of course!" Wen-Tehrom returned openly, "I apologize for staring. It is very beautiful, unlike anything that I have seen before." Her eyes left the robe and returned to Madrazi. "But you need little help from fine clothes. Wear it well in memory of your mother and may you have her happiness."

She rose and walked over to the robe and turned, "We will keep the marriage ceremony this very afternoon. I know that it seems abrupt, but we see no need to wait—after all, we have all been waiting for ten years. It will not be a large gathering, just our own household, but I am told that the ceremony in town was quite successful and well attended."

"I am ready," returned Madrazi, knowing it was the right thing to say, but finding that it was also true. She struggled to express the myriad of questions that ran through her mind. "But it is all so new. I hope that I do nothing to embarrass you. I do not know what to expect," she added hesitantly, hoping that the older woman would discern her intent.

Wen-Tehrom smiled in understanding. "I know, child. I hope that what we have planned suits your desires. After all, it is your wedding! Let me tell you all of it while you bathe. We have tried to arrange it so that your greatest task is to simply enjoy the hours ahead."

Madrazi felt an instinctive trust of this woman and rested on that feeling. She appreciated her new mother's suggestion; a hot bath would certainly ease her tension as well as remove the dust of the morning. She was shown through the middle door, and saw a brightly-lit room, with sunlight flooding the room through an opening in the ceiling. It reflected off of a series of pools at the far end of the room. The inviting gleam contrasted with the smooth slate floor. Colorful tiles lined the edge of the pools, but Madrazi's curiosity about their cunning designs was overcome by a desire to sink into the water's warmth. She did not hesitate, but quickly disrobed and slid into the delicious heat of the pool. Wen-Tehrom added perfumed oil from a small flask.

"Thank you," she sighed. "I have not felt hot water for two weeks."

"Enjoy it!" laughed Wen-Tehrom. "Lean your head back and close your eyes and I will tell you what will happen this afternoon."

The fragrance and heat soothed Madrazi's tense body as she obeyed and listened to the stranger who was to become her new mother.

"You and Shem will be wed outside, under the eyes of God. In the back of the house is a small grove of trees where he will await you with his fathers. We call it Methuselah's forest, because he walks and prays among the trees most mornings. The rest of the household will line up along your path as Pomorolac presents you to Shem. I will stand with you and tell you when to start."

After you have met under the trees, each step of the ceremony will be explained and you will find that you will follow it easily. We have been able to practice with your two sisters, and the men are becoming quite adept at this now."

She moved her stool aside and allowed Jahaz to kneel and begin to wash

Madrazi's hair. She felt the last residues of salt vanish and she was ready to commit herself to this new adventure.

Wen-Tehrom resumed. "Once you are together, Methuselah and Lamech will pronounce their blessing. Noah will invoke the Creator's presence as a witness to your vows. He will join your hands in the garland and pronounce the words of blessing over you, and you will forever be husband and wife. Then, the celebration will commence and continue for three days. There are no strange customs, ceremonies, or rites for you to memorize. The most important thing for you to do, my dear, is to enjoy the day and harvest good memories for your old age."

Her voice was as soothing as the water, and Madrazi felt her mind and muscles ease completely under their influence. Wen-Tehrom continued on with stories of her own marriage to Noah while Madrazi finished. She emerged refreshed from the bath, Jahaz wrapping her in a cool robe and following her to a chair at the other end of the room. Madrazi sat and her servant dried her hair and prepared her various ointments. Then they began to bring order from her hair, braiding in the white flowers supplied by Wen-Tehrom, resulting in a crown of fragrant blooms.

Madrazi had at times in her life brought out her wedding robe, stared at it, fingered it, and dreamed of its wearing, but never had she actually donned it. When she did, she knew that she had reached a place in her life that would always be remembered. The heavy silk brought the shipboard vision of her mother close once more, and the feeling brought tears. Madrazi walked to the window and stood in the sunlight letting her heart reach out, wondering if her mother was present in some way. How had she felt when she stood in this robe waiting to be joined to Pomorolac? Remembering their happiness, she found comfort in its warm smoothness against her skin.

"Your mother must have been very beautiful," said Wen-Tehrom, interrupting her reverie, yet seeming to have sensed her thoughts. "I have never seen a young woman like you. You will warm the heart of my son, and for that I am grateful."

Madrazi appreciated the kindness behind the words, but they broke the spell and directed her mind once more to her doubts and fears. Many had complimented her for her beauty, but they saw little, did not live in her body, and did not spend every day with its flaws. What would Shem think after he discovered them? Would he consider himself cheated? Was she really beautiful enough to keep him happy for many years?

In that mind it seemed like only a few minutes passed before Madrazi was led down several corridors and out onto a shaded porch. As she stepped out into a band of light across the head of the steps, she suddenly felt all the fear drain away. Something stirred deep inside and her mind no longer seemed aware. Dizzy, she clung to her father's arm. A twinge of memory lit his eyes as she looked up to him, and he smiled and said, "You are the vision of your mother many years ago. I hope that you and Shem find our happiness."

His voice sounded hollow. She held tightly to his arm and found that his familiar presence brought her back to herself. They waited there for a few minutes while Wen-Tehrom saw that all was in order. With each passing moment, Madrazi felt more and more in control. Then Wen-Tehrom returned, and with a glowing smile beckoned them to follow.

At her first step, the unsteadiness returned. Madrazi would later be able to recall in great detail all that passed during her walk down that path, but at the time she thought it a waking dream. All of her senses felt alive, but she sensed an alien presence forcing itself upon her. Her father gently held her arm for a moment, and his touch beat it back. She descended the steps, breathing slowly and willing her mind to seize control once more. But as she started down the path, her barriers were again easily breached. A part of her mind noted the people lining the path, but they seemed far away. At first, all she felt was the sensation of her mother's robe as it slid along the contours of her body. Its weight pressed against her and then its touch seemed to merge in her memory with that of her mother. More than a veil dimmed her sight, and she clung once again to her father's arm for support.

But the presence pressed upon her again with great strength. She felt disconnected from her father, the other people, and even her own body. As she weakened, she became aware that her mind was seeing depths to life previously unknown. All of her past was revealed as blindness and ignorance, and her pride shriveled. There was a temptation to give in, to dive into these new depths heedless of all else, but she fought against it. As she struggled, her perception of the outside world was altered. The path and the people faded into a long, dark tunnel. Light came from up the path toward her, but Madrazi willed it away. With that thought, she began to regain control. She saw the faces beside her, felt her father's hand, and saw at the end of the path a young man with indistinct features standing beside Noah, Lamech, and Methuselah. Although she felt as if she had walked for hours, she realized that they were not even midway to the end of the path.

Just as she regained confidence in her own senses, Madrazi heard a voice singing to the accompaniment of a small harp. Madrazi's steps unconsciously took on the slow rhythm of his music as the words floated over her.

White lace,
Veiled face,
The blush of hope shines through.
Young bride,
Starry-eyed,
For everything is seen as new.

The music refocused and strengthened the alien presence and once again she was overwhelmed. No longer did she sense her feet carrying her along; it was the music, drawing her deeper into a different world, similar to hers in surface appearances, but opening beyond sense into a limitless extent beyond. Madrazi was torn; she was attracted and repelled at the same time. Desire and fear fought within. The music continued.

She will know,
And walk below,
His banner spread above.
And know no shame,
To bear his name;
His banner over her is love.

Bridegroom,
Enters room,
With joy himself beside.
Thoughts stray,
Yet away,
When first he chose her for his bride.

As the words rolled over her, her desire for the new depths gradually began to overcome her fear of the unknown. Irresistibly, she was drawn farther into that alien world. She sensed darkness around her, but it was pierced by light from the head of the path. For a brief moment she saw four figures standing in the distance, watching her. Light enveloped them and flashed towards her, hurting her eyes. She wanted to flee, but the music carried her forward.

Time has passed,
But now at last,
The days have led to this.

Silent now,
The solemn vow
On which is set a sealing kiss.

The music faded, Madrazi blinked, and suddenly, all was as it was before. She shivered, and felt her father's comforting hand press lightly upon her arm. She looked up and saw that they were near their destination. Out of the corner of her eye, she saw Jahaz standing with Jakeh. Madrazi saw tears trace a path along her skin, but joy lit her eyes. Beyond them were Ithiel and Ucal with Japheth and his wife. Ham and Debseda stood beside them. Then her eyes shifted to the front and they stopped in front of the three elders and Shem.

Lamech was the first to speak. "In the beginning, God created us man and woman, saying that it is not good for a man to be alone. Today we celebrate the joining together of our son Shem and our daughter Madrazi so that they might have each other as they walk down the years of life. May God bless them as companions, with friendship, love, and honor for each other through trials and joys as long as life lasts."

He then stood aside. Madrazi was surprised, expecting a much longer speech. Methuselah stepped forward and spoke. "Our life is governed by choices. God chose Adam and Eve for life and joy. They chose rebellion and sin and lost both. But God did not leave them so. He offered another chance, and they clung to that promise in faith, knowing that one would come from their own seed. Cain chose rebellion; Seth chose life. We all face that decision, determining our path of destiny for all time. But other choices direct the twists and turns. Today Shem and Madrazi choose to walk together. In that line of Eve, they will play their part, make their choices, and live them out over the years. May God bless this choice and all those that they will face together."

Methuselah finished and moved aside to join Lamech. Noah then stood forward. He looked at Pomorolac and asked, "Does your daughter, Madrazi, come willingly into this marriage, forsaking her own family to stand as the wife of Shem, and do you her father agree with her in this decision?"

He answered, "We do, with joy."

Then, releasing his daughter's arm, he stepped in front of her, lifted away her veil and stood for a moment before her saying a silent farewell before standing aside with Lamech and Methuselah. Noah motioned to Shem, and he moved close to her side and Madrazi turned with him to face Noah. She felt the heat of his presence beside her and caught an indefinable aroma of a strange man mixed with that of cedar. Her heart began to beat faster and she looked rigidly ahead at Noah.

He looked first to Shem and asked, "On your word, and before God, will you take this woman to you as your wife, love her and provide for her as long as you both are alive?" In the sudden silence, Madrazi heard his voice for the first time saying, "I will, by my word, and with the help of God." She decided she liked the voice. It was quiet and calm and yet carried across the clearing.

Madrazi was still afraid to look over. Noah motioned to his wife and she brought to him a garland of white flowers with a faint air of sweet perfume. Noah held the garland in his two hands and lifted it into the air. He looked to the sky and said, "Oh God of promise and mercy, we beg you to bless the union of this man and woman. We pray for life, love, joy, mercy and the fruit of the earth and womb."

He then took the garland and gently lifted Madrazi's right hand and laid it in the hand of Shem. She trembled involuntarily as she felt the first touch of his strong fingers. Although her father had removed only her veil, the cool wind across her cheeks and the warmth of the new hand on hers made her feel strangely naked. Noah then wrapped the garland of flowers around their hands and said, "May this union be pure in love as these flowers are pure in color and aroma. May it grow and flourish as these flowers grow and flourish under the sun and dew sent by God."

The scent of the flowers and the clasp of Shem's hand brought warmth to Madrazi's skin. She felt blood rise to her face, but welcomed the feeling, knowing that there was no need for shame.

Noah continued, "May the God who hears all words and knows all hearts accept your promise to each other, and may He strengthen each of you to uphold and fulfill all that you have spoken today. May His blessing be upon you and your children and their children after them."

Then speaking louder to the assembled crowd he said, "I now bear witness that Shem and Madrazi are joined in marriage before God and man. Hold them in honor as is fitting for a husband and wife."

The crowd cheered, and immediately surged forward to embrace the couple. The noise jolted Madrazi and she felt as if she had just awakened. But the man close beside her, still clinging to her hand, was no phantom. She turned with him to face the oncoming wave and they were swept along in a swirl of people who were now her family and her life. She saw him now clearly beside her and wondered at the fortunes that had opened two strangers to the greatest possible intimacy. They were married, but had not yet spoken one word to each other alone. She wondered what he thought, and if he was disappointed in her appearance or manner.

She almost panicked at that thought, but remembered the words of

Methuselah.   She knew that they could find a common ground, in being brought together as strangers, if nothing else.   It was a place to start.   She looked up at him again and saw his face outlined in the sunlight.   She was not displeased.   He still held her hand, and feeling a tremor, he pressed gently upon it as he smiled.   His dark eyes turned fully to hers, interrupting the distraction of the crowd, and she saw both an openness that she guessed was reserved for few, and at the same time an acute appraisal.   That moment of communication was all that was afforded the couple as the press around them carried them to the banquet awaiting the celebrants.   But Madrazi was comforted by an assurance that he managed to convey in that one look.   She never forgot it, among the other memories that she collected from the rest of the day and night.

Chapter 12
FIRST IMPRESSIONS

Madrazi woke from a deep sleep in the morning, refreshed, but puzzled. At first, she could not understand what was wrong. She lay comfortable in her own bed, but the air was not salty and no sound of the waves could be heard. The light was strange. Sunlight filtered into the room from strange directions, and cast bars of light across the bed near her feet. As she lay still and moved into the world of waking, she shook off her confusion. She was no longer the girl in her old room. She was the woman of Shem and lay in his bed in his room—their room.

Not wanting to disturb him, she moved only her eyes and tried to see what she could. All the room was strange to her. She had not seen it yesterday and when they had arrived last night, neither was interested in the furnishings. After Shem had carried her into the dim light of aromatic candles, they lost little time exploring anything but their new life together. Her eyes had been occupied with her husband, and his with her, and her fears had been resolved in his arms.

Many who thought they knew the cold, controlled Madrazi would have been shocked at the strength of her passion. It had surprised her at first, then frightened her, but as it found a match in his, fear subsided and they both took satisfaction in each other. It was a confirmation of her new life. The nadir had been aboard Hakkem at the mercy of the sea and its false winds: everything since that night she had seen her mother had been an ascent out of the depths—an escape from her implacable foe. Never again would she venture out on the sea; she would learn the forest and live her life under its shadow. Her fears during those dark days aboard Hakkem had vanished like the mist in the sunlight. Her enemy would not threaten her again. With a secret smile, she glanced around the room.

It was a large room, with windows facing north to the forest. Paneled with fragrant cedar, she saw the skins of a lion and a bear on the floor. Antlers served as racks; the set within her vision bore a quiver of arrows. Thick candles on wrought stands had been snuffed late into the night, and a hint of their waxy scent still lingered. The wooden furniture was solid and dark. It was clearly a man's room, and Madrazi began to plan changes as she lay still. Turning her head slowly so as to not awaken her husband, she added to her mental list of alterations before she felt a stirring behind her. Fully awake, she turned and saw his dark eyes, watching without speaking or moving. She had the uncomfortable feeling that they had been watching her for many minutes, divining her thoughts.

"Welcome to our morning," he said softly. "This is the first time since I was a boy that I have woken to another pair of eyes in my room. But I forget, it is your room now—all that I have is yours."

"Then I am content," replied Madrazi, and although it was true, she felt a rush of modesty at their proximity under the thin coverlet. The darkness and emotion of last night had made it easy to be together, but she was now embarrassed, even though she knew that there should be no reason. She hoped that what he saw in the light of day would appeal to him as it had in the darkness.

"What are we to do now?" she asked. He did not reply, considering the various meanings of her question, and instead he gently ran his fingers along the line of her hair and brushed it back from her face.

"First, I want to enjoy your beauty," he said, lightly, but with an undertone of last night's passion." Sensing her nervousness, he added, "with my eyes."

For a few moments, he spoke softly and stroked her hair, and she began to relax. "All we need do is enjoy the next few days," he said. "People will make much of us, and we should allow it. That will satisfy everyone. But we will find time for ourselves, too. If you wish, we can take some now, and wander the grounds and talk. It is easy to share my bed with one as beautiful as you, but we are still strangers in so many ways."

"We are no longer strangers," she returned, her mind on last night, "but we must share our minds and hearts, too. It would be good to be with you alone. I have never been comfortable in the midst of a crowd, even if the occasion is one of joy. And although we have many years to grow together, I am eager to start."

Within a few minutes they were outside in the cool morning air. His hand was warm and she savored its touch. The sun was not yet high and the morning mist was cool. Few others were abroad. As they walked quietly up the path to the glade where they had met, she became uneasy. What had she seen yesterday? Had it been a waking dream? She could recall little. Once the celebration had started, her walk down the path had faded like an old memory; not immediate, but not gone, either.

As they meandered across the grounds, Madrazi saw that the forest was not as near as it looked from the front of the house. Between the grove behind the house and the forest was a large swale, and the forest itself had no clear boundary; its outermost trees stood like lonely sentinels in the meadows. At the head of the hollow stood a large barn that formed the apex of two long lines of pens, cages, and smaller outbuildings that angled to the northeast and northwest. Its size surprised her until she remembered the rumors of Noah's avocation.

Shem sensed her curiosity and explained. "This is where Father keeps animals we are studying. We investigate each kind and learn of its ways; what they eat, when they sleep, how long it takes to produce young, and how to care for them. He records his knowledge about their behavior in captivity, and I lend my aid by observing them in the forest. Together, we have come to understand much about all kinds of creatures. Father does the same with plants and trees, but most of that work is done in the fields and orchards in front of the house. As with the animals, we compare observations with what I see in the forest."

"I had heard that this work had earned your father much respect, and that his understanding of plants and animals was exceeded by none."

"Respect?" he mused. "Perhaps, in a way." He laughed and put away whatever thought had passed through his mind, but Madrazi sensed an undertone of bitterness in his voice. They walked past the barn and up the near line of pens. Everything was well designed. Food and water were readily at hand for the animals, with pens and enclosures grouped together around food stores.

Slightly more than half the pens were occupied. Many of the animals were familiar and included those useful to men—goats, sheep, cattle, donkeys, fowl, and even two young camels. Some she knew of secondhand, but had never seen. Near the end of the right hand line was a large pen built around a small pinnacle of broken rock. Inside she saw a marshy pool and two small crocodiles lying on the mud beside it. Madrazi instinctively shied away and Shem took advantage of her fear to pull her close. She felt the blood rising to her face, but enjoyed the warmth of his body against hers and decided that she had found a time and place for fear.

At the end of the line she saw a large wooden tank mounted on a sturdy framework, perhaps five cubits off the ground. Wooden pipes led from near its base around the back of the line of cages. She could see that the piping extended the entire length of the enclosures. A framework enclosed the tank itself, with four sails mounted in a circle on the front. They moved slowly around in the morning breeze.

Shem sensed her question before it was asked. "The tank is for water," he explained, pointing to the odd tower. "The wind turns the sails and pumps water out of the ground." Madrazi had been well trained in the design of ships and their associated mechanisms, so she had little problem in understanding its workings once Shem explained its purpose. But she let him continue. "Once in the tank, water moves through those wooden pipes to the troughs in the enclosures, saving us the trouble of carrying it to each cage."

It was an ingenious system of watering many animals. She recalled the baths in the house and Wen-Tehrom's words. "Is this another example of Ham's skill?" she asked, pointing to the tank.

"Yes, Ham is the master of designing and building mechanisms to ease labor; and since they usually work, Japheth and I encourage him as much as we can! Father saw the mechanism in Nimur and told Ham of its use. He was able to work out the construction, and it has proven well worth the effort."

They continued walking along a defined path that led into the forest. Before them on the verge of the wood was a large area enclosed by thin nets strung between the outermost trees. Drawing near, Madrazi heard the morning music of many birds. Walking closer, she saw flashes of brilliant color that complemented the sweet sounds. The netting enclosed a number of small trees and formed a large aviary. Madrazi recognized only a few of the birds inside. Looking in both directions, Madrazi saw no other dwellings along the edge of the forest, nor had she seen any the day before.

"What do you like best of your home?" she asked.

"That is hard to say," he answered. "This place is my life." He turned then to face the forest, struggling to explain. "I love my family, but that is only part of it. I readily admit being ensnared by the forest." He hesitated, searching for words. "It is a wonderful place, and I would rather be under its eaves living in a cave than in the largest home in town. You cannot know how it feels to be alone in the depths of shadow; only animals and birds sharing the majesty of the trees, the sun on the meadows, and the cold streams that refresh your feet after a day of exploring." Madrazi caught the passion in his voice and knew that she had just seen a glimpse of the man beside her.

They rose and walked a little closer to the trees. She stood silently beside him as he looked with eager eyes to the north. He stayed very still and she realized with a start that he was far from her at that moment. He walked in spirit among the faint sounds that emanated from beneath the shadows. He was attuned to its pulse of life and she was both curious and jealous. She hesitated to break that spell, but needed information if she was ever to share in it.

"I felt something of that yesterday, coming down the road," she said, pulling his attention back to where it belonged. "I was drawn to the shadows under the trees and I longed to stand and see nothing but the trees going on and on to the horizon. I wish to learn its ways."

"Then we must go, and I will show you," he said with a flash of fire in his eyes. Madrazi could see that her words had pleased him greatly.

"There are many new places that I would like to see. Does not your grandfather own a large home in Lamech? Surely the savor of the trees must be flavored by a taste of the streets of town."

"That is something that you will learn quickly about me, " he sighed. "Great-grandfather built the town and Grandfather and Father sit with him on the council. As the firstborn of Noah, people say that I may become an elder. But I have no longing for such a life. The people there..." He stopped, but not before Madrazi heard the passion rising in his voice and the blood to his face. He turned to her and forced a laugh. "I forget that I am no longer my own man. Do you wish to live in Lamech?"

Madrazi was caught off guard by his direct question, but her good sense overruled her emotion once again. "I wish to live with my husband to whom I have committed my life and my love."

They stood facing each other, dark eyes searching the deep green for the thoughts behind the words. He answered her with an embrace and as their lips met, Madrazi knew that her answer had pleased him.

She pulled back and looked up at him again. "But, husband," she added with a mischievous smile, "I will enjoy Lamech, too, and I will drag you along with me when I go!"

"I will endure if you insist," he sighed, "as long as my brothers do not find out that I am doing it under your orders!"

"No," she laughed, "that will be one of our secrets."

He moved closer to her and it seemed only natural that her head would find his chest as his arm drew her to him. With no hesitation, she threw her arms around him and pulled him close against her warm body. He felt her body relax against his, and they both reveled in the new feelings that they had waited long years to experience.

"Tell me of your home," he asked, gently, sensing better than his wife that this was not the proper place for passion. "Was it hard for you to leave the sea? I hope that the Great Forest can offer you some solace for your loss."

His words were ill timed. At that moment all her being was focused on the physical pleasure of the warm firmness of his body pressed against hers. No words could have caught her off guard as those did, and the heightened emotion turned instantly from pleasure to pain. With passion still ruling thought, she jerked away from him, hardly seeing the shock on his face. Her body stiffened, and in instinctive fear her vision seemed to burst from her unconscious mind and advanced to the edge of sight. Words erupted in anger with no conscious thought. "I hate the sea! I will be happy if I never venture onto it again, and happier still if I never see it!"

As quickly as it had come, the anger dissolved as Madrazi realized that she had broken the spell of the morning. An awkward silence stood between them, and shame swept over her. With it came an unreasoning anger at Shem for bringing out a part of her that she wanted to remain deeply hidden. She hurried to explain, trying vainly to atone for her display. "The sea is my enemy. It took my mother many years ago, and I cannot forgive that."

She started to go on, and stumbled over words. Fighting tears, her anger stirred again at her unseemly show of weakness. A small voice inside urged her to share her fear and her vision, but she could not. Its wounds were too deep, and they had only been married for a day. A few moments ago she had been so close to him; now she felt a stranger. What would he think if he knew such an evil omen was a part of her life? She looked down at the ground and hoped that her explanation satisfied him.

Shem was surprised at the intensity of her anger, but he sensed the depth and power of her emotion, though without understanding. Wanting to help, he was hurt by her retreat. But he knew that further prying would only raise more barriers.

Instead, he came to her in a smooth, fluid motion and offered his hand. She tried to force calm into her face, but it was too late. After a moment, he replied softly, as if afraid to transgress again. "I am sorry about your mother. And I am sorry that I brought to your mind such feelings on this day. It should be a day of happiness for you, not a memory of sadness."

New guilt tore at her heart when she saw how easily her display had hurt him. She must make amends and so she took his hand and pulled him into her arms. "How can this be a day of sadness when I have a husband like you to dispel the gloom? It is I who should apologize; it was not right to speak in such a way to you." His kiss was the satisfactory answer that they both needed, and Madrazi began to put away her fears, clung to his hand and let him lead her on.

They wandered back around the west side of the house past a large barn, smaller cottages, and several outbuildings that supported the work in the fields. There were grain stores and small buildings for livestock, horses, and poultry. Only a few men were about and they nodded politely to the couple as they hurried about their work. Shem explained some of the workings of the land as they walked along, and Madrazi listened halfheartedly as she reproached herself for her temper. Shem was evidently accustomed to speaking little, but made an effort to keep talking.

Madrazi saw his discomfort and forced herself to speak calmly. "How many people live here," she asked, attempting to restore normality to the morning. "I have never seen such a large farm. You must be able to feed hundreds."

Shem looked over the fields and shrugged. "I have always thought that this is quite normal. I have never known anything else. We send much food into Lamech; we sell some, and Grandfather distributes the rest to those in need. We are now ten in our family; the wives of Lamech and Methuselah were buried in a glade of the forest in my youth. Their other children do not live in Lamech, choosing instead the lands of Methuselah's youth. There are usually between forty and fifty servants and laborers, more during harvest and planting. Some come and go, but most of them have been with us for many years."

There was no offense in the words, but Madrazi sensed that he was holding something back. What offense had her question given? Could they not have a normal conversation? Shem looked towards the eastern sky and noted that the festivities of the day would begin soon. Madrazi accepted the opening and asked him about the events and sensed him relax as he talked of the things his family enjoyed. They were soon discussing their favorite games and the tension began to melt away. She sought his hand and gently stroked his fingers as they walked. He responded with a quick tightening of his hand, and she knew that they had at least reached a truce.

Their hands tensed together at a shout from one of the outbuildings. "You are late for your own feast, brother!" Japheth called, running up. "I would never have thought you one to miss an opportunity for good food, but I can see that you have been distracted."

There was some quality of his ready grin and obvious affection for his brother that won Madrazi's heart immediately. Before Shem could answer, she replied with a sideways glance at her husband, "I am so sorry that we were detained, brother. My husband lost track of the time telling me stories of his family." Madrazi kept her features placid and her eyes demurely fixed on the ground at his feet.

Her reply left Japheth wordless. Shem caught on more quickly and added, "Yes, brother, it took quite a while to explain the details of the day that Father caught you in the wheat…"

Madrazi looked up to see Japheth's face was a humorous mixture of surprise, alarm, and anger. Husband and wife both broke out laughing at the sight, and Madrazi hurried to say, "Shem was only showing me the grounds, and I was only attempting a little fun, but from the look on your face, I must find out more about this story...." She could not help laughing again, and his discomfort banished her earlier tension. The morning brightened again, and Japheth's face relaxed to a wry grin as both men began to laugh with her.

"So you have married a woman with quick wit, Shem. Beware!" But his smile and a hug disarmed his words. "I must walk with you some morning, too. I could tell you a few stories about your new husband!"

"Just make sure that you don't share them all with Mother or Father, unless you ask us first," said Shem. "Brothers must have a few secrets, too."

Together they walked back towards the back of the house. Madrazi was certain in those few moments that Japheth would be a friend. They were alike in sharp wit and ready tongue, but she could sense a gentleness and compassion that tempered his jests. Besides, it was clear that the brothers were close and conflict with Japheth would only create more tension. She held Shem's hand and was content to listen to their banter as they walked and learn more about both.

The morning was passing as they came to the large patio where everyone was gathered for an early meal. Tables were laden on one side, and everyone ate as they stood and talked together. Just as Madrazi thought that she could slide through the crowd unnoticed, Japheth pursed his lips and gave a shrill whistle that stilled all conversation and drew everyone's attention. With a loud voice he announced, "Behold! The bride and bridegroom return! In spite of little sleep, they choose to honor us anew with their presence!"

Madrazi felt the heat rise to her cheeks and saw Shem cast a dark look at his brother. She felt a blend of amusement and embarrassment, but Japheth ignored it and seizing a cup, he raised it and cried out, "A drink to the new couple. May all their mornings dawn with a golden happiness and peace that comes only to those who share such love!"

The jest gave way to sincerity, and the crowd on the patio raised their cups. Just as the blood began to recede from her cheeks, she heard him add under his breath, "Such love as can ignore sleep." His face was guileless, but hers was immediately red again.

Madrazi felt a warm, soft hand on her arm. She turned to Yaran, who shook her head with mixed understanding and annoyance at her husband. "Come with me, Madrazi. It is the privilege of a woman to withdraw gracefully from the crowd when need arises."

She shot a look at Japheth that seemed to dampen his enthusiasm for a moment, but then he shrugged and turned to Shem. "Let the women retire from the field, brother. We will enjoy the fruits of victory at the table." Shem looked at his wife helplessly and she nodded with a rueful smile while the brothers turned away. Yaran steered her though the crowd into the house.

She led Madrazi back to the women's room, sensing her need to be apart for a few minutes. As they sat together she said, "I am sorry if Japheth caused you embarrassment. He has a quick wit, but it often speeds from his lips without the benefit of thought."

"Please don't worry," Madrazi returned. "I deserved it." She went on to describe what had happened earlier, and Yaran was laughing merrily by the time the tale was finished.

"Beware, Madrazi," she said. "Japheth is seldom at a loss for speech. He will haunt you forever, now that you have bested him at his own game. Please let me know if it is ever too much. I know how to rein him in when he steps where he should not." The flash of her eye reinforced her words.

"I don't mind. I have always been around men and traded speech with them freely. Our home was isolated from the towns and my father has little use for unnecessary protocol. After my mother died, there were no women my own age to befriend." She hoped that Yaran understood.

"You will have women enough here, Madrazi," she returned. "But we, too, have a simple household and speak freely with each other."

Madrazi smiled her relief and finished brightly, "I have already seen that Japheth loves Shem, and for that alone, if nothing else, we must be good friends." She paused, and looked up at her new sister. "I hope that we will be."

"Of course," Yaran replied easily. "We will have little choice. Shem and Japheth have been so since youth, and we will have to follow where they lead. But I think that you and I could find friendship regardless of our husbands."

Madrazi was grateful but her curiosity stirred and she asked, "How long have you been in this house?"

Yaran looked uncertain for a moment, then replied, "It is hard to answer your question. I have been of the house of Noah since birth, but have only been married to Japheth for six years. My father worked for Lamech and Noah before he died, and my mother accepted a place here afterwards. We served here until my mother died seven years ago. Japheth and I had already reached an understanding, and when my mother died, it seemed best to go ahead and marry. It was uncomfortable for a time, changing from servant to daughter, but all have been good to me. You will find this a good house. Your husband is a good man, and we all have looked forward to this day for many years."

The women talked easily for a few more minutes. Madrazi told her a little of her life in the house of Pomorolac, and soon was ready to return to the festivities. "Thank you for rescuing me," she said as they walked together out of the house.

"Seek me out if you find yourself in need, again," Yaran returned with a smile. They had not been gone long, and as they returned to their husbands, Yaran gave her hand an encouraging squeeze.

With studied disregard for Japheth, Madrazi turned to Shem and asked, "Have you left anything on the tables for the bride? Perhaps we should investigate." She took his arm and steered him away, continuing to ignore Japheth. Just as he was getting ready to follow, out of the corner of her eye Madrazi saw Yaran intercept him and drop one lid in a wink. Madrazi knew that she could easily like both Japheth and his wife as she led Shem away.

The two had put her in a good mood, and she was again ready to enjoy the day. Madrazi sensed that this time was special and remembering Wen-Tehrom's advice, she threw herself into the day with an effort to be pleasant to all, and so add their own enjoyment to hers. But she kept Shem close as much as she could. She realized that in spite of her failure to keep her temper, she had enjoyed their brief hour in the morning, and a feeling of possessive desire was upon her the rest of the day.

Everyone passed the day pleasantly. Happiness naturally associated with a wedding mingled with sufficient food and drink to lift the spirits of all. Instead of work there was music, story telling, and contests between the men. Ham was the strongest man present and proved a better wrestler than even Ucal, who had inherited much of Pomorolac's strength. In a footrace held in the afternoon, Shem proved the faster by a good margin over the others and Madrazi watched with pride as he won. She was fascinated at his grace in motion; he ran with an easy stride that suggested even greater speed. Other games followed, but Madrazi kept Shem close the rest of the day and would not let him compete. After the evening feast, they gathered in the great hall, where Pomorolac told tales of his voyages that enthralled everyone for hours.

At a call for more, Shem turned to his wife and asked quietly, "Have you heard these tales before?"

"Of course."

"Then perhaps you could tell them to me some other time," he suggested.

Madrazi agreed with a conspiratorial nod and they slipped from their seats and walked quietly away, while the others remained to hear more. Japheth, sitting between them and the door, asked behind his hand what had kept them for so long, but Yaran kicked his ankle and smiled sweetly up at Madrazi.

Alone with Shem in the passages, Madrazi found herself suddenly more apprehensive about this night than the previous. The unknown was now known, but not fully. She was not sure which was worse. Shem was oblivious to her anxiety; he led her into their room and closed the door. She slipped away to sit at the foot of the bed, curled her legs under her, and motioned him over. He sat and his steady dark eyes seemed again to read her thoughts.

"You have been a wife for one evening and one morning. Lamech spoke of two becoming one—of making something new. What do you think of what we are creating so far?"

Madrazi reached into the question and her lips curled up slightly as she appreciated its perception.

"You are not the stranger that you were yesterday," she admitted. "At times we have merged and at times we have walked alone. I know you a little better and myself a little less. Everyone says that it takes time and I well believe it. But my vow is as good tonight as it was last night and as it will be tomorrow. One thing I have learned is that I remain quite willing to pursue your love."

"I promise that it will not be a difficult chase," Shem smiled. "You are the one person that I have no desire to outrun."

Chapter 13
UNCOUNTED COSTS

Men sweated and labored, shouted and sang. Gulls cried and dove around the ships and docks. Oblivious to the activity around her, Madrazi stood silent near the end of the quay in the midst of the waterfront flurry. The afternoon sun glinted off the rippled water below and flashed from the white sails of the fishing boats at the edge of sight. She took no notice of these things; she saw only the receding stern of Hakkem, and although her ears could no longer catch the sounds, her mind replayed the rhythm of her father's voice chanting the orders that were returning the ship to the open sea. The reality of separation was upon her and she was miserable. Her past was sailing far away and the future was uncertain. The man who was her future stood a half step behind her, respecting her mood.

Would she ever see her family again? Or Jahaz, Jakeh, or any of her old friends? The wind and sea were carrying the remnant of her world over the horizon, just as they had carried her mother away years before. Feelings of loss were augmented by an irrational guilt. For ten years she had been focused on the future; for the past weeks she had gladly embraced a new life with Jeriah, Noah, Methuselah, and the man who stood silent at her shoulder. Too late, she had discovered that in her pursuit of the new she had not fully counted its price—the loss of the past.

Its first intimation came when Pomorolac sent his eight crewmen back to Lamech with the baggage, a sign that he was anxious to return to sea. Despite her best efforts to prepare, the arrival of that day struck Madrazi hard. Her emotions, unlocked by the events of the past weeks, refused to submit easily to her self-control and she felt sorrow and a vague foreboding.

She had many questions about her new life, but the presence of her father and brothers provided a haven from which she could safely search for answers. She remained confident of Methuselah's love, of Noah's goodness and of her own desire for Shem. But she was beginning to see that she did not yet belong. She noticed a standard of speech and behavior that made her uncomfortably aware of her shortcomings. Pomorolac had warned her that adjustments would be required, but it was easier to talk about a nebulous future on Hakkem than to face it squarely in the now of her life.

When her father and brothers had announced their departure plans, Madrazi had seized the opportunity to escape for at least a few days. Finding Shem later that day, she had made her request, "My husband, my heart is heavy at my upcoming separation from my family. I would delay that time as much as possible. Would you allow me the grace of a few days to travel with them to Lamech?"

In their short time together, Madrazi had made the disconcerting discovery that Shem was a most perceptive man. His eye seemed to see through her own and into the guarded secrets of her mind. Afraid that he would see her other reasons for the request, she could not meet his eyes. But Shem was also a kind man and granted his permission with only a question. "Do you wish my company on the road, or would you prefer for me to meet you in town?"

"I would not chain you to the city for even a day," she had replied. "If you will allow it, please meet me in town and bring me home after my father sails." He accepted that without comment, but Madrazi saw that there was more in his mind than in his words.

Pomorolac was grateful for his daughter's company and told Shem that he could meet them at the Sea Gate at midafternoon of the third day, when the tides would be propitious. "When we reach town, we will stay at the inn of Eldad, and Madrazi can enjoy the company of his daughter once again."

Two days later, everyone was up early to see them off. Madrazi ate an early meal with her brothers and Jahaz. Jakeh came in some minutes later, then Pomorolac. Madrazi noticed at once that her father was tired and preoccupied; he ate nothing, but approached her and gave her an uncharacteristic embrace. Smiling wanly, he said quietly, "I am glad that you are coming with us today." She was not sure what to say, but returned his embrace and gave him a warm smile, hiding her concern about his appearance.

Noah, Wen-Tehrom, and Methuselah had gathered on the front path, and they offered Pomorolac their wishes for a safe journey. Noah took him aside and spoke quietly for a short time, and Madrazi saw her father nod briefly. Shem came out of the door a moment later. He bowed respectfully to Pomorolac and gripped the arms of Ucal and Ithiel. He kept hold of her hand as they walked to the road and as Madrazi looked back, she saw him standing there for some time, watching the party fade into the morning.

Madrazi felt full of things that she wanted to say to her family, but she could not find the words, and all of them seemed afflicted with the same malady. She could sense her brothers' disappointment at leaving behind the celebrations and joys of Noah's house, while her father's mind was clearly elsewhere. Her mood grew to match that of the men; the reality of their parting was before them and each step was a break with her past life. Pomorolac remained quiet and withdrawn. Jahaz was also despondent, her head was bowed and her step slow. Her responses to Madrazi's attempts at conversation were forced and flat. Finally, she stumbled back to Jakeh and walked with him the remainder of the day. Fortunately, the road seemed short and they arrived at the inn in the afternoon.

Gratefully, Madrazi found her heart lifting as they neared Lamech. Although tired, the anticipation of seeing Jeriah banished the gloom of the day and brought her a flash of happiness. She longed to share the events of the week, and Jeriah was the only person she had met with whom she was completely at ease. Perhaps an opportunity to talk would relieve her of the pent up emotions that swirled inside.

Once at the inn, Eldad welcomed them warmly, delighted to hear that they would stay for two nights. Pomorolac sent Jakeh back to the ship with instructions to begin preparing for the trip and Jahaz announced that she would accompany him. Jakeh bowed low to Pomorolac and turned to embrace Madrazi before he left.

"It will be a lonely and dull business back home without you, Madrazi," he said tenderly. "I will have no one to argue with about the step of the masts or the size of the sails, and I shall have to check all of the navigational calculations myself." His smiled turned serious as he said, "I will miss you. Your father will, too," he added quietly in her ear. "I wish you joy, prosperity, long life, and many children."

"I will miss you, also, old friend," she replied, still holding his arms. "Please take care of Father, Ucal, and Ithiel." Leaning to him, she whispered in his ear, "And please see to the happiness of Jahaz. My sadness is tempered by a new life; her's needs your compassion." She kissed him gently on his rough cheek and stepped back, finding no other words that would not bring tears.

After they had left, Madrazi saw Jeriah walking towards her with a bright smile on her face. Pomorolac seemed relieved at her presence. Bowing to her guests, Jeriah said, "Permit me master, to see to the needs of your daughter." Nodding his approval, Pomorolac left to follow his sons to the food, drink, and talk of the public room.

Jeriah led her friend back down the familiar halls to her room, and set down Madrazi's pack. "You are the most pleasant surprise of my whole week! I will not rest until I have heard every word of these past days. But first," she walked to the table and returned with a goblet, "drink this. Then we shall go talk the sun down."

Madrazi drank eagerly the same cool yellow wine that she had enjoyed before. It seemed many days since she had last tasted it and reminded her how much of her life had changed. Jeriah led her down a back stair into a small interior courtyard. Flowers and fruit trees surrounded the fountain in the middle and inviting seats were arranged along the path across the space.

"Come," she said, "This is my garden and the flowers are sweet this afternoon. Sit with me and tell me all."

Suddenly, Madrazi began to weep, then was instantly ashamed. But Jeriah, who already understood her well, simply embraced her for several minutes without a word. Finally, she loosened her hold, and looked at her friend's tear-stained face. "I will love you whether you talk to me with words or tears," she said, "but I might understand the words better."

Madrazi laughed through the final tears, and allowed Jeriah to fetch a clean cloth to dry her eyes and another cup of wine. It relaxed both body and emotions, and after the tears, words came easily. As Jeriah prompted her with questions, Madrazi told her of all that had happened.

"And now you come back to Lamech to seal the change; your old life will be gone when your father sails and the new will be truly upon you. Like a just-purchased cloak, your life is now brand new and exciting though it will take many years before it will fit with comfort."

"It would be much harder without you," Madrazi admitted, grateful for Jeriah's insight. In the presence of her friend, Madrazi felt a return of happiness. Her smile was mirrored on Jeriah's face, and they talked of inconsequential things until supper.

As they ate, Jeriah sensed her friend's new mood and talked of the next day. "Father has granted me time these next days. I will take you around the town tomorrow," she promised. "Or perhaps," she laughed, "now that you are a respectably married woman, you can escort me! I know the best shops and we will spend hours selecting all of the things that Shem will have to buy when he arrives. I am sorry that he will not bring you here to live, but we will see each other often, and enjoy the time all the more for the intervals of parting."

So passed the hours, and each minute seemed to the women a year in which their friendship blossomed. They talked about anything and everything, shared secrets, and went to sleep exhausted, but happy, at a very late hour.

Early the next morning, they rose and dressed quickly, and spent a glorious day wandering the streets of Lamech. Madrazi saw clothes, jewels, oils and perfumes, sandals and shoes, and other goods in the unending string of shops favored by Jeriah. Their time was their own; Pomorolac was doing business in town and preparing Hakkem for departure.

Late in the morning they met a young soldier and a woman in the market near the square. The woman greeted Jeriah warmly, but the soldier lagged shyly behind. Madrazi saw suppressed emotion in his eyes as they fixed briefly upon Jeriah. Jeriah turned to Madrazi. "This is Arbah, my friend, and her brother, Jared, son of Zered. He is the foremost warrior in Lamech, and is renowned even among the wise in Taspar. He has given us a great victory over Y'tor."

Madrazi saw a slight flush on her friend's face, and noticed the flutter of the vein in her neck, but she kept a polite smile on her face and turned to the brother and sister. Her mind recalled the news that had accompanied her betrothal, and it raced back through the recent events. "Thirteen days ago?" She asked. Jared nodded and Madrazi hastened to explain. "We saw the smoke of a great burning from our ship a few days before we arrived. If you have defeated Torech, then you deserve the gratitude of all Lamech. As its newest citizen, I add my thanks for your courage and skill."

Jared was slow to answer, so Jeriah interrupted. "Madrazi has become my good friend."

He turned to Madrazi. "You are too kind in your words, and credit belongs to others. Sechiall is Supreme Commander, and the men fought well."

Madrazi turned to Arbah and said, "If you are Jeriah's friend, then you are mine now." She smiled back her appreciation and the two friends continued on their way.

"So he is not only a great warrior, but a handsome man, and one who appreciates your beauty," Madrazi teased as soon as they were out of earshot.

Jeriah blushed lightly, and sighed. "I suppose that there can be no secrets between us."

"I meant no ill," returned Madrazi quickly, fearing that she should have kept silence.

"Of course not!" Jeriah reassured her. "I do like him and his family, but he is seldom in town and has not called upon my father."

"Give him time," Madrazi counseled, relieved that her friend had not taken offense. "Some types of courage come easier than others."

By the time they returned to the inn, it was late afternoon, and both women were as happy as they were tired. Madrazi was relieved to see a hint of a smile on her father's face, and he embraced her. Later, when they were alone, he told her. "I am glad, my daughter, that you have found such a friend as the daughter of Eldad. Many never do, and the lucky few find only one in a lifetime. My heart is easier about leaving you here knowing that Jeriah will lighten yours."

He then pressed a leather pouch into her hands. "I have paid a handsome dowry to Noah, and he is a man of great wealth," he said, "but you are a woman of independent ways. Please accept this as my parting gift to you. Use it to find pleasure in the shops of Lamech with your friend. And think of my love as you find happiness in its use."

Madrazi was suddenly nervous about carrying such a sum of money with her, and knew that she could never hide it from Shem. Reading her thoughts yet again, Pomorolac spoke softly, "I have discussed these funds with Eldad. He will invest them for you and keep an accounting for a small part of the profits. You will always have funds awaiting you here in town."

"Thank you, Father," Madrazi stammered. "Please make it so. You continue to provide for me, long after you will have gone. I will always think of you, regardless of what I am doing. Do you mind if I continue the evening with Jeriah?"

"Of course not, my daughter!" he laughed. "Do you think that I have no business to conduct? I cannot let this opportunity in Lamech slip by without gathering knowledge that will help our trade for years to come. Perhaps I can establish a partnership here in town and so find an excuse to come visit you occasionally. Eldad is interested and is a member of the guild, but these things take time. Perhaps we can cut a covenant in time."

"Make sure that it is one to your advantage, Father," Madrazi cautioned.

"Which of them are ever not?" he retorted gently, and they smiled together, sharing again their past life.

As he turned away, she could not resist asking him, "Father, what was the matter yesterday? Please do not hide the matter from me."

A flash of anger was immediately replaced by his most impassive look. He thought for a moment, then said, "It was nothing. I merely spent many hours of that night in conversation with Noah. We spoke of many things and I did not sleep. I was only tired. I am sorry that I gave you any cause for concern." Madrazi knew that he was withholding much, but she also knew that he had said all that he would.

Sleep was peaceful that night and the sun was over the city wall before she finished breakfast. Her father found her walking the courtyard with Jeriah and said, "I need to go on board Hakkem and prepare for the voyage. Come with me and say your farewells to the crew and to Jakeh and Jahaz. I regret now that I allowed Peniah to talk me into keeping her with us, but what is done is done. Comfort her while you can. I will return you to the quay at the appointed hour when Shem arrives."

Madrazi bade Jeriah farewell, and followed her father through the town, across the square, down onto the quay and across the harbor to Hakkem in the small boat. Mounting the ship for the last time, she saw the downcast glances of the many faithful friends that she had made growing up. She forced a smile and took the time to walk the decks, speaking to each man. She ended up at the stern with Jahaz. The hours were short, but the minutes long. Madrazi searched for words to speak to Jahaz and found few. Jahaz' silence did not make it any easier. Both women shared the misery of separation, but neither seemed to have the words to comfort the other.

Finally, as they watched the crew swing out the boat that would separate them forever, Jahaz turned to her mistress with red, puffy eyes and said, "If I were free, I would stay with you, Madrazi. You have been my life since your mother's death, and I do not know what I shall do without you. But you," she paused and looked strangely away to the east, "you have made a good choice. Trust my word. The house of Noah is a haven of peace and you will be blessed under his hand. That choice was made for you. Make it your own, and happiness will stay with you all your days. Farewell." With that she turned and went below, weeping openly.

The unexpected speech and her tears combined to empty Madrazi's heart of any remaining happiness. Her conscience convicted her for the hours spent with Jeriah with no time to spare for Jahaz. Her guilt was offset by the irritating confidence that all but she shared in her future. But it was upon her now. Stifling a tremor, she climbed down into the boat after embracing her father and brothers one last time. She did not recall her words to them, and sat stiffly in the bow of the boat with her eyes fixed on the quay of Lamech. With Hakkem shrinking behind her, the figure of Shem on the quay grew larger and clearer. As he helped her up the final step, he started to say something, then stopped, sensing her unhappiness and remained silent as he walked with her to the end of the quay to watch the ship slide into the distance.

As the horizon finally swallowed up the last white gleam of the sails, Madrazi turned away, happy that a veil covered her tears. Shem still did not speak, but walked beside her back up the wide steps and through the city gate. The black seats of judgment were empty and dark shadows stretched across the square. Finally he spoke. "We will go to the house of Lamech tonight, and leave in the morning." He paused as if to say something else, but then turned and led the way without speaking.

"This is the place," explained Shem, not knowing that she had been there once before. "Methuselah first built it, then gave it to Lamech as a wedding gift. Over time, we have enlarged it, and there is room for all of us when we stay in town. Lamech is here much of the time. The government of the city is more his concern than Father's or Methuselah's."

Madrazi nodded, "It is a beautiful home." She stopped herself from saying more, because she found herself wanting to ask him why it could not be their home. She could not help but believe that living in a great house in a growing city as the wife of a ruler's son, with a friend like Jeriah would be so much more enticing than the farm on the edge of the forest. But she knew better than to speak those thoughts to him.

They walked up the paved path to the door and entered to the bows of two servants. Upon discovering that Lamech was away, Shem made arrangements for the evening. Seeing the black mood that had engulfed his wife, he led her around the house, and told her stories of his family as they wandered from room to room. Madrazi appreciated the distraction and his empathy, but the mood was strong upon her. Seldom before had her emotions held such sway over her thoughts. Finally, he led her to a small, comfortable room in the back of the house.

"This has always been my room; I suppose that it is now our room," he said, "unless you wish for something more substantial."

Madrazi looked around and saw that the furnishings were plain, but adequate for both. There was a bed against the far wall and a tall wooden cabinet. The floor was polished marble, and its cold hardness suited her feelings. Once again she had to bite her tongue to keep from answering his question honestly.

She stood in the doorway just in front of Shem, desperately yearning for the comfort of his embrace, for quiet conversation, for anything that he could do to take away the gloom that stained her heart. She felt a desperate need to be one with him, to absorb his quiet peace and strength. But Shem was unsure of her mood; he felt her tension, but did not know how to respond. He tried; tentatively reaching out his hand, unsure of the right words. His eyes were on the floor and his face, troubled. Madrazi took his hand, hoping that her touch would bring to him what she needed. Finally he said, "There is much for us to talk of together, my wife, but there is a proper time, and it is not now. I know that your life has been taken from you and that you are not yet sure what will replace it. Give it time, and give me time."

She tried to keep her face blank, but her heart fell. She wanted his words, his mind, his heart, his passion. She wanted a husband, yet he was drawing away. She did not know what Shem wanted to talk about, but his reticence told her clearly that there were things in his heart that he was reluctant to share. Anger rose first, then shame, as she realized that she had done the same to him by refusing to share her fear of her vision the morning after their marriage. She sensed for a moment that both wanted to breach the wall, but the moment passed, and they were left standing there, strangers. Unbidden to her mind came the contrast between this difficulty and the ease with which she unburdened her heart to Jeriah. Was she a disloyal wife? Guilt added to the brew of feelings, and she looked away in fear that he would read it in her eyes.

They stood for a moment, each desiring words that were not there. Finally he turned away saying, "I will go and arrange for a meal tonight. I must go out for a few minutes."

Madrazi knew that he wanted to escape her presence and let him go without a word. They both knew at that moment that they would share a cold bed that night. She wanted to be a worthy companion, but was stumbling in blindness trying to find the path into his heart.

That determination was taxed further as soon as they returned to Noah's house. The very next day, Shem left, saying he would be gone for several days into the forest. New to the house and with the celebration of the marriage finished, Madrazi felt useless and in the way. There remained a hollow feeling from the still-vivid memory of Hakkem's sails disappearing over the horizon, and there was little to engage her energies and abilities. As a result her mind dwelt on loneliness, fear, and doubt.

In spite of her moodiness, her mind was still sharp. She saw indications within the house of some conspiracy from which she was excluded. She had been told to spend her first few days exploring the house and grounds and learning what she could. It did not take long, and boredom began to overtake her. The servants were respectful, but evasive when answering her questions. Wen-Tehrom, Debseda, and Yaran were busy and with Methuselah away, she was as lonely as she had ever been. Although often alone at her previous home, she had at least possessed hopes and dreams of her future; now that she was living it, disappointment dogged each step.

Two days before Shem was to return, Madrazi spent the morning wandering the orchards and vineyards, wallowing in self-pity. She felt oppressed and her temper was short. Seeking solace, she wandered towards the aviary, hoping that the singing of the birds would calm her. When it did not, she wandered back into the women's common room. She entered quietly and saw Wen-Tehrom and Yaran talking intently on the other side of the room. As she walked toward them, a board creaked and at the sound, they both started and looked over to her. Wen-Tehrom quickly regained her customary smile and invited her to join them. Madrazi sat with them and found herself listening to a variety of entertaining stories that clearly had little to do with the interrupted conversation. It took an effort to hide her frustration behind a bland smile and appropriate words of agreement to the lessons of the stories.

She knew that she had interrupted a conversation not meant for her ears. Why was she not trusted? How could she become a part of a household that seemed intent on treating her as an alien? As soon as possible, she retreated to her private room and wept quietly for a long time.

Chapter 14
REVELATIONS

The next morning Madrazi woke alone and cold. Shem remained away and she was glad—she was not ready to see him. Love could not be built on physical proximity; it needed a unity of mind and heart that had seemingly disappeared with Hakkem as she had sailed over the horizon. Madrazi did not understand why it was so; she only knew that when they had turned back from the sea and walked off the quay, the excitement and harmony were gone. What had she done wrong? It was worse now; the household that had opened to her with joy just a week before now seemed determined to shut her out. She was a stranger and felt it deeply. Yesterday had ended in gloom; last night she feared to sleep for the first time since that terrible night on Hakkem.

In their short time together Shem had created great conflict within her. He was a good man, one to whom she could easily give her love. She desired his and wanted to explore her own capacity to experience and share it. She had been so sure those first few days that he could unlock those doors. Yet in town she felt deep down that they were strangers. It was not a matter of likes and dislikes, or habits and desires, but something deeper; something that she could not grasp. She knew so little. What was his mysterious work in the forest? He had told her much about the forest, but never why was he constantly searching out the habits of its denizens.

A part of her wondered idly if an early child might help. After all, some of the patriarchs had fathered children when they were younger than Shem, but Methuselah, Lamech, and Noah had all waited much longer. She was not even sure how she would feel about a son or daughter, and knew that she was not ready to be a mother. Her common sense agreed, and told her that it would not help. A complicated marriage did not need additional complexity. No, she would restrain fertility until she had resolved her current problems.

It was not just Shem. There was an undercurrent in the household—a purposeful, organized, and directed effort to exclude her. She was no fool. She had eyes and could read the faces and gestures of others. Already she knew many puzzles, but could not yet connect them. People in Lamech perceived Noah as a dabbler in natural knowledge, wealthy and able to idly pursue whatever his interests happened to be. Yet Madrazi quickly detected the falsity of that view. Beneath the gentle, considerate, and kind elder, she saw a hidden strength, resolve, and courage. Other evidence appeared during her lonely wanderings around the grounds. There were too many men for the work. There were vast fields, orchards, and vineyards. Cattle, sheep, horses, goats, and donkeys ranged in pastures to the south. She knew more than most about allocating labor, paying men, and still having money left at the end of the venture. Here, there were clearly excess men. Her curiosity stimulated, she had begun counting workers over the past days and tried to learn their faces and names. Not only did their numbers change from day to day, but she saw new faces as well.

In spite of these concerns, she had pledged herself to Shem and could not back out of the bargain. She had never broken her pledge before, and would not start now. Besides, there was a part of her heart that really wanted to please Shem and find happiness in creating a life with children, meaningful work, and its reward of wealth. It was true that they had found pleasure in physical union, but she knew that would pale without intimacy in mind and spirit. However, one afternoon spent in silent tears was enough. She rose, dressed quietly, and wandered outside into the first light of morning. Her feet were drawn to the grove where she had exchanged one life for another and forever joined herself to Shem. What kind of bargain had she made?

A soft footfall interrupted her morbid reflection. Had Methuselah returned early? She turned, startled. But instead of the expected face of her Granpapa, she found herself looking into the soft brown eyes of Noah. "My daughter," he said gently, and laughed as to himself, "You are my daughter now and yet we hardly know each other. Except for our given oaths, we might as well be strangers. And my house is strange to you, its people are not your people, and so many things have changed for you in such a short time. It is unsettling to walk away from all that you know and follow an unfamiliar road. This I know well. And how are we to judge a new life when it has so little in common with the old? It is much like being lost in the dark."

"Truly you have seen my heart, sir," Madrazi replied cautiously, disconcerted at his frank words. His voice was kind, but his eyes, like Shem's, seemed to measure her as he spoke.

"A small part of it," he returned shrewdly, "much of it stays hidden at your behest." He continued to look into her eyes and she had the uncomfortable feeling that he saw through them to her inmost thoughts. She dropped her eyes, but his next words took the sting out of his accusation.

"But in a strange place and among new people, your heart is often all that remains private. If you will, come with me today. It is my desire to share some of my own heart with you; to show you my gardens, my animals, my lands. And to speak with you of your new family and to explain that which is not clear to you. Will you grant me this day?"

"You need not ask, sir," Madrazi replied carefully, relieved that she might gain a key that would allow entry into this house. "It has been my custom to obey my father in everything and trust to his wisdom over my own."

Noah considered her answer, and replied. "In this world, the wisdom of Pomorolac is often worthy of great trust. You will find mine different after its fashion. You will understand me better if you know that I hold the beginning and end of true wisdom to be in the Creator. Pomorolac seeks insight into the hearts of men, and any advantage to be gained from his knowledge. I prefer insight into the heart of the Creator, for then I see my own heart more clearly. Apart from Him, the wisdom of men comes to nothing. When we first came to this city, men accepted this and gladly followed Methuselah and Lamech. But much has changed over the centuries. Some, like your father, retain a measure of virtue and give grudging respect to those who still follow the Almighty, acknowledged for the sake of custom and tradition, but little else."

He placed a gentle hand on Madrazi's arm, directing her to the house, and she said nothing, for she honored the father that she knew more than the one she did not. Yet she found his honesty refreshing. What would her father's life mean to him after he died? Pomorolac himself never seemed to know the answer to that question and his daughter was at a loss for words. But she would not agree with Noah for the sake of flattery. So she kept silent and listened. As he had said, her heart was her own.

Noah led Madrazi into the main hall and called for bread and fruit. No one else was present and so they sat and ate. Her feelings remained confused; his words about Pomorolac stirred her resentment towards Shem, the household, and her new life. Noah was clearly aware of her state, for he strayed from their previous conversation and began to tell her of his coming to Lamech. He had been a mere boy then and consumed with the excitement and joy in the great undertaking of building a new town with his father and grandfather.

Madrazi was drawn into his story and listened carefully. "Many hundreds of years of my life went into that effort, and if I chose, I could take pride in what we made, for there is much about Lamech for which I could justly receive praise. I postponed marriage for the sake of the town. I took my place at an early age among the seats of the elders, and loved the white stone beauty of the city above the sea. I was proud for many years to sit with my fathers in the place of judgment."

He paused and sighed. Madrazi sipped her tea and watched him carefully from the corner of her eye as he spoke again. "I said earlier that I understood something of what you are feeling. And so I do. Many envied the life that I had built—admittedly on the strong foundation provided by my fathers. But like you, I found that it changed in just a few short days; days that I can never forget. Years of labor for Lamech left me hollow and I became convinced that all my efforts were futile, empty, and all of my accomplishments but dust. Would any remember what I had built in generations to come?"

"There is a numbness that comes from the slow habits of years, that can only be shaken by decisions made in moments. I faced such a moment, made my decision, and have found what I lacked in Lamech."

Madrazi was thrown off balance by the sudden change. She recalled her own quick decision to accept Shem's proposal, and felt a glimmer of understanding. Yet his meaning remained as unclear as everything else in the household. She remained attentive because Noah was clearly leading to some point. Perhaps he wished to drive home a lesson first. He smiled briefly, as if seeing her mind once more, then slowly sipped his tea. When he continued, his eyes were staring into the distance.

"That decision—that moment—changed my household, setting it apart from all others, to the extent that we migrated to this place. Methuselah claims that you are a far-seeing woman. As such, I am certain that our life here has proven confusing. You have seen the leaves blowing but have not yet felt the wind. I am sorry that I could not come to you earlier, but this is the first day I have been free. Tell me, now," he asked shrewdly, "what weighs so heavily upon you?"

"I am an ordinary woman," she replied, avoiding his question, "but you are a great man among this people, with lands, wealth, and honor, yet you talk as if you live under a great burden, and one difficult to share."

Noah looked at her carefully, "You contradict your first assertion with your second. But you are correct. I have only my family and a few servants willing to bear it with me."

"I am now a part of your family," she said simply.

A faint smile touched his lips as he held her eyes. "Yes. Perhaps Methuselah's flattery was justified. You will pursue what you think right with great courage and determination. But neither Shem nor I command your heart. You give or withhold that by your own choice."

His words aroused mixed emotions in Madrazi. But she would not be distracted. "Then tell me clearly of this burden and what demands it makes," she countered. "Then I can choose."

Noah nodded, but did not speak. Having finished their food, they rose and

Madrazi followed him out of the house and back to the bower where she had been joined to Shem. Noah continued on without speaking until they reached the aviary at the forest's edge, and even then he stood silent for several minutes. Finally, he gestured her to a wooden bench on the near side of the aviary and sat beside her. Then he spoke softly and the morning songs of the birds seemed to add harmony to his words.

"It was only one hundred years ago, and yet it seems so much longer," he began. "I had been troubled for many years by the tide of lawlessness sweeping the earth. Even in Lamech, men's service to the Creator had become a matter of duty, without joy. Eden was a myth of generations past. Adam was dead. So were Seth, Enosh, Kenan, Mahalalel; even Jared had passed. Enoch no longer walked among men. Methuselah was old. Lamech and I were ensnared by our city. My brothers and uncles followed after the world just like other men. I had no sons. The promised line was dying.

Evil flourished, whether in the open, bloody deeds of the Nephilim, or in the subtle contempt of selfish hate masked by courtesy. Men openly lusted for what they did not have, and they began to take from the weak rather than pray for their needs. Even I had begun to question whether the Creator still had regard for the affairs of men.

My dark thoughts would not abate, would not be diverted, and would not let me alone. Finally, there came a time when I beheld dark, troubling dreams. In a black mood I left my house, with nothing but a little food and a blanket, and plunged into the loneliness of the Great Forest. I was determined to stay until I found an answer and the meaning of my dreams. I wandered in the wood for several days until I came to a clearing about a half day's march from here.

It was dusk and I stood inside the trees at the edge of the clearing and watched silently as animals fed on the rich grass. I felt a peace and tranquility beyond my reach. As soon as I stepped from the trees, it fled with the animals. My thoughts were still darker as I said to myself, 'so men destroy peace wherever they go.' I walked across the meadow to a stream on the far side. Making fire for the night, I spread out fresh boughs and lay down to sleep. But my sleep was full of the same dark dreams and a foreboding of doom."

Madrazi was entranced by his story. She had forgotten her earlier suspicion and listened intently. He had evil dreams, too? She interrupted him without thinking. "I understand. I know such a dream. It killed my mother..." she stopped, embarrassed that her words had run ahead of her mind, and wishing that she had kept silent. But Noah seemed not to hear, lost in his own narrative.

"I woke in the hour before dawn full of fear. The fire had burned to coals and I gathered some branches to renew it. Turning after gathering another armful of wood, I saw the fire suddenly burst into flame with a light that was not fire. It flashed first like lightning, turning the clearing into noon for an instant and then slowly fading. I fell facedown on the ground, for I was convinced the Creator had seen my doubt and was come to slay me.

"But a voice said to me, 'Peace, Noah. Arise to hear my words. Keep them in your mind and heart and guard them as your greatest treasure.' Then He said, 'I am going to put an end to all people, for the earth is filled with violence because of them. I am surely going to destroy both them and the earth.'

I trembled in fear and though I stood as bidden, I hid my face behind my cloak. I knew that the judgment was just and that I deserved death with the rest because of my doubts. I wondered when and how the Creator would do this and I was sure that I would be the first to perish that day.

But he knew my mind and spoke again to me. He said that the days of men would be one hundred and twenty years, and that my life would be spared because of His favor. And then He spoke these words to me, 'So make yourself an ark of gopher wood; make rooms in it and coat it with pitch inside and out. This is how you are to build it: The ark is to be three hundred cubits long, fifty cubits wide and thirty cubits high. Make a roof for it and finish it to within one cubit of the top. Put a door in the side of the ark and make lower, middle, and upper decks. I am going to bring floodwaters upon the earth to destroy all life under the heavens, every creature that has the breath of life in it. Everything on earth will perish. But I will establish my covenant with you, and you will enter the ark–you and your sons and your wife and your son's wives with you. You are to bring into the ark two of all living creatures, male and female, to keep them alive with you. Two of every kind of bird of every kind of animal and of every kind of creature that moves along the ground will come to you to be kept alive. You are to take every kind of food that is to be eaten and store it away as food for you and for them.'

I seemed not to hear the words with my ears, for the wonder and glory of the light overwhelmed me, but they were imprinted on my mind as if written in letters of fire. The light faded and I was left on my knees facing the sunrise. All that day I sat and considered what had been said. Why had I been chosen? Why not Methuselah, or Lamech, my father? But I had heard the voice, and I faced a choice—obey the heavenly vision or refuse it."

Madrazi found she was holding her breath. In a moment of insight, she saw clearly the hidden power behind his gentle voice and soft eyes that she had suspected before. She found empathy in her heart for the struggles of this good man and his search for answers. She understood the haunting presence of night visions and felt with him the desire for release and resolution. For a moment, she wanted to believe his words without reservation—the faint touch of a stranger within begging for release. She struggled to settle her heart and listen.

Noah's voice grew hard. "I made my choice! I resolved that day to obey or die in the attempt. That place was holy ground. I built an altar on the spot of my fire and returned to Lamech. I knew with certainty that I would build the ark in that same forest clearing.

But the task was great. I had no sons, but I believed that God would provide them. I did not know how to build such an ark, but I was confident that God would show me. I did not know how to feed and care for so many animals, but God was my teacher. When I returned, I gathered Lamech, Methuselah, and our wives together and told them of the heavenly vision. They listened to all that I had to say and they accepted the words of the Creator. They pledged to help me accomplish the task and go with me into the ark. But when I related the vision to the other elders and leading men of the city, they laughed and called me mad. I persisted for a time, for who knows? Perhaps men would repent and God would spare the earth from His terrible wrath. At first men laughed and thought that maybe I had seen some strange deluding vision. But they would not believe the words of warning. Their hearts grew hard and they demanded that I cease speaking of it. At one point, men of the city were ready to banish me from the council.

Finally, I realized that they had made their choice. I presented the truth and they rejected it. What should I do? To build the ark required that I live near the clearing, but I needed the trade of the town and its harbor for trade with other cities. Also, I held out a hope that some of the men would eventually repent, given time. Even now I hold this hope—that men will repent and that God will turn from his terrible anger.

My search for a new home did not take long. It had to be accessible to town and to the clearing. This vale was pleasant, fertile, and under the eaves of the forest. The land has proven rich and the forest supplied many good things. It is only a day's march from Lamech and less than that directly to the clearing. Many of our servants came with us, and most have remained faithful. Those that keep faith to the end shall have the opportunity to come with my family.

My first task was to plan. I spent an entire year thinking through the instructions from the Creator and making lists of all the work to be done and planning the priority and sequence of each task. Designing and building the ark loomed large, but I had to also gain knowledge of all kinds of animals and their care. When I thought of all the different kinds, I realized that was where I needed to start. So, I began cultivating and breeding animals common to man; cattle, sheep, poultry, horses, oxen, and donkeys. Once we were familiar with them, I began trapping and caring for wild animals to learn their ways. Our knowledge increased rapidly as Shem grew; he has proven most adept at observing their ways in their own surroundings.

Beyond these challenges, others have continued to arise. If the ark was built and the animals gathered, how would we provide food and water for them? How much food would we need? How could we store so much without spoilage? Would there be sufficient room in the ark? How could water be stored and kept pure? These were some of the hundreds of questions I asked myself that year."

Madrazi had been drawn in by Noah's narrative, and found herself caught up in the numerous problems such an undertaking would entail. True to her upbringing, she had automatically begun her own mental lists. It was a heroic tale, a great enterprise. But as Noah's words faded, their power diminished, and she came back to herself. This was no great adventure; it was a fantasy. The hero claimed a commission from the Creator. She was attracted to the challenge, but his story ran contrary to all of her wisdom. Why would the Creator destroy the earth that He had worked so hard to bring into being? Could He bring about its destruction, even if He wished it? This would all happen in twenty short years? Madrazi was torn. She felt a strong sympathy for this man—a good man, now her father. But how could he be right? Could she commit to his vision wholeheartedly? Uncertain, she held her peace and waited for him to speak.

When he saw that she did not respond, he nodded sadly and continued his tale. "Almost at once, I discovered gold in a valley north of the forest. It freed me from commerce and paid for our house, our servants, and gave me time to devote to my task. After we had started the construction of our house, I left my wife and servants to continue, and traveled to the port of Nimur. There I spent three years learning the art of building and sailing ships. I am not the craftsman that Pomorolac is, but I daresay that I have learned much from those whose work is highly regarded."

Madrazi nodded her agreement, for her father had traded secrets with the wrights of Nimur and she knew their reputation.

Noah smiled at her expression and continued, "I hid my status, and worked as a common laborer in a shipyard, and became familiar with the tools and techniques of the most skilled men. I learned to work with different kinds of wood and learned which were strong and which resisted the sea. Gopher wood of the Great Forest was highly regarded, although teak, locust, or mahogany would also have served. But I resolved to follow the words of the Creator in every detail. The dimensions given in the heavenly vision are larger than any ships built, even in our modern day, but I learned enough to realize that it could be done. Fortunately, I needed an ark to preserve life, not a ship to sail fast or far. It only needed to house people and animals, to store food and water, to let in air and light and keep out the sea."

Madrazi's love of ship design drew her back irresistibly into Noah's tale. Years spent in Pomorolac's shipyard, with some of the finest craftsmen to be found anywhere—even Nimur—enabled her to understand his words better than most. Though extraordinarily large, she had to admit that the ratios of the ark's dimensions were sound, and she found herself thinking of ways to compensate for the size by adding strength in the framing and in the joining of the wood. Noah smiled briefly as if reading her mind once again and continued.

"After leaving Nimur, I began planning and building a shipyard in my clearing. Our settlement had been completed by the time I returned and the work in the clearing well underway before Wen-Tehrom gave birth to Shem, then Japheth and Ham. As my sons grew into men, I finished preparing the clearing in the middle of the forest—a shipyard far from the sea. I began to cut wood and cure it. I learned how to make various kinds of pitch. Back here at our house, the servants and Wen-Tehrom were busy building a settlement, clearing and planting fields, and maintaining our ties with the town.

When the boys turned twelve years, I took them each in turn to the clearing and showed them the altar and asked their commitment to the heavenly vision. For each son I offered a sacrifice on the altar, and together, we found their gifts and the tasks they would assume. Ham is a skilled workman in wood and governs the construction of the ark. Japheth is a farmer and finds new ways to preserve and store food. Shem studies the ways of animals in the wild, and is my right hand. He also oversees the men and the labor. Our servants work both here and at the clearing, but they are not enough, so we have hired men from Lamech."

He turned again to Madrazi. She felt once more the pull to be a part of his venture—a great undertaking that would push her abilities beyond their limits and achieve things that people would speak of for centuries. The blood of Pomorolac, master explorer, ran in her veins and in that moment she knew a hot desire within to join Noah and become a part of his dream.

Noah stood, helped her up, and they began to walk back towards the house. He clutched his hands behind him and bowed his head as they paced together. As they passed the animal enclosures, he spoke again, his voice changed. It was grave and she could hear worry in his words. "The wheels of time turn. Twenty short years remain until the fulfillment of the heavenly vision."

Up until that point, Madrazi had been carried away with the challenges of designing, building, and equipping such a vessel. Her mind raced to consider and solve problems of strength, balance, and stability. But his words arrested her thoughts and returned her mind to the sinister purpose of this great undertaking. Noah must have sensed it, for he stopped, turned to her, and said. "You are now caught up in that race—to complete all these tasks before judgment comes. Now you understand much about our family that you did not before. We do not pursue pleasure or wealth. We pursue a mission in which our very lives hang in the balance. This is no longer our world; it has been given over to destruction. We walk in it as strangers, knowing that a new one waits beyond destruction and despair. And should we succeed, what do we face? Grief from the loss of all we now know. Terror from enduring the Creator's wrath. Fear from a voyage into the unknown. And what do we have? Only the promise of the Creator."

He faced her squarely and she felt his eyes pierce her soul. "You have choices to make, but some have already been made for you. Your destiny is tied to Shem. That choice was made for you. But in your secret heart, the commitment to our effort remains your own. You can work with your body and mind and fulfill your oath and obligation to Shem. But your obligation to the Creator can only be met by your willingness to commit yourself in faith to His words in your most secret heart. No man can command that."

The sun was now high overhead yet she could not remember the passing of the hours. Had the words not come from Noah's own mouth and had she not seen the lucidity of his eyes as he talked, she would never have believed any of it. She was not sure that she believed any of it now. But his face was not that of a liar, and it was clear that his family—her family now—accepted this tale and were acting upon it. Her earlier enthusiasm was drowned in the cold reality of those words. All the world? Destroyed? It could not be! How could the entire world be destroyed? And why?

In the midst of her questions, her mind was suddenly assaulted with shadowy images of her own vision. She glimpsed again the destruction of everything by the sea, just as Noah said. A tremor ran through her. Was the vision that she hated so passionately a glimpse of Noah's prophecy? How could it be if his words were not true? How could there be any similarity between his prophecy and her vision if neither were true? Had she not already escaped the sea? Now it threatened her again. Confusion swamped her, but one thought came clear: from that moment she linked Noah's prophecy with the vision that was her bitter enemy. The thought hardened her heart against Noah and his quest.

Noah sensed her turmoil and remained silent and still. Finally, uncomfortable over the lengthy silence, Madrazi asked one of the questions running through her mind. "Why must this happen? I know that many men are evil, but many men are good. My father is a good man. My mother was a good woman. There are many left who use honest measures, tell the truth, and act with integrity. Why should God do this thing?"

Noah sensed her deep emotion and replied gently. "One of the things that I enjoy about the forest is the sweet water we find in springs under the trees. It is clear, cold, and pure. In the mountains to the north, the springs are different. Some of the ores from the mountains contain salts that wash down into the springs and make them unfit to drink—sometimes even deadly. We have proven this to ourselves by taking a pinch of those salts and adding them to a jar of the forest water. It too becomes unfit. It does not take much, but as the salt dissolves and is hidden in the water, the result is impure. So it is with men and evil. Evil may be hidden and may be small, but any amount, hidden or visible, contaminates the man and makes him impure in God's sight."

"Any amount of evil pollutes the whole man?" She asked. This was entirely foreign. She had always assumed that men's deeds were weighed against each other; the good canceling the evil, and many being neither.

"Yes."

"What of you?" she asked quickly before realizing the disrespect present in such a question. She fumbled to apologize.

But Noah only laughed. "Do not be afraid, Madrazi. I am the first to admit that no man is unstained by evil. Even men that others call good and righteous."

"Then why do you not also perish in this coming destruction?" she asked boldly, deciding not to be put off.

He took no offense. "Only God's promise to me separates me from the condemned. If you want to know the reason for God's choice, I cannot tell you. It is a question that I have wrestled with for one hundred years, without any clear answer. Why should I survive and others die? For who knows my own heart better than I do? But I have one answer to my questions. I have heard the voice of the Almighty speak to me. I cannot make that experience yours, but I can tell you that when I remember that voice the fears and questions seem to melt to nothing."

Madrazi stood silent again, torn in her thoughts. This was her family. Her oath had committed her to be a part of whatever they did. And yet, that secret part of her heart that Noah had so readily discerned could not accept the extent of what he was saying. It was so easy for him to speak the words, but impossible for her to imagine as truth. What was she to do? Once again Noah read her thoughts.

"Do not think that I or my family did not struggle with this calling. We still do. It is not something that can be comprehended and accepted in a short time. But I do ask you to trust me—trust that I have told you the truth, and that God's word is true, too.

I hope that at least you will now understand the sense of urgency, the effort, and the heart of those in this house. I do not learn about animals and plants for the joy of the knowledge, though many think so and consider me strange for doing so. I learn those things to make certain that when animals and plants are taken aboard the ark that they will survive the judgment and live to inhabit a new world after the old has passed away. Ham does not work with wood and metal for profit or pleasure. He labors to build an ark that can carry us safely through whatever wind and wave might assail us. And although Shem loves the forest, he spends his hours there in order to complete my work. Soon, he will take you to see and you can judge for yourself. Perhaps you will see something that you can do to help."

Noah gripped her hand for a moment, and then he walked slowly away leaving Madrazi to face her thoughts alone. Suddenly the faces of her father and brothers sprang to mind. She called out to Noah and he stopped and turned back. She ran to him and asked, "What about my family?" Before he could answer, understanding flooded her mind and she asked, "Is that what you discussed the night before he left?"

Noah nodded and sighed. "Pomorolac was my kinsman even before you agreed to marry Shem. I told him much of what I have told you and warned him of the judgment to come. I begged him to bring his family back to Lamech before the day arrived, and join us on the ark. He listened with respect to all that I said, but it was clear to me that he did not accept the truth of my words. I asked that he reconsider my words in the future, and told him that he is welcome to come to us at any time. Do you think he will?"

She shook her head, unable to answer. He started to say something else, but thought better of it and left her reeling in a chaos of thought and emotion.

Chapters 15
REACTION

Madrazi's feet moved without aim or volition, her mind hopelessly tangled. She wanted desperately to consider the morning objectively, but Noah's words had roused too many emotions. Her only consolation was in finding answers to her questions about the household. Little wonder she did not fit in! Her eyes were fixed on a good life, children, land, wealth, and security. Theirs were on a race against time and a coming destruction. She could not gainsay Noah's faith. Whether or not this prophecy was true, he certainly believed it with all his heart and his family was united behind him. She could not change any of them. Any argument that she could raise would have been debated many times already.

But neither could she accept that the ground, now so firm beneath her feet, would be gone in twenty short years. She was trapped. Noah was right in that. She had given her word to Shem in the presence of witnesses, and was committed to his life and fortune until one of them died. For a time, she was angry with Noah and Methuselah, but the pact was sealed and anger was fruitless. More alone than ever, she walked back toward the forest through the aviary, now crying softly, emotion victorious. Even the birds seemed to sense her distress and muted their cries.

Finally, the tears slowed, and she found herself on the verge of the forest path. She followed it for several steps until she came to the first forest giant overlooking the path. Gradually as she stood leaning on the tree, her mind reasserted itself. Could the story be true? It seemed impossible to her rational mind. The Creator would not destroy his creation. People were not that evil. The sea had raged for centuries and could not cover the vast expanses of land she knew existed. With some relief she told herself that she disbelieved Noah's story because her rational mind knew it to be impossible.

At that moment, the memory of her vision intruded again and disrupted her well-ordered thoughts. She caught her breath. Had she seen Noah's prophecy all those years ago? But the vision was a thing of evil; a private omen that had stolen her mother, not some word from a loving Creator. She had spent years hating and suppressing it and now Noah threatened to breach those walls and have her live in its open presence, the fearful specter of crushing waters beside her every day. She had no strength for such a task. It had taken all that she had just to keep it at bay.

Anger boiled up. It was only coincidence, nothing more! *I hate it! It is not true. It is not true.* She kept repeating this in her mind while her fingernails dug at her palms. *It could not be! It must not be! Push it down! Seal it away! Rebuild the walls. It is my own heart. It is my own mind. He cannot have it!*

In her anger, she thought of her father. He knew that it was impossible. Noah had admitted it. Noah had not been able to change his mind. But now she was married to a man who was giving his life to a futile task. What could she do? Apart from that flaw, she had to admit that he was a good man and would probably be a good husband. True, they needed to become accustomed to each other, but she was certain deep down that he was someone to walk with through the centuries. In that thought, she saw a ray of hope. They were bound to each other for life—for hundreds of years. What were twenty short seasons to that?

With that thought came a ray of light. The future was her hope. She could submit to her husband in his family's foolishness for a few short years. Give him body and mind, and all her best efforts to keep the hope of a good marriage alive. She would weather the inevitable storms. At the end, this prophecy would show itself false. Shem would be hurt, perhaps devastated, but he was young and strong and he would have a strong wife to help him through the chaos of a life gone awry. They would have to face a new future—her future—squarely. They could leave this place and make a new life in Lamech. She would have proven the worth of her vows and earned a voice in ordering that future. Beyond the present darkness was a normal, peaceful life, one without wild prophecies, arks, and animals. She had endured Peniah for one decade; surely she could endure this for two.

Madrazi found a measure of peace in that thought, though she wondered for a long time how Shem would react to the failure of the prophecy. It would surely destroy Noah, so great was his faith. She shuddered at the unhappiness and disappointment that would engulf the family when the time came. Would despair swallow Shem? He would sink, but how far? Could she keep enough of a hold on him? Would she be strong enough to anchor him?

It would be difficult; but she drew herself up straight and squared her shoulders. She had accomplished difficult tasks before. She would perform this one. She would honor her given oath to Shem. She would stand by him and do whatever she could to support him and his family, no matter how strange the task. She owed him that much, and to Noah and Methuselah. She felt the old iron resolve and promised herself that she would keep that iron at the center of her soul.

For the next two days, Madrazi wandered the grounds into the cool verge of the forest thinking again and again of Noah's words, hardening her disbelief in the prophecy and focusing instead on the dilemma of her marriage to the prophet's faithful son. Was it wrong to support her husband for the sake of a better future, if that support was a lie? How could she keep her sworn oath, be honest with herself, and find love in her marriage all at the same time? Was it better to deceive herself or her husband? Noah himself had said that her heart must be her own, but Pomorolac had drilled honesty into her from childhood and the contradictions troubled her.

Over those days alone, she managed to reach an inner truce. She was glad that Shem had been delayed; it gave her time to marshal her resources. Whatever she chose to accept or reject about the prophecy, Noah was right about her bond to his family. As the wife of Shem, she owed him obedience of body and mind, even if her heart could not join his in pursuit of a prophecy of doom. She could not escape this obligation; duty was a part of her very being. A failure in that duty to herself would be worse than withholding part of her heart from her husband, at least in regard to the prophecy. If her solution contained a tinge of deceit, then it was only for his good, for her marriage, and for their future. She could bear that guilt for the hope of a better life ahead.

Having found her answer and stilled her conscience, Madrazi laid her plans. If she was to have her way twenty years hence, then she must initiate the steps that would even now begin to lead them into that path. She must overcome the stiffness between them, earn his love, and forge strong links in a chain that would pull him through the dark times ahead.

"While they strive toward escaping this prophecy's doom, I will make sure that I escape the prophecy, with my husband beside me," she vowed to herself.

She began immediately. Watching for him that afternoon near the edge of the forest, she ran to meet him with a smile and an embrace. Since they were under the trees and out of the sight of others, she lengthened the embrace and held him close for some minutes. Then she took his hand and led him through the yards and toward the house for rest and refreshment. He stopped outside the back door to wash his head and when he had finished, she sat him down and washed his feet. The soft eyes in his dark, handsome face seemed to accuse her, and she turned her face away. Rallying her strength, she set her face in a smile, seated him at a small table in the kitchen, brought him food and drink, and sat with him as he ate. She filled his ears with casual talk of the doings of the household in his absence, and when he had finished, she led him away to their room.

Gratefully he removed his cloak and lay down upon the bed, stretching his full length and relaxing his frame. More compact than Ham, his long, lean muscles contained the strength of a much larger man. There was much about his manner that reminded her of a wild creature. He was always alert and aware, and seemed to possess uncanny intuition and insight. Even now he was uneasy; Madrazi feared that he sensed the purpose behind her submissive demeanor. She must distract him. She lay beside him and then suddenly rolled over on top of him and brought her lips to his. He returned her kiss as his arms closed around her. In their passion she knew that she held power and was determined to use it. She relaxed against him and felt his tension ease.

Propping herself up, she looked into his eyes. "Do you find it strange that our bodies have such an ease in unity while our minds do not?" she asked quietly. "My hand seeks yours, my lips seek yours, and the heat of our passion rises without effort. But words do not come easily for either of us. Unity in mind and spirit may be difficult, but I believe it a worthy goal for a man and woman. Neither of us will be completely happy until our thoughts and feelings are joined as easily as our lips." She knew that she was pressing him, but to remove any sting, she also pressed her body against his.

Shem hesitated a moment, then laughed. "Yes, it is true that the body runs before the mind and the spirit lags behind. I agree that intimacy in all things is a worthy goal. I have only to see the happiness of my own parents to know that. Our lips give us only a taste of the promise of what is possible in time."

"It will take more than time," she said. "We must try, even though it is hard. I am willing."

"As am I," he replied softly.

"Then you must trust me," she returned gently. "Your father told me of his vision and the work of this house to fulfill the conditions given to him by the divine word. We should have talked of it sooner."

He nodded, apparently not surprised at Noah's action. "Yes, we should have, and I spent much effort in trying to find a proper time and place to tell you. But I did not want to spoil your enjoyment of the wedding feast, and when we were in Lamech, you seemed so sad at parting with your family that I could not bring myself to add to your burden. There were times when you were probably ready to hear, but I was not ready to speak. I did not know how you would react to my words. We have seen only ridicule and rejection by all around us, and the name of Noah means little to people that he has attempted to save through his warnings. I have seen in this ultimate ingratitude more of the justice of the Creator's sentence than in anything else I have known."

His intensity surfaced in his final words and Madrazi caught an intimation of hidden fires that he kept locked away. But she did not draw back and let his passion feed her own. Purposefully, she let it show as she shot back, "I am not of those in Lamech who mock your father. I think that he is a great and good man. I am your wife, and the daughter of your father. I have freely committed myself to you and your future. Do you think that our marriage was the choice of Pomorolac? If I had not agreed, then he would never have consented. I was my father's right hand in his home. He did not need to, or even want to be rid of me. I consented because I trusted Methuselah, and because I believed that we could make a good life together."

Madrazi paused and caught her breath. Tears lurked near the surface. The truth of her words threatened to renew her own inner conflict. She calmed herself and said, "I would be your right hand if you will let me. It may be hard, it may take time, and there will be days…" she paused, forcing herself again to speak evenly. "I am not weak. Please let me be your wife."

Shem was silent for a moment, and she thought she had offended him. But he turned with new respect in his eyes and said plainly, "I was wrong to misjudge you. I am sorry. I should have spoken immediately. I will try to avoid that mistake in the future."

Encouraged, she buried her face in his shoulder and breathed in the scent of the woods as she clung to him. "You were not entirely wrong, my husband. I do not know what to think about what Noah has said. It is too much for me right now. I cannot understand how such a thing could be. But I am your wife and I have pledged my life and future to you and I will never dishonor that pledge. I am yours and will do all I can to help you and support you."

Those words were as honest as she could be with him, and she fervently hoped that he would not press her further about what she actually thought of the prophecy.

He nodded slowly and spoke almost to himself. "Yes, sometimes I myself cannot accept the reality of what is to come, but I trust in the word of God to Noah." He brightened. "If you are to help then you must see all that we do. Would you like to come with me to see the ark? I will tell you all that we have done and show you all that we have yet to do. You were the right hand of your father. All know that Pomorolac is a master of ships and the sea. Lamech told me that the ship which brought you to me was the finest that he had ever seen in our harbor. If you have the skill to have served him effectively, perhaps you could find many ways to help. I am overwhelmed by all that there is to finish, and twenty years seems too little time."

Madrazi softened her voice, "I will help, and I will come to see the work as long as you pay more attention to me than to your work! If there is work for me, then let us discover it together. And if the proper tasks do not show themselves, at least we will have a few days alone in the forest. I would learn of its ways. Would you teach me?"

She knew that she had succeeded in touching another chord within him. He brightened immediately, and said, "I would show you all that I have learned. Under the trees, I find peace, and in the solitude of its depths, I believe that I walk with God. That joy I would share with you!"

The night comforted them both. It was again one of warmth and passion, blended with the satisfaction of new understanding. Life seemed to reach a new equilibrium, and Madrazi awoke to his hands stroking her hair the next morning. They roamed the grounds, talking and learning of each other, letting friendship enter their marriage. It was easier than Madrazi had imagined; there were many ways in which they were alike. They were both strong, independent people, both reticent to mingle in crowds, but committed to their few friends. Madrazi was used to being with men and her analytical mind and indifference to the day's customs made speech between them easier.

During the days that followed, Madrazi found the others becoming more open, too. She was now a part of the secret, the conspiracy, and she began to discover how powerful that bond was. A few mornings after Shem had returned, Madrazi found herself alone in the women's atrium when Yaran appeared at the door.

"I'm sorry," began Yaran, "I didn't know anyone else was here." But Madrazi's laughter was contagious and Yaran's face lit up with a humorous smile.

"Come and sit for a moment," urged Madrazi. "This house is like a hive of bees. At least in here, I thought that I would be out of the way."

"Are you sure you want company? Wen-Tehrom has told me that Noah has spoken with you about his prophecy. I was raised in this house and never knew anything else. But you must bear the burden of the prophecy on top of uprooting your life for Shem. If you want time to yourself, please tell me. I will not take offense."

"I have been with myself too much," replied Madrazi. "You said before that we would be friends, and if I must live in the midst of such confusion, then I will need friends."

"I am your sister and will be your friend. Tell me how I can help you?"

"Tell me of the household. How is it run? What do the men do? What must we do? What must I do?

"I am hardly one to tell you your place," smiled Yaran. "You are the daughter of a mighty man, wife of the eldest son. I am but a servant who found his brother's love."

"Then I will tell you something about my place," returned Madrazi. "I think little of predetermined rank. A person is the sum of their thoughts, words, and deeds. I think more of a slave with a strong mind and will than of the most exalted noble who is stupid and lazy. Men and women must make their own mark with the time and gifts that they have. Are not all equal as children of Adam? No, Yaran," she continued, "in time we will be friends or not by what is in our hearts, not because of our husbands."

"I think little of such things, myself," admitted Yaran, "but there are others who do, and I am mindful of them. A servant married to a son has caused questions in the past and some resentment, but Japheth loves me and I bear it easily."

Madrazi only nodded at the warning, realizing that she knew little of the woman beside her, and even less of the others. She warmed to Yaran, however, for her confidence was proof of her desire for friendship.

Yaran continued. "The men's work is of necessity concentrated on the building and equipping of the ark. It is said that you will visit it soon."

Madrazi nodded, impressed with Yaran's knowledge of the doings of the house. With such knowledge to share, she would be a valuable friend.

"Methuselah and Lamech tend our interests in town," she continued, "but even though he is their son, it was Noah who received the vision from the Creator, and his fathers grant him preeminence in our family. His fathers attend to the business of the council and guard his place on it. Methuselah founded the city and Lamech is its namesake and the chief elder, if there is such a position. At the least, he is chief in the minds of the leading men.

But in this household, all acknowledge Noah as our head. Each of his sons has proven valuable according to their gifts. Ham is the master of wood or metal. He truly sees what he makes even before he starts, and his hands follow his mind without fail. He designs, he obtains what material he needs, and then he builds. A better craftsmaster does not exist in this part of the world. He grasped all that Noah learned from Nimur and improved twofold upon it. A quiet man, he prefers his own company to that of his brothers, but he is friendly enough in his own way. Debseda shares his desire for privacy. Do not be offended if she seems distant."

Madrazi nodded, recalling that she had hardly passed more than a few words with Ham's wife. Yaran was a marked contrast and Madrazi listened eagerly.

"I love Japheth with all my heart, and my opinion of him is colored by that love. Shem is the deep forest; Japheth the waving meadow. I have never been so sad that he cannot cheer my heart and bring laughter to my lips. He likes you, but has the uncomfortable suspicion that you are too intelligent for a woman. Japheth enjoys being more clever than those around him. In the affairs of the family, my Japheth turns his attention to the food and supplies we will need on the ark. You must ask him more about that. He will appreciate showing off his knowledge, especially to you.

What can I tell you about Shem? He is like his father. Noah hides his strength under gentleness and compassion. Shem has the same strength, deep within, waiting for circumstances to bring it to the surface. He is the hardest to know, but I feel that he knows the rest of us better than we would wish. He is a man of the forest, a mighty hunter who fears nothing. As to our mission, Noah must learn how to care for the multitude of animals that must come into the ark. Shem goes into the forest and into the mountains to find what they eat, how they sleep, how they bear young, what they fear, how much water they need, how they tolerate cold, heat, dryness, or dampness. As he learns, he helps Ham design places for them on the ark.

Because the men are busy with their tasks, the women run the household. That is one reason we live together. With the help of our servants, I tend the orchards, groves, and vineyards. Debseda is mistress of the fields, Wen-Tehrom of the house. You may share the responsibilities of the others or you may find others that suit your gifts."

Madrazi heard her sister's tactful question inside her statement, and replied, "I do not know what I shall do. From what I saw when I arrived, the fields, groves, orchards, and vineyards would only suffer under my hand. I do not desire what is yours or our sister's. I am still floundering in the deep waters of Noah's prophecy and must find my feet before I engage my hands. I do not desire to be the cause of enmity in our family."

She turned from Yaran and stared at the morning framed in the windows. Her words troubled her heart, for she knew that as long as she lived among these people rejecting Noah' prophecy, that she would be rejecting all of their work. And had she not just said to Yaran that people were the sum of their works? Was she not then rejecting the people? Such thoughts made her uncomfortable, and she feared that Yaran might read her doubts in her eyes.

But if Yaran suspected her doubts, she kept it hidden. She excused herself and left Madrazi alone. Yaran had provided valuable information and seemed friendly enough, but from her references to the Creator and her implicit belief in Noah, Madrazi suspected that they could never find the intimacy of spirit that she had discovered with Jeriah.

Chapter 16
FOREST PATH

That afternoon, Shem announced that they would go to the clearing and see the ark the following day. Madrazi's maritime interest was piqued; she was curious to see how such a monstrous vessel was being built, but her interest was offset by her anxiety over being dragged into the family's obsession. Fortunately, Shem spent the remainder of the day with her, teaching her the names of the various trees and vines at the edge of the forest and her interest stifled any discontent.

Rising early, they started their journey with the sun. Shem led the way north from the back of the aviary. A well-traveled but narrow trail wound into the forest and the noise of the birds was quickly swallowed by the majestic silence of the gray stillness under the trees. At first, Madrazi could see only a short distance ahead, but Shem moved with such confidence that Madrazi became convinced that he could have seen the path on the darkest night.

His acute vision was only the first of a series of facets of her husband that began to unfold before her. She realized that he was a creature of the forest and did not come fully alive unless under its boughs. She marveled at the changes that came over him as soon as they entered the woods. He seemed to glide along the forest floor with hardly a sound. She tried to emulate the way he walked, but felt awkward every time that she stepped on a stick or scuffed some leaves and broke the silence. It was not oppressive to walk in silence, for their quiet allowed them to hear the faint sounds that Madrazi would have otherwise missed. The trees seemed to speak to Shem, but Madrazi was an interloper and understood little other than the wind in the leaves and the creaking of branches. She vowed that one day she would come to belong among the trees as much as her husband.

The sun climbed, the light increased, but always the forest remained a place of shadow. Beds of ferns bordered the path in the hollows; in some places they stood higher than her head and formed a green canyon along the trail. They passed a large, fern-bordered spring beside the trail, but neither desired water and so they kept on. Imperceptibly, the floor of the forest sloped gently upward, as the path wound in and around small hills and hollows. After a few hours sunlit glades began to appear and the undergrowth thickened. Bright flowers bloomed in the grass of the glades, and birds and small animals played in the trees.

Shem would stop on occasion and silently point to a squirrel gathering food or to various markings in the dirt. Invariably he would be able to explain to her exactly what had happened, and when, from a quick glance at the marks. Seeing her interest, he took more time at the next stop and explained exactly what each track meant and how he knew its age from the condition of the edge, the dust inside the track, or the overprint of another. Madrazi was enthralled. It was a new language, one that she had not known to exist before that day. As they continued, she found that she could now recognize some of the marks on the trail and took pride in demonstrating her new knowledge to Shem.

By mid morning, the forest thinned and the slope of its floor became more noticeable. The roof of the forest opened and the sun, riding higher in the sky, beat down on their heads. Madrazi was ready to ask for a rest when Shem led her down a short side trail that ended against a small hillock of bare, weathered rock. Trees spread their limbs over the thick grass of the dell, and at the base of the hill a spring bubbled out into a small pool.

Shem reached for a cup carved from an ox horn hanging from a knob of rock. Rinsing it out, he filled it and offered it to his thirsty wife. "Sit for a minute," he said, indicating a smooth rock next to the pool. "This has long been one of my favorite places. When I sit here and stare at the sky in the water of the pool, I forget town, I forget the house, I even forget my work on the ark. I lose myself in its reflections and am free to think about anything." He hesitated a moment and then with an embarrassed grin admitted, "When I was younger, I used to daydream about you."

Madrazi stared at him, grateful for the confidence. In one short morning, she was learning much about the man who was her husband and she was eager to continue her education. Shem did not notice; his face had softened with old memories. When he finally noticed her stare, he blushed. "Great-grandfather offered vivid descriptions of you as a young lady," he explained sheepishly. "He took me to this place years ago, after he returned from your father's house. I sat on that stone as he described you in great detail and said that he had found my wife. As he talked, I stared into the pool and thought that I could see your face far away in the water. Afterwards, I came often to see if I could see it again."

"Did you?" she asked, her curiosity aroused. It seemed strange to her that a self-sufficient man like Shem would waste his time yearning for her. She was flattered and pleased.

"No," he answered, "but I remembered what I had seen with Great-grandfather, and found this always a place of peace where I could dream unfettered."

"What did you dream?" Madrazi asked, eager for another glimpse of his heart.

"Only the foolish imaginations of the truly young," he equivocated. "I have discovered in a few short weeks that it is not good to create the image of another person without knowing them because reality eventually overwhelms imagination."

"But imagination gives anticipation and hope when there is no knowledge," Madrazi shot back. "I have spent time during the last ten years dreaming of my life with you, what you would be like in appearance and manner, what we might enjoy doing together, how many children we might have."

"And what have you learned now that knowledge has replaced imagination?" asked Shem, his own curiosity aroused.

"Imagination builds hope, but hope joins experience in knowledge that gives comfort in the present and more hope for the future. Both hope and knowledge are needed to build a love that will weather the years. Love is better in shared knowledge with two than in the imagination of one. Would you not agree?" she asked, running her hand softly along his cheek.

He pulled her hand down to his lips and he kissed it gently. "You are right again. I bow to your superior understanding. Let us never cease to build our love."

It was a small step, but one taken together. They smiled in that mutual understanding and without another word rose and hiked back up to the main path. Shem resumed his silent progress through the trees and glades and Madrazi followed, content for the moment.

The sun was high when the path wound up the steep side of a low ridge. Shem had not stopped since the spring, and Madrazi was breathing heavily when the path reached the level ground on top of the ridge. Going on a little further, they reached a break in the trees and finally Shem stopped to let her rest. Just below was the head of a path leading steeply down into a vale much lower than the side of the hill they had just climbed. A vast bowl of grass lay at the foot of the ridge, and in the center was an impossibly large mass of dark wood.

Shem did not speak; words would only interfere with her first sight of the ark. Madrazi accepted his silence and stepped in front of him to see more clearly. He placed his hands lightly on her shoulders. Even at that distance, the ark was a magnet to her eyes. Both Shem and Noah had described its construction in some detail, and seeing her knowledgeable interest, Noah had even shown her his drawings, but nothing could have prepared her for the sight. She had seen ships built and sailed for many years, but never one like this. It was at least five times as long as Hakkem and more than twice as long as the largest ship that she had ever seen. There were no sleek lines in its shape, only the massive, ugly, angular bulk that told of its task—simply to float and survive angry seas. The lack of masts and the customary accoutrements of a ship's deck added to its squat, ungainly shape. Then Madrazi saw men walking across the clearing and realized that her first grasp of its size was still not accurate. The dark mass filled her eyes and held them for untold minutes in silence. As she watched, the dark wood shimmered and her eyes seemed to see in its mass the destroying sea of her dream. Never had it intruded so clearly upon her waking mind. She shut her eyes and tried to send it away.

Shem felt her stiffen, then shudder under his hands. He wrapped his arms around her and his touch broke the spell of the moment. The ark stood again inanimate, with no sign of watery destruction or fiery abyss. With an effort, Madrazi dragged her eyes away from the massive wooden structure, and concentrated instead on the panorama. Far away on the northern horizon ran a long line of low red mountains. The trees thinned against the lowest slopes of the mountains, but formed a solid green mass marching back to the clearing. Forcing her eyes to skip over the ark, she saw the clearing itself was hundreds of cubits across from east to west and roughly oval in shape. Its grass was thick and green. The ridge where they stood formed the southern boundary. At its west end, the same ridge curled north, sloping down and ending at a small stream that formed the northern boundary, overhung by encroaching trees. A road ran down the western hill into the clearing from Lamech, unseen in the distant haze.

Immediately below her, through the trees at the foot of the ridge, she could see an orderly line of nine buildings. On the far right were three large barns set apart from the smaller structures; quarters for the workers, she guessed. Beyond the last of those buildings on her left was an open space leading up to the road. On the far side of the road was a long low shed, open in the front, with pungent smoke rising from brick chimneys to the rear. Other buildings and sheds lay beyond it and around to the east, some partially obscured by the ark.

Try as she could, Madrazi could not long avert her eyes from that dark dominating monstrosity. It was thick and squat, not at all like the graceful ships that she had helped design. The men working around it and on it were as ants. At its east end, its bulk reared a full thirty cubits into the air and a roof covered the uppermost deck for twenty or thirty cubits back from that end. She could not tell from its boxy features whether it was intended to be the bow or the stern. Back to the west, the upper deck was open and she could see the clutter of ongoing work. Nearly halfway down its length there was an abrupt step down to the middle deck, which extended almost the complete length of the ark before stepping down again to the lowest deck and then to the ground.

Madrazi had expected the work of constructing such a great vessel to capture her interest and engage her mind. But this was no ship and its appearance left her cold. Furthermore, the bizarre contrast between seeing the vessel in its woodland surrounding added to her distaste and she shivered involuntarily. Shem, misreading her reactions, tightened his arms around her waist. "I understand," he said. "I have been here for many years and still cannot stand here without awe of what it is and what it means."

But what Shem found an object of awe aroused only disgust and fear in his wife. She had seen a premonition of death at her first sight of its bulk and nothing could change that. Its size was certainly awe-inspiring, but its shape brought to her mind a giant coffin; the shadowy interior recalled too clearly the black abyss of her dream. Noah had presented it as a repository of life, yet she could only see the threat of extinction to all else. Why must millions die? Neither could she shake the incongruity of a seagoing vessel sitting in the depths of the forest. Her newfound love of the trees and the quiet places magnified her repulsion. The ark allowed the intrusion of the entity that she hated most into the quiet glades of the forest that she so desperately wanted to love.

Madrazi reminded herself of her plans but was forced to reassess the cost of the upcoming years. Shem obviously took pride and pleasure in the ark's construction, and she could not let him see her feelings. As she had learned to tolerate fear of the sea for the sake of her father, so she must apply those lessons here. She steeled herself and smiled weakly. "You promised to show me everything," she prompted in as normal a voice as she could muster.

Shem moved back in front and led her down the path back under the trees and out of sight of the dark shape. The respite helped her recover her courage and she flashed him a more genuine smile at the bottom of the hill. They walked on in silence as the gathering noise from the clearing ahead grew louder and clearer.

The path ended at the back of one of the smaller buildings, but Shem kept walking. He waved at the three larger ones as they walked past them. "Here we keep animals that help in the work of construction, and that help us test our ideas for housing them in the ark. We also store food for the workmen in the last barn and provide a place for Japheth to try his ideas for preserving and storing food for the voyage. These smaller buildings house the workers."

Remembering another puzzle, Madrazi asked, "Do the men of your house work in both places? I kept seeing different men at the house and did not understand why."

"Yes, you have sharp eyes. There are two groups of men who work here. The older men have been with our house for many years, and work willingly out of love for Noah and the promise of safety for their families in the ark. But they are not enough to complete the work and so Lamech hired strong young men from the city who work here for wages. We pay better wages than they could find in town and so most of them ignore the goal and perform their tasks without complaint. Even though most reject the prophecy, they work hard and we treat them well and make progress."

"Do you offer them a place, too?" she asked curiously.

"We would take any that were willing," he replied. "There will be room and provision on the ark for more than one hundred people and the men of Lamech could build their own havens if they wanted. There are ten of us and forty-six servants. We could easily take another four score if they would come. The men who work here are warned every day by the labor of their hands, yet they still refuse the Creator's words. People in the city do not even talk about the ark now, except as a rude jest."

As the couple rounded the last barn they met Japheth coming out with two men. He stared in surprise for an instant and then broke into a lighthearted smile. With a mischievous twinkle in his eye, he looked directly at Madrazi and said, "Brother, it has never been such a pleasure to see you! After a week with rough men and dirty animals, my eyes are lightened by your appearance."

Shem was used to Japheth's humor, but Madrazi could not help but smile in return. Japheth had a way of lifting the spirits of all around him and his irrepressible good nature took Madrazi further away from the dread she had experienced on the hilltop. She had not seen him once angry or gloomy and was convinced that she seldom would. There was always a smile in his bright brown eyes as if he found everything and everyone a source of humor and delight.

She responded lightly in kind, "I have come to offer you advice on shipbuilding. There is not one clean line on your vessel."

Japheth bowed low in mock humility, "Oh mistress of the paths of the sea, it would indeed be a worthy task to add beauty to the function of our barge, but you will have to take those questions up with my esteemed father and large, short-tempered, younger brother. I will be content to bask in the warmth of your smile and leave the difficult tasks to those of sufficient strength. If you wish to intrude upon my domain, then perhaps you would prepare the noon meal."

Shem protectively took his wife's arm and led her away from the barns. He pointed at the last of the quarters. "We will have a room to ourselves in that house. But first, come with me. I have something important to show you." Madrazi followed cautiously, for she detected a change in Shem; a sense of something she could not discern.

He cut across the meadow, and the sun shimmered on the grass and a light breeze ruffled the thin blades. Shem kept his head down but walked in a straight course for the far trees. Madrazi stopped to pick some yellow flowers and fell behind. When she caught up, he was near the verge of the trees at the stream. He spoke not a word and Madrazi sensed a weight upon him.

By the edge of the running water, a cairn of smoothly stacked flat stones stood alone in the sunlight. Just beyond were the cool inviting shadows of a quiet pool and large oaks on the other side. Madrazi's attention was first drawn to the beauty of the scene, but Shem halted a few steps away from the stones and stood silent with his head bowed. Madrazi stopped abruptly; the stones seemed to forbid her presence. She felt a tingling on the back of her neck and suddenly realized that this was the very place where Noah had encountered his vision.

Her own feelings were very mixed. This patch of ground was sacred to Noah and Shem, but she felt no grandeur or glory. Suddenly she realized that it marked a place that would force a delay of her dreams for the future for twenty years. Resentment began to build, but she tried hard to suppress it. The ground and altar were clearly important to her husband and so she must treat it in the same manner regardless of her own feelings. After all, it was just a patch of grass and a pile of rocks. Yet she could not help but feel something else, looming on the boundaries of her conscious thought. She grew increasingly uncomfortable. Shem stood silent. Was he going to stand here all day?

Finally, she could take no more. Gathering her courage, she interrupted Shem's reverie. "You honor your father. This must be an important place for him."

He turned, and she saw a flash of impatience and emotion in his dark eyes. Was it anger, frustration, or something else? But he quickly hid it and walked away a few steps before turning to her. His keen glance settled on her eyes and made her look down in shame. She should not have broken his silence. Bracing herself, she awaited the expected storm of anger. But he merely replied, "And for me," and walked slowly away towards the buildings.

She turned after him and watched him stride off for a moment. Shaking her head, she followed without a backward glance, wondering if she would ever understand him.

Chapter 17
STRANGE SHIPYARD

Bread, wine, and a short rest refreshed the couple. Shem said nothing about the stone altar, but Madrazi knew she had offended him in some way. For a time they sat silent on the shaded porch at the front of their quarters. The sun was still high but had already begun its westward trek. A breeze ran across the tops of the trees and settled into the meadow. Madrazi watched the grass bend, as if bowing before the ark. She was also watching the men come and go, and tried to count them. Finally, she gave up. "How many men work here?" she asked, tentatively, hoping that Shem was not still irked.

"Usually no more than sixty," he answered, seeming to thaw. "We have had more in the past, but it is getting harder to hire men from town. But we knew long ago that our men would be few, and so we have become skilled at making our work more efficient. Careful planning of each task as well as the sequence of work enabled us to make do with fewer men. Early on, most of the effort was directed at cutting, curing, and shaping wood. Only then did we move most of the men to construction. Father laid out the whole process at the beginning. In that sequence, we try to keep each man on a specific part of each task. Repetition eventually allows them to do more work in less time. It has worked surprisingly well throughout the construction; it helps that the ark consists of many identical sections of framing and planking. Thus we prepare the same number of the same size and shape timbers over and over again. When one section is complete, the same crew starts another; each man doing the same work over and over again."

"That would certainly save time and labor," Madrazi admitted, "but how many sections are there, and how did you discover what size to make them? How do you connect them? What interior support is needed to make them seaworthy?"

Shem laughed and held up his hands. "You will have to talk to Ham if you want every little detail. But I will answer as I can. You must understand that the ark does not have to sail in the fashion of your father's ships. Think of it instead as a giant box, 300 by 50 by 30 cubits. Since it has three decks, you many think of it as three boxes on top of each other that are approximately 300 by 50 by 10 cubits each. We frame and build sections for each box that are roughly 50 by 10 by 10 cubits. Though each section is the size of a small ship, they require no special shaping or curvature and every one is exactly the same."

Madrazi found her initial fear of the ark slipping away. In addition to her desire to please Shem, the work was intriguing and turning her mind to its details helped distract her from her earlier fear. She imagined herself as one of the workers—focused on the task at hand and trying hard to ignore its purpose. As long as she could submerge herself in the work, her fear receded. She imagined confidently that she could maintain that state of mind. After all, the functioning of any shipyard was so familiar that she could picture much of the work without seeing it, and the idea of doing such a large job with minimal labor intrigued her. Her father had always had more than enough men to build and repair his ships and had never faced that particular challenge. It was more than that; as Shem had said, most of Pomorolac's ships were little larger than one of the ark's sections. Moreover, she found comfort in Shem's acknowledgment of her intelligence and experience and his evident willingness to forget her offense at the altar. So she found it easy to smile and take his hand as he helped her up.

"Let me show you first how we prepared the wood," he offered.

Madrazi kept her hold on his hand, ignoring the stares of the men, and walked with him toward the north side of the clearing. As they walked around the ark, she stared more closely at the giant timbers half sunk into the ground upon which the hull rested and asked Shem how they had been emplaced.

"Laying the foundation was hard work," he admitted. "We needed massive tree trunks that were fifty-five cubits long and did not lose much girth over that length. Fortunately, there were many large trees on the edge of the clearing and we only had to drag a few from out of the forest. Setting them level and true from one end to the other was the work of many months. Ham made sure that the entire foundation was square by adjusting the positions of the trenches until the diagonal lengths were equal. The hardest part was moving the weight. But Ham eventually perfected a machine that could lift one of the trunks and sway it into place. We now use a smaller version to lift heavy timbers onto the higher decks of the ark."

He pointed and she saw a large timber A-frame standing on the edge of the highest level. He continued, "Instead of building one complete level at a time, we stagger them to make the lifting easier. That also allows us to build in the storage bins, containers, vats, pens, and cages as we go. The stern will be finished last. Like the bow, Ham is building a double hull there for added strength."

"How could you be confident that it would all fit together building from one end to the other?" she asked. "When Father builds ships, there are always adjustments to make as the work progresses."

Shem pondered a moment. Finally he said, "The simple design makes it easier to be precise. Noah drew many designs and built several small models during the early years. The last one was three cubits long and many of the problems that would have arisen were solved in those models. Besides, Ham is an exacting workman. He is here more than either Japheth or I, and he closely supervises everything from the cutting and curing of the wood to the joining of the smaller timbers. Once the men realized what he demanded, they worked hard to be exact."

They were now opposite the open stern of the great vessel. As Shem talked, Madrazi stopped and stared down the length of the vast cavernous interior of the lower deck. She saw a clutter of wooden structures of all sizes instead of the dark emptiness she had expected. Some were as simple as large boxes or vats; others grew more intricate as her eyes became accustomed to the dim light. Shem's gaze followed hers. "All of the cages, pens, and enclosures for the animals and storage compartments for food and water are built in as we go. We may walk through and see tomorrow: the men will be finished with their work and we won't be in their way."

She nodded acceptance, her eyes still captured by the maze of intricate woodwork that extended beyond the range of sight. As she was staring, she saw a broad-shouldered man with black hair emerge from the dim interior and walk towards them. He was carrying a large chest of tools by a broad leather strap over one shoulder. Madrazi was sure that she could not even lift the box, but the man did not seem to notice its weight. Seeing the couple, he hesitated, but then came forward, stepped lightly down out of the ark, and nodded respectfully.

Shem introduced him. "This is Meshur. He is Ham's right hand." Meshur looked both pleased and embarrassed at these words. "This is my wife, Madrazi," he said to the man who bowed low.

"Welcome, lady," he said somewhat awkwardly. He paused, not quite sure what to say next. Madrazi noticed his reticence and spoke quickly to set him at ease. She had been around men like Meshur all her life and she knew what they would speak of and what they would not.

"Thank you, Meshur," she said. "This is indeed a wondrous work that speaks well of your skill. If you are Ham's right hand, then I bow to your ability, for it must be great."

The shy smile broadened at her words. As she suspected, he took great pride in his craft, and his hands and arms proclaimed that he was no stranger to heavy work.

"It is my privilege to work with Master Ham. I have learned more from him in these short years than many master craftsmen acquire in a lifetime."

"Have you always wanted to be a builder?"

Meshur nodded gravely. "Ever since I was a boy. Before I came here, I worked for my uncle. We constructed many buildings and even helped set the standing stones for the circle of the heavens north of town."

"That would be exacting work," Madrazi agreed. "I built a small circle at my old home to learn the paths of the heavens. But the only stone was the gnomon in the center. All else was wood."

Both men stared at Madrazi. She felt a twinge of amusement. Evidently Noah had not discussed her achievements with his son, and no one expected a mere woman to know what the wise still struggled to learn. Madrazi pretended not to notice their looks, but felt anew the pride in that achievement. She added modestly, "The daughter of Pomorolac was expected to know the courses of the heavens."

Shem shook his head slightly and smiled slowly. He wondered what other surprises his wife had in store. Madrazi returned his smile and then turned back to Meshur and talked about his work for a few more minutes, ending the conversation as he began to look ill at ease.

"You have an easy way with men," observed Shem as they watched him walk away.

Madrazi was not sure how to interpret that statement. Her upbringing had been different from most other women. She had assumed that Shem knew all about her past. But she knew little of his. How could she expect any more from him? It would take time, but they had many years and the time at the spring that morning had proven that it could be done. She sensed another opening to talk, but wondered if his observation contained a hint of disapproval. She did not want to risk angering him, so she replied cautiously. "I was around my father's men all my life; in the shipyard, on board his ships, and in much of his business. I have traveled far, and stood beside him in many towns."

He said nothing and in a flash of insight, Madrazi remembered his words by the spring and realized that much that his knowledge of her was built on Methuselah's stories of a young girl who still had a mother. He knew little else except the bare outlines of her mother's death, her later work with her father, and her isolated life. How could he know how different the woman was from the girl of Methuselah's tales? She had much to tell him, but realized that this was not the time or place for such intimacy. Instead, she changed the subject, asking him the first question that came to mind. "I helped my father enough in his projects to understand the frustrations of cutting and shaping large beams and planks. I am curious to see how it is done here. This vessel will use a whole forest of trees."

In answer, he gestured ahead and led her towards the stream on the far side of the clearing. "The first thing that we did was mark and cut appropriate trees in the forest. We found several large groves of suitable trees within a few hours walk and have harvested most of them. These were sawn into lengths where they fell and dragged out of the forest. Even now, we have several men who can look at a living tree and tell you exactly how many beams and planks that can be coaxed from it."

As they walked across the clearing, Madrazi could see several broad and rutted paths winding out into the woods from beyond a stout timber bridge over to her right. A long narrow shed had been built beside it on the near side of the stream. Nearer to them was a much larger shed filled with stacks of finished timbers. Shem ignored the larger structure and led her on to the other. As they drew near, he waved his hand at it. "This is our cutting shed. We use the water to power our tools."

She followed him and looked through the open shed up and down the stream. She had heard of such contrivances to grind grain, but had never seen one. They strode straight into the shed; like many of the buildings it was composed simply of a roof upheld by thick pillars. A flat table ran in front of them from one end of the shed to the other, and directly over it was a running hoist attached to a heavy beam. At the east end of the building the table ended in a shallow ramp. Walking around it, Shem led Madrazi to the verge of the stream. The paved stone floor under their feet gave way to a steep bank. On their right a quiet pool glinted in the sun, at its foot, the water ran over a weir and down a manmade channel just below them. That water turned a large wooden wheel positioned across the spillway. An axle ran from the center of the wheel into the shed, where it ended in a small wooden wheel with a thick leather belt around it. A confusion of shafts, pulleys, gears, and belts occupied the space between the stream and the table. Madrazi understood enough to see that the water eventually turned a large round iron saw suspended just above the table under the hoist.

Shem did not wait to be asked. "The axles are joined by the leather belts allowing the saw to be engaged or disengaged by this lever." A wooden handle extended from the maze of machinery. "When the saw is turning, we pull wood along the table with the hoist and quickly cut a smooth, flat side. We can cut a beam or plank in this way in much less time than we could by hand and it needs little finishing after. Fortunately, gopher wood is soft when first cut, though it cures to great hardness. We discovered iron for the saws in the mountains, near out gold mine."

Madrazi did not try to hide her surprise. In all the work that she had witnessed in her father's shipyard, she had never seen wood cut in this way before. Even though her old friends could do the job quickly and efficiently with a two-man saw, they could not hope to match the speed of this machinery.

Shem continued, "After all four sides are cut square, the beams and planks are taken outside and buried."

Her curiosity was again aroused. "Why do you bury the wood?"

Shem replied, "Father learned that trick at the shipyard in Nimur. Certain types of wood, including gopher wood, cure and harden more completely when buried for a season. We bury them in the sand here."

Thy walked back down the length of the shed, and beyond it Madrazi saw a large area of sandy dirt, pierced by open trenches. Beyond the open trenches was a series of stakes that marked the filled trenches. "Stakes are placed at each end of a trench, and notched each week to tell us when to unearth the wood. After we dig it up, we stack it in the next shed to finish curing in open air."

They walked out of the cutting shed, past the sandy plot with its lines of trenches and to the larger building where the timber was completing its curing. Once past it, Madrazi was hit by a strong odor that she had only noticed faintly before. The west wind had pushed it out of the glade and back toward the sea, but the wind shifted and the pungent aroma became stronger. The scent was so familiar that she had ignored it at first, for pitch was one of the smells that defined a shipyard. But her eyes were drawn across a patch of open ground to another shed at the far west end of the clearing. Brick chimneys reared above the roof. Walking closer, she saw brick ovens built into the shed from the rear, with long, narrow, fired clay vats positioned on top of the fires. Rising smoke from the vats sent out the familiar aroma.

Shem smiled. "The scent of the pitch seems to fill the entire forest at times," he apologized, "when the ovens are active and we are cooking either one or the other."

"I have often seen men make pitch," Madrazi interrupted, "but I did not know that there was more than one kind. What uses do you find for them?"

Shem explained. "The first is very thin, almost like water, and soaks into the wood when it is hot enough—a finger width or two into cured beams and planks. As I'm sure you know, untreated wood will not float indefinitely in water. Eventually it becomes too heavy. Different kinds of wood float for different lengths of time, and cured wood floats longer than that freshly cut.

But when we take the cured beams and planks and immerse them in pitch, it hardens to a shield that allows them to float easily for many years. Cured wood is brought here as we need it, and is placed in rope slings at this end of the building and lowered into the pitch. A hoist overhead moves the planks through the vats and they are lifted out at the other end and stored to dry. Then we carry or drag it to where it is needed."

"What does the other blend of pitch do?" she asked.

"The second pitch is thicker and binds to the dried surface of the first. We use it to overcoat exposed surfaces after we build and caulk each section. It will keep the wood from water damage and is supposed to resist boring by sea worms. This is another skill that Noah learned from the wrights of Nimur. After it dries for many days it becomes dark and hard. It is why the outside of the ark is so dark."

"Father also had trouble with worms in the past. He began to plate the bottoms of his ships with thin sheets of copper." Madrazi said as they walked back to the building where they were staying.

"We hope that the pitch and the natural curing of the wood works, too," admitted Shem. "Even if we had thought of that, we could never find enough copper to cover the bottom of the ark. Did it work well?"

"Oh yes. But he has to replace the sheets every few years."

Shem nodded thoughtfully as they continued lazily across the grass. Madrazi's earlier tension continued to ebb away. She and her husband had found something of mutual interest, and she was determined to hold onto the easy accord they now felt.

"How do you make the pitch?" she asked. "When father needed pitch, he would collect the sap from pine trees and boil it for many hours. After the trees were drained, they were burned slowly beneath the soil to make charcoal, and the powdered charcoal was mixed with the boiling sap. But we only used it to coat the outside surface of the ships after they had been built."

"We make it in a similar fashion," smiled Shem. "However, we found that different kinds of trees, varying amounts of charcoal, and different lengths of time over the fires changes the final product."

Encouraged by her interest, Shem took Madrazi's hand and led her up the road that climbed the low hill at the west end of the clearing. Madrazi had to shade her eyes against the flaring sun, but at the top of the hill they turned and saw their own shadows cast far back along the road. The clearing below was illuminated by the late afternoon light. It poured into the open end of the ark and lit the swarm of men finishing the day's work. Shem touched Madrazi's hand and she turned to him. She could sense his curiosity and knew that she must speak. But not knowing what to say, she turned back to the clearing and stood silent for a while longer, watching the light fade. As it did, the opening of the ark suddenly became a doorway to darkness and once again the menace that she had felt on the hill smote her heart once more.

It happened so quickly that Madrazi had no time to react to the sudden chill that assaulted her soul. She could not tear her eyes away from the dark maw and sensed the destroying waters within that black cavern. Shem sensed the change and attempted to pull her close, but she was stiff and unresponsive. Anger at her untamed feelings flared and it took all of her self control to bottle up her conflicting emotions. After a sharp internal struggle she silenced her fear, returned his embrace, and fumbled for words to relieve the silence.

"I'm sorry. This day has overwhelmed me," she said, sharing the first thought that came to mind. "I enjoyed walking together with you through the forest. I believe that I could easily love it, and I wish to know more. We saw something of each other at the spring, and for that I thank you."

She dared not speak of the ark, lest she lose control again and hurt her husband. Yet she stammered on, knowing that she must say something.

"Noah's story has changed my world and I struggle with his words. I thought that leaving my home and family and marrying a man who I had never seen would be change enough, but I was wrong. Perhaps these are too many transformations for me in such a short time. I want to be a part of your life. But the life you offer is so much different from what I expected. I wanted to stand beside you to build a home, bringing sons and daughters into the world and making a life together. But you ask me instead to build a new world, as sole survivors of the old. I will try to support you and your family as best I can, but I beg you for time and patience."

Shem nodded. He sensed her frustration, but understood that he saw only a part, and did not yet fathom its depths. Afraid that any words would only increase the tension, he simply stood quietly beside her until the sun faded and gathering shadows in the clearing muted the ark.

Chapter 18
DARK VESSEL

Before they had finished preparing breakfast the following day, Japheth called out from the doorway and came straight back to the kitchen. "I smelled the food," he volunteered. "Since I am staying all day, I have some time to waste, and another breakfast is as good a way to do it as any. What are you two going to do in what little remains of this day?" He immediately sat down at the table and watched Madrazi shake her head as she began to pull out another plate and cup.

"I am going to show Madrazi the interior," Shem answered. "If there is time, I need to retrieve a litter from the beaver colony at the old cutting. Are any men still working inside today?"

"None that I know of." He grinned at his sister-in-law. "Perhaps Madrazi can inspect her quarters and tell you what colors she wants for her rugs and curtains."

"The color does not matter so long as the rooms are not next to yours!" She laughed, as she poured him some tea. The brothers laughed with her and Madrazi felt a brief stab of jealousy at their easy friendship, but her common sense rescued her as she realized that she should be grateful that Japheth did not see her as an interloper. She wondered idly why neither of them seemed to be close to Ham. He was the youngest, but only by two years, yet he seemed to always be apart. She admired his skill and craftsmanship: he was the kind of man who Pomorolac would have placed in command of one of his ships, or even his shipyard, despite his youth.

After they finished eating, Japheth wandered off to the barns and Shem led Madrazi across the grass to the front of the ark. In the morning light, she did not feel yesterday's sense of doom, but her fear hovered in the recesses of her heart, ready to spring up at any time. A broad ramp led up into the cool shadows of the lower deck. She stopped just inside, feeling the dark walls and ceiling close in about her. Resolutely, she shook off her anxiety and followed Shem as he led confidently on.

Nervous in the dead silence of the dim interior, Madrazi began to ask questions. "How will you provide light inside when all is complete?"

"The sun will be enough. It will enter through a series of windows built into the top deck all the way around the vessel, just below the roof."

"Then how will you keep the water out?"

"Have you been inside our barns at the settlement?" She nodded. "Good!" he exclaimed. "Think of their windows. They are similar to those that are being built into the ark. Covers for the windows will be mounted on the inside of the ark, mounted inside grooves. They can be slid open or shut as needed."

Madrazi recalled the open slots around the top of the barns' walls, framed but not covered over with planks. She had seen the windows only partly open, obscured by panels mounted parallel to the openings. Long poles extended down from the panels that could be pushed or pulled to open or close them.

Shem explained, "The real problem is not the amount of light. In the barn, we used the same ratio of window space to interior space as the ark. Even when the windows are partly closed, light is adequate for both animals and humans. The harder task is distributing the light throughout the ark."

"That is true. There will be many portions of the vessel that will be dark all the time."

"Not as many as you think," Shem corrected. "We are building large hatches in the decks that will be our primary access from one level to another. Those will allow some light down to the lower levels. Even so, we will make use of those areas that will remain dark. Many animals live their lives underground. We cannot bring a part of the land for them to live within. But we have found that in captivity, these animals can survive comfortably in cages above the ground as long as there is little light. They will inhabit the darker recesses. Other animals, such as bats and the cold-blooded creatures enter a state of sleep or near sleep if conditions are kept cool and dark. Part of the difficulty in designing the ark was allocating spaces for those needs."

Madrazi's eyes had now adjusted to the dim interior and she had to admit that she could see well enough. But she still did not like the dim silence and broke it with an observation. "Father worried about lighting in Hakkem, when he designed her," she said. "He was concerned that light would not reach the lower deck. Of course he did not want the widespread use lamps for fear of fire, although they are necessary at times. But he found other ways to provide illumination. Below decks he used polished copper mirrors positioned near the hatches to reflect more light into the interior."

Shem stopped short and laughed approvingly.

Madrazi mistook it for something else and turned upon him in anger. "And what is so funny about that," she snapped.

"No," said Shem still chuckling. "You misunderstand. Your idea has great merit and I was thinking of the response from Ham when I innocently suggest that he might have overlooked such a practical solution. Besides," he continued turning to her, "I could never laugh at any idea from such a beautiful woman."

Madrazi faced him, but her anger died when she saw the light in his eyes. It seemed quite reasonable to meet his embrace and lift her lips to his. His smile as he released her was sufficient for her complete forgiveness and taking his hand she let him lead her on.

Encouraged by his approval, Madrazi continued. "Father also found another way. In some parts of the oceans, there are light giving plants or animals that form skims atop the water. He placed them with seawater inside empty water barrels and they lit the recesses of the lower decks."

Shem laughed. "Perhaps you should have married Ham. You both have quick minds for problems."

Madrazi felt a surge of passion; anger mixed with desire. She knew that she would find no better man, and the conflict between love for him and disbelief in his father's prophecy stirred a dangerous brew of emotion that she chose not to control at that moment. She simply reached out and pulled him to her with all her strength. Holding her body tight against his, she replied in a strained voice, "I want no man but you!"

Those words seemed to freeze the couple in place for a long minute, eyes fixed upon eyes. Shem did not know why his words stirred such deep feelings in his wife, but he had the sense to keep silent and just hold her close for a few minutes.

"That is my wish, too," he said finally, feeling her heartbeat slow, "forgive my foolish words."

Their bodies parted, but their eyes remained locked. "I cannot refuse you," she said automatically and she realized that part of her struggle was the truth in those words. Shem held her again in grateful wonder, while Madrazi felt tears wash across her eyes. The powerful emotions she felt for him were hard to reconcile with her ingrained habits of aloof independence and guarded feelings. She wanted to give herself completely, but there was much that must remain buried. She sighed, stepped back, and the moment was gone.

Shem led her farther in and they climbed the first great ramp that led to the second deck. There was more light on that level and they were near the latest construction. Madrazi began to look more closely at the storage bins, cages and pens. She stopped and turned in all directions, seeing the multitude of enclosures. "How many animals will be able to fit into this craft?"

"That was a difficult question. Father and I worked many years to classify the different kinds of animals, both wild and tame and to distinguish those that will need to be on the ark to survive the judgment of water. Over fifteen thousands will be on board when we are finished."

Madrazi stared at him, astounded. "Fifteen thousands! How will you possibly fit so many animals inside? This vessel is large, but how can it hold so many?"

"Easily." Shem shrugged. "We too, were first surprised. Then we realized that our thoughts were of cattle, sheep, horses, and other domestic animals, and those full grown. Most animals are quite small and will take up very little room. A very few of the largest animals will take up disproportionate space, but for every one the size of an ox, there are many tens like mice. We will also take young animals; they are smaller and will have a longer life in the new world. All together, the animals will only take a little more than half of the available space aboard. The hardest part is planning where each kind is to go to match their needs for light or dark, food and water, and convenience in caring for them."

Madrazi was still skeptical. "What about air? How will the small windows on the upper deck supply sufficient fresh air for the animals below?"

"Easily. We built our barns at home with the same ratio of windows to interior space. In the barns the animals have both adequate light and air, even when full and with the windows more closed than open. Our biggest concern was that air would move directly from one window to another and not circulate among the animals on the lower decks. But in the barns it flows freely throughout, removing the heat generated by the animals and bringing in fresh air for all. Depending on the temperature, we can adjust the size of the openings and keep the barns quite comfortable. Besides, Ham is prepared if the windows do not provide enough air for the entire ark; he has designed two flues that extend from the lower deck through the roof along the midline of the ark. They will draw air from the deepest recesses of the lower deck to the outside, forcing air down from the upper decks."

They continued along the vast middle deck. As Madrazi became used to the size of the ark, she began to see, with a practiced eye, the craftsmanship evident in even the small details. All of the wood was smooth and even. The intricate joints were well fitted, and the heavy framing that would obviously impart great strength to the vessel in any sea also served as support for the various cages and bins. Her father's men could have done no better.

A little farther into the depths of the second deck, they came upon a long row of cages set less than two cubits away from the wall. Behind them was a narrow, shallow trough slanting toward the wall and slightly down towards the bow of the ark. Glancing up, she saw hoppers suspended from the ceiling over every fifth cage.

She turned wordlessly to Shem and he grinned. "The boxes are grain stores. They are open on top and have a trap door in the bottom that can be opened and closed with a pole. The bamboo chutes carry grain from the base of each hopper into the five cages below. The bamboo is sized in diameter proportional to its length, allowing almost identical volumes of grain into each cage. Feeding the animals in five cages takes only a poke from a pole and a few moments."

Madrazi looked at him and queried, "Ham?"

"Of course! Ham and father have worked hard to design everything to minimize work; we want to be able to care for all the creatures even if only a few people remain fit to do so. With the hands of all, it will be quite easy."

"Why are not the cages built into side of the ark? Would it not be more stable and waste less space?"

"The trough behind the cages is for cleaning up animal waste. The bottoms of the cages are wooden slats and waste will fall out of the bottom of each cage onto the slanting boards and then into the trough. If necessary, we can wash the contents of the trough overboard; it is thickly coated with pitch and should remain waterproof. If that proves impractical, we can clean them with shovels and move the waste to vats built into the lower deck. Earthworms will compost the waste and take care of the problem for us."

Madrazi had not yet considered all of the problems the animals would present, but it was clear that her new family had. For a moment, several humorous remarks ran through her head, but Shem seemed quite serious, and so she kept them to herself. Shem was oblivious to the small smile that passed her lips and continued to explain.

"Our experience has taught us that the pens of many farm animals do not need frequent cleaning. If they are constructed with trenches or troughs to allow the runoff of urine, and if the solid wastes are removed regularly, a thick layer of straw will compress and provide an adequate bed for the animals for more than a year."

The couple continued along and came to the ramp up to the upper deck. The hatch was ten cubits across and forty long. Like the previous one, a ramp extended up one side to the upper deck, allowing them to climb into the sunlight. Only at the back of the ark was the roof complete and the vessel completely enclosed. But after spending some time on the lower decks, the sun here seemed bright and Madrazi stood blinking and enjoying its warmth upon her head.

Remembering Japheth's jest, she asked, "Where will we stay? Don't I need to tell you what color scheme I desire for my curtains and rugs?"

"Follow me, beloved," said Shem, bowing before her. "Our family will have cabins built at the back of the top deck, with a large communal area for eating and a place for the women to talk while the men work."

He dodged gracefully the well-aimed kick and led her back around and across scraps of wood and boxes of tools. They passed beneath the edge of the roof and he pointed to partitions that were almost complete. Their ceilings ended well below the level of the windows; Madrazi guessed that this would allow better lighting and air circulation, as well as provide storage space. There were four rooms to be built into either side of the ark and a large open area between them. Beyond the rooms, the wall of the ark reared up to meet the roof above the windows. Just below the windows, a narrow parapet ran completely around the perimeter with regularly spaced ladders reaching down to the deck.

Madrazi stood in the middle, looking around. The roof was high above and the windows threw strange shadows across the floor. Looking up at Shem, she asked, "I see eight rooms. Are we to be separated for the duration?

"That is not my desire. We intended sleeping and day quarters for each couple and I will insist on your presence with me for the one if not the other."

Madrazi arched her eyes at her husband and then lowered them with a slight bow. "I am yours to command, my husband. Shall you choose our rooms, or shall I?"

Shem smiled at her teasing tone, but shook his head. Looking away he said, "I may be older, but Ham is building the ark and you may have to be prepared to take what is offered."

"As long as you are present, the accommodations will be delightful," returned Madrazi, pulling his arm against her body.

Shem turned and took her once again in his strong arms. He said nothing, for Madrazi had decided that his lips were better occupied against hers than with wasted words. Shem pulled gently away and buried his face in her hair as she buried hers against his chest.

"Your beauty overcomes my control so easily," breathed Shem.

"Is that a complaint or a compliment?" queried his wife, wondering why he did not notice that her own was just as easily breached by him.

"Every other man in the world would think me mad if I spoke it as a complaint, but I am not accustomed to being so easily distracted. In the forest, such a lapse could cost me my life."

"Are we in the forest, now, my husband?" asked Madrazi softly, lifting her lips to him again.

Wisely, Shem did not answer with words.

As they later were walking towards the front of the deck, Madrazi saw an area, five cubits square, paved with close-fitting, slabs of slate. "Why are these stones here?" she asked.

"They will be the foundation for a brick oven. If the motion of the ark is not too great, we can cook. There will be a ready supply of firewood kept in these bins," he said, pointing to boxes built into the sides of the ark across from the paved pad.

They continued back into the sun, which was beginning to dip into the west. Instead of walking down the great ramp, they came to the edge of the unfinished upper deck and sat near its edge, looking down the length of the ark. Far below them, miniature men moved cured timbers through the pitch vats, and stacked them outside to dry. A light wind caressed their faces. With the loaf and wineskin that Shem had brought, they made a noon meal together, looking out across the tops of the nearer trees.

Madrazi reflected on her morning as they ate silently. She was astounded by what she had seen; no vessel like this had ever been built. Beside it, Hakkem was a rowboat and many of her father's older ships were scarcely longer than the beam of the ark. But it was not the size alone. The design and workmanship were as good as any she had seen, and she was experienced enough to realize that the addition of the numerous cages, pens, clever storage bins, and provisions for feeding and watering the animals had increased the difficulties of construction many fold. Her respect for Ham had risen with each new device she saw.

But she could not treat the great vessel as merely a wonder of Noah's creative ability and Ham's skill. Rather than distracting from its dark purpose, its construction only served to heighten the inner conflict stirred by Noah's tale of prophecy and doom. Her mind had examined the evidence and found it wanting, yet the massive bulk beneath her seemed a tangible denial of her conclusion. Once again she was torn: did this carefully-constructed marvel mean that the words of Noah were true? Or was it a monstrous hoax that threatened not the world, but merely the universe of her marriage?

Shem roused her with a light touch. "What are you thinking?"

"The ark stirs fear in me," she replied honestly, "I am trying to understand it."

"That is not surprising. After all, it is a symbol of destruction for all that we hold dear in this world. Your fear proves that you understand that. You must try to remember that for us, it is rather a refuge. But come with me this afternoon, and I will take you away from it and show you more of the forest."

As they crossed the heavy bridge and entered the trees, Madrazi left the ark and its fears behind. A short ways into the forest, the path diverged. Shem took the first one to the left. It was overgrown and had not been used for several years. Scattered small trees in the path already reached Madrazi's head, but they were still thin and sparse. Her feet enjoyed the feel of the thick grass and the flowers in the sunlit patches were colorful and heavily scented. Peace seemed to emanate from the trees and form a tangible protective presence around her.

Once again, she marveled how silently and easily her husband slipped along. She tried to imitate his steps, but in spite of her best efforts, her feet would find a stick or her clothes brush against the undergrowth. Once, when she was concentrating on where to place her feet, she ran into him, but hid her embarrassment in silence. She soon grew accustomed to his irregular gait; he stopped frequently to scan the trees ahead. In less than an hour, they came to a large clearing in the trees. Amid bare stumps and piles of long dead branches, the forest was beginning to reclaim the land.

At the near edge of the trees, Shem reached out a restraining hand. He was absorbed in his surroundings and she was almost an intruder; a nuisance. He brought his mouth close to her ear and whispered, "There is a colony of beavers in the stream at the far side. Over there," he said pointing a finger, "are the tops of their houses. They look like small domes of sticks and mud."

Madrazi's eyes followed his finger and she saw small piles of wood in the middle of a wide shallow stream. Just downstream of the piles was a rough dam of sticks that slowed, but did not stop the flow. Shem breathed into her ear again. "We must be silent now if we are to see them. They are watchful and easily frightened. Follow my footsteps exactly."

They set off along the edge of the clearing, staying just inside the larger trees. The ground there was carpeted with dead needles, and Madrazi belatedly realized that he had chosen the path that would minimize both sound and visibility. Had she known more, she would have perceived that they moved against the wind as well. Shem went slowly and silently; his wife placing each foot where his had been and trying to avoid any noise. Along the perimeter of the clearing they made their way, slipping from tree to tree and then stopping to evade the attention of any creature present in the clearing. As they approached the other side, Shem slowed even more, stopping every few steps to watch. Finally, he drew Madrazi alongside him and pointed without speaking.

A short distance ahead, on the banks of the stream, she saw several brown animals balanced on their hind feet and broad flat tails. They were almost the size of a half-grown sheep, and were looking warily about, but had not yet sensed the two humans hidden by the trunk of a large tree. As they resumed chewing on the branches at their feet, Shem crept quietly towards the next trunk. With a suddenness that alarmed both Madrazi and the animals, he stopped and let out an exclamation. Although his voice was not loud, in the silence of the clearing it seemed a shout to Madrazi's keyed up senses. Her eyes were on the beavers, and at the sound of his voice, she saw them immediately dive into the water, stopping only long enough to slap the water with their tails. Giving up on any attempt to move silently, Madrazi hurried forward to see what had alarmed her husband.

Without a word, Shem pointed to the soft ground in front of him. In a damp depression that ran parallel to the stream, there was a line of prints crossing from the clearing into the forest. The tracks were larger than her feet, and spread out to the front; the three large, clawed toes leaving deep prints in the mud. Several cubits separated the tracks, and Madrazi knew they marked a large creature, and from her husband's reaction, a dangerous one. The hint of fear in Shem's eyes frightened Madrazi more than the size of the tracks.

After a moment, he spoke. "These are the tracks of a giant hunting lizard. We have seen them in the forest along the mountains to the north, but never this far south. Some reach twenty cubits in height, and they are fierce killers, with no fear of man. They devoured three of our servants who worked at the gold mine until we hunted and killed those in that valley. Four other men were hurt badly in that hunt. They move faster than a man can run and they have eyes like an eagle. If there is one this close to the ark, then our men are in danger and I must kill it before it kills some of them. Come! We need to get back immediately!"

The tracks appeared to head to the east of the ark, and Madrazi blurted out, "Why cannot we follow these and see if they truly do go near the ark?"

Shem stared at her, amazed, and shook his head. "Without weapons, the only thing we could possibly find is death."

"What kind of weapon can you use against such a large animal?"

Shem replied impatiently as he dragged her back towards the path, "We killed those at the gold mine with arrows dipped in venom. If you can get a shot into their eyes or open mouth, the poison works quickly. They quickly lose their ability to move and die in less time than it would take you to run fifty paces. If you miss, but penetrate their thick skin with the arrows, they still die, but live long enough to do damage." Madrazi, who finally began to understand that he spoke from experience, shuddered.

Without another word he walked quickly back along the trail to the ark.

No longer as concerned with silence, Shem was not running, but was moving at a pace that forced Madrazi to trot every minute or so to keep up. Madrazi attempted to ask several more questions as they went, but for a while, he ignored her, preoccupied with his own thoughts.

But as they neared the bridge, he spoke, avoiding her eyes, "I must gather a party today and prepare for a hunt tomorrow. You will return to the settlement with Japheth in the morning."

Madrazi felt a sudden blaze of resentment. He was not asking; the order was terse and uncompromising. He had never before spoken to her in that tone of voice. She was excited, tired, and still frightened at the same time, and she resented his tone.

"Why can I not come with you? I can keep up in the forest. I am not afraid."

"Perhaps," he allowed, "but I could not concentrate on finding and killing this creature with you present. I would worry too much for your safety and any distraction might kill us all." His voice softened for a moment, then regained its earlier tone. "Just do as I say and I will come home in a few days. Who knows? We may have nothing to do. The lizard may wander back to its own ranges by itself and leave us in peace."

Madrazi followed silently, knowing that he was right, but still angry. Her place was beside him, and she was consumed with curiosity to see such an animal. She had heard tales of the giant lizards from her father and his men, but had never seen one. Indeed few people did, since they usually avoided men, living in remote wilderness. But she held her tongue with an effort and followed him back into the clearing.

Chapter 19
WALKING AWAY

Madrazi had been persistent, but Shem, adamant. In spite of her best attempts after returning from the forest, Shem had insisted that she leave the next morning with Japheth. Preoccupied with the task ahead, he had been short and impatient and would listen to none of her arguments. She had been left alone all night and was in a foul mood by morning. She felt angry and abandoned. Resentment at his rejection and fear for his safety created an uncomfortable conflict within. He would be walking into danger, and she was being forced to run away.

Now she sat at table, picking at her food and feeding her temper. In marked contrast, Japheth, a grin adorning his face even at the early hour, sat and ate a healthy meal and ignored her mood. "Good morning, sister," he had said upon arriving, with a voice that matched his smile. "Are you ready for an unforgettable day of my company?"

Madrazi had muttered a 'good morning' and said nothing more. Japheth ignored her, enjoyed a large breakfast, and finally pushed back and looked across to her. "Shem has already left, sister," he said gently. "If you have a surfeit of anger, why don't you send it out after him and not let it spoil our day. If you hurl it hard enough, perhaps it will catch him, though he moves quickly when he has reason."

Madrazi wanted to snap a sharp reply to him, but underneath his jesting, he spoke truth. There was truly no call for her to inflict her ire on him if Shem was its cause. "But I wanted to go with him," she said instead, trying to explain. "I would stand with him, but he will not allow it."

Japheth laughed out loud, "Well, I for one am grateful for his common sense. Just think! If he had let you go, then I might have been forced along, too, and I have no desire to hunt anything that can also hunt me! You are my best excuse to avoid a long, tiresome, and dangerous day or two in the middle of the woods. We would probably have to sleep there, too, probably on rocky ground with my luck! No, sister. It is better that you stay here and provide me an opportunity to miss this adventure."

"Are you afraid?" she retorted, instantly regretting her words.

But Japheth just laughed. "Of course! Shem is the one with all the courage. I inherited all of the wit and intelligence. I am smart enough to be afraid of something that can kill me much easier than I can kill it. Shem on the other hand, has the heart of the lion, but the mind of one, too. So he goes out with nothing but a bow to slay a monster that any reasonable man would leave alone."

Then more seriously he added, "Don't worry about Shem! He is more at home in the forest than any beast and has no rival with the bow. These animals attacked our servants at the gold mine. We hired a hunter, but he only got more men killed before managing to slay just one of the beasts. Shem took over, killed the other three, and I was the only person hurt."

"What happened?" Madrazi asked, curiosity overcoming her anger.

With a quick, but exaggerated look around to ensure that no one was within earshot, he put on a serious face and confided, "It was bad!" Then shaking his head with a hint of a grin, he continued, "My knees were bruised from knocking together!" They both laughed at that, and it broke the tension. Madrazi decided that she could not remain angry in the face of her brother's relentless, good-natured jesting.

"Very well, brother," she said in a determined and more cheerful voice, "we will let the hunters hunt, and we will enjoy the beauty of the trees and your keen wit as we return to a refuge of comfort, good food, and good company."

But in spite of her speech, she could not help but think that each step they took would place her farther from her husband, who was courting deadly peril.

Japheth laughed again, seeing that he had won. "I knew that a sensible woman like you would see things my way. Enjoy your breakfast and we'll be off in a few minutes." And then, as if perceiving her mind, he added, "Do not worry yourself about Shem. There is nothing in the forest that he cannot master."

"You already told me that."

"You are still anxious."

The climb up the ridge was steep, but once they topped the summit and started down, Madrazi felt the oppressive darkness of the ark lift and began to enjoy the sunlight, the trees, the birds, and the good company of Japheth. He was unlike Shem in almost every way. Where Shem was reserved and serious, his brother was incessantly talking in his light-hearted fashion. Even in the forest they differed. Japheth strode down the middle of the path unconcerned about the noise he made.

But it was a change that suited Madrazi. Also, she had not yet had an opportunity to talk to either Ham or Japheth about the prophecy and the ark, and she wished to know their minds and why they followed their father. She did not understand her own husband completely, but it was clear that his heart was as fully committed to the prophecy as his father's.

Since Japheth had been tasked with providing food and water for the ark, Madrazi began to question him about his work.

"What will we eat on the ark?" she asked, lightly.

"We will feast each day on only the best dainties. You will only have to cook and carry the platters to my place, and of course, bow down as you serve me."

Madrazi tried not to smile, but failed. "I am serious, Japheth! If we are imprisoned on that boat for a long time, how will we keep enough food unspoiled? I suppose that if we are on the water, we could contrive to eat fish, but the taste of fish grows old quickly. My father has told me that water begins to grow unpleasant after a few months in a cask, and that bread goes bad, too. Only meat preserved in brine seems to keep for any length of time."

"I will personally assure you that fish will not be necessary," returned Japheth, snorting as if offended. "I have worked for many years to discover which foods can be preserved, how to do so, and how long they will keep. Fruits and vegetables can be dried and then kept for a long time, too. Others have been doing this for many years; I had only to ask to learn how. Apples, raisins, dates, apricots, and peaches are among my favorites. The juice of lemons and limes can be collected and stored in casks for some time. Potatoes, onions, gourds, and yams all do very well as long as they are stored properly. We store them at home for more than a year with ease. And meat is not the only thing that can be preserved in brine; cabbages, cucumbers, and other vegetables can be pickled and will then last. Even eggs can be preserved in that fashion. When brine is not attractive, honey is a good alternative. My favorite berries can be kept indefinitely in honey."

Madrazi had never heard of honey being used as a preservative. But he just grinned and said, "You might be surprised at my knowledge, sister." He waved his hand airily. "You might be even more surprised that it comes to me so easily."

She laughed out loud as he kept talking, "The cows and goats will be kept on the upper deck with us so that we can more easily enjoy their milk. If they give well, we can have butter and cheese, too. We can dry enough meat for the animals that need it. We could easily dry and jerk enough for several years. If not, many of those animals can live on grains for a period of time."

"What about the people? Will we have enough?"

Japheth grinned. "You think that I would allow your husband to go hungry? Shem is rarely short-tempered, but withhold food for a day or two and he becomes a different man. I could not subject you to that! I have planned for over one hundred people to eat well for two years. I don't think that we will be stuck aboard for that long, and I expect that we will have plenty. Think of all the food that we take to Lamech. We grow much more than we need, and I have always had plenty for my work. There will be no shortage."

Madrazi remembered something Noah had said and asked, "But if the face of the earth is to be destroyed, then there will be no food on the new earth when we leave the ark, maybe for several years."

"That is why a section of the upper deck will house seeds and cuttings of everything from grapes to grain. We will be able to plant and harvest in the new world as soon as the waters recede. Even if it takes time to bring in a good crop, we will have enough food to last three years at need, and that does not account for what we can get from the land. The animals will be set loose on a destroyed world, not a barren one. Many animals and people eat seaweed. If the sea covers the land and then recedes, does it not appear to you that seaweed and various fish will be left behind? The purpose of the judgment is to destroy life; many animals that we will release will be able to scavenge the bodies of their dead comrades."

She had to admit that Japheth's explanation was sensible. Her family had made various kinds of seaweed a part of their diet for many years. "What else will the animals eat on the ark?" she asked. "They cannot go without food and water for two years."

"Water is easy," replied Japheth with a shrug. "Ham has built compartments into the lower deck of the ark that will hold nearly two hundred thousands baths of water, probably more than we will need. He has fashioned central supply tanks into the roof of each deck that this water can be pumped into, using the strength of oxen or donkeys. From there, its own weight will carry it to the troughs for the animals, saving much work. We have also built almost five hundred strong casks, each holding ten baths of water, for our own use. These will be stored near our quarters on the upper deck. We will pump water from the stream to complete our supply shortly before the day arrives. It should last long enough. We may have to strain out the living things that grow in water after a time, or even boil it over the stove, but it will be fit to drink."

"But what will you feed all of them?" she persisted. "Shem told me that there will be more than fifteen thousands of animals on the ark."

"Most animals can eat grasses and grains."

"But how can you fit that much hay and grain aboard?"

"It is not as hard as you think," said Japheth, with a touch of irritation at her interruptions. "Noah and Shem have discovered that many animals accept substitute foods into their normal diets for short periods of time without distress. They adapt to new situations more readily than many believe. Even so, grain does not take up much room, and hay can be compressed. I have learned to make wafers of compressed hay that are much smaller than bales of the same amount."

"Horses, cows, and many other wild animals with similar eating habits can subsist on diet of mostly grains like oats and bran, not hay. For a time, they even do well with beets and citrus pulp and a small amount of hay. This is not their typical fare, but they need only survive on these for a short time. Even if we took nothing but hay to feed all of the animals, it would only require a fifth of the total space in the ark. Replacing the hay with grains and other substitutes shrinks that need almost in half. There will be plenty of room for all your clothes, sister!"

Japheth could not stay serious for more than a few minutes at a time, and seemed to enjoy teasing her—probably because she returned it so easily.

"As for our other passengers, Father has discovered that those creatures that eat fruit will do as well with fruit juice. We can store these as concentrates or preserve fruit as jams or jellies. As long as they are sealed, they will keep many months. Hummingbirds will feed on sugar water instead of nectar; like many animals they have amazed us with how easily they can change their diet. We have some monkeys now that eat only fruit in the wild, but will eat grain mixed with a little fruit in captivity."

"Are you going to try to feed hay or grain to the giant lizards, or lions, or bears?" she asked, with more than a little sarcasm.

"There is no need. There are many sources of meat for those creatures. We are bringing dried meats for the animals. When mixed with water, it will be palatable for most of the captive animals. Those that won't eat meat preserved in salt can eat meat preserved in honey. If none of that suffices, then they can have fresh tortoise meat; we will take live tortoises on the ark. They don't take up much room, and won't run away!"

They both laughed, and Japheth continued his tutoring. "If we are not able to catch fish from the ark, we are bringing our own supply of fresh fish for the fish eaters. We have found a kind of fish that burrows into the mud of riverbanks and lakes. When the water retreats, the mud dries but the fish sleep in their little mud balls until the water returns. If we dig them up and store them dry, they will revive in water as much as two years later, giving us fresh fish."

"What will you feed the birds," Madrazi asked, now curious to explore the man's knowledge. He took life so easily that it was hard to believe he knew so much about anything. She was discovering facets of his life she had not expected.

His knowledge continued to roll easily from his tongue. "Some sea birds, like penguins, albatrosses, petrels, boobies, auks, gulls, and terns survive on the open ocean, and we have no need to accommodate them on the ark. However, we will have to make room for others that live primarily on land, and those that live near the water, but need refuge, such as loons, grebes, and pelicans. Many of these will eat fish, but they often eat whatever they can. Many birds and lizards enjoy crickets, and thousands can be kept in very small cages. They multiply rapidly, and will keep our passengers fat. Other birds eat insects, as do many bats, and Ham has derived an ingenious way of feeding them."

"I'm surprised that you would give him the credit," she teased.

"Well," he said slyly, "if I thought that I could fool you, I probably would not even mention his name, but once you hear how this device works, you will not fail to see his hand. We will build several enclosed grain silos on the middle deck near the cages of birds and bats. They will be filled with grains contaminated with insect eggs. From the silos we will build wooden pipes that run through these cages. In each cage are several holes in the pipe." He paused to make sure she was following his explanation and continued when she nodded.

"When we want to feed the insect eaters, all that is needed is to pump a bellows into the silos, and blow air through the pipes. The insects are forced into the pipes with the air and escape through the holes into the cages. The birds and bats get to catch them as they pop up through the holes. Not only do they get their meal, but they get the fun of catching it, too!"

"Won't the slow birds get hungry?" Madrazi asked, innocently.

"No," he replied laughing, "they'll get faster."

Japheth had the best of her once again. Since they were walking through a meadow, she stopped, stooped, and plucked a flower and handed it to him with a flourish. "The prize for the victor," she said. He accepted it with a bow, but then held it back out. "Beauty always triumphs over wit," he said.

They walked along and Madrazi continued to listen to Japheth. He was good company. She valued his companionship and he provided it easily. He was incapable of being depressed or sad, and his joy was contagious and lifted her spirits. She was able to put away her frustration with Shem and simply enjoy the day. She also found a new respect for his knowledge and skill. Best of all, she was adding to her store of knowledge about the household to which she was now bound.

"Japheth," she asked after some time had passed, "why do you devote your life to this work? Do you ever wonder about the prophecy?"

He sensed the depth of feeling behind the question and for once looked serious and thoughtful. Finally he spoke. "There are three reasons that drive me along this path with Noah. The first is simple. I am his son and his blood. To not help Noah achieve that which he has set out to do would be a blood betrayal that I cannot contemplate. The second is also simple. I love my father as a man, and even if I was not his son, I would follow him. There is a special power in Noah that few fully perceive but which cannot be denied. He has a greatness about him and a great task has been laid out before him. It is my honor to be able to join in his work and share a small part of that destiny." Madrazi nodded. She could readily sympathize with those reasons. She had always stood by Pomorolac when others thought him insane to chance the wide oceans.

Japheth paused for a moment and then continued. "Finally, I believe the words of the Creator are true. I have not the ability to understand His ways like Methuselah, nor do I have the power to talk with him like Noah, but I know that He is present, and I know that His love and mercy are a part of my own life. It is hard for me to explain. I do not carry the sense of His presence that Shem does, and often I blunder through life without regard for His will. But I blunder in the right direction, and I know that I will see more clearly on the day that I join the fathers. It is enough. I am a simple man, and my faith is simple, too." He paused for a moment and shrugged, "It suffices for me."

Madrazi had no response. His reasons were sensible and she understood how strong the bond of blood could be. Through Shem, she was now bound to Noah, too, but Japheth's simple faith was not enough to overcome the conflict in her own life. She needed something else, but had no idea how to obtain it. She was trapped in a venture doomed to failure, but could not walk away. Aside from her vows of marriage, like Japheth, she sensed the greatness in Noah. He was a man to follow and believe. What was missing?

As she wrestled through the complexities of her dilemma, it struck her that there was one difference between her and her new family. In all honesty, she had to admit that she did not possess the same faith in the Creator that Japheth, Shem, and Noah had all expressed. She would not deceive herself. Was that deficiency the source of her problems? If so, it was even more frustrating—she could not force herself to have it, and did not know where to look.

These thoughts led to another idea that chilled her soul. Was this belief in the Creator the real wall between her and Shem? Would she only possess a part of him, because the rest belonged to the Creator, and to the very prophecy that threatened her future? She shuddered. If so, it was a wall she had no strength to breach or wisdom to circumvent. How could she ever achieve happiness with Shem if she was always denied the essence of his soul? The thought shook her to her core, and in a panic she wondered if Shem had already seen the same thing and decided against a relationship of love and intimacy, and was willing to settle for one in which he would merely tolerate the one who would bear his children.

Japheth saw the look on her face and mistook it for something else. He sighed and said, "Did I not tell you already that Shem would be fine. You will see. He will be home in a few short days, and then you will be happy again."

"Yes," she agreed mechanically. "He will be home in a few days." But she wondered if she could ever again be happy in her marriage. She walked on, the taste of ashes in her mouth.

****

She awoke disoriented. The fire was low and the lamps out. Wind carried the chill of the heights into the valley and its cold seeped through the tightest doors and windows at night. She pulled the quilt closer and let its warmth settle over her skin. It became harder to keep her body warm, but the fire that lit her heart remained constant, only mellowing with time. It struck her that those who wanted love most desperately seldom found it. Its secret was so contrary to men's wisdom that it eluded many. It still shamed her that it had taken so long to understand—many wasted years.

She sighed and saw the young woman asleep in her chair, her sewing draped over her lap. She was gifted with the needle, making patterns and pictures on cloth that caught the eyes of the few who saw them. She was a misfit— not belonging to the new south or the old north. She had searched for truth and found banishment. Then, as an outcast, she had found the truth she sought, at the price of discovering another kind of alienation—the old ones were so strange, and her short years were insufficient to comprehend them. But she was loyal, accepting life as it came, willing to serve, and asking little in return. After all, they had given her a life and a home. Over the past two years, she had sat and stitched pictures on cloth as the old woman created a tapestry of words.

She sighed again. She had always loved the embroidery of colorful thread on smooth cloth. There had been a robe...

Chapter 20

UPHILL BATTLE

Green, red, and golden silk thread had been embroidered together into an intricate pattern of flowers around the collar of the robe. The pattern continued down past the silver clasps and along the front on both sides before circling the hem. Sunlight seemed to emanate from the golden centers of the bright red flowers and light the interior of the shop. Pulling the robe about her, Madrazi let her mind wander back to that day, ten years before, when she had plucked flowers in a sunlit glade of the forest as she and Japheth talked their way home following her first visit to the ark.

How slow the days, but quick the years! She had forgotten her anger and forgiven Shem in her relief at his return after killing the great lizard, but the incident had created or revealed a barrier between them that she had never been able to surmount. They would fumble towards each other as if in a dark room, but never quite touch. So she had settled for something less than the ideal of her dreams and had soldiered on as best she could.

Shem had tried: even after that first fight, he had brought home one of the lizard's teeth. At first, she had not thought it very attractive, but Shem had carefully dried it in the sun, coated it with a light pitch, and wrapped it in an eye-catching pattern of gold wire. On a gold chain, it made a unique piece of jewelry and one that allowed her to brag about its origin, and as she forgot her anger, she came to enjoy it. She was wearing it today. The pale yellow tinge of the tooth and the bright gold of the necklace were set off quite well by the robe.

The years had passed as a blur of conflicting emotions. Love for her husband had deepened with time, but it was diluted or tainted by her cynicism and disbelief in Noah and by her own secret plans for an alternate future. She had also grown distant from the family. In the first few years, there had been a degree of companionship with Debseda, for Madrazi suspected that Ham's wife harbored her own doubts. Admiration for Ham had helped, for Debseda was fond of flattery, whether of herself or her husband. But as Madrazi came to know her better, she found a taste of Peniah's spirit in her sister-in-law, and she retreated from that friendship. Yaran and Wen-Tehrom enjoyed such a close relationship that Madrazi felt that she would be intruding in trying to draw near to either. At least the time of waiting was now half complete and she had managed to remain a dutiful wife.

Ever since that day with Japheth, she remained convinced that the Creator was somehow at the root of her unhappiness. Her childhood frustration with Methuselah's religious narrowness was magnified by that of the entire house. She would never claim something that she did not possess, and she did not possess their enthusiasm for god. She did her best to observe the traditions and rituals of the family for the sake of harmony, but such efforts left her with a vague discomfort. Fear of the ark had its place, too. She had seldom returned to the clearing during those years, but the initial fear engendered by the dark vessel seemed able to reach across the forest and find her wherever she was. All would be well and then some woodwork in the house, some remark from one of the others, or the sight of caged animals would bring it all back.

So for ten years she had lived two lives: an outward union with the family that masked an inward hardening to Noah's prophecy and her equally rigid plans for a future that would leave the ark a useless monument rotting in the depths of the forest. That secret barrier limited the depth of unity between Madrazi and Shem and time alone would never remove it. Only the removal of the ark and the prophecy would allow that, and she feared that such a small spark of love as she often felt could not survive that long without being fed or renewed.

One of the few bright areas of her life appeared during her second year in Noah's house. Desiring to see Jeriah, she volunteered to assume responsibility for carrying food to town. It allowed her to be useful, kept her far away from the hated ark, and gave her time in town where the strains of family life eased. Permission had been readily granted: it was not a popular task, and so for the past eight years she had made the regular trek at the head of a line of mules to Lamech's storehouse. From there, the elder supervised the selling of one part and the distribution of the rest to the poor of the town and surrounding countryside.

Initially, the greatest obstacle to the undertaking was her fear of Lamech. He was aloof, a man of great power that seemed to emanate from his very being. All who encountered him felt it and responded with either respect or fear. Madrazi had been uncomfortable in his limited presence at Noah's house: she had the uncomfortable feeling that he could read her thoughts, and avoided him lest he discern her heart. But the desire to see Jeriah conquered any anxiety at dealing with him, and so she made her first trek at the head of a train of provisions.

The afternoon held several surprises for both Madrazi and Lamech. Madrazi never took any responsibility lightly and so had assumed that her help would extend beyond simply walking to town while skilled servants guided the mules along the road. It was late and she was tired, but when Lamech told her that he was taking food to a widow who lived outside the walls, she turned immediately to help prepare the packs. She did not see Lamech's slow smile, and it had disappeared before she turned back to him. Within a few minutes they had packed a mule with grain, oil, dried fruits, and fresh vegetables, and set off together.

He led Madrazi down quiet side streets to a small gate in the east wall. Lamech led the mule down a winding path, while Madrazi walked behind. The path led around the city to the north, towards the sea. Soon they arrived at a windblown hollow facing away from the town. Below was a small clay and thatch home. Following an overgrown path, Madrazi saw a few goats browsing the coarse vegetation, while small children in ragged clothes kept them away from the few rows of the small garden scratched into the rocky soil. As they emerged into the clearing before the hovel, a woman came out of the house and waved a greeting.

Lamech led the mule down to the front of the house. As the children ran to greet them, Madrazi was shocked to see him not wave them away, but bend down and pick up the younger ones. He held each of them up over his head for a brief time, greeting them by name. He seemed uncaring of the dirt that found its way from their unwashed bodies onto his fine robes and his voice was completely different from the one used with the townsfolk. The woman bowed low before him. "Welcome, great elder!" she said. "We are all grateful to see you on this day. But who is this that comes with you?"

Madrazi came hesitantly forward and Lamech introduced her. "This is Madrazi, wife of my grandson, Shem. It is she who brought the food into town today and she insisted on coming to meet you and your children." He paused, and before turning to the mule said, "The peace of God be upon you and your house, Hazira."

Then he untied the ropes and lifted the heaviest of the bundles off of the mule. Madrazi lifted a smaller bag of grain off of the mule and followed behind. They entered a dim room, with simple bare wooden furnishings on a bare dirt floor and Madrazi wondered how people could live in such surroundings. Unsure of herself, she set down the grain beside the bundle Lamech had carried in. She was uncomfortable amid such squalor, but felt a strange sense of fulfillment. The children were as shy with Madrazi as she was with them, but they were quite comfortable around Lamech. After talking a moment to each one, Lamech walked back to unload the remainder of the food with the children trailing behind him. Madrazi turned to follow them when the widow came to her and clutched her arm. Her eyes glistened with tears. "Thank you," she said. "You are a great lady, and yet you come to us with kindness and bring life for my children."

Madrazi was curious. "Does Lamech come here often?"

"Oh yes," replied Hazira, drying the tears from her cheek. "Ever since my husband died three years ago. We would have all died long ago if it were not for his kindness. He is a great lord in the city, but he is like an angel of the Creator to us. Even now, I find it hard to believe that he is so gentle with the children; the other men of the city would not want to be touched by them, yet he embraces each one and calls them by name. Often he brings gifts for them, and he is the only joy that they know."

Madrazi had been raised with the belief that poverty was the result of laziness, but as she looked around, it was evident that this woman worked hard to keep her house, raise some food, and care for her children. Madrazi was ashamed of her careless opinion and her heart softened to think that she could help this family. In addition, she felt a sense of accomplishment not experienced for many years and a resulting determination to continue this work with Lamech as long as she could. Before they left, she had learned the names of each of the children and had coaxed a few words from the oldest girl.

Preoccupied with the needs of the family, Madrazi did not notice Lamech's smile of approval as they led the mule back up the path to town. After some minutes, she ventured to ask, "How many families do you feed?"

"What you brought today will feed a dozen widows and their children for a month or more. I had to come to this home tonight because they have had nothing but goat's milk for three days."

"Thank you for allowing my help," she said, gathering her courage. "May I continue? I never realized..." she stopped at a loss for words and hung her head, thinking of many uncaring years behind her.

"I understand," returned Lamech gently. "I have found that in giving to others, I am always rewarded in full. And if an elder of the city cannot help the helpless, then what good is the responsibility of the office?"

Madrazi had always thought of the council as exercising power and making decisions of law and commerce, not helping the poor. Evidently Lamech had a different view and her surprise was augmented because he was not just an elder of the council, but clearly esteemed above the others in the eyes of most people. Madrazi felt that he had opened a door for her to a place that few were privileged to see, and in that understanding she forever discarded her fear of him.

As the years went by, Madrazi found satisfaction helping Lamech bring food to people who otherwise would have starved. Her respect for him grew as did his for her. Her efficiency and skill were applied with energy and she took much of the burden from him. After a time, she marveled that she had ever thought him distant and cold. She could not talk to him as she could to Jeriah, but their friendship did not require many words. His compassion extended beyond food; he gave respect and affection to those who received it from no other person. Helping the helpless became an escape from her problems at home.

Jeriah was another haven. It became Madrazi's habit to stay in town for several days whenever she brought food. Jeriah would willingly lay aside her own work to spend those hours with her friend. The years only confirmed what both had felt for each other on that first day, and their friendship grew richer and fuller as the years rolled by. They became closer than sisters and Madrazi fancied that Jeriah was the mirror image of her own heart. Thankfully, none of the family opposed the time they spent together; indeed, much later Madrazi realized that Shem had been relieved that she had found a source of happiness while he was engrossed in his father's business.

Now Jeriah held the shimmering robe to her own shoulders and spun around. Skilled hands had continued the patterns of flowers across the back in a pleasing design. Madrazi accepted it back from her and held it around her body again, enjoying the soft caress of the linen lining on her neck. Jeriah stood by and laughed. "That is the first smile I have seen on your face all day. If you do not, then I will buy this just to keep the smile."

It was hard not to be in a sunny mood around Jeriah. Madrazi realized that the day was beautiful, the robe was flattering, and she had three more days in town with her best friend. The merchant stood by silently beaming. He knew that any words of his would only lessen the chances of a sale. But the women were not novices to business. Keeping her eyes away from him, Madrazi turned to Jeriah and frowned. "Well," she admitted, "it is a nice robe, but it seems richly priced for such a coarse weave. Where are the gold fasteners? I would like to encourage commerce in Lamech, but would not my family's reputation be diminished if I made such foolish choices in my buying?" Madrazi hoped that the look on her face was sufficiently innocent.

Jeriah understood immediately, a look of concern crossing her face. "You are right, Madrazi! You must not diminish the respect of our leading elders.

What would people think if they thought that Noah could not select a prudent wife for his son? And how could Pomorolac ever trade in this region if it was known that his own daughter paid dearly for ordinary merchandise?"

The shopkeeper could not hide his alarm or his silence. "Please, please," he said soothingly, "do not speak such words. This is one of the finest cloaks to be found in Lamech. Perhaps I was mistaken in the price that was mentioned before. Did I say eleven? Forgive me, I meant nine."

Madrazi ignored him and kept her eyes on Jeriah. "Oh," she managed a tinge of unbelief in her voice. "I thought that he had said seven."

"I was certain that he did!" returned Jeriah seriously, "Perhaps the poor man has trouble in his speech. Do you think that it might be some kind of sickness? Perhaps we should leave this place. I do not want to buy clothes in a shop ridden with disease!"

The merchant wanted to react in anger, but the innocent expressions and sincere tones worried him. It would be best to inflict them on another shop, and quickly, but he must not allow the daughter of Noah or niece of Dajus to spread rumors about his. "Of course I said seven," he spoke, forcing cheer into his voice. "But only because this robe deserves to be worn by one of such beauty."

"Very well," Madrazi said with a vapid smile, "I cannot resist your kindness." She handed him seven silver coins and he bowed as they walked through the door. Once outside and safely down the street, they broke into laughter.

Jeriah's cheer was contagious. "First a smile, and now a laugh. Stay with me a few more days, and I will have you back into a proper mood."

"Am I really that bad," Madrazi asked, but she knew the answer already, and Jeriah was a good enough friend to say nothing. Madrazi hated to admit, even to herself, that she had put herself to a task that overreached her strength, but the months passed slowly beneath the edge of the forest, and the next ten years lay before her like an endless road. She had hoped that her conflict would subside as the years rolled by and her life grew easier, but it was ever present and the thought of living a lie lay like a festering sore upon her conscience.

But at least today she could put these things aside. "Come, Jeriah, I have made arrangements for our meal today in the courtyard of Lamech." They were walking up the path to the front door when Lamech emerged and approached them. The two women bowed to him, and he broke into one of his rare smiles.

"Welcome to our home, daughter of Eldad! You honor us with your presence."

Jeriah returned his smile. "The honor is mine, elder," she replied correctly. "Many thanks for your gracious invitation."

Instead of walking on past, he paused with a twinkle in his dark eyes for Jeriah. "I have heard it said that Jared called upon Eldad. I wonder what his errand entailed? Surely Eldad is too old to fight in the army." A warm smile was on his face, in contrast to the shocked look on Jeriah's face. Madrazi suddenly understood, and laughed aloud, and Jeriah's face colored and speech deserted her. It was not often that she lost her composure, and Madrazi smiled again at that.

When Lamech saw her embarrassment, he added gently, "May happiness attend your ways, daughter. Jared is a worthy man, and I hope that the Creator's blessing will attend you both."

He drew away, and Madrazi turned on her friend. Before she could speak, Jeriah interrupted, "Please, I was going to tell you at our meal when we were alone."

Madrazi hugged her immediately. "I am so happy for you, my sister. You deserve every bit of joy that he can give you. I hope that you find it in his love."

As the women embraced on the street, tears of happiness mirrored in their eyes. Once alone with their food, Madrazi demanded the entire story and they spent the afternoon sharing the excitement and anticipation of the coming marriage. They were still in Lamech's house as the sun began to sink behind the city walls, so Madrazi sent a servant to inform Eldad that Jeriah would stay with her that night, and the women ate and continued to plan the wedding and Jeriah's new life.

It was late and they had talked of so much that both were tired, yet still their emotions ran high. Suddenly Jeriah asked a question that, upon reflection was reasonable enough, but which caught Madrazi totally unawares. "How is it that you can be so happy in my marriage to Jared, when you have found sadness in your own?"

She immediately regretted her words, and cried out, "Forgive me, my friend! I should not have spoken!" But her shrewd question had exposed the raw center of Madrazi's heart and she felt her carefully constructed walls crumble away. All of the misery of the past years burst out uncontrolled, and Madrazi wept freely for many minutes. Jeriah tried to comfort her, weeping, too, in distress and sympathy.

After some time, they pulled apart, and Madrazi found her voice. "Do not regret your words, sister, for perhaps your ear is what I have needed for some time. I will open my heart to you, but I must ask that my words remain for you alone."

"In that, too, I will prove your friend," Jeriah replied simply.

Madrazi hesitated, but the thought of bearing another ten years alone, loosened her tongue. "You perceive well that my heart is divided. For, in truth, I love Shem, and would be all to him that a wife should be. In some ways I have succeeded, but in others, not. There is a thing that comes between us like a black darkness, and though I fight, I do not easily endure it."

"Do you remember when we first met? You told me much about this city and its history. Do you remember the events more than a century ago that led to discontent with Noah and his moving his family to the Great Forest? Of Noah's prophecy and the trouble it caused?"

Jeriah paused, thinking. "Well, all that was before my time, but I have heard the story many times. His tale spread some consternation, for many laughed until they saw that he was in earnest and then they became angered at the accusations of evil. Lamech has always been one of the most upright and pure of the cities of the earth, and the leading men heard insults in his prophecy. But he has served well since, and most have forgotten his words. Those who remember laugh it away as an old joke."

"No one in Noah's household laughs," replied Madrazi seriously. "They all believe it to this day, and insist that its fulfillment is but ten short years away. Noah told me his story right after my wedding to Shem, and I weighed his words with care, for I still hold him in the highest respect."

"As is proper for a daughter to such a man," added Jeriah.

"No!" Madrazi disagreed vehemently. "My heart is my own. I give him this even though I cannot accept the message of his prophecy."

"And such is the division of your heart," mused Jeriah.

"Yes," Madrazi admitted, "The prophecy is at the root of my bitterness. I live a lie. I determined that I could not accept the truth of what he told me, but I found that I belonged to the son of the prophet, and a son who is committed to his father's vision. I want a future with Shem, and so I wait for the years to pass."

"What will the future hold when the appointed time comes, and nothing happens?"

"I fear that it will break Noah and Wen-Tehrom, and that their remaining years will be short and full of regret. Ham is like Lamech; he is strong in mind and body, and he will find himself in spite of his disappointment. I cannot tell about Japheth, but I fear for Shem, that his heart will be crushed for the sake of his father if not for his own, for he believes the prophecy implicitly."

Madrazi sighed and went on. "In the days after I heard Noah's tale, I spent several days alone and finally resolved for the sake of my oath, if not my love, to be a wife to Shem for those twenty years: to live a lie and to be there for the dark days. I resolved to be at his side to direct him away from despair and then into a future that would emerge back into the sunlight. But my strength is not limitless, and the years weigh me down with cares. I cannot live with a divided heart!"

Jeriah said nothing, but her eyes spoke her sympathy, and Madrazi was encouraged to continue. "There are nights when I lie awake and wonder what would happen if the prophecy were true. Noah is a righteous man. If the Creator were to speak to anyone, then Noah would hear." She hesitated, and then looked down and spoke softly, "And I am haunted by my own past."

Jeriah sensed that the root of her fear and unhappiness was finally being exposed. She leaned closer to Madrazi and said, "You can tell me. I am your friend."

"I know," Madrazi forced a crooked smile, "but it is still hard." She took a deep breath and forced the words to come.

"In the days following Great-grandfather's visit to my home many years ago, I was overwhelmed by a vision of fear that has stayed with me ever since. It killed my mother, and pursues me always; I am sure that it will be my death."

Madrazi paused again, regaining a measure of control. Keeping her voice and face steady, she related in a few minutes the details of her nightmare and its terror. Before she had finished, sweat had beaded on her brow and her hands were shaking. Jeriah sat in rapt fascination and listened. She felt as if she were experiencing the dark wave herself, so vivid was Madrazi's description.

"And so, my dearest friend," Madrazi concluded, "I am haunted by the possibility that this dream is a vision of the future in which I will be destroyed by the prophecy of Noah. Against my doubt in the prophecy, I cannot escape the similarity between this dream, which I have never related to Noah or Shem, and the words that the Creator gave to Noah."

"But even if that were so," interrupted Jeriah, "would not you go into the ark with Shem and your family and so escape the destruction?"

"I don't know. Perhaps my doubts will ultimately prevent me from entering the ark. Perhaps circumstances will prevent me being there at the right time. If god has determined the day and manner of my death, who am I to resist it?"

"Perhaps you are seeing the doom of another."

Madrazi paled, "No! I could not wish this doom on anyone else. I would rather be destroyed than carry the guilt of hanging this evil upon another."

"Then maybe the dream is only a possibility," mused Jeriah, "a warning to heed the words of Noah and commit yourself to his work. I do not wish that to be true, for it would mean that I would see you less and that we would be ultimately separated by this flood."

"Not if you came with me," Madrazi blurted out.

Jeriah sighed. "Even if I believed the words of Noah, I do not see why Noah should want me to come."

Madrazi interrupted. "Noah is a generous man. If we asked him, you could come. He tried to warn all the people of Lamech many years ago, but was rejected. He bears the city no ill will. Indeed, if other arks were built to save the entire city he would rejoice."

"I can see that you love your father and husband," said Jeriah, "but I too have a duty to mine. Have you not heard of Jared's conflict with Noah? Of Noah's rebuke in the public assembly years ago? Jared does not forgive easily, and his pride would never allow him to approach Noah even if he knew the words to be true."

Jeriah thought for several minutes and then smiled, "You have shown me more of your heart than you think. If you will listen to the advice of a friend, then I think that you must keep doing as you have begun. It is the only practical answer to your problem. It is only for a few more years. When the prophecy fails, Shem will seek a new life—perhaps here in town. If you love him and commit yourself to his work now, then your life together then will be rich in love for many years. It may take time for him to overcome the disappointment of his wasted years, but you can help him through those sorrows. I know that your heart is divided, but there is no lie, there is only love for your husband. And you will have my friendship always when the days appear dark. My marriage will not change that. I will always be here for you."

Madrazi bowed her head, grateful for the love that Jeriah offered. There was wisdom in her words and she felt new strength to continue her battle. Emotion had muddled her thinking. She would never give up on the future again. What if the years were long? She had a friend here—one with whom she could share all of her heart. She had only a few more years to struggle and the promise of centuries of happiness together with Shem beckoned.

Chapter 21

INFILTRATOR

Pashtur slipped through the trees, careful to make no sound. The fading light of day brought deep shadows to the forest, and as darkness swept over the woods, a silent tension seemed to emanate from the very trees themselves. He glanced around and wondered if the tales of his childhood about living trees could be true. The forest held danger, even for those well prepared. Other than the eldest son of Noah, Pashtur had never met anyone who was truly comfortable within the depths of the trees. But Pashtur was at least skilled at moving silently and unseen and he crept on, parallel to the men on the road.

He was not afraid of being seen under the shadows of the forest, but sound traveled far and the men he followed would recognize a manmade sound for what it was. He wondered once again if he was being foolish, but there was something unusual in any group of men starting the trek to Lamech this late in the day, and this was a suspicious group to begin with. Besides, he did not like their ringleader—a new man named Balech. So as they walked along the road, he shadowed them and tried to catch as much of their speech as he could.

Balech had joined the work crew six months ago, at once establishing himself as someone to be reckoned with. He was strong and able when he felt like working and he had a commanding air that attracted weaker men. He had served in the army, so he said, and he told many convincing stories of death and destruction, although it was difficult to believe that he had personally killed as many as he claimed. He was frank about his motivations; he would work for a few years here to enrich himself and then return to the army when the prospect of a suitable battle presented itself.

His brash words, disrespect for authority, and tales of women and wine attracted some of the weaker men. Others came into his circle by the instinctive recognition of another troublemaker. Balech avoided any trouble with Noah's sons, but reverted to his true self as soon as they were absent. His men formed a close group and there were rumors that they smuggled strong drink into the forest and maintained a cache in some small clearing. Pashtur did not doubt it; some of the group were always absent, although they all hid their drinking well.

To their credit, most of the men did not like Balech. They thought him an arrogant braggart, but after his first two fights, men left him alone, for he injured his opponents when it could have been avoided. When some of the men warned him that Meshur would put him in his place, Balech replied that his skills would overcome whatever small advantage of strength that Meshur possessed. "I have dealt with many enemies more dangerous that that ox," he laughed. "But he is Ham's favorite, and I need the wages for a few more months. Perhaps when I am ready to leave, I will give everyone a free demonstration of my talents."

Pashtur's dislike of the man was fanned to hatred at those words. He eagerly reported them to Meshur, hoping that his cousin would beat Balech senseless and drive him away in shame. But Meshur had just shrugged. He had grown in many ways in the years with Ham, and had become more and more consumed with the task. "Let the braggart talk," he said to Pashtur. "As long as he does his work and does not interfere with others, I do not care about his words."

Pashtur could not be satisfied. There was something about Balech that raised his fear and suspicion and he made it his business to spy upon him and his circle of friends. Meshur was too busy to see how Balech was disrupting the workers. The man was always too careful to be caught in any overt action, but he actively subverted those that he could when the opportunity presented itself.

Pashtur felt that he was the only one that saw Balech orchestrating an ever-increasing chorus of complaints among the men. Such talk distracted at best and slowed progress. It certainly kept Noah's sons busy mediating conflicts, soothing outbursts of anger, and overcoming the inefficiencies that only seemed to increase by the week. To learn more, he had begun to hang on the fringes of Balech's group; never really accepted, but perhaps a likely recruit. But his well-known relationship with Meshur kept the little man from every becoming a part of Balech's party.

So Pashtur found himself slinking through the verge of the forest, fighting to keep pace with Balech and his men on the road. Deathly afraid of discovery, Pashtur strove to avoid noise as he picked his steps through the gathering gloom while striving to hear snatches of the talk of the unsuspecting group.

His persistence was finally rewarded when the entire group stopped suddenly as Balech rounded in obvious anger on one of the men. Pashtur managed to creep in closer while everyone's attention was focused on the shouting Balech and the unfortunate man retreating before him. Pashtur heard Balech's angry voice, "...*make certain that changes are coming... right side.*" The man held up his hands and replied, but Pashtur could hear only the appeasing tone, not any words.

Balech spoke loudly again, "...*Lamech...Sechiall will make... rewarded well*."

Pashtur shifted and his tunic caught briefly against a tree. The noise of a slight tear froze him in his steps. Balech was scanning the woods and he began to move in Pashtur's direction. Sweat broke out on Pashtur's face. He thought about breaking and running for the camp, but the men would see the movement, and even if they did not catch him now, they would find an opportunity some day to get him alone in the forest. Balech was nearly opposite his position on the road, and Pashtur tensed his body to spring into a sprint before he could be cut off.

Just then, one of the other men came over to Balech. "I too heard something, Balech," he said quietly, "but it might have been Shem. He is a ghost among the trees and if it is Shem, he is probably well hidden and will not be found in the dark. Besides, he is as skilled with a bow as any man you have ever seen in the army. I don't like the idea of him looking at my throat right now over the shaft of an arrow. If we keep a good pace on the road, he cannot keep up with us unseen. We can discuss our business when we get out of the forest and onto the road to town."

Balech nodded reluctantly and they waved to the others and set out at a fast walk down the road. Pashtur breathed again and waited a few minutes until they were out of sight. Then he returned to the road in the failing light and walked slowly back to the camp, wondering what the words of Balech had meant. What did the Supreme Commander of the army have to do with a common laborer like Balech? How was Lamech involved? What was the reward? And what changes were coming? He could make no sense of any of it, but he promised himself that he would talk with Meshur tonight.

Meshur would think little of it, but he would remember, and if it occurred to him that Balech was trying to hinder the work, he would surely send him away—preferably with a good beating. Pashtur decided it would be well worth the wait to see Meshur's hard fists push Balech's boasts back down his throat.

****

The crackle of burning wood was loud, but as the young woman watched, the old one slept on. Keeping odd hours was hard, but the young woman owed much and she had made a promise she would keep. Stepping lightly over to the couch, she arranged the quilt, making sure the frail body was covered and warm. It was becoming more susceptible to the cold—a sign that death was not too many months away. How was it that death struck those that deserved life? Those men who had cast her out— men not yet even fifty years old—deserved death. The old woman had lived more than ten times that, but the world would be the better if she could remain centuries longer. Death came to even good people, like the mighty men of old she had read of in the scroll. Death came, and set in motion things beyond the understanding of even the wise.

Chapter 22
DEATH DREAM

The black water and red fire engulfed Madrazi. She awoke sweating and screaming. She shuddered uncontrollably. It was the most vivid visitation since her mother's death. Even waking, she felt trapped in that world, struggling to return to her own. Eyes wide, she saw the gray shadows of the room echo back the dark images of crashing waters, reality and vision merging in those moments of transition. Finally, they faded, leaving her weak and spent. During her fifteen years in the house of Noah, the vision had not once invaded her sleep, but living in the midst of Noah's prophecy kept it always hovering at the edge of consciousness. Now that it had breached those barriers, she tasted anew its fear.

Lydia, a servant, rushed in the door. "Mistress, what's wrong?" she cried, staring at the wild-eyed woman. Madrazi realized that she must have cried out.

"Death and destruction, girl," she replied without thinking. She blinked twice, and saw the familiar shapes of the room swim back into focus. Her face and voice only added to Lydia's alarm. She stood petrified, staring as if at a stranger. Her servant's fear helped Madrazi gain a semblance of control over her own.

"Please don't say such things," begged Lydia. "We are safe in your father's house. Your husband shall return today and you will be comforted."

With great effort Madrazi twisted her face into what she hoped was a smile. "It was only a dream, Lydia, go back to sleep."

Once the girl left, Madrazi relaxed her face and felt the tears start. Nothing could entice her to risk sleep now and she walked unsteadily to the window. The new moon was low over the plain to the east, and day was not far off. She huddled in a chair, pulled a quilt around her legs against the late night chill, and watched the stars dim, pondering the meaning of what had been loosed on her imagination. What did the dream portend? Was Shem dead, even now as she sat crying? Knowing that something of unspeakable horror was imminent and yet not knowing what form it would take or in what direction it would strike was like being locked in a darkened room with an angry adder. Madrazi shuddered as new tears stained her cheeks.

Finally after the darkest shades of early morning passed, she saw red gleams paint the horizon. Rousing herself from the chair, she dressed and tried to arrange her hair and wash the tears from her face. She must hide her fears from the household, but the effort knotted her stomach, and she wanted to be alone. Something was far wrong and like one condemned, she waited only the sentence of execution.

Softly she opened the door and walked somberly down to the great hall. A quick bite and drink and she could slip out the back and have at least part of the morning to steady herself before Shem arrived. But Noah and Wen-Tehrom were already up and eating their morning meal, talking quietly together. They had not yet seen her and she stopped in the doorway and wondered if she could slip out unseen.

Starting to slide back into the hall, Madrazi halted, struck by the almost tangible love that flowed between the older couple. It was evident in the very way that they sat, leaning towards each other, talking softly. Affection was in every gesture. Could she ever share that kind of love with Shem? Before she could tear herself away, Wen-Tehrom saw her out of the corner of her eye and called softly. Madrazi obediently walked into the room and Noah seated her at the table. "Shem should be back this morning," he said. "I know that he will be eager to see you."

Madrazi forced a smile. "And I, him. We are planning a feast for the workers. They have completed the second level and are making good progress toward finishing the third. They have worked hard and it seemed an occasion for celebration."

Once Jeriah had married, Madrazi had returned to helping Shem with his work, carrying food less often to Lamech. Her time with Jeriah had of course decreased and her stays in town had diminished to one or two days. But when they were together, Jeriah seemed quite happy and Madrazi drew comfort from her friend's fortune. She was now married to a man who held the respect of all in town and it seemed sometimes to Madrazi that Jeriah had achieved the very life that she had innocently envisioned before coming to Lamech.

Jared had at first been uncomfortable in Madrazi's presence, but she liked him and in time, won his acceptance. He certainly was not blind to the deep friendship of the two women; Madrazi had acted for Jeriah's dead mother during the betrothal and wedding. Eventually, a strong mutual respect paved the way for a comfortable friendship, and Madrazi would have liked him for what he provided her best friend, even apart from his own excellent qualities. Though never easy to talk to, she thought him a good man, much like her own father in character and conviction.

Noah brought Madrazi back to herself. He nodded and agreed, "Yes, the work has progressed well these past few years. The ark should be finished in less than two more. Then we must begin to lay in provisions and prepare for the creatures."

Madrazi's opinion of the ark had not changed. Like any other distasteful task, she tried to ignore those feelings and do her best to help her husband—a labor of duty, not love. She did appreciate the opportunity to be more with Shem, and as her hard work earned his gratitude and respect, she found that she valued his opinion of her. The work had provided a point of commonality, though they were still far from the unity they had so optimistically sought after the wedding. But a comfortable companionship was better than continual friction and she knew that most women were lucky to achieve so much. As long as she concentrated on her husband rather than the hated ark, she managed to retain a degree of equanimity.

So she politely nodded to Noah and began to peel an orange, gently inserting her fingernail and hoping that the skin would come away easily. Before she could finish, there was a loud clatter at the front door and the sound of wailing on the front porch. Shem burst in, pale and distressed. Startled, her finger pushed halfway through the fruit, but her attention was riveted on her husband. Tears stained his face and he was laboring to control his weeping. His clothes were rent from shoulder to hip and the two servants with him sank to the floor, arms across their faces. Seeing his face, Madrazi's heart froze and the memory of the night's terror came rushing back: the devouring sea lurking in the dim corners of the hall. She did not notice the mangled orange, dripping its lifeblood onto her clothing.

"It is death, Shem." It was a statement, not a question, and his surprise overcame his distress momentarily as he looked at her and nodded.

Noah rushed to him and helped him to the table. "Gather yourself, and tell me, my son." The calm in Noah's voice arrested Madrazi's emotion and penetrated Shem's distress. He clenched his hands as he sat down and looked at his father.

"It is Lamech, Father. Barak and I found him dead on the main road near the intersection of our road to the clearing. He had been slain by the sword, and his belongings were gone. Shuhi and Zephed were dead beside him. Barak and the servants thought that it was the work of bandits, but the signs were not clear."

Even in her distress, Madrazi caught a moment of hesitation in his last words and wondered what he was not saying.

Noah sat down abruptly, stunned. Wen-Tehrom rushed over and put her arms around her husband and son and held them tight. Madrazi felt like a stranger in the house—no part of this family, and yet a spectator who could not leave. Her own tears flowing freely, she rose to give comfort to Shem. At that moment, she stopped short for a step, struck with an overwhelming conviction that the specter of death was not yet satisfied, and she wondered what other ill news would be inflicted upon them.

She touched Shem and he looked up, tears falling freely now and neither could speak. Instead they clung to each other tightly for some minutes. It seemed incredible to her that the powerful presence of Lamech would no longer wait for her in town, or that she would no more watch him comfort the children of the poor.

After a moment, Shem seemed to gather self-control and looked at the woman in his arms with some curiosity. "How did you know?" he asked her quietly, not wanting to disturb his father's grief.

"Later," Madrazi returned, "when there is a time and place for us to talk. Yet I fear that Lamech is not alone, my heart tells me that more evil news awaits."

At that moment, Ham and Japheth rushed into the room, roused by the early morning commotion. Alarmed at the scene, they hesitated, unsure what to do. Shem broke away from Madrazi and hurried over to quietly give them the news without disturbing his parents. Madrazi set her face and forced her feet out to the back courtyard, to be met by Debseda and Yaran. She told them, hoping that her words were appropriate and left them to go to their husbands.

They went inside, but Madrazi continued. She knew what she must do though she did not want the task. But it was better for her to inflict pain than Shem or Noah. Steeling herself, she walked back into the grove between the houses and the park and found Methuselah walking among the trees praying, as was his habit in the morning hours.

Coming alongside him, she slipped a hand into his and looked up. "What is it, my child," he asked. "What sorrow do you bear?"

"Sorrow for you, Great-grandfather," she said hesitating. She looked down and continued as she felt the old arm quiver beneath her touch. "Shem has returned with evil news. He has found your son Lamech and his servants slain on the road. I am so sorry to be the messenger of this news. It is hard to carry such a burden to one that you love so much."

Methuselah surprised her by simply sighing, "And it is hard to hear such bitterness from one so young. Come, child, let us go and comfort the others."

Her surprise must have been evident to him, for as she searched his face he continued. "Do not concern yourself with me, child. My comfort is in God and I draw closer each day. Lamech now dwells with Enoch and I will join them in the presence of God ere too many more years have passed. I have lived too long. But for the happiness that you have brought me by marrying Shem, I would have been glad to pass over many years ago."

Methuselah's words took her aback, and she wondered how well she really knew the old man. After all, he had lived a lifetime before she had ever met him. She shook her head and put aside those thoughts to ponder later. She would later remember his words with comfort, for they seemed so strange to her then. By the time they entered the house, she had composed herself to try to help the others. Methuselah embraced Noah and Wen-Tehrom in turn, and passed among the sons, laying his hands on them and speaking softly to each in turn. His calm pervaded the room, and when they were settled, he spoke.

"We have seen the righteousness of man depart from this earth. God has warned us through Noah of the coming judgment and we have been diligent to prepare the ark according to His word. We have prayed and hoped for God to turn away from His anger, but also obeyed in preparing the ark of our salvation which, when finished, will with finality condemn this evil generation. Lamech would have shared in that deliverance, but God in his love has chosen to save my son from the coming wrath by taking him now. Do not fear for him! His faith was steadfast—an example to us all as the time draws near. We will mourn our dead for seven days and bury his body in the hope of the promise of a new life. Then we must put away sorrow and obey the commandment of the Judge of all the Earth."

The family gathered together around Methuselah and joined hands. He raised his face in prayer. "Oh, Mighty Creator! We have seen your deliverance of Lamech from this evil generation. You have confirmed his righteousness by sparing him the judgment of destruction. Bring him into the presence of your spirit and reunite him with righteous Enoch and the fathers. We praise you, Judge of the Earth, and acknowledge your mercy to Lamech all of his days in granting him faith to believe your promises and to make them more valuable than life itself. Preserve us, your remnant, in a similar faith from this wicked and perverse generation."

He paused and finished, "God is our strength and shield. We will bury our dead and go on as Lamech would wish."

The next few days were a busy time. The bodies of Lamech and his faithful servants were brought home and buried in the glade of the forest where his wife and the wife of Methuselah had been laid. More flowers were planted to join those that clustered around the graves of the women. Work in the household stopped as everyone joined in mourning and fasting. The women

wore dark, plain clothes, and Noah and Methuselah wore the robes that they
had torn together on that first morning.

A messenger had been sent to town immediately to carry the ill tidings to
the council. After reading the message sent by Noah, Dajus and Subtur called a
solemn assembly. The news of Lamech's death was proclaimed, and seven days
of mourning were decreed. On the eighth day the town would assemble again
to publicly honor Lamech, and join in worship. Jeriah later told Madrazi that
many had taken to the streets to show their grief. Lamech had dedicated much
of his life to the city that bore his name, and he had been respected by the
wealthy and poor alike. News that Lamech would be buried in the Great
Forest saddened some who wished him to rest in the town that bore his name,
but those that knew him remembered his wish to lie beside his wife.

Madrazi recalled little of that ceremony except standing in the public
assembly for a long time while the rich and powerful of the city praised Lamech
as one of their own. She found it hard to reconcile their speeches with her own
special memory of stern Lamech smiling and playing with the widow's children
the first time they had carried food together. After the ceremony, the family
spent the night at Lamech's house and then left early the next morning. They
walked slowly and arrived home in the cool of the evening. The following
week passed quickly; everyone was busy making up lost work. Shem remained
withdrawn and quiet for a number of days and Madrazi left him to his sorrow.
She did not know what words she could give him that would help, so she said
little.

By the first day of the next week, life at the settlement had returned to
something close to normal, and Shem began to shoulder the concerns he had
laid down the moment he had discovered his grandfather's body on the road.
One morning after breakfast, he led his wife out to the verge of the forest.
They allowed the peace of the trees to settle upon them as they walked under
their shadows. Finally, without looking at her, Shem said, "When I came into
the house that day, you seemed to know what had happened before I spoke."

Madrazi had been dreading this question and took a moment to gather her
thoughts. She had hid the omen of destruction from him for fifteen long years,
and an honest answer was long overdue. But she feared his anger when he
learned of her evasion. Guilt, augmented by her openness with Jeriah five years
earlier, compounded her reticence. But it was time and she must face her duty.
She owed him the truth and she was ready to pay the price of whatever
punishment he demanded.

Neither looked at each other nor were their hands together. Madrazi sat
on the grass, pulling her knees to her chest, and began slowly, "The answer you

seek has its origin in years past. When Methuselah first came to our house, I found a happiness in his presence that I had never before known and have not known since. I have loved him from those days."

Shem nodded; all knew of the special bond that existed between his wife and Methuselah. Madrazi continued, "As soon as he departed, so did my happiness, and that very night I beheld in my sleep a vision of death and destruction. It terrified me then and its dread pursues my every day. I cannot explain why it came or what it means, but it brings the chill of death to my soul with each visitation."

Shem had not expected that answer, and was more surprised than he showed. He saw the truth of her words in her glistening tears and a sudden desire to take her in his arms overwhelmed him, but something deeper stayed his hand. He sensed an importance to this moment and knew that he was finally beginning to see into the hidden depths of his wife's heart. She choked, her throat closed, and for a moment, she could utter no word. Shem stood quietly in front of her with his head bowed, waiting. Gradually, the spasm passed, and she could breathe again.

"The dream came often at first, and more clearly each time. Only the comfort of my mother saved me from the onslaught of those first days. But it came a seventh time with greater power, and that morning the sea took my mother. I do not know how I survived those years; many days I think that it was only to taste greater sorrow and pain. That same dream came upon me again in the early hours of the morning you came with the news of Lamech's murder. I did not foresee his death, but death was in my heart and I saw it on your face before you spoke."

She stopped for a moment, waiting for his words of condemnation. The air was heavy, but somehow the telling of that much made it easier to continue. Shem had said nothing yet, but he had not turned away, either. So she went on in a softer voice, "Even now it weighs upon me; Lamech's blood was not the end of it. There is more to come."

Shem felt his heart go out to his wife, but still he held back. Sweat beaded on her forehead and he saw blood welling from her palms where her nails pressed into the flesh. Madrazi mistook his silence for a just accusation of her deceit. He had been her husband for years and she had withheld this evil that cursed on her life and threatened his happiness. She hung her head, but struggled to go on. A mist was before her eyes. To speak the words would be to invoke the curse and to open the doors to destruction. But she sensed that if she withheld the truth now, she would never be able to release it or be released by it. She wanted to expel her anguish in one scream of rage and terror, but forced her voice to speak, instead. In halting words, she described her dream.

She stood up then, emptied, her sight cleared and once again before her husband. She felt weak and sick, but somehow the better for having exposed her curse before him. Expecting the worst, she looked up to face his anger. But his face neither accused nor condemned. There was only her pain reflected in his eyes, and Madrazi was stunned to see a sheen of tears. His hand came up and slowly and gently he let his fingers traced the lines of her tears before brushing back a stray strand of hair.

"I am truly sorry," was all he could say, and she was not sure whether he was sorry for her pain, sorry that she had not trusted him sooner, or sorry that he had forced her to tell him now. Perhaps Shem himself could not have told her which, then.

But he gestured her to sit again in the grass and he sat with her. They watched a dove fly from the forest out into the meadow to search for seeds. Insects renewed their buzzing, and birds, their songs. Shem's hand took hers and his touch imparted strength. Madrazi felt her tears stop, her breath come easier, and her heart settle back to its normal rate. Still Shem was silent and she wondered what form his reprimand would take. But instead, he just sat there with a stem of grass between his lips. Madrazi could see the magic of the forest dissipate his tension, and she gave herself to simply feeling, seeing, and hearing. Gradually, the same spell overcame her, allowing her muscles to loosen and her fear to evaporate in the soft breeze.

After some minutes, Shem looked at her and unexpectedly said, "I have been preoccupied all week with a weight on my own mind and have not been able to speak to anyone about it. Will you listen?"

Madrazi looked up at him, surprised. A request for help was the last thing she expected. Strangely, that trust was more comforting than anything else he could have done. She felt unworthy of it yet uplifted by its free offer. For his trust betrayed nothing less than a love that could cover her offense; a love that she knew was undeserved.

"With all my heart, my husband," she replied. He nodded, understanding the emotion behind her inadequate words.

"I need your wisdom. Lamech was not killed by bandits. I have told none other of my suspicions. I do not wish to burden father, and no one else would believe me. Please listen and tell me what I should do."

Madrazi did not feel very wise at that moment and knew that she had no authority to instruct her husband, but nodded and gripped his hand as he continued. "I have had some time to think about what I have seen, and my thoughts have been able to overtake my sorrow. Most of the bandits that used to infest this region have been killed or driven away by our army. We have never encountered them in all our travels to the ark or to town. So any bandits that might have killed Lamech would have been far from their usual haunts."

"You know well that I love the forest and have learned to read its stories in the signs of animals and men. I searched for such signs as I walked the place of his death. It was plain that one man—a powerful man skilled in the use of the sword, killed all three. There was no sign that Lamech or his servants tried to flee, and so I believe that they knew the swordsman. Also, Lamech's dead hand clutched a silver clasp with a small bit of cloth. It was not from his own clothing or that of his servants. It must have been from the murderer, but it was not the clothing of a bandit."

"You suspect murder by enemies known to him?" she asked to make sure that she understood.

"Yes," said Shem slowly, "but I cannot speak accusations on the basis of guesses. Who would believe me? Those who do not know my skills would scoff at my ability to tell a story from a few marks on the ground." Madrazi nodded in agreement, for though she had seen him interpret signs on the forest floor on occasion, she still had difficulty believing the ease with which he did it. He could follow an animal or man by such signs for miles.

Shem smiled grimly at the agreement in her eyes and continued. "It is a serious thing to bring a charge of murder before the council, and to do so without evidence or witnesses will bring only shame. My mind is not subtle, but I ask myself who has reason to want Lamech dead, and who has the skill with a sword to kill three men so swiftly and efficiently?"

Madrazi felt her heart go cold. The best swordsman in Lamech was Jared and everyone knew of his ambitions and their thwarting by Noah. But as quickly as the thought entered her mind, she rejected it. Jared was not that kind of man, was he? Was her thinking clouded by her love for Jeriah? Unwittingly, her face reflected her thoughts.

Shem saw it, and said, "Yes, my first thought also turned to those that want power on the council and both Jared and Sechiall are skilled with many weapons. But," he paused, "I cannot believe that Jared would do such a thing. Whatever else, he is a man of honor. He is no murderer. Sechiall, however..."

Madrazi agreed, "Jeriah would not join with an evil man. I have been with Jared many times in her company and I agree. He is not capable of such a thing. I have met Sechiall briefly. He is like a son to Jared, but I did not like him, nor does Jeriah."

Madrazi dared not tell her husband of the one time she had been alone for a few moments with the Supreme Commander. His bold leer and thinly veiled suggestions would have insulted a prostitute, but he completely disguised his manner upon Jared's return, and Madrazi knew that any accusation would probably separate her from Jeriah and send Shem into a deadly rage—one that she feared he would not survive. She believed Sechiall capable of any evil.

"Have you thought of talking with Jared privately, and asking his help?"

"How can I?" asked Shem. "He has no cause to believe me or to help me. He holds some of Father's words from long ago as a grudge, though the other elders agreed. And if by chance he was involved, then he would have reason to kill me, too."

Madrazi considered his words and replied, "I know that Jared wants power in the council for the army, for the army is his life. But he is the kind of man who will achieve his goals by honest means. If he was willing to murder to gain what he wanted, he could have done it long ago. The army has been loyal to Jared for many years and the support of Taspar is his for the asking. Please consider talking to him. Perhaps he would be willing to help you—if for no other reason than to absolve his name from suspicion. If you spoke to him privately, then he could not believe that you had any motive other than a desire for truth and justice."

Shem studied the ground in front of him, weighing the advice. Madrazi was struck by a notion that her husband and Jared could have been friends, given the opportunity. They were similar in many ways, but had never had a chance to discover it. Finally he spoke. "What you say is reasonable, my wife. I will consider it. But please say nothing now."

"I will do as you ask, my love," she replied seriously, "and I will consider these things in my own heart." She paused, once again struck by the incongruity of her husband sharing his deepest confidence with her after she had just finished demonstrating her unworthiness. Words tumbled out. "Please forgive me for not sharing my heart with you sooner. I should have trusted you." She almost felt like confessing her doubts about the ark and prophecy to him, but could not. Shem sensed her reluctance, but let it go.

He stroked her hair with a gentle hand and lifted his eyes to hers. "Methuselah says that marriage is walking a path together. We have taken another step, my love, and we will take many more, each in its time. I love you, and value your companionship and help. That is why I keep walking."

Madrazi could find no words to say. Her tears blurred the quiet stillness of the morning, and she felt as far away as ever from understanding her husband. But he was with her, he loved her, and thoughts were not really needed now.

Later that day they walked hand in hand out of the forest. The birds beneath the netting of the aviary watched them pass with scarcely a cry. Once out from under the trees, Madrazi felt the peace of the last hour vanish and her earlier fear returned redoubled. Shem caught her mood in the sudden tension of her fingers, and stopped.

"What is the matter?"

"I do not know, but I feel the fear again."

"I am with you," he said, quietly.

When they entered the common room of the house, they found Noah and Wen-Tehrom talking softly together. Methuselah stood nearby with his head bowed. The force of their emotion was palpable, and Shem gripped Madrazi's hand as they walked forward. Upon seeing the couple, Wen-Tehrom turned away to hide her tears. Madrazi's heart turned to stone within her and she braced herself for the dark news.

Shem's hold tightened as he, too, sensed what was coming. It was Methuselah who walked slowly over to the couple and embraced Madrazi without words. "Excuse us, my son," he asked, and Shem immediately moved away. Madrazi searched his face, but Methuselah averted his gaze and led her outside to his retreat under the trees. The sound of their footsteps echoed in Madrazi's mind as she dully followed the old man. There was some comfort in Methuselah's presence, but she had no strength. As they drew within his grove, Methuselah finally spoke.

"Madrazi, please understand that I love you more than any daughter and will always do so. Yet just as you came to me a few days past, now I must hurt you, and that brings pain into my old heart, too."

"Great-grandfather, just tell me. It is worse to fear in ignorance. I know that something terrible has happened, for the same fear that I knew at Lamech's death has returned."

He bowed his head. "My beloved daughter, we received a dark message today from a trader in Lamech. It seems that ships were sailing on the open sea a few months ago when an unusual storm rose up without warning, scattering them all. This trader was on one of the ships and related how his vessel barely escaped destruction. It was some days before it could return to the place where the other ships had been. None of them were found, but they did find the wreckage of several. One of those destroyed belonged to Pomorolac. Your father and brothers and all on board were not to be found."

Madrazi froze inside and her mind returned to her mother's death so long ago. "So the sea has swallowed up all I loved," she said as the tears flowed freely. "Why could it not have been me?"

"Because choices were made to deliver you from the sea, my child," replied

Methuselah as he held her, and she was never sure if he whispered those words to her or to himself.

Chapter 23
POWER

An unusually stiff breeze from the ocean rippled across the harbor and up the short reach of the plateau to the high white walls. The sun had set over the water and darkness was rushing out to sea to swallow the one red gleam of day that remained. Neither wind nor darkness stirred the cloaked figure standing near the low parapet of the roof of the Hall of the Council. Despite eyes open to the vista before him, Subtur's vision was turned inward: the cold, analytical skill that had won him the respect of older, more experienced men, searching for answers. He noted that winds had become more unpredictable over the past few years, but did not a restless nature reflect man's restless advancement?

Thought was impaired by emotion. But emotion was hard to suppress. Lamech had been a friend, a mentor; the only man in the city whose wisdom and insight surpassed Subtur's own. That murder had stirred uncomfortable emotions within Subtur, including a chord of fear, but Subtur forced it aside. After all, Lamech's death was not some poignant passing to be mourned—it signaled a dramatic alteration in the balance of power in the city that none yet seemed to appreciate. But then, they lacked his skill and wisdom.

Life in the city was many different things to its citizens. Almost all saw it in terms of their experience. Those sought peace, pleasure, and power in the petty sphere of their small lives. Only a very few chose to weave the apparently unrelated daily events into the tapestry of civil discourse that defined the pulse of political life. Subtur did, and did it better than most...no, all. Dajus saw part, but was distracted by avarice. Jared saw a small part, but ultimately was a follower, not a leader. Lamech had understood it well, but was gone. Methuselah and Noah had the ability, but had become detached over the past decades. Only one other seemed to have the potential—Sechiall.

The man was young and inexperienced, but there was certainly an instinct, a purpose, even a ruthlessness that Subtur perceived hovering just beneath the surface. The young protégé's skills may have blinded Jared, but in spite of his desire for greater military influence on the council, it was Sechiall who seemingly grasped the intricate subtleties of using such power once it was attained. Thinking back, Subtur could remember that every one of the boy's bland suggestions were always to the point.

Night had now truly fallen. The streets were empty; lights in the houses nearby proclaimed the evening meal and night-shrouded revelry. The stiff wind still blew off of the water, but it was not the air that suddenly chilled Subtur's blood. What if Sechiall was behind the death of Lamech? Jared would never countenance murder. Subtur was certain of that. But if Sechiall was playing his own game for power…? With Lamech dead, it was hanging in the air, ready to be grasped by anyone wise or strong enough. Subtur intended that he and Dajus would be the first to the prize. But was there another competitor?

What would the council become if Sechiall was added to the equation? Dajus and Jared had assumed that Sechiall would content himself with the workings of the army, leaving the governance to the more experienced men, and voting with them when necessary. After all, the tradition of respect for wisdom ran deep in Lamech. But was it Sechiall's tradition? He was an outsider, a child of men like Torech of Y'tor. They had all assumed that the civilizing influences of the city had turned him from his birthright. But what if the blood of the Nephil ran true in him? Would he attempt to seize power? How? Jared controlled the army; Dajus commanded the allegiance of the wealthiest and most influential merchants, and Subtur was respected by all.

But Lamech had been a keystone in the life of the city. He was strong and wise and had held the structure in place by the force of his character and will. No man could completely take his place. If someone wanted to shift the distribution of power, Lamech's death was a masterstroke. It opened many more doors of opportunity than almost any other event could. Was Sechiall wise enough to see that? Was he ruthless enough to pursue it? Subtur shivered again. These new thoughts disturbed him, but they could not be ignored. He must talk to Dajus, soon. But first, he must make sure of his own opportunities.

Now the half moon and bright stars shone bright in the darkness. What unheard message was carried in the beams that danced from star to star and then echoed back to earth? Their dance was intricate, and Subtur thought for a time of the depths of knowledge and wisdom that remained to be plumbed by man. If by some insight or intricate code men could perceive their hidden meaning, then perhaps the heavens would be open to voyages to the stars. Subtur was certain it was possible; simply seeing what man had done on earth opened hope for greater things. Remorselessly, the stars sent their unending message streaming across the heavens, teasing the wise with possibilities.

But for now he waited, attuned to his own wisdom, not that of the heavens. Soon he perceived the shadowy figure of a man moving along through the shadows below. It turned into the courtyard beside the building, and Subtur soon heard the puffing of Dajus as he ascended the outside stairway and made his way over to the dark form of his friend.

Before either could speak, a disembodied voice whispered right behind them, "Good evening, revered elders."

Dajus and Subtur both startled at Sechiall's greeting. Dajus spoke first, "And good evening to you, Commander. I hope that you frighten our enemies as easily."

Sechiall laughed softly, "Our enemies are less than they once were..." he paused meaningfully, "thanks to the unfortunate activities of bandits in our lands. The army will search diligently for the killers for many days, but I fear that they will have disappeared completely into the Great Forest. But enough of the past. Let the dead mourn the dead. Men of action must look to the future, and of course, we need men of wisdom to guide our deeds."

Subtur spoke. "We may plan for the future, now, but implementing those plans may take time. Events have put opportunity in our way. Let us not waste it by haste."

Sechiall agreed. "I can be more patient than you imagine, elder. But times of waiting are also times for planning. Lamech was the strength of the council. Methuselah is close to death, and that eccentric Noah, avoids the town. He is not concerned with affairs of the council. Torech is still building his army, conveniently pushing you to action. It is time for the army to have a place on the council. That was our original agreement."

Subtur demurred. "That agreement did not anticipate the untimely murder of one of our own. What if Methuselah and Noah voice suspicion that Lamech's death originated within our own town? Regardless of the truth, people will wonder and may question our motives if we act precipitously. In a time of such doubt, do you think that they will turn to an outsider? We must find a way to avoid that problem. Perhaps replacing Lamech with a merchant or trader for the present will ensure our final success."

Sechiall controlled his anger with an effort. "Of course, elder, whatever action we take must conform to the wishes of the leading men." He paused in thought, and then smiled. "But what if the death of Lamech was not a simple murder by robbers, but instead a plot of Torech—an assassination of one of our council? If evidence could be gathered to show this, then it might be appropriate for the army to take a more active role. How could we not set our faces for war if Torech has taken the infamous step of murdering our leading elder?"

Dajus rubbed his hands. "Such a plot would rally the men of the town to the army. But we must have evidence: bare assertions will convince none. If it were produced, then the need to protect the remaining elders would force us to bring the army more closely into our councils. And you are right, Sechiall. Such an insult from Torech could not go unanswered. But many would speak against precipitate action. How do we answer them?"

Subtur checked his urge to strike Dajus. Though clever enough, his ally was again congratulating himself for someone else's idea, while missing the signals of danger. His suspicion of Sechiall deepened, while his respect for his ability rose. "The time is not right. The commander is young and in a time of crisis, the city will look to the wise."

Sechiall sprung his trap. "That concern will be alleviated by following the tradition already established by the council with Lamech's own approval. The new member will have a provisional seat. The army will undertake deliberate preparations to crush Torech. Such preparations will take several years. During that time, the men of the city will forget the complexities of today and put their thoughts towards defeating Y'tor and the benefits and riches that must come from that victory. In a short time, people will become accustomed to the new arrangement and the sight of vigorous leadership by Dajus and Subtur will soothe the fears of all. Of course, the new provisional member of the council will take a very humble role in public during these troubled times. Especially since most of his efforts will be in drawing up a plan for the final defeat of Torech."

"But what of this evidence?" demanded Subtur, frustrated that Sechiall had anticipated his objection.

"We will start the hunt for the assassins immediately," returned Sechiall smoothly. "And by good fortune a picked group of my best warriors will find them in the wild. They will put up a good fight, so in the end we will be forced to kill them. But their bodies bearing the armor and weapons of Y'tor will be brought before the council. And at least three of my most reliable men will hear their confession to this terrible deed given with their last breath, and testify before the council to its truth. Who can question us then?"

Subtur nodded slowly. He did not like the way in which Sechiall was redirecting their careful plans, but he had to admit that it would probably work. But Sechiall was pushing too hard. Subtur determined at that moment to talk to Dajus in private and make further arrangements for Sechiall after Torech was defeated. Jared would get his seat on the council at the cost of his holding Sechiall on a tight leash. Sechiall might be clever and ruthless, but Subtur decided that he and Dajus could undercut him at the right time. Finally he spoke, "I have considered all that you have said, Commander. If the army can supply this evidence, and the leading men see the need for the destruction of Y'tor, then we will support a temporary change on the council. However, we cannot risk a deadlocked vote. We must convene an assembly and be sure that either Noah or Methuselah cannot come within the prescribed time limit."

Sechiall smiled grimly. "I anticipate your every wish, elder. I have a spy working for Noah. Noah often goes into the forest for days at a time. When next he goes, my friend will send word and we can call an immediate assembly. Methuselah will make it in time, but the message to Noah will go to his house and be delayed. But we must act now! You must authorize a search for the assassins. Surely the men of the town will agree once the evidence is presented, and they will praise your foresight in deducing the possibility and sending a patrol south so quickly."

Dajus interjected, once more causing Subtur to grind his teeth. "It is a good plan. The time of mourning for Lamech is done and the men will begin to think about the future and not the past. Go tonight and find your evidence quickly. Then we will convene as soon after that as fortune allows."

The two elders slipped back down the steps and out the darkened door. Sechiall remained for some time on the roof, watching the moon trace its path across the sky. If it was true that the god of war lived in the moon, then surely he was smiling down on Sechiall this night. He returned the smile with wolfish delight.

After they were out of sight of the rooftop, Subtur touched Dajus on the arm, and they walked another direction together in silence. Dajus was becoming impatient, when Subtur turned into the familiar side street and led him into the inn of Eldad. Eldad met them inside the doorway and bowed low. "How can I serve my kinsman and friend?" he asked. "I must close my doors in an hour," he added apologetically.

"Peace, Eldad," responded Dajus. "We have come to enjoy a quiet drink together as friends. However," he added, "we would appreciate a table alone, where we can speak privately."

"Of course, elder," returned Eldad. He led them across the great room to a small table in a quiet corner. No one would be close enough to overhear, and the men who remained were caught up in watching a game of dice before the fire.

Subtur sat without a word while Dajus controlled his impatience. Eldad brought them their drinks and left. Subtur turned to Dajus after letting his eyes scan the room. "Sechiall is clever, and certainly has spies about. But what could be more innocent than two old friends sharing a drink at the end of their day? When he finds out, he will think that we are merely celebrating our arrangement with him."

"Why should we care if that young pup knows that we are talking?" asked Dajus irritated at Subtur's foolishness.

"Because that young pup is a wolf, not a dog!" returned Subtur forcefully, while thinking to himself, *your lust for wealth and power have blinded you, fool.* He leaned over the table and whispered, "He has not hesitated to slay an elder of Lamech. Why should he stop with one? I tell you, Dajus, I don't like this! We had a good plan—but then Zered died before his time. We should not have let Jared's impatience bring Sechiall into this. Jared is one of us; one that we could control. He never would have used murder, and Lamech's blood will haunt us across the centuries, no matter how successful we are! His blood in upon our heads, and he was a good man. *And one who could not be played by Sechiall as you have been tonight.*"

"Of course he was," replied Dajus calmly. "He was my friend, too! Do you think that I would ever condone such an act? It is not only evil, but foolish and full of risk." He leaned across to his friend. "But Subtur, his blood is not on our hands—Sechiall murdered him without our knowledge and probably without Jared's, either. We must think of our city, our duty, our opportunity. It is the place of the wise to accept reality as it comes and find new ways to bend it to good ends. If we do not walk a short ways on this path with Sechiall, he will murder others and become another Torech. He is powerful and ruthless, but young and inexperienced. He thinks he is clever, but he is not subtle.

We can control this situation, but only if we play the game with care. If we must bear some guilt for Lamech's blood, it is for the good of our city and our people. Who better than the strong and wise to do so? We will walk this dark path until we watch Sechiall fall off into one of the many pits that line the road. Then we will seize the new reality and ensure the prosperity and peace of our town for years to come."

Subtur stared at his cup silently for a few minutes. "I suppose that you are right, Dajus," he said finally, "but it is a high price. Have care lest it is we who find ourselves in a pit. Sechiall has nothing to do with wisdom, but he has the cunning of a wolf and will not hesitate to shed our blood, too. His sword did not respect the wisdom of Lamech! Beware that it does not thirst for yours! Let him destroy Torech for us, and when he returns, we will use Jared to rid our town of his evil. In return, Jared will get his seat on the council. If it is clear that the only choice is between Sechiall and Jared, I think that even Noah and Methuselah will support Jared."

"We will both be wary," replied Dajus, finishing his drink. "But Sechiall is merely a soldier. We have time to consider a foolproof trap for this wolf. His own lusts will betray him. It will be a difficult time for the next few years, but the end will shine all the brighter for the present darkness. We will lead the council of Lamech regardless of what happens."

Leaving a gold coin on the table, he rose and the two men walked out into the night of Lamech.

****

The old woman woke, warm and rested. The younger was still asleep in her chair, her wrap pulled close around her. She must have awoken and replenished the fire; it leapt with joy as it consumed the new wood. Oh, the folly of men who think that they can light a fire of evil and not be consumed by it in the end! They imagine they can embrace a serpent and escape its poison! For the serpent is cunning and traps men in their pride. Only by opposing evil can it be overcome. Even the simplest man can do that! Sometimes only a simple man can, but evil strives to entrap those inclined to oppose it...

Chapter 24
MESHUR'S CHOICE

Meshur paused from his work, irritated at the intrusion. Shaping the flange for a feed chute was delicate work and he disliked interruptions. But Pashtur's eager look told the big man that he would not be left alone until his cousin had his say. Sighing, he put down the chisel and the wood and waved Pashtur to a seat on a block beside him. The waterskin was close by and Meshur satisfied his thirst before sitting down. Pashtur was looking furtively down the length of the deck, making sure that no one was close by.

"Cousin," he whispered in his best conspiratorial voice, "I have to tell you what I heard this morning." He paused and looked sideways at Meshur. "I heard a rumor yesterday that Supreme Commander Sechiall wanted all of the hired laborers working for Noah to return to town. Balech is the source of this talk; he was in the army and I believe that he is Sechiall's spy. It is said that the men are needed in the army to fight against Y'tor, but I overheard Balech telling one of his friends that it will distract Noah from his duties and thus weaken him on the council. Sechiall has only been on the council for three years, but he wields much power secretly."

Meshur grunted. "I have no interest in the army or political intrigue. I like working here. I have learned more in seventy years from Ham than I could have in hundreds of years with your father, had he lived. The son of Noah is the most talented craftsman in this region! I will work with Ham as long as he will have me. When I finish here, I can return to Lamech and become the richest craftsman in the city, even if I learned nothing more for the rest of my life! Balech is a dog, and he and his pack of complainers should keep out of my way. If he tries to tell me what I need to do, we will see if he has any real friends to carry him back to town!"

Pashtur was visibly alarmed. "Cousin! Do not speak so loudly. Balech has more friends than you realize, and powerful ones at that! Do you think that your great strength would help you against a man like Sechiall? If he did not have you killed in the dark of night, he might decide to do it himself. From what I have heard, Sechiall's strength is a match for yours and you have no skill with sword or spear!"

Meshur felt his blood rise at that. "Fine! Then let this great warrior come out to me with empty hands and we will settle our differences like men. I would welcome a test of strength with him. If he were not the favorite of Jared, he would be nothing! Jared is a good man; I do not understand what he sees in that yellow-haired foreigner."

Neither man heard the soft steps approaching. "Fools!" The harsh voice of Balech echoed against the walls beside them. "Sechiall is the Supreme Commander of Lamech's army and will soon sit as the Chief Elder on the Council. Why should an important man like that bother himself with a dog like Meshur—the lackey of the son of a madman? You understand nothing! Sechiall could bring about your death with his bare hands or with the snap of his finger and a quiet word to any of a thousand men. He has loyal men in every place."

"Including here?" asked Meshur quietly, standing up.

"Of course! You must consider what your life is worth and choose your allegiances wisely."

Meshur was not a man to talk when talking was not called for. Those who did not know him well did not know how quickly he could move his bulk. Balech learned when a rock-like fist slammed into his mouth, hurling him to the deck. Meshur followed Balech's fall with a quick step and seized the front of his tunic pulling him up with an easy motion. Balech's eyes showed fear, pain, and surprise. Blood trickled from the corner of his mouth and dripped on Meshur's knotted arm.

Meshur pulled Balech's face close to his and snarled, "You will not tell me what I must or must not do. Run home to your master and tell him that I will say the same thing to him in the same way, should he have the courage to face me! Now begone! If I see you here at the end of the day, I will finish this."

He looked around at Balech's stunned followers. "Do any of you wish to take up your master's fight?" All looked down and began to back away. Meshur snorted and shoved Balech back into the nearest, the force knocking both of them to the deck. "Take your friend and leave. What I said to Balech will be true for any traitor in this camp. Noah pays a better wage than you can get in town and he has treated every one of you with more respect and consideration than you obviously deserve. Cowards are welcome to leave, but men who know their own mind will stay here with me. Make your choice!"

None of the men that had followed Balech so eagerly wanted to test Meshur's anger, especially in the enclosed space. With fearful backward glances, they helped Balech up and retreated as quickly as possible. Meshur watched them go, and turned to his cousin. "Follow them with your usual skill and subtlety, Pashtur. Find out what they do and how many leave camp. I must find Ham."

Pashtur nodded, and slipped after the retreating men. Meshur found his way to the rear of the upper deck where he had last seen Ham. He began to think of what he had heard and done and wondered how Ham would have dealt with the men. But he had no patience for men like Balech and was not sorry that he had struck him. He hoped that only a few of the worst of the men would go with him, but he feared that Balech might have been able to influence more.

Ham straightened up and wiped the sweat from his face when he heard Meshur call his name. A rare smile played upon his lips as he watched the broad shouldered young man approach. Meshur had proven to be more than just the hardest worker on the ark; he was easily the most skilled. Ham hoped that he could convince him to take refuge aboard the ark. He would make a fine addition to the new world. But as Meshur drew closer, the grim look in his eyes demanded Ham's attention.

Meshur hesitated for only a moment and then related to Ham what he had heard and done, beginning with the conversation overheard by Pashtur on the road to Lamech. It was clear that he expected some censure for his precipitate actions, but he kept his head up and his eye steady as he spoke. When he had finished, Ham smiled again. "Do not worry, my friend. I have ached for an opportunity for Balech to provide an excuse for me to do the same! I am only sorry that I could not have seen it!"

Meshur exhaled, thankful that Ham understood. "Balech has infected the minds of some of the men. We may lose more than Balech and two or three of his cronies. If too many leave, it may be hard to complete the remaining work."

Ham shrugged. "We have made excellent progress, especially over the last twenty years. It is true that much work remains, but the ark will be done sooner than I thought. At need, we can bring more of the men from the house to work here. Even if all the hired men left with that dog, there are enough men at the house to complete the heavy work that remains. Most of what is left will require skilled hands, not strong ones. Either way, you are worth all of that crew, Meshur!"

Meshur tried to hide his embarrassment and pleasure. Ham was an exacting master and seldom had praise for any man's work. Meshur did not think that unfair. Ham criticized his own work more readily than other men's, and Ham's errors would have passed for good work for most. None working on the ark could match his skill, whether in devising intricate plans or shaping a large beam. Meshur's talent, second only to Ham's, enabled him to see Ham's ability better than any other. Those few words of praise made every month of his seventy years of work worthwhile. "Thank you master," was all he could say.

Ham looked appraisingly at the younger man. "Do not call me 'master' any longer, Meshur. You are worthy of this great task that has already cost us so many years. From this day, call me 'friend,' for truly we will work together as friends and complete the work with or without the men of Lamech."

Meshur could only stare in amazement at Ham's words, but he held out his hand, and Ham gripped his wrist. No other words were spoken, but none were needed. Meshur turned away, smiling and did not realize that he was aimlessly wandering until he found himself at the back end of the lower deck. Shaking his head, he made his way back to work. Ham was the most skilled, the most intelligent man he had ever known. That he had earned the friendship of such a man with his own skill and strength only added to his determination to push himself well beyond his present ability.

For a short time he enjoyed his new status, and worked harder to please Ham, his friend, than he had to please Ham as his master. But his happiness was fleeting. Three weeks later, he was preparing to return to work from two days in town. He was ready to return; the work had progressed more smoothly with Balech and his gang absent, but Meshur had been severely disappointed in some of the deserters—men he had shared work with for decades. But he did not waver. Ham had honored him beyond all expectation with his friendship; he now had a trust to fulfill. The bond of friendship was something Meshur valued and he knew that Ham did not offer it lightly.

Pashtur met him at their usual place outside of the small west gate and the two cousins started off along the familiar paths that they had learned as boys through the fields to the north of town. Circling around they reached the road at a shaded spring several miles from the front gate of Lamech. It was the meeting place for men going into the forest to work, but today only six met them. They were all good friends of Meshur, and had worked for Noah from the beginning.

Meshur frowned. "Is this all? Where are the others?"

"Twenty left with Balech," replied Nebo, "and all of the others have been approached by Balech or his friends and warned to stay away from Noah and the Great Forest. We were threatened, too, but we have no close family here, and decided to continue. Noah has treated us well and he pays well. But men with wives and children are fearful because of Balech's threats."

"What?" thundered Meshur. "What has our town become when women and children are threatened by worthless dogs like Balech? Why is he not taken before the council and punished?"

Pashtur caught his arm. "Because cousin, Lamech is dead! Noah and Methuselah are seldom in town, and Sechiall has the support of Dajus and Subtur. Balech is Sechiall's man, and only fools like us dare to defy him."

Pashtur's cold tone of voice broke through Meshur's anger. But before he could reply, the men heard the sound of trotting horses. They looked down the road to see a patrol of warriors riding back to town. The workers stood silent by the side of the road as the warriors drew close; Meshur did not try to hide the contempt he felt for them. But instead of ignoring the laborers and continuing to town, the line of riders suddenly wheeled, quickly encircling the workers. Spears forward, they watched while their leader dismounted and stepped forward.

"I am Captain Oman. Who are you and where are you going?" he asked roughly.

Pashtur shot Meshur a warning glance and stepped forward. "We are simple laborers, mighty warrior," he responded respectfully. "We are on our way to where our task awaits us."

"And where might that be, little man?" queried the captain with a sneer. "Perhaps in a clearing of the Great Forest? He chuckled and his men no longer hid their smirks. Pashtur stood wordless. "I have heard of you," continued the captain. "You are the sneak and the spy. My comrade Balech gives a very complete description!"

Meshur could contain himself no longer. "If you are a comrade of Balech, then you too must be one of our brave warriors that threatens the terrifying enemies of Lamech—the wives and children of honest men! We have no business with you. Stand aside and we will be on our way."

Oman laughed coldly. "You talk too much, ox!" he said, turning his attention to Meshur. "You are going back to your homes in town where you can find useful work. I have killed my share of men, and I would be content to add you to that list right now!"

Meshur faced him and taunted, "Then lay down your spear and come at me. If you are such a great warrior, surely you can defeat a poor laborer like me with the strength of your arm alone. Or is it strong only when holding weapons against unarmed foes?"

Oman's face blazed with anger. He drove the point of his spear into the ground and dismounted. "Stay, captain!" said the man next to him, quietly. "There is an easier way to handle this. You are needed for greater things."

That man dismounted beside his captain. Stepping forward quickly he drew his sword and pressed the point against Pashtur's belly. "You will obey your superiors, ox, or I will open your cousin right here. I have skill with a sword, and can guarantee that he will take several days to die, and that no man in Lamech will be able to save him."

Meshur stopped short. Pashtur's face was deathly pale and beads of sweat gathered on his forehead. With a sick look of fear he looked at Meshur with a silent appeal.

Oman visibly restrained his temper and retrieved his spear. "You are right, Kenah," he said to the man holding the sword to Pashtur's gut. We have more important things to do."

He turned to the workers. "You will all return to town now!" he ordered in a cold voice. "You will never enter the Great Forest again and you will never seek out Noah or his sons. Should you do this, we will hunt you down wherever you are, and we will slay you all! Shall we start now?"

Meshur tried to hide the conflict within. How could he betray Ham? He had spent decades of hard work to win Ham's respect and trust, and now he was being forced to throw all that away? But if he did not, how could he live with himself if he let his own cousin die before him? That was a betrayal, too: a bond ultimately deeper than work and pride—a bond of blood.

The choice was clear, but not easy. Without a word, he stooped and picked up his pack, and turned back to town. The other men silently followed, and Kenah sheathed his sword, allowing Pashtur to catch up with the others. The small man was still sweating and could not hide his trembling. The soldiers mounted and walked their horses behind the laborers with a menace evident only to the eight men.

Back in the privacy of Pashtur's house, the two cousins sat silently for some time. Pashtur regained his tongue first. "Thank you, Meshur. He would have killed me. I saw it in his eyes. There was nothing we could do."

"I have betrayed the greatest trust ever given to me. I have proven myself unworthy of any other."

The big man moved to the table and picked up a pitcher of wine in his massive hand and began to drink. Red streaks appeared on his cheeks and dribbled down to stain his tunic. Pashtur saw tears mingled with the wine, and quietly rose to leave. He would talk to his cousin in a few days. Let him drink now and forget. With time he would see that there had been no choice, and would understand that he had nothing to be ashamed of. Pashtur shuddered when he remembered the point of Kenah's sword straining against his skin, and the cold look in the man's eye that left no doubt to his desire to force it all the way through.

Suddenly Pashtur found that he hated Noah. True to his nature, his thoughts swiftly found his tongue. "It is not really Balech, this Oman, or even Sechiall that are the real problem," he blurted. "If Noah had been content to live in Lamech and perform his duties, then Sechiall and his animals would never have been able to gain any authority. Lamech, Noah, and Methuselah would never have countenanced their kind."

Pashtur caught his breath and sped on, unaware that Meshur was focused on the wine, not his cousin's chatter. "Certainly the town is deprived of much strength and justice with the passing of Lamech," he continued, "but Noah and Methuselah seemed to have left us to the mercy of evil men, allowing Sechiall to use Dajus and Subtur to spread his corruption. Noah has been ensnared by his obsession with this ark!" Pashtur paused, the fear in his eyes returning. "This ark was the reason that I almost died on the road today! Don't you see?" Meshur did not respond, sunk in his own self-pity. Pashtur's face grew hard. "I hate Noah!" he declared with the forcefulness that comes after fear. "I hate the ark!"

That statement roused Meshur to the point of a glare, and he started to think of how to answer his cousin's ranting. But Pashtur would not be stopped. "I am glad that we have been delivered from his folly! Never will I suffer the humiliation that I did today for something so preposterous!"

With that declaration, he turned and fled the room. Meshur watched him go. More than anything else he wanted to go to Ham, but how could he explain. He knew in his heart that his hands would never again caress the smooth joints and solid beams of the marvelous ark. The gathering darkness of the room suited his mood and he sat in a corner. It was a large pitcher.

****

Shades of red and orange shimmered across the coals. Shadows crept back out from the corners and consumed most of the room. Yet the light from the dying fire would not be extinguished by the darkness. Even in darkness, there is always some light and when one coal fades away, another unexpectedly glows brighter. So it has been and so it will be. We are each just a small part of things, thought the old woman watching the intricate dance of the embers, and small tasks consume our days, rendering us oblivious to the great events unfolding around us. Yet significance often has little to do with appearances...

Chapter 25
DYING LIGHT

Madrazi slumped in her chair by the window as the sun sent shadows slowly around the walls. Methuselah was sleeping lightly and as the light fell upon his face, she could see the deeply-etched lines of age with startling clarity. She was now often in his room, attending to his few needs. As it had become clear that he was failing, she had asked to be allowed to care for him and none had the heart to refuse her. Her vigil with Methuselah was an escape from the storm that had broken upon the house over the past two years. With the desertion of the laborers, an impossible burden had fallen on the family and their servants. Every man was needed in the forest and the women had to absorb the labors of both household and farm. Madrazi helped where she could, but recently all her time had been dedicated to the care of her failing friend.

Over the taxing months, the household had been held together by Wen-Tehrom. Madrazi had been amazed at her unflagging spirit. She organized the work fairly, took the greatest share upon herself, and kept the peace whenever a frayed temper erupted. She always had a smile and a word of encouragement, and with Yaran's able assistance the essential work had been done. Strangely, the turmoil did not seem to affect Madrazi; the recent years had left her callous and indifferent. Lamech's death had been more costly than she first expected—no more caravans of food were sent to town and her visits with Jeriah were few and far between. The spark in her spirit sank low until Methuselah's condition had led her to Wen-Tehrom's room to request the task of his care. Despite Methuselah's impending death, the time spent in his presence had stirred her heart once more to life and she began to shed her own cares in devoting herself completely to the old man.

As her mind exercised its accustomed introspection, she realized that one could not be with Methuselah and remain mired in self-pity and sorrow. There was something about his company that chased those shadows from her heart. In his presence, selfish emotions were banished, and her energy was renewed in turning to the needs of his comfort and health. If the other women noticed the change in Madrazi's face, they said nothing, but Wen-Tehrom secretly rejoiced and Shem was unable to hide his relief during his infrequent hours at the house.

Madrazi did not notice. She was just thankful for the opportunity to help her great-grandfather, and did not really care that her strength might be needed in the fields and barns. Although the roof of the ark had been completed more than a year earlier, the desertion of the hired workers had taxed everyone sorely. Many of the servants who remained were older, and could not work at the pace of the younger men from town. Ham was seldom at the house; doing the work of many men in completing the remaining pens, storage bins, and quarters aboard the ark. He drove himself night and day; the desertion of the hired men had apparently hurt him more than any one else.

From Shem's infrequent visits, Madrazi knew that Japheth and his helpers were already loading food, seed, and all of the uncounted items needed for care of the animals and life in the next world. Shem and his men were testing the containers that would hold water; the larger storage compartments built into the lower deck and the smaller ones and drinking barrels on the upper deck. Shem was even able to rouse Madrazi's interest in Ham's design of a screw pump powered by oxen that moved water from the stream up into the ark. Noah worked as hard as any, reminding all that the day was coming soon. He prepared the captive animals, but had been unable to capture more, and even with the cages full, there were only a few hundred of the thousands that would be needed aboard the ark.

None of the family had traveled to town recently. Shortly after Lamech's death, evidence had been presented of Torech's culpability, resulting in Sechiall's elevation to the council and the decision to prepare for war with Y'tor over Methuselah's objection. Noah no longer had time or interest for affairs of the city. Madrazi had tried to maintain Lamech's charity to the poor, but soon found she could do little, and the indifference and even opposition of the townsfolk ended her efforts. She had not realized the obstacles that had been overcome by Lamech's power, and did not know whether to hate or pity the men who let others suffer by their selfish negligence. However, she did not completely abandon Jeriah during those dark days, though the changes in Lamech discouraged frequent travel to town. Where once people had been open and courteous, now they were suspicious and uncaring. Jeriah did not seem as attuned to the transformation as her friend and excused what she did see with the town's preoccupation with war preparations. Certainly Jared was away much, training an army that had swollen with young men eager for the glory of conquest.

But Madrazi's world was now limited to Methuselah's rooms. She sat in the midst of a storm, aware of its gathering clouds, but ignoring the portents; for they seemed insignificant compared to the impending departure of her beloved friend. At his side, she was untouched by the outside world and had little sense of time's passage. She clung to her time with him because he was all that remained of her past, and she was not ready to abandon it for the demands of the future. Her hatred and fear of the ark had been replaced by apathy; she no longer cared about its construction, the frenzied work of the women, or the problems in town. Her world was that one room and her life was the old man who lay dying.

After serving as a source of strength for the family in the years following Lamech's murder, he had taken a turn for the worse after the council meeting that had installed Sechiall. He had not been in town at all for the past six months, and gradually became indifferent to the affairs of the household. Recently, his strength had begun to leave him, and for the past two weeks, he had been unable to leave his bed except for a few minutes during the morning and evening. He wanted little food, but slept much; waking at odd hours of the night or day, ready to talk for a few minutes or hours until he fell back asleep, exhausted. Soon he would awaken no more in this world.

She started, coming fully awake. She did not remember falling asleep—the passing of light and darkness held little meaning to her anymore. She looked at Methuselah and was surprised to see his old eyes clear and bright. There was something strange about his face, but it was more sensed than seen. "Granpapa," she cried softly, "you look much better. Did you have a good rest?"

"Soon, my child, I will have enough of rest," he replied slowly. "My time is near; I see strange, but beautiful visions in my sleep now. Before I depart, I have words that I must leave with you."

Tears welled up in her eyes as she leaned nearer to him. "I will hold them always in my heart with all your others. You know that."

He heard the anguish in her voice, and smiled faintly. "Peace, child. Do not grieve for me. I go to my fathers and my son. I will stand before my Creator and see His face, as did Adam. I am content." He breathed deeply and continued. "But that is not what I need to say. You know that I chose you for Shem and made certain of your marriage. I know your struggles; wife to Shem, yet doubting the prophecy of Shem's father."

He shook his head at her look. "No, child, do not fear. That part of your heart is your own, but you have given everything else in good measure to your husband and family. Guard your heart from the hardness of deceit. It will come to truth in its own time. Only make sure that nothing stands in its way." He coughed gently and she gave him a sip of clear water as she felt tears run down onto her lips.

He lay back for a moment, and then spoke again. "It is most ironic: I, who have no doubts of my grandson's vision, will not see its fulfillment; while you who cannot bring yourself to believe, will! Your doubts will be dispelled in a new reality—your new reality. Remember then that another choice will face you—the only truly important choice you will make."

He sighed, and rested again for a few moments. Madrazi sat attentive and wiped the tears from her cheeks, waiting for his next words. Her mind seemed abnormally clear and she knew that she would never forget these moments.

"Child, your choice has never been faith in the words of Noah. You will see them come to pass with your eyes, and go into the ark and survive the judgment of God by the choice of others; Noah, Shem, me. Your test of faith will come only after you see that truth. That choice will be to believe or not the One who delivered the prophecy to Noah. Find a new life for your soul, just as Shem and Noah will deliver your body alive into a new world."

"How will I know where to look?" she asked.

"When the time is right, you will be shown, and then you will find that which you will always treasure in your heart, just as I treasure it in mine. For now, cast aside all doubt, love your husband, help your father, and keep my memory. Remember that I chose you, but my choice was that of the Creator before it was mine. I am old and the old is passing away. You are young, and your great-grandchildren will fill the new Earth. A new life needs a new heart. Consider well what I have said."

He paused and slowly drew breath. Smiling weakly he asked, "Do you trust me, Madrazi?"

Remembering those words of long ago, she lost control and sobbed, "Of course, Granpapa."

"Good!" he exclaimed weakly. "Do not forget. Best friends trust even when they will not see each other for many years."

As he spoke, a change seemed to overcome him. Madrazi saw a strange light in his eyes, and it seemed to grow and infuse his whole face. The lines were gone and peace was in his features. With a gasp, she realized that this was what he spoke of seeing in Enoch long centuries ago. It was true! She could never refuse him anything, but the light told her that his God was speaking through him, too. She would hold his words. In honoring Methuselah, she was obeying God. She did not understand it, but its truth was undeniable.

Madrazi gathered her thoughts and leaned close the peaceful face. Softly she spoke, but with a conviction that she knew was heard beneath the words. "I swear to you, Methuselah, that I will remember your words always. I swear to you that I will do all that is within my strength to help Noah and Shem. I will set aside my doubt and rest in your words. This I promise to you—you can depart satisfied that your choice was not in vain."

Madrazi knew that her words, like those at her wedding, were binding her with new cords to a life that had perplexed her for twenty years. But in a moment of awareness, she realized that she could do nothing else. No confusion, no selfishness, no pride would interfere with this promise as they had blighted the previous years. The shame of that thought and the emotion of the vow brought new tears, but they seemed to bring calm instead of turmoil.

Methuselah smiled again and reached out his hand. She held the weak and fragile fingers. His voice grew stronger. "I am content. May you find the peace and joy that I have now. I am leaving, but God will always be near to you, and I will await you in His presence."

He leaned back and relaxed and was asleep again in a few minutes. Madrazi waited to pull her hand from his, and left the room quietly. Instinctively, she knew that Methuselah had completed his life with these words, and she ran to find Noah and Wen-Tehrom. Her stricken expression told them all they needed to know and all three hurried back to the old man's bed. Noah's entrance roused Methuselah one last time. As Noah gathered him into his arms and pulled him close, Methuselah spoke again. "God is faithful. He will do as He promised. Put all your trust in Him." Madrazi had entered the room behind Wen-Tehrom and saw the old man look directly at her over Noah's shoulder. "She was the right choice," he said clearly. Then as they watched, his eyes saw beyond the room. "My father, I see you. I come."

As Noah held him in his arms, Methuselah's body slowly relaxed. Wen-Tehrom held Madrazi close for a moment and then guided her out of the room to leave Noah alone with his grandfather. The women wept together as they made their way to the great hall and sat down. Madrazi leaned on the table, pillowing her head in her arms. An exhaustion of body and mind combined with a hollow sadness deep in her soul to steal what strength she had. She remembered little, but Wen-Tehrom's hand on her head as she slumped over the table and wept uncontrollably for many minutes.

When the tears had run their course, Madrazi began to be aware once again of her surroundings and of the arms of Wen-Tehrom around her shoulders. She looked up at the older woman with red eyes, silently asking questions for which there were no answers. Wen-Tehrom ignored them and spoke softly. "My daughter, we all know of your devotion to Methuselah, and your care for him in these final days has been a labor of love. You have been a gift from God, making his final days easier. I do not know what words passed between you, but I have never seen such contentment on his face. I will never forget your love for him."

"I did love him," Madrazi choked. "We were so different, but my life was enmeshed in his and...I cannot understand. I hate death! I have lost so much that I loved...I am so alone." She bowed her head again, ashamed of her words.

"You are not alone in this world," said Wen-Tehrom, "as long as I remain alive. We who remain are bound together in love for Methuselah, and for each other. I am not the woman who gave birth to you, but I will be your mother if you will have it. Noah is not Pomorolac, but he feels the same. We know that we cannot be all that they were to you, but there is no reason why our life together cannot be good, and cannot hold love. There is already more there than you realize."

Madrazi was past responding at that moment, but she later remembered those words with gratitude and marked that day as the time she truly became a part of that family.

They mourned Methuselah for only three days, and buried him beside Lamech. "Our task is too urgent, and Methuselah will understand," said Noah. We will honor both of our dead in the new world." Although loath to spare anyone from the work, Noah sent word to Lamech of Methuselah's death, and said, "I have completed my duty to the council and people of Lamech. My face is now turned away from the old and to the new."

Chapter 26
LAST WARNING

The few allotted days of mourning for Methuselah passed, but Madrazi's grief could not be eradicated in days, or even weeks. Rather than attenuating her emotion, the passing days seemed to intensify it. So many feelings were colliding in her heart. There had been little time for grief, though she was sure she would mourn Methuselah for the rest of her life. His final words and her inability to comprehend them added to the emotional mix. And underneath simmered the warnings of both Methuselah and Noah that the time was near. One way or another, her efforts of the past twenty years would be tested, and doubts in her course engendered by Methuselah's warnings did little to help. She still did not believe Noah, but neither could she disbelieve. She told herself that it did not matter right now; she was bound inseparably to this family and its pursuits by her word. So she drove herself each day and found exhaustion kept her mind firmly on the hour at hand.

Shem had become an anchor during her turmoil. His presence, his kind encouragement, and his small courtesies all helped counter the loneliness of loss. He did not offer many words—he seemed to know that they would be pointless, but he shared as many hours with her as he could and as her black mood lessened, she came to realize that Methuselah's death affected him deeply, too. So she attempted to offer him comfort and in that found her own equilibrium returning.

There came a morning when Shem intercepted her before she could plod off to the barns. There was a hint of happiness in his face and before she knew what was happening, he surprised her, lifting her off the ground into his arms. She returned his kiss by reflex, and suddenly found that one was not enough. With a laugh, he let her down, but did not let go. "Madrazi," he said, with a hint of teasing, "would you care to accompany me to Lamech tomorrow morning? I wish to buy a warm cloak, and thought that we might find two of the same weave."

She had no words, taken aback at both his speech and his manner. Perhaps he understood her need for distraction, but there was something else; some resolution that he had reached. She suddenly wanted nothing more than an escape from the lonely work and from the oppression of her pent up emotion. Lamech would offer both. "May I call upon Jeriah?" she asked tentatively.

"Of course, my love," he returned. "I anticipated your wishes, and I have finally decided that I will take your advice and speak to Jared. I know that they are to leave soon to fight Y'tor and I want to see him before they go. I have thought about the death of Lamech for these past five years, and cannot escape the conclusion that his killer was Sechiall. I have finally decided that Jared deserves that knowledge, whether he chooses to act upon it or not."

Madrazi better understood his mood. Having wrestled long with that problem, its resolution seemed to have cleared away some tension inside. Then his face clouded for a moment. "I have something else to say." He was suddenly nervous. "I know that Jeriah is special to you in a way that no other person is. I know that you doubt the coming of destruction..." He silenced her with a glance as she started to protest or explain, and continued, "but I ask you to consider for just a moment that it may be possible. If it *might* happen, would you not want your friend with you? I have asked Noah, and he has told me that if you make this offer to Jeriah and she accepts, that she would be welcome, with her husband."

Madrazi winced inside. If there was anything that could ruin the benefit of a trip to town, turning her mind to the prophecy and the ark would. At the same time she knew that she should be grateful. For Noah and Shem, the offer was a genuine act of sacrifice and love. Fortunately, she understood that well enough to keep her anger from showing. Instead she suddenly resolved to let nothing ruin an outing to town with her husband, and upon that decision she felt her spirits lift.

They were still high when they arrived at Jared's door the next day. Servants, recognizing Madrazi, welcomed the couple inside and hurried away to find their master. Within minutes, both Jared and Jeriah were greeting them—Jeriah warmly and Jared with some stiffness at Shem's presence. "Welcome to our home," Jared said formally. "Please accept our sympathy at the loss of your father, Methuselah. He was a man of dignity and honor, and his death impoverishes all our lives."

Shem inclined his head. "We are saddened by his passing, and grateful for your kind words. A light has truly passed out of this world, but we celebrate its presence in the halls of his fathers." He glanced at his wife. "We had business in Lamech, but we desired your company." Both men knew well that he meant that Jeriah and Madrazi wished for time together. "We had learned that you march on Y'tor soon, and wanted to wish you safety and success."

Jared nodded. "We leave in two days. I must go tomorrow and make final preparations." He paused uncomfortably, ready to be done with the encounter.

Shem spoke up. "I know that you have much to do, and that our wives will want time together. Perhaps, Madrazi," he said turning to her, "you could meet me later at our house."

Then he turned back to Jared, "But before I take my leave, Commander, would you grant me a few minutes of your time?" Jared and Jeriah could not hide their surprise at those words. Jared recovered first and nodded. Knowing Shem's purpose, Madrazi took her friend's arm and asked, "Could we enjoy the morning in your garden?" Jeriah arranged her face into a smile, nodded, and walked out with Madrazi, leaving the men alone.

Jared hid his thoughts behind an impassive face and gestured to Shem, "Please come and sit, and enjoy a cool glass of wine." The commander bowed Shem into the open door and then spoke, "Be welcome here. I must find us some wine so that we may drink and talk together."

Alone in the room, Shem felt its tasteful sense of sanctuary and walked slowly across it. Pools of light from polished lamps did not quite invade all of the dim corners, or disturb the essential quiet of the room. It had a rugged comfort, and the orderly arrangement of the furnishings spoke of a disciplined decorator. Clearly a warrior's room, weapons and armor adorned the walls, and an engraved wooden frame with a scroll mounted in it occupied the spot over the fireplace. Shem walked across to it and saw that it was the commendation Jared had received the day that Noah had rebuked him for his desire to bring the army onto the council.

Shem turned away from it; both men would be embarrassed by that memory were Jared to return now. He slid to the left to get a look at a series of wooden shelves let into the far wall. About half of the shelves were filled with writings—not the scrolls common at that time, but with small books. Shem had heard of stitching fine parchment together inside a protective covering of wood or hide, but had not seen any so fine. The leather-covered wooden covers were engraved and dated, each a different year. Shem realized that the entire collection formed a record of many years. He turned as he heard Jared's soft footfalls outside the door.

"Writing is my release in the evenings," Jared explained, nodding at the shelves. Shem accepted the golden cup while Jared stared at the shelves and continued, "Scrolls are too cumbersome to take into camp, so I limit my scribbling to these. The covering protects the pages from the elements."

"The exteriors are exquisitely crafted, Commander. May I ask what covers the interiors?" Shem's curiosity was plain: although all in Lamech were educated, it was not common for a soldier to practice the art of writing.

"For better or worse," replied Jared, smiling grimly, "I have changed the army of Lamech into something to be feared by our enemies and respected by our friends. Over the years I had the fancy that warriors from some other place or time might be interested in our story. So I have kept the story of these years for them—and for me." He shrugged his shoulders and turned to Shem. "But you did not want to see me for these insignificant works. He turned to the fireplace and both men's eyes caught the scroll mounted there. Jared stiffened, but Shem broke the moment.

"Commander," he began formally, but then paused. "Jared," he began again in his soft voice, "I know we are not friends and our paths would not cross but for our wives, but I come to you with my opinion of you as a man and I will speak to the man I believe you to be. If I am mistaken, then I am sorry, but a man must rely on his judgment. Will you hear me?"

Jared looked at Shem with searching eyes. It was true that they did not know each other, but the plain words and honest tone stirred his respect. He might dislike Noah, but there was no reason to hate the son, and there was something in those dark eyes that he trusted. Though he and Shem had spoken infrequently in their previous encounters, Jared's job was to know men, and he had heard of Shem's prowess with the bow and courage as a hunter. Any man that could face and slay a large hunting lizard was a man, indeed. As their eyes met, Shem's were now as hard and searching as Jared's. Trusting his instincts, Jared decided he could talk honestly with the man facing him.

"If you speak truth, I will hear."

"Good!" exclaimed Shem, "I have hard things to say, and have not the diplomacy of my fathers. Having spent my life in the Great Forest, I know only its ways, not men's clever speech. Please do not be offended because I lack such skill."

"I am only a soldier, so I also am accustomed to the unadorned truth. Speak on."

"Before you fight a battle you consider many possible outcomes of your actions, do you not?"

"Of course! Success demands no less."

"Then consider the possibilities surrounding the death of Lamech."

Jared stiffened, but Shem continued. "We are told that Torech had him assassinated, but what are the other possibilities? Bandits? Soldiers from another enemy town? Or perhaps enemies closer to home? There is no doubt he was murdered. He and his servants were slain quickly by a man skilled with the sword."

Jared bristled. "Why do you say man?" he demanded harshly. "My soldiers slew three men of Y'tor who confessed to the murder."

"I found Lamech and his servants on the road!" returned Shem just as sharply. "Around the bodies there were only the tracks of one other man. I have spent my life in the forest, learning to read its signs and I know how to read tracks. And there is another piece of information that I have not shared. I reveal it now to you because of my hope in the kind of man you are." He held out his hand and Jared advanced and looked. Lying in Shem's hand was a small piece of brown cloth with a small silver clasp at one edge, and a dirty stain. The soldier recognized the stain as blood, long dried.

Shem said nothing, but continued to look at Jared as he took the scrap and eyed it closely. Then he continued. "I found this clutched in Lamech's hand. What one man would benefit most from Lamech's death? What one man would benefit from the blame being placed on Torech? And what one man has the skill with a sword to kill three strong men in the time it takes us to speak of it?"

Jared said nothing, eyes fixed on the scrap in his hand, mind racing. Finally he stirred. "You think that I had anything to do with this?"

Shem smiled grimly. "Do you think that I would be here now, saying these things if I did?"

Jared measured him carefully, new respect in his eyes. "Yes," he said at length, "I think you would."

"I appreciate the compliment, Commander, but I have no wish for revenge."

"Then why come to me?"

"Because I do believe that you had nothing to do with it," returned Shem emphatically.

"Now you pay me the compliment. But I ask again, why come to me?"

"If this deed was done by one in Lamech, I think that you could discover his identity easier than I," returned Shem. "Also, if your war with Torech is being used to some end other than the legitimate defense of the city, should you not be concerned about the waste of your men's lives?"

"What would you have me do if I discovered truth in your words?" asked Jared. "Do you seek me as an instrument of vengeance on your enemies?"

"No. God will avenge Lamech if vengeance is necessary. In fact, I ask nothing at all of you except to ponder what I have said. You will do what heart and honor demand. I came to you because I believe a plot may exist in our city and that you have no part in it. How you choose to meet this challenge is for you, not me. I have made my decision to follow my father and his prophecy. Its day draws near and the affairs of Lamech are no longer my concern."

Seeing the look on Jared's face, Shem continued, "I know that all in Lamech reject Noah's vision from long ago, but I would leave you with one final word. For the sake of your wife, if you will, there is room on the ark for any who choose to believe the word that God has spoken through Noah. Farewell, Jared. May God open your heart and give you wisdom."

Shem turned to go and Jared followed him to the door of the house. They stood for a moment without speaking, but each seeking something in the eyes of the other. After a moment, Shem nodded slightly to himself and turned away. Jared returned to his room and sat down. He still clung to the scrap of cloth, and now he stared at it for many minutes. He knew the cloak that it had been torn from. Long ago it had belonged to him.

Was any of this possible? Shem knew little, or he would have brought charges to the council. But why had he come to him? If this were true, then the blood of Lamech had irrevocably stained all the carefully crafted ambition of his entire life. How could he turn his back on his dreams? But what good were his dreams if they were dripping with the blood of an innocent man? And what kind of man had received the hopes and dreams of his youth and turned them to murder? Jared sat in the chair and stared at the clasp for a long hour before resolutely putting it away.

He was still sitting when he heard Jeriah bid farewell to Madrazi. Her footsteps echoed in the hall, and then she was standing before him. "Is all well?" she asked.

He shook himself from his reverie and replied, "Yes, my wife. I have discovered today that I misjudged a man. Your friend found a good man and I am sorry I did not know it sooner."

"I found a good man, too," said Jeriah. "You have given me happiness in these short years, and I look forward to all the rest. What words did you pass with Shem?"

"Most were about business with the army, but he spoke in friendship of something else..." he paused, wondering if he should tell her of Shem's offer. Finally he spoke, "He said that the day of Noah's prophecy draws near, and offered us a place in their ark against the coming destruction. Yesterday I would have laughed at such a thing to his face, but I could not after seeing into his eyes. It brought to mind something that I had forgotten."

"What is that, my love," asked Jeriah.

"When Zered fell ill, Noah and Lamech were the only elders to come to him. They talked with him alone the day before he died, and I was surprised, for I never counted Noah as a friend. When I went in to see my father after they had gone, he had changed. Where before he had preferred Dajus and

Subtur, he then praised Noah and Lamech as good men and friends. He even told me that he was foolish not to attend to the words of Noah, although it was too late. I always thought that the nearness of death had disturbed his mind, but now I wonder. What think you of this prophecy?"

Jeriah paused to gather her thoughts. "I know that Noah and his family believe it to the point of separating themselves from a prosperous life in Lamech. I cannot accept it myself, but sometimes I cannot help but wonder what it would mean if it were true."

Jared paused, and then spoke. "My love, life is full of uncertainties. If anything happens to me in the upcoming battle, go to Madrazi with my blessing. I believe that her house would be open to you, and that you would find refuge there. Her husband is a good man."

Jeriah looked at her husband thoughtfully. He did not seem himself, but the words were sincere. Perhaps the strain of the coming battle was wearing him down. "Peace, husband," she replied softly. "We will have many good years together and I am content. Shem is not the only good man in Lamech."

Late that night, Jared found himself in his refuge, searching through the books before him. He selected two and sat down. Slowly he opened the first and the words brought back the relief of acceptance into the brotherhood of warriors that he had discovered after crossing swords with Pohtile that morning long ago. That day had shown him that his life had only one purpose, to fight and defeat the enemies of his city. The coming days would tell whether or not his preparations had been adequate. He was confident in his abilities and those of his men, but what of Sechiall? What if Shem was not mistaken? How else could he have had that bloodstained piece of his old cloak?

He opened the second book and refreshed his memory on the events surrounding those early years; the coming of Sechiall, his early training and the promise of great things. Perhaps there was a clue in these words—some forgotten incident or word from the past, insignificant at the time, but now ready to reveal its meaning. Something that would connect with the words of Shem and form a logical path along the trails of his memory: something that might explain without convicting him of treachery, or even worse, of being a foolish accomplice to a treachery that he had not even seen. He brought out ink and a clean, new book and started recording his thoughts hoping to capture what lurked on the edge of thought. Writing away the night hours was an easy habit. Sleep was out of the question, but this wakeful night brought no clear answers.

****

The minutes passed and the glow of the fire diminished slowly. The flame consumed the next to last stick, reducing it to coals and then sputtered, almost going out. But there was one last unburned piece of wood, and the flame found it in time. It flared briefly then settled into the steady glow of orange fire. From her couch, the old woman watched it burn down until only the shimmering dance of glowing embers could be seen. The fire searched for fuel; people searched for...people searched for their heart's desire, but often did not stop to discern what that might really be. Others knew all along; some found out just in time...

Chapter 27

CLASH OF HONOR

Sechiall and Jared rode together ahead of the long columns of marching men. Other riders ranged miles ahead and out to the flanks, scouting the terrain and returning to report regularly to the commanders. In keeping with Jared's take-no-chances temperament, all were alert to any possibility of ambush or enemy scouts. Sechiall was grimly exultant in the efficiency and strength of Lamech's army and his mood seemed contagious as the men marched in disciplined order behind. Their challenge was clear, and their confidence high. The years of preparation under Jared's firm hand had been worth the wait.

"What do you think Torech will do?" he asked Jared lightly, "Come out and fight, or bottle himself up behind his walls?"

Jared was silent for a moment. "I would burn the fields, stay behind the walls and force us to spend time a long way from home. With a small raiding force lurking somewhere outside of town to cut our path back home, he could make life difficult. But Torech has not that patience. He is cunning and a good fighter, but always overconfident. What would you do?"

"You know me," Sechiall grinned, "I would come out and attack as soon as possible, and keep attacking until all my enemies were dead."

"Yes, and I think that like you, Torech will think about the battle instead of the war. He will come out to us. After our last battle, he knows we can fight, but his fear has been dulled by time, and we have helped his bravado by remaining behind our walls all these years. He will probably outnumber us again, but not by as many as he did last time. We have a good idea of his strength, but he has little of ours. Torech has never invested in spies. But the money that has gained us information about his army has been well spent—we know what he has and how he uses it. If he attacks and sees us retreating, then be sure that he will press his advantage relentlessly. He is a great warrior, but predictable."

"It will destroy him. We are fortunate that Y'tor has no Jared. Your ice and my fire make an unbeatable combination. In a few hundred years perhaps Taspar will beg to be our ally and Lamech will be the capital of a great kingdom—our kingdom. With Supreme General Jared as my right hand,

Lamech will become known and feared all around the earth."

"Perhaps," allowed Jared. He seemed to hear the words of Sechiall with new ears. Sechiall had always been boastful, and spoke of ambitions beyond his reach, but Jared had long since ceased to pay it any attention. But after Shem's eyes and words.... He could no longer ignore what was now plainly spoken.

Though he was not yet sure what path to choose, he was determined to discover if there was any truth in what Shem had said, so he kept Sechiall talking. "I am still surprised that Torech was foolish enough to murder Lamech. It was fortunate for the town that you and your patrol were able to track the killers, but it is unfortunate that they resisted and could not be interrogated more carefully and brought before the council for judgment."

"It would not have been any different," returned Sechiall easily in his well-practiced lie. "We produced bodies of Y'tor's warriors for the council. Oman, Gatar, and Kenah all witnessed my testimony of the confession of the last one before death overtook him. All the men of the city were satisfied, except that dotard Methuselah. But he is dead and Noah is unwilling to show his face in town! Your vision is achieved, Jared! After Torech is destroyed, we can build our army into a regional power. Y'tor will be a colony of Lamech, and its men will be forced to fight with us. In a few years, wealth and power will be ours for the taking."

He continued, his eyes blazing with an inner fire, "You can sit on the council with me, Jared, and we will control those fools Dajus and Subtur. The day of the wise is ended. The day of the strong is upon us. Let us seize it!"

"We have to defeat Torech first, Commander," Jared observed dryly.

But underneath his words, he felt the pull of Sechiall's vision. And Sechiall himself was compelling. So young, yet such a masterful man; confident, bold, and cunning. Almost a son... but what else? Why had Shem come to him? Why did he believe that Jared's honor was more important than ambition? Like Noah, he had darkened what should have been a bright day. All it had taken was a silver clasp on the torn and bloodied fabric of a cloak—Sechiall's cloak—one that Jared had not seen for five years. Such a small thing, yet from the moment he had touched it, he felt his hands stained with innocent blood. Was his dream worth the murder of a good man?

If Shem had spoken the truth, then Sechiall had murdered an innocent and good man to achieve power. If one, why not more? What would constrain him? If guilty, he had proven that he held little respect for tradition, custom, or established order. Jared needed to discover the truth. How it mattered! Had Shem seen that, too? Why had he waited so long? Why were his words so easy to believe? There must be room for doubt, and Noah was the key. Now he must use it.

"Your vision is large and bold, Sechiall," replied Jared quietly after the two had ridden for a few more minutes, "but it requires victories, and the first will be the hardest. We must defeat Torech in open warfare, and then we can worry about Noah. He is a powerful man in Lamech and the reminder of the old order under which many prospered. He cannot be manipulated as can Dajus and Subtur. How will we defeat him? I see your hand in the desertion of most of his servants—many of them are now marching behind us. But that will not stop Noah. Once he gives up his preoccupation with dreams and visions, and returns to Lamech, he will be a powerful man. After all, he is the blood link to the origin of our town."

"Yes," agreed Sechiall, his passion running ahead of his tongue. "We will need to defeat Torech and Noah in the same fashion—with the sword! Torech will be more difficult and will take an army. Noah will be easy, and I know a few men that we can trust to do the job and keep their silence."

Jared's blood ran cold as Shem's words echoed in his mind, accusations drumming in time with each step of his horse. Achieving power was one thing, but murdering a righteous man like Noah was not warrior's work. Sechiall had just proven that Noah's life was not sacred; Lamech's would not have been any different. Jared still did not have proof, but he had few doubts. He felt his carefully-crafted image of the world begin to shatter. But he kept his face still.

"You have planned well, Sechiall. I will see to our march, and we will talk more of this later."

He rode back down the line of marching soldiers, hardly seeing the salutes of the men. Through all of his confusion, one thought beat upon him. *Shem was right! Sechiall must have killed Lamech and used it to bring about his opportunity.* Could he share in such a victory? Or would innocent blood on his hands haunt him to the end of his days? Delonias would never stoop to such things. Perhaps he could help. If after the battle, Jared rode to Taspar.... No, he must face this as he did all other problems—head on.

Ten days later the army of Lamech halted at the mouth of a shallow canyon that opened onto the plain above Y'tor. Jared had chosen this site with care. A short ways back from their camp, a side canyon branched off to the west and he had seen the possibility of ambush scouting the area years ago. To be successful, Torech must now learn of their presence. To that end, he had allowed the first scouts to return to Y'tor but then had issued orders that all others be killed. His own scouts were well trained and he was confident that none would get through their net to warn Torech of their preparations at this site.

The two commanders sat in a large tent over bread and wine and contemplated the days ahead. Jared had recovered his equanimity, and hid his thoughts from Sechiall by concentrating on the battle ahead as he considered inwardly how to deal with Lamech's death.

"Torech must come now," said Sechiall. "He knows we are here and will be before his walls in two days. A day after that, and I will ride into his city, carrying his head on my spear. Y'tor will be ours. Torech's life is mine, but if our plan succeeds, then his sword will be given to you before the council by your Supreme Commander!" Then Sechiall's brow furrowed. "What will we do if Torech will not come out? I once had a wise teacher who told me to plan for every contingency."

"Men like Torech are often provoked into unwise actions," said Jared, his mind not on Torech. He paused a moment, in thought, and then roused himself and continued. "If he doesn't come up onto the plain to fight, then we will leave half of our army there out of sight of the town and take the other half right down to his gate and taunt him. If he doesn't come out to fight a force less than half of his own, then his hold on the town is weakened. He rules by fear. If he is seen to be afraid, then his power is diminished."

Later that evening, Jared returned from his inspection of the outposts. They were alert and understood the necessity of keeping a careful watch this close to Y'tor. Pickets, the fastest runners, were scattered out along the plain between the ravine and town. Any movement from town would result in warning quickly being passed along to camp. An uneasy peace settled on the men as the more experienced sought sleep after eating their fill and the less experienced sat together talking of the great feats awaiting them the next day.

Jared too partook of an uneasy peace. Not sure of what to do, his heart was now sure of the truth of Shem's words. During the past few days, he had thought of several schemes to broach the issue with Sechiall, and rejected them all after consideration. He was not a man of great subtlety or a schemer. He was a warrior, and so he finally decided that in keeping with himself, he would question Sechiall directly. He did not relish the anticipated argument, but at least his heart was now at ease.

Last night, standing in the late night darkness alone, Jared had decided many things—foremost among them that honor was better than power. As he stood alone under the black expanse of the heavens he felt the call deep in his soul from the brightness of the stars. For a moment, he had an inexplicable feeling that the stars were small windows to a much greater light that lay beyond the darkness. He knew then what he must do. The stars seemed to bring back old words from Delonias. "Duty, honor, and courage are the marks of a true warrior. Anyone can take up a sword to kill, but there must be a difference between a warrior and a brigand."

His mind turned to the future. Jeriah would understand. Perhaps they could leave Lamech after this battle and he could take service with Delonias in Taspar. But first, he must be sure. If Lamech's death had been a coincidence, then Sechiall was not a murderer and could perhaps be turned away from his hatred of Noah and his plans to kill him.

With a clear mind, Jared squared his back and walked into the tent. "Commander," he began formally, "I have a report to make. All is in order, and victory awaits you tomorrow."

Sechiall nodded. "Of course, my friend. We will be celebrating the death of Torech this time tomorrow."

Jared glanced at the orderly and then back to Sechiall. "May we speak alone, Commander?"

Sechiall waved the man away and told him to take the guard outside the tent entrance away with him. "What is it, Jared? Do you have some further idea for our triumphant return to Lamech?"

Jared steeled himself against the power of those blue eyes. "No, I have a question!"

Sechiall was taken aback by his tone. "Ask."

Jared opened his hand and the lamp reflected off of a small piece of silver in his hand. "Did you kill Lamech?" The words hung in the air between them, and Jared saw the blue eyes harden as they measured the words and the man.

Sechiall reached his decision in seconds, but in spite of his long knowledge, he misjudged the older man. Relaxing, he smiled and waved his hand in a casual gesture. "Of course I did, Jared. Lamech was the largest obstacle to our desire for power. Once he was removed, and we fixed the blame on Torech, we opened the door to our dreams. We will rule, you and I. Noah will die under the same sword that drank his father's blood, and then nothing will stop us."

Jared's eyes were as cold and hard as his voice. "Your dream, Sechiall! Delonias sent a serpent to me, not a man. Torech is the enemy of my people. I will fight tomorrow and we will win, but when we return to Lamech, I will speak to the men of the city. If they do not kill me for my unwitting help in your deeds, then I will leave and go elsewhere to seek a life that has more to it than power and pride."

Sechiall's face changed. For a moment, Jared saw both anger and surprise there, but anger won. There was a hint of incomprehension, too, and Jared wondered at his years of willful blindness to their different moral codes. Their friendship and shared ambitions had always made those differences seem trivial, but now the true gulf between them stuck Jared like a fist. Honor must drive his life; in Sechiall, the lust for power burned away the veneer of principle. Jared saw Sechiall's thoughts in his eyes. Fear was there, too. If Jared went to the men of Lamech and exposed the plot, Sechiall would be branded a murderer and his adoption into the town would be terminated along with his life.

Moreover, Jared would probably not suffer for his murky role, for that would implicate the two elders. Besides, he would be needed to keep tight rein on the army if Sechiall was punished. That was inevitable: the life of an outsider—a murderer—would be easily forfeit in the name of justice. Dajus and Subtur would, of course, lead the cries for his head and deny any association with him in the heinous killing of their beloved peer. Sechiall's eyes blazed; Jared wondered if he was more incensed by the threat on his life or by the threatened loss of the power almost within his reach. Sechiall's hands trembled, but Jared stood still with the resolve of a strong man who knows and follows his heart.

Although Sechiall's first response was to lash out with fist or sword, he controlled his emotion and attempted to reach the man before him. "No, Jared," he replied in a cold voice. "It is your dream. Do not be angry because I am able to see the end of the path even if you do not. We are superior! The rest are sheep and need us. Talk and delay achieve nothing; only strength and the will to use it. We have that strength. Do not resent me for having the will when you did not. Torech is an enemy and you would gladly kill him. Lamech was an enemy and I gladly killed him. Noah is an enemy and I will kill him, too. It's that simple!"

Jared was unrelenting. "You are wrong! Torech is a warrior. Lamech was the foremost elder of our town. Noah is a good man, and also an elder of our council. If Lamech was an enemy to be slain with the sword, why did you not challenge him in the square instead of murdering him on the road?"

Sechiall snarled at this shrewd question. "Because the sheep of Lamech do not understand power and cling to their religion and traditions for peace and security. They do not understand that peace is won in blood and security maintained by fear. Fear is sent forth by power. Surely you understand, Jared. You have prepared me for power for many years and you would have been content to hold a part of that power in your own hands as my friend and father. But now you turn on me. What am I to think?"

"Uncontrolled power is of no service to anyone," replied Jared coldly. "I prepared you for power within bounds, Sechiall. Virtue, honor, integrity. These are not just words to be used to manipulate others. They must have meaning, or we are no better than men like Torech."

"The only flaw in Torech is his inability to project his power as far as his eyes see," returned Sechiall quickly. "If we had not defeated him, then he would have taken Lamech by now. No, Jared," he laughed, "there is only one choice; conquer or be conquered. The difference between Torech and Sechiall is that I shall conquer and he shall be conquered. Anything else is an illusion."

"Then there is a greater difference between you and I than either of us realized," replied Jared bitterly. "For I live to serve my city, not to rule it to my whim. I will not allow Lamech to be subdued by Torech, no matter what face he may wear."

The men faced each other: both bathed in the tension erupting from the discovery that years of friendship were empty, and the tension itself was leading to a blood resolution. Jared was not afraid. Sechiall's hand twitched and Jared knew that they were on the brink of swordplay. He waited for Sechiall to make the next move. Only surprise and good fortune would grant Sechiall life after that, and surprise had been lost. Jared could almost see the internal debate in Sechiall's face, but it passed, and suddenly pain and confusion appeared instead.

His taut muscles relaxed. "Perhaps you are right," he began haltingly, his hands held out to his mentor. "I am young and my heritage fights within me. My instincts are my father's and overpower my thought at times. The battle is before us tomorrow and I see nothing but blood right now. But if we do not fight in harmony, then Torech will win everything. He must be destroyed! After the battle, let us sit and reason together. You were always my teacher, Jared; I freely admit that I have more to learn. We can talk more easily in the aftermath of victory than in the tension before battle." He made his final play as he saw Jared waver. "We owe it to our men to overcome one hurdle at a time."

Jared was caught off guard. He had seen the thought flicker in Sechiall's eyes and had been ready to draw his sword. Conflicting emotion strung his body with tension. What Sechiall said was true. If the commanders disputed, the men would not be ready for battle tomorrow and there would be no chance of executing his carefully planned strategy. Sechiall noticed his hesitation.

"Listen, Jared," he said slowly, "I swear that after the battle tomorrow, if we both live, that I will resign my post to you and whatever we discuss will be done with you as Supreme Commander of the army. I am willing to put my life in your hands. Is that not enough? All I ask in return is that we first complete a task that all men in Lamech desire."

Jared could not refuse this offer. It surprised him, and made him doubt the words his own ears had heard earlier. But the offer was more than reasonable. "I agree, Sechiall," he said slowly. "We will lay this aside and destroy Torech tomorrow. Then we shall talk. I will see you in the morning." He turned his back on Sechiall and left the tent.

Sechiall paced his tent for some time. He was angry and afraid; not quite able to believe that Jared had changed so much. He lay down upon his blankets and thought back to the first night in Juloch's tent. The boy was now a man. But the same determination shone hard as iron in his face. He remembered that night—all seemed without hope. A slave to inferior men, destined to serve them with a sword, but without will and power of his own. He had nothing then but a burning ambition, an indomitable will, and the inborn knowledge of his innate superiority that was his heritage.

Men were not Nephil; they were weak. Most men made themselves weak by the things they called virtues: honor, duty, and integrity. He sneered at these and at Jared. He was disappointed in Jared's weakness and betrayal. He had no such weakness. He had found long ago that the single-minded pursuit of individual goals was strength, and that this strength was greater than any skill with spear or sword. Men used virtue to keep the strong from using the weak. And so he had kept his nature hidden from all. But the mask had been pulled aside. A pity—but too late to matter. Tomorrow would bring blood and death, and they would only feed his strength. There could be no weakness.

Jared too, was awake in his tent. Thoughts never before considered flowed through his mind. His dreams had cheated him. They had subtly lured him down a road that ended in murder. Shem and his silver clasp stood as a last warning, and he had taken heed. Suddenly, more than anything else, he wanted to talk to Noah. His mind hardened. Whatever happened, he would never allow Sechiall to attack that good man. If necessary, he would stand before Noah with his own sword. Strangely, the contentment that he felt in his heart overcame regret at what he was forsaking.

His mind wandered back to his wife. What would Jeriah think? She was a strong woman. She enjoyed the life he had built in Lamech. Sufficient wealth, prestige, respect; but they might be lost if he continued down this path. No! Once she understood the circumstances, she would support him, even if it meant losing those privileges. If they had each other and his honor, a new life could be built. Tomorrow it would start—a different life, but one that now filled him with anticipation.

Only one thing remained. Jeriah must know, even if the misfortunes of battle overtook him. He lit a lamp and set it on his camp table. The guard outside his tent took little notice; Jared was a man who took little rest when battle was upon him. Inside Jared worked industriously with his fine brush, committing his soul to the pages in front of him. But suddenly he stopped in the middle of a word and stared ahead of him. If anything happened to him, how would Jeriah even receive these words? He could no longer trust Sechiall. Then he relaxed. Juloch was the answer, of course.

The hour was late when Jared had finished. He carried the small package under his cloak as he walked around the encampment; an encouraging word for this man, a sharp reminder to stay alert for that. Finally, among the pack animals, he found Juloch's, with the pack made ready for the new day, lying on the ground beside the horse. Jared slipped his leather case inside the pack and quietly walked back to his tent. It was all for nothing, he told himself. Tomorrow he would surreptitiously retrieve it after the battle. It would not do to let Juloch think that his master had lost his confidence. He shook his head as he walked through the silent darkness back to a wakeful hour before the beginning of a new day.

Chapter 28
THE VICTOR

The camp was alive and active well before the sun rose the next morning. Men hurried to eat, strap on armor and weapons, and find their assigned places. Despite the appearance of confusion, Jared's trained eye saw the order of a trained army and he took satisfaction as a payment for his decades of discipline and work. Having trained for years and marched for days, his men were now ready and eager to fight. From a small rise near the mouth of the canyon, Jared smiled grimly at the preparations in its shadowed depths before forcing himself to scan out onto the dawn-lit plain. Torech would be here soon. A fierce opponent to be sure, but Jared was certain that he had no inkling of Lamech's strategy—one that would trap Y'tor's army between the hammer and anvil. This time, there would be no escape.

Though confident of victory, Jared relied on his innate caution as the battle drew near. Overconfidence would lead to Torech's defeat and Jared was determined that it would play no part in his own victory. His scouts ranged far out onto the plain and into the surrounding hills with orders to slay any man of Y'tor. No fires were allowed, and men spoke and worked quietly. In the gray half-light the companies formed up smoothly, marching either to the canyon mouth or following Sechiall around the first sharp turn into the branch ravine. Sechiall had said little to Jared and appeared subdued and respectful, and so Jared had put aside the conflict of the previous night and set his mind onto the hours ahead.

After the ranks had marched out into position on the verge of the plain with the canyon mouth at their backs, Jared mounted his horse and rode among them, making sure that each company had marked its path of retreat correctly. They had spread out in battle line; to all appearances ready to move out after the morning scouts reported back. Jared hoped that Torech would congratulate himself on his rapid march from Y'tor during the night, and conclude that he had caught Lamech off guard and pinned against the hills behind them. In the light of the early morning sun, no movement was visible on the plain before him and no report had yet come from his outposts. So Jared dismounted and walked along the front of his men, trading comments with many.

Now one of his men appeared running quickly along the front of the hills. It was the chief scout, Zarmesh. He had been with Jared from the beginning, and had proven his worth many times. He halted before Jared with a grin. "Torech is coming, Commander. They march now up onto the plain. You should be able to see them soon, for they move quickly."

"Good!" exclaimed Jared. "Send word to Commander Sechiall," he said to a messenger standing ready. He turned back to Zarmesh with outstretched hand. "Good work, friend. Go back and make sure your men are all well hidden. Wait to move into position until the ambush is sprung. And keep a few men hidden to circle back and watch the city."

Zarmesh grinned his answer. Both knew that Jared had repeated these orders scores of times and both knew that Zarmesh understood them after the first hearing. But both knew that part of being a soldier was repeating orders until even the dullest man in the army understood them perfectly.

Jared watched him fade back into the rocky walls of the hills. He felt a surprising peace in the face of battle. Reaching resolution with Sechiall and his own future seemed to have stilled any of the usual pre-battle nervousness. His mind was firm, and he knew that what he was going to do was right. He was no murderer and would not allow Sechiall to turn him into one. If his dream must die, then he had no one but himself to blame. He would defeat Torech, do his duty to the city, and then leave. Jeriah would understand. He was a lucky man to have her as a wife. With her at his side, he could be and do many things. He would also be sure to see Shem before they left. He owed him a debt—Shem had stopped his slide before it became a fall into an abyss of evil. With these resolutions he gave himself completely to the battle.

A buzz of excitement rippled among the men gathered in front of the canyon. Already the rigid lines of Torech's army had formed up and could be seen marching rapidly towards them. Jared had stationed scouts at the top of each side of the ravine and instructed them to make sure they were visible against the sky. His men here were ready. Their strategy depended on the actions of Torech. If he held back to assess the battle, then Lamech would advance slightly from the canyon pretending to offer battle on the plain. When faced by Torech's charge, they would retreat in fear back up the canyon. If Torech led the first charge, the task was simpler. They would maintain their position, as if hoping the canyon walls would provide cover, and then fall back in apparent dismay. Some would throw aside weapons and run screaming their fear—straight back to fresh supplies of spears up the canyon.

Jared had guessed that Torech would not hold back and he guessed correctly. Men in the front row braced themselves against the wave of warriors led by the yellow-haired giant visible even at a distance in the middle of the line. The gap closed quickly and the two armies met with a clash like a breaking wave. The sound carried far into the ravine. Y'tor's warriors saw Lamech's men try valiantly to stand firm, but break and begin retreating up the canyon. Jared shouted to rally his men, but was carried along with the ebbing tide. Some men threw down their weapons and began running away, crying out in apparent terror. Torech's mighty voice was heard over the din ordering his men to press on and destroy the enemy. Jared could not hide his grim smile as he let the crush carry his mount back up the canyon with the men.

Now! They were passing the opening to the side canyon and the men of Y'tor were already exulting in an easy victory. They pressed hard against Lamech, but the narrowing walls forced them to slow, allowing those of Lamech to regroup. Archers hidden in the rocks began to take a toll of the attackers. Torech roared his war cry and spurred his men into the final effort that would break this stand and finish the fight. They followed, leaving their flank exposed to the side canyon. Then, just as had been planned, cavalry led by Sechiall crashed into the rear of Y'tor's troops and cut deep into their formation. Foot soldiers followed hard upon the advantage won by the horsemen and widened the breach, slaying those thrown off balance by the charging horsemen.

Within minutes, Torech found himself surrounded: enemies front and back, and steep walls to each side, with pesky archers raining death down on the bunched Y'torians. Calling for his men to regroup, He had them form a shield wall that would protect their retreat out of the canyon and to more favorable ground. But just as they began pushing against Sechiall's force, Jared launched another attack with his own reformed troops. The shield wall crumbled at the point of attack and Jared and his men began splitting the ranks of Y'tor, pushing within sight of Sechiall, who was busy raining death down upon his enemies from his black mount.

Any other army would have surrendered then, but Torech was inflamed by the fighting lust. He lunged back into the breach, shouting curses and swinging his heavy sword. In the cramped confines he killed or wounded men with every stroke. Men of both sides halted their charge and braced themselves to hold their ground. As a result, the turmoil cleared momentarily with Torech facing the front ranks of Lamech. Blood lust had contorted his face and blood dripped from his sword. He was even more terrifying at hand and brave men recoiled back. He roared his challenge and watched the front ranks of Lamech falter.

Immediately grasping the situation, Jared swung down from his horse and shouldered his way to the front of his men. His servant Juloch found himself on the opposite side of the excited animal and tried to calm him before hurrying after his master. Jared was already amid the thick of Lamech's men, pushing his way forward. His face was set and hard, and he knew that his sword must quickly halt the carnage and more importantly, the spreading fear. As he pushed to the front, men of Lamech and Y'tor began to recognize that a battle of champions was upon them and spread ranks as best they could. During this momentary pause, men on both sides caught their breath and locked eyes with individuals across the sandy ground, seeking opponents for the next round of battle.

Juloch shoved the reins of the horse into the hands of the nearest soldier and began to push his way forward after his master. But the way was blocked solid by men gathering to watch the spectacle unfolding before them. Juloch had to content himself with climbing atop a boulder and peering over the heads of his comrades.

Jared stood facing Torech. The Nephil king was fully a head taller than his opponent and his armor barely contained his wide shoulders. Sweat and blood mingled on his face and his eyes were still full of rage at the ambush; his mouth twisted into a snarl. As if by common consent, soldiers on both sides moved further aside and left room for the two generals to face off. This was their fight and none would interfere.

In the sudden silence of the moment, Torech raised his sword. "Name yourself, then prepare to die under my feet!"

"Jared, son of Zered, Battle Commander of the host of Lamech."

Torech laughed at him. "So you are the famous Jared, that toy of Delonias. He spat. We finally meet after all these years. I cannot believe that you would actually come out and fight. I was sure that you would hide behind your boys until I slew them all. I owe you for a small setback many years ago. At least it will be quick for you, and your widow can boast that you fell at the hands of Torech!"

"If Torech's skill with the sword is as great as his boasting, it will indeed be a hard fight," replied Jared quietly. Torech was not only larger than Lamech's commander, but his reach was longer by at least two hands. But Jared knew his own skill and was confident that it was greater than Torech's. His fearless eyes surprised Torech, who was accustomed to looking at frightened opponents. Looking on, Juloch was less confident. He knew Jared's skill, but the tales of Torech's feats were legendary.

Torech did not wait. He advanced quickly in a powerful attack. Jared parried with his shield and deflected the backstroke with his own blade. Men murmured at the strength of Torech's attack, and at the complete absence of one from Jared. But Juloch knew that his master was learning from what he saw. On the third exchange, Jared found an opening, moved his wrist slightly, and saw with satisfaction the point of his sword brush Torech's shield arm, opening a small cut.

Torech took a step back and gathered himself. He stepped forward again in another attack. Keeping his shield high, he executed a series of sweeping slashes with great strength and ferocity. But Jared coordinated the motions of his shield and sword with his feet and avoided the brunt of each blow, using his own shield and sword to deflect the force remaining in Torech's wasted blows. Although Jared was smaller than Torech, his strength was much closer to the larger man's than most would have imagined, and his shield arm remained steady under blows that would have staggered most men.

He was content to be patient, awaiting an opening. Torech was strong and fast for his size, but the lightning quick reflexes that had so impressed Delonias those many years before had not deserted Jared, and Torech could not catch up to him. During the early exchanges, Juloch noticed that Torech moved too far out of line with his feet at the end of his sequence. He knew that Jared had seen it, too, and once sure of the pattern, he would begin to turn it to his advantage. Juloch grinned as his master did exactly that on the next pass: defending as before until Torech started his final stroke, then stepping quickly to his right. Torech's blade whistled within a hand's width of his head, but before Torech could take a step to right himself, Jared's blade moved again in a short economical stroke, and another, deeper cut appeared on Torech's arm.

Juloch's fear waned and he settled to watch the rest of the encounter. He had seen his master fight many times, and the outcome was certain, now. Even Torech seemed to perceive it; his early confident look now changed to one of wariness. He was surprised to discover someone his strength, size, and ferocity could not immediately overcome. The wounds on his arm were not severe, but Juloch knew they were an irritation, and the giant's prestige was oozing away with his blood. From his perch upon the boulder, he could sense Jared growing more confident. It was just a matter of time. The watching warriors on both sides now began to press in closer, and Juloch lost sight of his master. He jumped down and began to push his way forward.

Out of Juloch's sight, Torech paused to gather himself for a new assault, and Jared seized the opportunity to press his own attack. He moved his shield arm quickly toward Torech while keeping his feet planted. Torech's eye was on the shield, not the feet, and he reacted as hoped by raising his shield. Jared immediately sidestepped and slid the point of his blade under Torech's shield, while deflecting Torech's hurried counter with his own. Not a debilitating wound, it pained the giant, and he realized he could bleed to death if this continued.

As they circled, Torech searched for an opening to a quick victory; Jared looked for another mistake. Torech stumbled in an ill-timed attack, and Jared's flashing sword missed Torech's throat by a finger, but left a gash in the side of his face. Torech stopped short, a look of shock and confusion in his face. The men were pressing closer, eager to see the finish, and Jared knew that he must end it quickly. He froze momentarily at the look of shocked disbelief on Torech's face, but before his body could react, he felt a fire in his left side in the gap between the front and back plates of his armor. His body stiffened and he felt an arm holding him upright, close to the body behind him. He tried to speak, but only blood came from his mouth.

"Here is my answer to your question," hissed the familiar voice in his ear. "You are weak, but strong enough to threaten me. Since you will not survive this battle, then I see no need for us to discuss our differences later. I am the victor."

Jared's body could no longer support his weight and he felt himself slump to the ground. Sechiall stepped around him and as across a great distance, Jared heard him call, "Now cousin, let us finish this. Death or victory!"

The noise of the battle drifted beyond Jared's hearing. As he lay back, strangely relaxed, he saw the deep blue of the sky above him, and from far away and long ago heard his dying father's voice clearly. "Yes, Noah warned me again that God would judge the world for its rebellion and evil."

He recognized his own voice in reply, but felt shame at the remembered arrogance. "Did he offer an escape, Father?"

The answer sounded clearer, "Noah said that the Creator would show mercy to those who turned from their evil deeds and believed in His promise of a deliverer from the line of Seth."

His own voice echoed now in his head, "But Father, I have turned from my evil deeds. I have repudiated evil at the cost of my dreams. I am willing to believe in God's deliverance. I cannot help myself."

"That is well, my child," he heard through the bright sunlight that seemed to now surround him.

As Juloch broke through the front line of men, he saw the huddled figure on the ground and two giants vying for the field. Sechiall had not Jared's skill with the sword, but he was easily the match of a tired and wounded Torech. And Torech was having trouble holding his shield high enough. His arm and side were oozing blood from the nicks of Jared's blade and he was visibly tiring. Sechiall felt the advantage pass to him and he unleashed a powerful attack. Torech parried the first blows, but stumbled back under the weight of Sechiall's advance.

Just when Juloch thought it over, Torech seemed to regain a measure of strength in a desperate panic. He swung his sword like a club in wide sweeping arcs. His strength remained. Any of those blows would have smashed most men. But his timing and coordination were gone, and Sechiall had been trained by the best. He waited for his moment, caught Torech off-balance, and slipped the point of his sword in below the shield, deep into the unprotected thigh. Blood streamed down Torech's leg and he found that he could not move. Desperately he swung again and stumbled, falling to his knees. He did not see Sechiall's next short, powerful stroke.

Sechiall picked up the head of Torech and held it aloft with a great shout. Lamech's warriors took up his cry and redoubled the fury of their attack on the men of Y'tor. It was too much, and without their great leader the men of Y'tor despaired and fled. But all of the pickets and outposts of Lamech had formed a line across the mouth of the ravine, and the horsemen of Lamech pressed hard against the back of the fleeing mass. Within a few minutes, the remnant of the pride of Y'tor had thrown down their weapons and was surrounded by a guard of Lamech's men.

Juloch was blind to the celebration, weeping openly over his master. Recriminations sprung into his head. Why had he not fought his way to Jared's side immediately? He had broken through only to see Sechiall standing between his friend's body and Torech. The fierce leader of Y'tor was now a headless body, bereft of any threat. But it was too late to save Jared. Juloch held his master for many minutes, ignoring the conflict around him, before gently laying his body back upon the ground. He wiped the stain of blood from his lips. Jared's face was still and peaceful, and Juloch wondered at the fading light in the dead eyes. As he laid his master gently on the ground, his trained eyes saw blood on the leather between the front and back armor plates. Gently moving the body, he saw that the wound angled to the front.

His sorrow swallowed by such a rage as he had never felt before, Juloch sprang to his feet and ran to the Supreme Commander. Men were milling and shouting around him, watching as he impaled the head of Torech upon his spear and waved it aloft for all to see.

"Sir, sir," shouted Juloch, fighting his way to the center of the press, and his voice caught Sechiall's attention. "What is it, Juloch?" asked Sechiall expansively, still flushed with victory.

Juloch controlled his tears, but not his anger, "They murdered him, sir; they murdered Jared! He was fighting with Torech and the battle swirled around them just before you arrived. Jared was struck from behind in the side. Curse the men of Y'tor! Death to their city!"

Sechiall twisted his face into a look of outraged fury. "So!" he called loudly enough for all to hear. "The dogs cannot even honor the warrior's code. Let us avenge our Commander with the blood of the city! Let no fighting man of Y'tor escape! And let Y'tor become the vassal of Lamech for as long as time shall last! They will serve us or everything in that city with life shall spill it before we burn it around them!"

The men gave an angry roar of approval and fell upon the unarmed captives, hewing and slashing until none were left alive in the blood-soaked sand. Juloch led the rush in his fury and covered his feet with Y'torian blood until there were none left alive to slay.

When they had finished, Sechiall lifted his arm and called for order. "Let us bury our dead and burn our enemies. We march on Y'tor tomorrow and woe to that accursed city for the vengeance of Sechiall shall take them all! Jared!" he shouted holding the head of Torech high, "We shall avenge you!"

So the army that streamed through the gates of Y'tor was that of Sechiall, not Torech, and the spirit of Sechiall inflamed them as Jared's never had. Their old iron discipline vanished as if it had never existed. The few men remaining in the city had opened the gates to the army and come out to beg for mercy, for they knew that they could not defend the city. Sechiall rode at the head of the column of Lamech. He ignored the old men bowing before them and led his troops directly into the center of the town. There in the main square and lifted up his spear, still holding the head of Torech and all the people of the city fell down before him. Juloch stood near the front and watched the despair of Y'tor with quiet satisfaction. Anger still burned within him.

Sechiall's next words met his approval. The eyes of all were on Lamech's commander as he turned to his men and shouted, "The blood of Jared shouts for our vengeance! Bring every man that is of an age to fight into the square."

The army of Lamech spread out by units and soon were hurrying men, young and old into the square. Then Sechiall turned to Oman and said quietly, "Take as many men as you need and take all these outside the city walls and spare none!"

"As you wish, my lord," replied Oman, and turning signaled for men to follow him. After they had gone, Sechiall went to the raised platform that stood in the center of the square. Its steps led upward to Torech's throne, and Sechiall mounted them slowly but firmly. At the apex of the small pyramid, he walked around the throne once, admiring the gold inlay and the filigree that formed a golden canopy over the back. It was his now, and he sat down into that throne as if it were always meant for him. Torech had, after all, only been a steward for the greater king. He motioned for quiet and it was granted instantly.

"Hear me, Oh people of Y'tor! Torech your king is dead, slain by a better man! Who shall not hail Sechiall as King in Y'tor?"

Amid the wails of the women were heard weak shouts of "King Sechiall, King Sechiall."

Sechiall accepted it as his due, and then shouted, "My first command is that food, drink, and women be brought for the men of Lamech. Bring only your best. In the morning I will talk to your elders and arrange my rule."

Then turning to the men around him, he said, "Find the house of Torech and prepare wine, food, and women fit for a king!"

Gatar answered him, "It shall be done as you command, O King of two cities!" Sechiall was pleased with this reply and waved him away with a generous smile.

Chapter 29
JULOCH'S JOURNEY

Juloch opened one eye and stared though the blurred opening onto an unfamiliar world. Closing it again brought no relief—with waking came pain: pain from an aching body, a head trying to burst apart, and the deep, gripping emptiness of profound loss. Fifteen minutes. That was all it had taken to become separated from his master, leaving his back exposed to the shameful death that no warrior should have borne. If only Jared had been killed by Torech in open battle; that would have been honorable, it would have won him acclaim by his city. But the few minutes that Juloch had not been able to stay with him had made the difference, and he would never be able to forget or to forgive himself.

Juloch remembered, and supposed that he always would, rushing frantically onto the scene, only to find the life draining from his master at the edge of the titanic struggle between the two blond giants. He supposed that sight would haunt him all of his days. How could he live with himself? Victory had not helped. Slaying unarmed men of Y'tor had not helped—it only left him with a vague sense of shame. Drink had not helped, though he could not remember ever having more than he did last night.

Raising himself halfway up against the weight of his bloated body, he looked dully at the woman lying unconscious on the floor. She had not helped, either. Guiltily, he wondered if her husband had been among those that he had cut down in a wrath that left him without clear memory; only disjointed flashes of upflung arms, beseeching looks, and cries for mercy. And blood, blood everywhere. He shook his head to clear it of those memories, but they remained, accusingly.

Staggering to a basin in the corner of the room, he gathered water into shaking hands and dashed it against his burning face. Like icy knives the droplets cut through much of the fog and washed the scum of drunken sleep from his eyes. Looking again around the room, he again felt shame. The behavior of the army—his behavior—went against everything that Jared had drilled into them for decades. Realization of that betrayal brought tears; but paradoxically they cleared the fog of emotion. He might be a man without a master, but he was a man.

Sunlight filtering in through the windows brought additional clarity. Juloch stripped off his stinking tunic and poured most of the pitcher of water over his head and body. Digging through his pack for clean garb, his hand hit a familiar hard shape, and not daring to breathe, he pulled the leather case from among his clothes. Too stunned to notice his nakedness, he staggered back to sit upon the bed, new tears flowing down his cheeks. Jared's engraved leather wallet was as well known to him as his master's cynical, knowing glance. Only Jared could have placed it there. No one else handled his master's writings. Jared had once stated casually that he would cut the arm off of any man who touched them, and there was not a man present who did not believe that he would and could do so. Even Sechiall had not been privy to Jared's writings.

Why had he placed them in his servant's pack? Had some premonition warned him? What danger threatened? For no reason at all, Juloch looked around. He remembered gratefully the dull days of lessons shared with Jared in their youth, and now he thanked each hour. He felt an intense need for privacy with this reminder of his friend, and was aware of a coalescing dislike for Sechiall and his cronies. Juloch could not have explained his feelings—after all, Sechiall had been like a son to his master, but he had learned over many years to trust his instincts, and he would continue to do so.

He must get outside of town, where no chance encounter could reveal the existence of these writings, and where he could sift through them in privacy and mourn his friend. Sechiall knew of their existence and would know the case for what it was if he saw it. That thought, too, made Juloch strangely uncomfortable. Dressing quickly, he strapped the case under the outer tunic against the small of his back and wrapped a cloak loosely about him to remove any hint of its outline. The distraction had done much to remove the effects of the wine, and Juloch quickly found his way into the side street that ran by the front of this home. Staring each direction to get his bearings, Juloch saw to his left the street open onto the town square. Keeping it always to his left, Juloch wandered side streets until he reached the wall.

No side gates were open, but Juloch felt no apprehension as he strode toward the men loosely guarding the main gate. The men greeted him as he approached, and Kenah appeared in the door of the guardhouse, running appraising eyes over Juloch. Juloch felt a shiver of fear at his stare, but did not know why.

"An early morning, Juloch," Kenah began. "I thought that you would have enjoyed yourself for another day or two like all the others. You have not been tasked with any duty."

"Ah, my captain," replied Juloch smoothly, his instincts guiding his speech,

"I am as grateful as any man for the provision made by our Supreme Commander, but my conscience will not let me indulge until I have fasted a day in solitude in memory of my master. With your permission, I will sit overlooking the waves and remember all the good days and gather them firmly into my mind, so that Jared will not be absent among us forever."

Kenah nodded, with some understanding. "Only be careful, Juloch. Who knows if some man of Y'tor may be slinking around the countryside looking for an easy vengeance?"

"Let it be another of the filthy murderers of my master, and I will welcome his attentions," replied Juloch, grimly.

Kenah nodded and stared after him for some minutes as he walked sturdily away from the gate.

Juloch walked moodily away from the city with no clear direction in mind, only a desire to be away from prying eyes. Time passed without notice and the midday sun found him sweating atop a small hillock away from town, overlooking the endless sea. A careful sweep in all directions told Juloch that he was utterly alone. The entire countryside seemed to have lapsed into the same stupor as the army of Lamech following the destruction of their enemies. He opened the secret clasp: none now, save perhaps Jeriah, knew how, and set it down in his lap. He lifted the cover and saw two of Jared's books lying closed inside. One of the books was current, but the other was old—thirty years by the date. A piece of parchment, hurriedly folded, sat atop them, and Juloch opened it to find his own name at the top. Reading quickly from right to left, he saw a message which threw him into great confusion.

'Juloch,' it read. 'If you are reading this, then I am dead. If you are not now alone, then put this away and keep it secret until you have a chance to read it.'

Juloch glanced around again, just to make sure that no hidden watcher was spying on him before reading on.

'Please keep the knowledge of this from all, especially Sechiall. If he presses you or otherwise suspects that you have my journals, then you must escape with all speed and take them to Jeriah. It grieves me to have to say goodbye in this fashion, old friend.'

Jared's mark was at the bottom of the page, but then there was more, as if an afterthought.

'If you find yourself an outcast of the army, I believe that you can find sanctuary with Noah. Go to him with my blessing and serve him as you served me.'

Juloch sat very still. Why would he find himself an outcast from the army he had served so many years? Why should the writings be withheld from the Supreme Commander? And why would Jared speak well of Noah? Or command his allegiance to the man who had stood in their way for so long?

Now Juloch had always been a quiet, purposeful man. None but Jared thought him astute, and he had little skill with the spoken word. But he was shrewd, and a man with good instincts. Following those, he opened Jared's current diary and began to scan backwards from the last entry. Captivated, he skipped back many pages until he saw the record of a conversation between Jared and Shem, Noah's son. Then he carefully read forward through the last page, not noticing the passage of the hours.

Various emotions gripped him as the pages sped by. Shock, fear, and rage washed over him, until finally as the shadows lengthened behind, a deep emptiness washed over and left him limp and shaken. Sechiall's betrayal was complete. With Jared dead, the way was open for him to seize power in Lamech. Dajus and Subtur would be his tools, and Noah would be slain, like Lamech. Juloch saw nothing to stop him.

Suddenly, a thought struck him with terrifying certainty. Sechiall had not sprung forward to support Jared. Sweat beaded on his brow as he realized that Sechiall had only to quickly slay any nearby Y'torian soldier, push the body forward, and then leap against Jared, and slip his already bloody knife in the gap of his armor. Murdering the Y'torian before he killed Jared was the perfect cover. And most would remember his fight with Torech, not a quick, subtle movement immediately before. Men saw what they wanted to see, and no one would imagine Sechiall harming his best friend.

Could Sechiall have done such a vile thing? Looking back through the eyes of Jared's book, Juloch found no trouble believing it. The Supreme Commander had slain his best friend—no he had slain his greatest obstacle, and Juloch's best friend. Rage washed over him. Jared had stood in Sechiall's way, and now the way was clear. Tears of anger and regret flowed then and Juloch wept for his friend, cursing and vowing vengeance with each paroxysm. It was many minutes before he could think clearly.

Common sense finally reasserted itself. He had decisions to make and no one but himself to rely upon. He must start now. Could he single-handedly avenge Jared by killing Sechiall? Unlikely. Even if he got through the guards, he knew too well that Sechiall would be hard to surprise or slay. Could he avenge Jared by thwarting Sechiall's plans? That, too, would be difficult, but Juloch judged it the easier of the two tasks. How to do it? He must think. But the sun was waning, and he needed to return without exciting suspicion. Kenah was close to the Supreme Commander, and was by nature a careful man.

He wondered balefully if Kenah knew of the murder of Jared and approved.

Even so, Juloch managed a wan smile for the captain and his men at the gate. Kenah could not help but see the red eyes before Juloch bowed his head and continued into town. With some trouble in the fading light, Juloch returned to the house to which he had been assigned. The woman met him at the door with a fearful glance and clean clothes. She had anointed herself with some kind of aromatic oil or perfume, but Juloch did not care. The scent of meat cooking somewhere in the back was more attractive to him. His actions of the previous day and night now seemed vile. Shame swept over him at the sight of a woman who must be filled with a grief as great as his own, yet was trying so hard to make herself pleasing to him again to save her life and place in the town.

He attempted amends. Bowing to the woman, he said, "Please forgive what I did to you last night. Revelry and sorrow make poor partners. I suffered great loss from this battle, but I will not dishonor you again."

He looked up to see wonder in her eyes. She looked at him more carefully and saw the stains of tears and the redness that she knew blurred her own sight. Ever since the news of Lamech's victory and the sure knowledge that her own husband would never return, she had felt only a great numbness. The previous night was a fog, blessedly blurred by wine. But it shocked her that the first emotion she now felt was one of great sympathy for an enemy, yet a man, and one bearing great pain like herself.

Tentatively, she put one hand up to his face and touched the rough cheek. "My husband was also a man with honor in him," she said softly. "If we understand each other, then let us deal with each other in that way. Please sit yourself and I will serve you food and drink. I am no longer afraid."

Juloch nodded, not knowing what to say. But there seemed no need for she led him to a table lit by a dim lamp, and served him meat and water. After she had finished, he said, "Please come and join me, for I am but a humble servant, and am not accustomed to being treated like a man I am not."

She nodded again, and came and reclined across from him. There were few words spoken, but no need.

Finally, Juloch said, "Please bring some blankets. I will stay here tonight. You need not fear. No man will disturb you." She quickly returned with both blankets and cushions, and Juloch arranged them on the floor. Then he brought the lamp over into his corner and sat down to think. Having an organized mind, Juloch thought carefully through what he needed to accomplish. First, he must escape the town with Jared's books. Then he must avoid recapture by any possible pursuit. Then he must make his way to

Lamech before any messenger might arrive with orders for his arrest.

Getting out of town had proven easy today, but what duties might be assigned to him tomorrow? He might be kept in the middle of this town for days. When would Sechiall remember Jared's writings and wonder where they were? A search would easily reveal them. If he was to leave, it must be immediately. He must have a horse, and he must ride—but not the direct route to Lamech, where better horsemen might overtake him. He could go either west along the coast or east around the hills. The former was the easier course, and so he must take the latter. This would bring him to the great east road which would then take him home.

He had failed Jared once. He must not fail him in this. The books would be given to Jeriah, who would see that justice was done.

Once his mind was made up, Juloch had no second thoughts or hesitation. His friend Yur was on duty outside the walls with the horses, and that was all that he needed. He found a small ewer of wine and set it quietly by the door. Silently he listened at the door of the sleeping room and heard nothing but the regular breathing of a woman enjoying the forgetfulness of sleep. He decided to leave his armor here; he wanted to travel light, but he caught up a short sword and strapped it around his waist under his cloak.

Once outside in the street, he remembered to splash a little wine on his face and let it dribble down onto his clothes. Then he moved into the shadows against the buildings and slipped through town until the torches announced his proximity to the front gate. Confident that Kenah would be off duty, he stumbled out into the torchlight and walked with exaggerated purpose towards the guards. They heard him before they saw him, and jumped up with their weapons ready. Holding up the ewer, Juloch called out in a too-loud, conspiratorial whisper. He saw the weapons drop and grins replace the wariness on their faces.

"'Tis only Juloch," one said to the other.

"Aye," breathed his comrade, "but I have seldom seen him this deep into wine!" Then in a louder voice he cried out, "Halt, Juloch! You should be enjoying the embrace of one of these Y'torian widows, not wandering the dangerous streets."

The other laughed with him. "Was her passion too great for you, old man? Perhaps you should tell us the house where you are staying. If she is that much of a woman, then you may need some help!"

Juloch sighed in relief. This would be easier than he thought. Playing along, he answered, "I have done my duty for Lamech already. It is time to drink with Yur and tell him of my victories. Let me out, young dogs! Have you no respect for your elders?" He cocked his head to one side and stared at them quizzically, then stumbled slightly forward.

"Is Yur with the outguards tonight?" asked the first casually.

Juloch slurred his answer; "No, horses."

Perhaps we should carry him out and find Yur ourselves," said the second to his comrade. "This man would end up in the sea if we let him out alone!"

"Insolent pup!" interrupted Juloch. "I can find my way across the heavens on a dark night over a sea of wine!" Then he changed his tone abruptly. "No one to talk to but Yur.... No one understands.... Women don't know anything." His face took on the twisted look of one trying hard to prevent the coming of tears.

The guards looked at each other in obvious sympathy. "It has been a hard week for us all, old fighter," replied the elder of the two. "Go along with you, but be careful in the dark."

As Juloch walked away, he heard the other say, "Better that he had died with Jared, than to endure such loss. Maybe some wine and a friendly night with old Yur will help."

He walked swiftly across the open land towards the encampment where the horses were being kept, only pausing to set down the ewer once out of sight of the gate. When he could see the light of the horse guards' campfire, he stopped and tested the wind. It was from the northwest and so he slid around to the southeast, careful to make no sound, so as to come upon the horses from downwind. After long, careful minutes, he was among the horses, making soothing sounds and patting the nearest to calm them down. Most of them calmed easily, but one kept its ears up and swung its head around as if trying to scent something. Juloch patted it on the neck and spoke quietly. The animal calmed, but remained alert.

He knew many of the horses, even in the dark, and he quickly found a strong mare that he had ridden before. Unloosing her halter rope, he led her down the line to the shelters that stored the equipment. It was the work of only a moment to bridle and saddle her. Juloch paused, uncertain. If he rode east now, then there would be little doubt as to his direction. If he rode through the camp, they would see him going west and chase in that direction. But it would also alert Sechiall immediately, instead of sometime on the morrow.

He chose to gain time, and led the horse back down the line. Stopping at the end, he waited, listening. Something felt wrong, but he was not sure what it was. He could hear no sound, and it would take an exceptional man to stand quietly for so long. Finally, he shrugged to himself and turned to swing up onto the mare. The moon had now risen and cast its faint silver light around him.

"Halt, old man!"

The voice was Oman's and it came from only a few paces away.

Juloch never hesitated. He was in the saddle in a blink and the mare needed no encouragement. She shot away, and had thundered a dozen paces along before Juloch felt something hit him in the left shoulder. He turned to look and in the receding distance saw Oman with bow bent again. Juloch leaned out over the mare's neck and kept his face buried in her mane. That sudden move kept the next arrow no more than a whirring sound above his head and the next fell well behind the speeding mare. There was yet no pain, only numbness in the back of his shoulder, and Juloch knew that he must put distance between him and the city. He had lost his advantage of time, and now must try to avoid pursuit. He did not know how Oman had been there; he must have been following him from the city. It really did not matter now. Only escape did.

But escape was not merely a matter of headlong flight. Juloch pulled the horse up and dismounted after a few minutes of running. Quickly he took four squares of rough cloth from the back of his saddle and wrapped the mare's hoofs with them, tying them securely in place with cords. He would be much more difficult to track now, and would need that advantage. Before remounting, he gritted his teeth and ran his right hand awkwardly along the arrow. Fortunately, it did not seem to have penetrated very far. It must have struck a glancing blow on his pack and cut along his back before sinking into his shoulder. It even felt loose. A swift tug brought pain, but the arrow came out easily enough. He tore rags and roughly bound the wound as best he could, and then remounted and rode on into the gray night.

The sixth morning found Juloch finally on the verge of the great east road. He had ridden at night and hidden by day at first. He had washed and bound his back and shoulder as best he could the first day, but it was hard to reach and the pain in his left arm made it even more difficult. The bleeding had stopped the second day, and Juloch began to hope that he would shake off another scratch with just another scar. But the third day he had awoken in the evening with a fever. His weakness frightened him and by the fifth day he labored just to saddle the horse. No longer hungry, he quit eating, but could not get enough water. There seemed to be a haze before his eyes, and he was no longer certain of why he was here. The last thing that he remembered was the sound of the horse's hoofs on the road as it plodded west.

Since Methuselah's death, Madrazi had remained detached from the work that swirled around her. That morning, she had left the house and its chaos behind and walked aimlessly away out on the east road. She usually wandered into the forest, but today she wanted to see the rolling hills to the south. The sun cast its long morning shadows and the grass was already dry as she started to cross the road. Glancing to the east, she saw a horse standing with its head down in the middle of the road and a misshapen lump lying beside it. Curiosity brought her closer; then fear made her run as she realized the shape was a man.

He was sprawled face down on the dirt of the road and covered by a tattered, bloody cloak. At first, she thought him dead. When she reached and turned him over, she saw to her shock that it was Juloch. Her surprise almost overcame her fear. She knelt and felt the blood pulsing through his neck and she realized that he was still alive, but badly hurt and feverish. Running back toward the house she saw two of the men walking out to the fields and called to them. In a short time Juloch was in a clean bed in the house.

He was burning with fever and as the women carefully removed his torn, dirty, bloody clothes, they saw a cruel wound on his back and shoulder. It was red and inflamed and smelled of infection. Wen-Tehrom and Madrazi boiled water and washed the wound with goldenseal and myrrh, then bound it with soft clean cloths. Juloch sank into a troubled sleep, his face flushed red. For the remainder of that day Madrazi sat with him, keeping cool wet cloths against his forehead, trying to calm the raging sickness.

Later that morning one of the servants who had helped bring Juloch to the house peered in the doorway. Madrazi motioned him inside and he tentatively stepped across the room. "I found this strapped to the back of his saddle, my lady," he said quietly. He handed her a leather case, a little more than half a cubit square and maybe a span thick. It was finely tooled leather and there was no obvious way to open it.

The servant spoke again, "He has traveled for many days, pushing hard. The horse is exhausted, and would not have gone much farther." He paused and stared at the sick man. "Do you think that he will live?"

"I don't know," Madrazi replied. "The wound itself is not severe, but it is inflamed and stinks of infection. If he can resist the fever, perhaps it will heal. But it is too early to tell."

"It is Jared's servant, is it not?" the servant asked, with a little hesitation in his voice.

"Yes. His name is Juloch and he has been his master's friend for all of his life. I fear for Jared and the army of Lamech. Why would he be alone, wounded, and a day's march east of his best route back to town?"

Madrazi shook her head. "We know nothing yet, but his presence cannot be a harbinger of good news from the south." The servant nodded and looking at Juloch again, shook his head slightly, and left the room. Madrazi pulled a chair from the corner of the room up beside his bed and continued to change the cloth on his forehead every few minutes. But he lay still and unmoving the entire day.

It was deathly quiet; the hour between twilight and dark. Gray embraced the room, and Madrazi rose to light a small lamp. As she turned back she saw him stir and gradually his eyes found her. His dark eyes were unfocused, but now open. She saw them gradually absorb the surroundings and finally, with a seeming effort, the questioning blankness was replaced by recognition.

"Rest quietly, Juloch," she said softly, returning to her seat beside his bed. "You are safe in the house of Noah, and we will care for you."

He relaxed slightly, his face pale and wan, the skin waxy and sunken around the bones of his face. She put a hand behind his head and gently lifted it, holding a cup to his lips. He drank weakly, his eyes grateful. As awareness returned, so did the pain. "There is rest in the tea," she said. "The pain will diminish, but your wound is badly infected. Sleep, now. I will be here beside you."

He started to speak, but Madrazi put a gentle finger across his lips. "Sleep now; we will talk tomorrow."

He sighed as the poppy seeds in the tea took hold of his body and he relaxed back into sleep. True to her word, Madrazi stayed with him all night. After caring for Methuselah, it seemed a small thing, and she napped through the night as he slept heavily. Occasionally he would cry out in some strange dream, but she heard no coherent words.

Madrazi woke in the morning light with Juloch's eyes fastened upon hers. He was still pale, but the fever seemed to have abated during the night. There was a hint of strength in his features that signaled a return to full health. "I will be back soon," she said and left to get him something to drink.

He took a little wine mixed with water and relaxed back against the bed.

His eyes were clear, though his voice weak when he said, "My lady, thank you for your care. You are like an angel to me. Please. I have much to tell the Lord Noah. Is he here?"

"No. He is away at present, but will return in a few days."

"Then I must tell you and you must tell him." He sighed. "I don't know what days are left to me. Will you speak my words to him?"

"Certainly. But you have long years left to you yet. You look much better this morning."

"Maybe," he replied, "But I feel something inside…. Have you time to listen? I have a trust to my lady, Jeriah. You must assume it for me. Promise me. I have failed in so much; please do not let me fail in this."

Madrazi was touched by his intensity and bitterness, and replied, "Inasmuch as I can help you, I will. You know that Jeriah is a sister to me, and I would help her without any oath to you."

"That is true. My master was always glad of your friendship." He lay back for a moment on his pillow, eyes losing their focus. With an effort he gathered himself and asked, "Is my master's case safe?"

"Yes. It is here, but I did not see how to open it."

"Bring it to me," he commanded weakly.

Madrazi did so, and as she supported its weight, he feebly reached around the back and slid a hidden catch forward. The opposite side fell open and she held it in trembling hands. Juloch spoke again. "Inside are two of my master's books. One contains his most recent writings. There was also a note to me. Please read it."

As she did, her own tears welled as she thought of Jeriah. Her world—the one that Madrazi had so often envied—had been shattered by one battle. She loved him so much; how could she live without Jared? Madrazi wondered how she would react if Shem were killed.

Juloch saw her shock and grief, and said, "My lady. What you have read is only the beginning of ill news. There is more written here and more for me to tell. Please promise me that it will all reach my master's wife."

"I will bring all your news to her." She trembled at becoming a messenger of such sorrow to her friend. Jeriah would never want to see her again after such an encounter."

"Your husband's visit to Jared is recorded in the second book," he said. "Everything that happened between that time and the eve or our battle with Y'tor is recorded there. But much has happened since that Jeriah needs to know."

Juloch could not speak for many minutes without resting. So he spent the balance of the morning reciting in short bursts the details of events leading up to the great battle, its terrible tragedy, and its wanton aftermath in Y'tor. He did not spare himself in the telling. Then he told of his discovery of Jared's message and his escape and flight through the wilderness. He did not seem to recall how he had come upon the road, and Madrazi marveled that he had ridden so far with such an injury. Many times she thought that he would lapse back into unconsciousness. But the will to deliver his message was strong inside and his courage was indomitable. Madrazi's heart was torn over the blame that she thought he unjustly assumed, but she said nothing, knowing that she must let him tell his story in his own way.

Shortly after noon, he finished. Madrazi gave him more tea mixed with the draught, and watched as he sank back into sleep. Then she spent the afternoon reading the journal of Jared between changing the wet cloths on his forehead. She was astounded at the impact that Shem's words had made upon Jared, and there were pages upon which he had recorded his deepest thoughts and feelings. At times she was ashamed for the ability to see the heart of the husband of her best friend, but she could not put it down. The depth of evil manifested in Sechiall was appalling; even worse was the betrayal of her own family by Dajus and Subtur. She wept softly for the betrayal of Lamech, and wondered if the two traitors understood what doors to evil they had thrown open.

All at once Madrazi recalled her naïve questioning of Noah so many years before. If even the leading men of the city were this evil, then judgment from the Creator was truly warranted. And what did she deserve? She shivered and quickly subdued these thoughts, turning her mind to Jeriah.

With Jared's death, what would happen to Jeriah after the return of the army? A widow with means should be able to live a good life in Lamech, but many years earlier Sechiall had briefly pressed his attentions on Jeriah. Once he had discovered her interest in Jared, he had been nothing but correct and respectable, but Madrazi had seen herself the two faces of the man. It was inconceivable that Sechiall would press his attentions so soon after Jared's death, but then she realized that it was equally inconceivable that he would have coldly murdered his mentor. Madrazi decided that when Shem returned from the ark, she would ask him to go with her and offer Jeriah the safety of their home.

Juloch ate a little bread that night and slept well, though the fever returned in the middle watch. But the next morning, he seemed better, and even sat up in bed for a few minutes. Shem arrived home that morning. He had traveled all night, but he had the same quiet, steady look as when he had slept many hours. After giving him a succinct summary of Juloch's words, Madrazi let him send her to sleep the rest of the day while he sat with Juloch.

The fever attacked again that evening, and in spite of everything that they did, it raged on and grew worse through the night. Shem and Madrazi could not defeat it. In spite of their care, the wound grew angrier; Juloch's shoulder was black and swollen. Shem's face hardened when he examined the wound late that night, and although they cleaned it again, the fever raged on, burning away the life that lay before them. In his final delirium, Juloch murmured only the names of Jared and Noah, but his words were disconnected and made no sense. With the graying of the sky before dawn, he seemed to settle down in the bed and breathed easily one time. Then, nothing. Shem steadied Madrazi with his strong arms as she realized that Juloch was no more. In silence the couple stood drawn together by their fight for Juloch's life, and the minutes seemed like hours before the first rays of the sun lit the gray gloom.

Chapter 30
OMENS

Yur stood stolidly in the hallway of the house of Torech with his spear planted on the paved floor beside him, pointing at the high ceiling. It was the fourth day since the great victory and order had been fully restored. The men had run wild the first night and the pent up emotions of battle and slaughter had led to the murder of several women and the robbing of more than one merchant. But Sechiall had acted quickly and decisively, publicly killing a few of the soldiers as an example to the rest. As a result, the soldiers had been more restrained and the citizens of Y'tor had been more willing to share food, wine, housing, and women. And after the first few days, most of the men were too drunk or tired to cause trouble.

Yur wondered again what had brought him to this station. He was not in Sechiall's circle, nor had he ever been friendly with Sechiall's lieutenants. But Oman had come to him two mornings ago and had ordered him to clean himself up and report to Torech's palace for guard duty. It was a poor trade for the easy job of caring for the horses outside the walls, but Yur had learned long ago not to question orders and had taken up his new duties with apparent equanimity.

Standing guard was not exciting, but it did give Yur a chance to think. His mind was not quick, but it was canny. So much had changed. After the fall of Jared and defeat of Torech, the army had taken the town, and Sechiall had proclaimed himself king. Then his friend Juloch had disappeared two nights before. Speculation was that he had wandered outside the walls drunk and sorrowing and had thrown himself into the sea to join his beloved master. Yur was uncomfortable with that explanation, and missed his friend, but had no time for inquiries with his new duties.

The door opposite him rattled and was thrown open and Yur came stiffly to attention, eyes staring sightlessly straight ahead pretending not to notice Sechiall, framed in the doorway. He appeared in a good mood, but did not acknowledge Yur or the other men standing guard. That was another difference between Sechiall and Jared, but Yur did not care. He did not like Sechiall and correctly assumed that it would not be a good idea to attract his attention. Looking past the new King of Y'tor into the room beyond, Yur saw bars of morning light lying across the woman on the floor. A new one this morning, Yur noted to himself. She had a blanket half pulled over her, and would have been beautiful were it not for the bruises just starting to show color on her face. She had evidently learned firsthand about her new master last night.

Sechiall looked happy, and he should have, Yur thought. He was master of this town, the victor over one of the most feared warriors in the known world, and the commander of one of the best armies. Yur had been a soldier when Sechiall had first arrived in Lamech, a gift from Delonias, a slave in the care of Juloch. He had immediately attracted the attention of Jared, and for some reason Jared had taken to him as to a son. He was certainly a great warrior, but Yur did not think he was a great leader. He inspired fear, not love; obedience, not loyalty. He was certainly not the man that Jared had been. But those thoughts were invisible to the man who stood not eight cubits away from him right now.

Sechiall's attention was drawn to the long hallway. A second later Yur heard the measured, firm tread and metallic rattle of an approaching soldier. Keeping his head straight, he darted a sideways glance down the hall. The imposing figure of Oman marched up to Sechiall and his strong arm extended in a precise salute.

"Hail, commander," he said loudly, "I pray that your night passed in pleasure and rest."

Sechiall bared his teeth in a vicious grin. "Come and see for yourself, Oman."

The two men left the door open behind them and walked into the room. The woman was attempting to gather a blanket around her nakedness and leave, but Sechiall stopped her with a sharp word. Yur's keen eyes saw her cringe before his command, and Sechiall laughed as he ordered her to drop the blanket and bring wine. There was no defiance left in her, Yur noted. She immediately bared her body and blankly walked outside of his range of vision, returning a moment later with two golden goblets. With a bow she offered them to the men and stood waiting. With a nod from Sechiall, she finally left.

Sechiall stood before the open window across from the door. Silently he stood and patiently Oman waited behind him. Finally, Sechiall stirred, "Oman, how speak the men?"

Oman hesitated and then pointedly turned away and shut the door. Yur heard the bolt slide into place and was overcome with curiosity to hear what Oman had to say; gossip from the commander was always a good currency in the army. On the wall facing him was an air vent. Noiselessly, Yur slid across the hall and took up station with his head beside it. He could hear most of the conversation, even though the men sounded as though they were in a deep hole. He kept alert, ready to ease back to his post if anyone approached.

From deep within the room, he heard Oman speak. "Oh mighty king, victory and its spoils have opened the eyes of the few that might have been blind. Without Jared to enforce his antiquated ideas of discipline and deportment, the men have discovered that the fruits of victory are sweet indeed! Those that dared complain were taken outside the city by Gatar. The rest are impatient to return to Lamech where you will be truly king of two cities and the warriors will finally enjoy the full bounty of rewards offered by a generous ruler."

Yur bristled at those words. Oman had always been an opportunist and his loyalty to Jared and his home city easily overcome by the promise of personal gain. But he stifled his anger and listened intently.

Sechiall was speaking now. "Yes, Oman, almost all of our obstacles have been removed. Jared is dead. Torech is no more. Lamech and Methuselah have joined their fathers. Noah and his sons pursue their foolishness with their ship in the forest. Dajus and Subtur will be easily bent to my will. We have only to return and claim what is ours."

There was silence for a moment. Then Oman spoke quietly and Yur had to strain to hear. "Did you find what you were searching for among Jared's belongings, sir?"

Sechiall spoke quickly and with some heat. "No! Curse him! Why couldn't he keep his thoughts inside his heart where they belong? I went through everything carefully and it was not there."

Oman spoke soothingly. "Then Juloch must have stolen it and taken it with him to his death."

Yur's curiosity was now fully aroused. Juloch had been his good friend, and perhaps he could learn more about his death. Maybe Oman knew more than he was telling the men. He strained to hear.

"Do not worry, Sire," said Oman in a calm voice, "You know my accuracy. Juloch is dead and his body and everything with him has been lost in the wilderness. We know this as surely as we know anything now."

"But have you seen his body?"

"No. But I would wager much that no one ever will."

"You are," replied Sechiall ominously.

Oman quickly changed the subject. "You are taking part of what is yours, today. Then we will return to Lamech and take the remainder. It is a day of joy, Sire. Do not let petty annoyances distract you from the great achievement that is yours."

"Today is also a test for our men, Oman. They must know that the claims I make today will be claims for Lamech as well as Y'tor. The flush of victory has cooled. The wine and women of Y'tor have become stale. Today they must respond with their minds, not simply the hot emotion of the moment. And when we return? Then their resolve must be as iron in the face of the old order, its symbols, its leaders, and even their own families."

"That is true, Sire," spoke Oman, "but you will see that all is the same with the men. You slew Torech. You won the battle. You avenged Jared. You led them into this city. You gave them the spoils of victory. You released them from the restraints imposed by Jared. Having experienced that freedom, they will not go back. You will see this with your own eyes today."

Yur felt anger blaze within him again. But it faded just as quickly. What Oman said was true. There had been a release from restraint that even the older men felt. They had not embraced it as readily as the younger soldiers, but most of them had come around and the few that did not, like Yur, knew they must hide their true feelings or die. The metamorphosis was irreversible.

Sechiall sounded pleased with this answer. "Assemble the men around the city square in one hour. If there be any of the citizens of Y'tor that offer complaint or refusal to my terms, let them immediately be slain in full view of all, and let their bodies be thrown before my throne."

"It will be as you command, sire," answered Oman.

"Excellent!" exclaimed Sechiall. "When the new order is brought to Lamech, I will need able men to help enforce my rule. You, Gatar, and Kenah will all enjoy the high rank and the other privileges that you have earned. But there is more for the one who excels in loyalty. I need now a captain of my bodyguard. Once people in both cities have become used to my rule, then Y'tor will need a governor, my personal representative in whom I can place my trust."

Yur felt contempt wash through him. Oman would receive his prize. He would be powerful, but he would never be the man that Jared was, or even Juloch for that matter. But Sechiall liked sycophants. Yur would keep that in mind. As he listened, he heard footsteps approaching the door. Without noise or abrupt motion, he slid back across the hall and resumed his post with the wooden look of incomprehension back on his face. A moment later the bolt slide back and the door was thrown open. Oman bowed before Sechiall and turned and walked rapidly back down the hall. Sechiall's eyes swept across the hall, hardly noticing the statue-like guard across the hall, and then he returned to his room and shut the door.

In a few minutes, he reappeared in his best armor and in the royal robes of Torech. Yur noted that they were too large for Sechiall, but he would not comment on that, and did not think anyone else would either. With a wave of his hand, Sechiall had the guards stationed along the hall form up behind him and march down the great hall to the entrance. There, another group joined them under Oman's watchful eye and the new king of Y'tor marched across the square and mounted his throne as his guard encircled it with spears.

As Sechiall stood before the assembled elders and people of Y'tor in the square, he announced loudly the conditions of his rule. First he called for a large blanket to be spread before his throne. Every adult of the town was required to bring two gold pieces or twenty of silver and place them in the blanket. From there they would kneel before the throne and swear fealty to Sechiall. Their name and contribution was noted by a scribe overseen by Gatar, and each entry was the price of life for each of Y'tor's people. Each soldier of Lamech watched intently as the coins began to pile up on the blanket. Sechiall had spread the word that this money would be divided among the soldiers, minus a tenth for the upkeep of the high places and shrine prostitutes, of course.

But the people of Y'tor were not angry. Sechiall had shown them a taste of terror and then had restrained his men. Citizens that swore the oath to Sechiall would retain their lives and most of their property. A heavy tithe would be due to the crown each year and the expenses of the army would be paid by the merchants of the town. In truth, his demands were not much different than those of Torech, and Torech had ruled long enough to accumulate much hatred among the people. As a result, Sechiall was pleased to see an enthusiastic response to all that he said. Even louder cheers echoed after Sechiall promised trade with Lamech that would profit both towns.

By the time he had finished speaking, the shouts of "King Sechiall! King Sechiall!" were as loud and strong from the people of Y'tor as they were from Lamech's soldiers. Sechiall had intended to leave a full five hundred men in Y'tor, but after seeing the demeanor of the people, he decided that two hundred would serve. Kenah could stay, order the business of the town and keep peace while the others returned to Lamech. Most of those remaining would settle here, where they would enjoy privilege and wealth not available in Lamech. They would be the core of the new army in the city, and Sechiall decreed that each of them would receive a house and two wives from the women of the town.

After dismissing the crowd to their homes, Sechiall called the commanders before him. They were told to assemble the men and prepare to return to

Lamech that very day. His work complete, Sechiall sat back and allowed the adulation of the crowd to wash over him as he turned his mind to the future. Yur kept his own feelings about the future well hidden.

Eleven days had passed since Jared kissed her, mounted his horse, and rode out of the gates at the head of the army. Jeriah had become increasingly restive during that time, and had spent many hours pondering Jared's meeting with Shem, and his words about Noah and his prophecy. Madrazi had once offered her a place on the ark, even though neither really believed that the prophecy could be true. But Jeriah had recognized the gesture as one of love and had appreciated the heartfelt affection of her friend. That Jared had spoken of anything that had to do with Noah at all was surprising.

Something that Shem had said had troubled her husband all that day and the next, and unexpectedly he had not chosen to share the source of his discontent with his wife. Instead, he had unwittingly left her with the same feeling, and it had only intensified over the past days. She had even considered walking all the way to the house of Noah and seeking Madrazi's counsel and comfort. But she had never been there and told herself that it would be ridiculous to go now, especially over some vague feeling.

During the late morning of the eleventh day, she experienced a sudden chill and felt faint and dizzy. Calling two servants, she retired and rested in her room until her strength returned. Later, she was able to continue her activities. But a feeling of dread began to creep over her and she felt herself drowning in some unseen fear. She could not eat and was restless all evening. She warmed a cup of wine to help her sleep, but lay staring at the dark shadows on the ceiling.

Gradually, the shadows gained definition and resolved themselves into moving waters. Instead of lying on her bed, she found herself standing on a beach. Immediately her fears were soothed, for it was a peaceful scene. Moonlight reflected its silvery gleam off of the gentle ripples and the sand was silver beneath her feet. As she watched the rhythmic lapping of the waters near her feet and felt her tension melt in the soothing sound and sight of the peaceful waters, she became aware that Madrazi was standing alongside her, also staring at the water. Jeriah was delighted. She turned to welcome her, and ask where they were, but found that she could not speak. That was frustrating because Madrazi had not even noticed her presence, and that hurt her feelings. But Madrazi stood silent and still, watching the waves roll towards them. The vista seemed familiar to her, but she could not remember having been there.

For some time they stood together. Jeriah was not sure whether her heartbeats measured moments or hours. Her entire body felt deliciously listless and relaxed. Suddenly, she heard a swift intake of breath. Madrazi stood rigid now; her body bathed in silver light that now appeared harsh and unfriendly. Her eyes were large, her fists clenched, and her mouth opened as if to scream. No sound came, and Madrazi made no move. Jeriah turned back to the sea, searching for the source of her friend's fear.

As Jeriah watched, she noticed that the surface of the sea had begun to recede. Her feet felt the ground vibrating gently; sand grains rolled across her feet. The surface of the water had become black and unreflective, and rolled back away from the sandy sea floor with increasing speed. Water flowed as a smooth sheet to the horizon where it began to build, reaching high enough to blot out many stars. There was no air; it was gone with the water. Madrazi stood stiffly beside her; Jeriah knew that they shared the terror she now felt to the core of her soul. A corner of her mind was trying to recall where she was, knowing that the information was there, but tantalizingly beyond reach.

Breath came again, wind blew her hair away from her face, and the black mountain began its great fall onto the beach where she stood. As it sped towards her, the very ground opened before its onrush, and the red glare of subterranean flames reflected off the face of the wave. Suddenly, recollection hit her. She knew where she was, and turned accusingly to Madrazi, wanting to know why she had dragged her into this vision of horror.

But as she turned, she saw the air around Madrazi begin to shimmer. The harsh moonlight of a few moments ago began to be transformed into a soft golden light that shone against the darkness of the night. The light enveloped Madrazi, and seemed to permeate her entire body. But despite its appearance, Jeriah found the light cold; as it grew brighter and richer, it hurt her eyes and chilled her soul. She felt a deep, instinctive terror that overcame even her fear of the black waters or red fire.

But she loved Madrazi and could not completely turn away. As she continued to watch, she saw her friend begin to fade; the light was taking her away. Madrazi's body became translucent and the light shone through and around her. Jeriah felt an infinite sadness at the impending loss of her friend, but was still repulsed by the light. Just as she turned to run away, Madrazi's eyes turned to her, burning bright with love, her hand reaching out and touching Jeriah's. Part of Jeriah wanted to grasp the hand tight and leave with her friend, but a primal fear of the light welled up inside, and Jeriah snatched her hand away. It suddenly struck her that it was foolish to reject escape, but by then it was too late. Madrazi was gone. The light faded, and as Jeriah turned, the chasm opened beneath her feet and the water fell out of the sky and enveloped her in darkness.

Screaming, she found that she could still move and breathe, and a dim light filtered in through the window. It took several minutes to realize that the stark terror of the night was not real and even then Jeriah could not stop trembling. She no longer wondered at the fear she had seen in Madrazi's face that afternoon when she had related this vision. But why had it invaded her life? What dread event occasioned it? Madrazi had told her that she was always buried beneath the wave in her dream. Why had Madrazi been rescued from the destroying sea while she remained to face it? Answers eluded her, and her mind refused clear thought.

As she shook with convulsive sobs, the thought came sharply to her that she should go to Madrazi immediately and ask her help. Perhaps her friend could interpret the meaning of the dream; perhaps even Noah could—after all, he was reputed to be a prophet. She must. The dream was a warning. Only by fleeing now could she save herself. She even climbed down from her bed and began to throw on her clothes. The decision made, she felt a great relief she could not explain.

But as she dressed, she stopped short and began to laugh at herself. Here she stood, a grown woman, the wife of one of the most important men in Lamech, fleeing in the middle of the night to the home of a madman because of a bad dream. For a moment, she seemed as two women; one standing there laughing, the other desperately urging her forward. Then she shook her head and disrobed slowly before climbing back on the bed.

But sleep would not come. The feeling of fear returned and she sat in the dark, unable to sleep. She simply could not run away to her friend, but she was lonely and she was afraid. All she could do was clutch the sheets about her as she sat crying softly. Would morning ever come?

****

Gray dimness gradually began to replace the night blackness. The young woman stirred, then slid her head to the other side of the chair and began to breathe deeply and regularly again. The old woman watched her for a moment, then settled back as the pre-dawn light seeped into the darkness of the room. It had been many months since she had slept for an entire night; recently, she had been living on short naps throughout the day and night. Soon, she would lay her body down for its final rest and discover the true outcome of all of her choices.

She shook her head slightly in memory of the older days. Men planned and toiled, devoting their years, their energy, and even their blood to achieve the visions that had captured their imagination. What they did not realize was that their most intricate plans were only a small and simple part of the tapestry woven by the master planner. 'In spite of our best efforts, all men eventually bow to that superior force,' she mused to herself. Often the most significant events within grandiose plans are the simple choices made by simple people in the midst of the chaos. How can one be prepared to face an ultimate choice?

Chapter 31
CONQUESTS

Five days after they set out, an exhausted army camped a short distance from Lamech. Sechiall had pushed them hard. Yur assumed his now familiar station outside Sechiall's tent, careful to avoid any error. Oman had continued to watch him closely during the entire march, and although Yur could not understand the reason, it seemed that he had earned Oman's suspicion. He had not yet made a connection between the captain's attitude and the disappearance of Juloch.

Oman was not a man to cross; he was vicious and had keen instincts. Yur did what he was told without complaint. He maintained the same look of blank, unquestioning stupidity on his face that Oman expected, and hid the sharp observations that he made with eyes and ears away with the even sharper conclusions in his head. His mind was not as quick as Oman's, but it was no less incisive. His intelligence had been sufficient to disguise itself, and had done so well, as evidenced by his still being alive. Had Oman suspected Yur of being any brighter than he looked, he certainly would have planted a knife in his back.

Yur assumed that there was some significance to the pace, but knew better than to inquire after the Supreme Commander's motives. He did observe, though, that the rapid march maintained a paradoxically high level of emotion and excitement along with a great weariness. Yur wondered how Sechiall intended to seize power in Lamech, for there was no question that he would. How could he proclaim himself king of Y'tor and return to Lamech as a mere military commander?

His patience was rewarded when he heard Sechiall's picked men spreading instructions carefully through the camp later that night. The army would make a triumphal entry into the city and would march in formation to the square of the elders where they would form up and support Sechiall in his demands. With the elders cowed into submission, Sechiall would have his power. In return, the soldiers would become the elite citizens of Lamech, lording it over the merchants and traders who had for so long looked down on them. Still jubilant from their victory, the men were receptive to Sechiall's promises.

'Finally the army will receive the honor and recognition that it deserves.'

'The merchants and traders will have to make way for the conquerors.'

Comments like these circulated throughout the camp, carefully instigated by Sechiall. Skins of wine from Y'tor had been packed away under guard, and were now passed around the camp with the evening meal. Not enough for anyone to become drunk, it relaxed the men and made them cheerful.

Gatar had been sent ahead the previous night to Lamech. Yur had overheard enough to know that he was carrying instructions to the elders about the coming day. However, Yur was certain that the elders did not guess just what they would be letting inside the gates. From what he had overheard, Noah would not even be present, making him the most intelligent of the remaining elders in Yur's opinion.

He felt a twinge of regret apart from his active dislike of Sechiall and his lieutenants. With Jared in charge of the army, and Methuselah, Lamech and Noah directing the council, life in Lamech had been good, if perhaps a little dull and religious. But Yur found himself thinking as he paced up and down under the stars that whatever its shortcomings, the old order had been far better than what was coming. In those late hours, Yur decided that he would leave Lamech at the earliest possible time. He could take service in the army of Taspar and then thumb his nose at Oman and Sechiall. That issue decided, he continued his pacing, content. Let the fools in Lamech embrace Sechiall. He would not be there to see their inevitable regret.

Camp broke early the next morning. Men grumbled as they polished armor and weapons. Captains strode briskly among their men, and each man was warned to look his best. They were ordered to maintain a precise formation marching through the town and then to form a solid perimeter around the square of the elders. The cavalry was sent to its quarters outside of town to care for the horses; only Sechiall would be mounted for the entry into town.

Shortly after dawn the army was on the march. The sun behind them glittered off the gleaming white walls of Lamech until they were dimmed by the long shadows of the approaching army. Near the city, the highway on the plain was wide enough for ten men abreast and the thousands of legs moved in unison behind their new master. His black horse was large and thickly muscled almost to the extent of deformity, but the raw strength of the mount seemed an appropriate throne for the mighty Sechiall, still carrying his spear. Banners of the army were prominent in the front and drummers scattered throughout the ranks increased the beat to a fast march as they drew near the gate. Yur was stationed in the front rank of guards marching directly behind Sechiall. Sechiall trotted ahead, circled his horse, and surveyed the willing ranks winding out to the edge of sight. Then he brought the horse back and held it in a stiff walk as he led his army through the gates.

Yur's sharp ears picked up the mutterings of the Supreme Commander. "Very well, Jared. You opened the door, but I will step through. You have a grave of honor, but I have two cities and the promise of more. The cub has returned as the king!" Yur kept his face impassive, but his resolve to leave Lamech at the earliest possible moment redoubled.

Sechiall kept his horse at a brisk walk. The morning sun threw his shadow far down the avenue before him as he rode into the city. A crowd had gathered. Men and women were cheering and waving banners. Sechiall had kept his grisly trophy—Torech's decaying head mounted on his spear. As it became visible to the waiting throng, a great roar arose. "Torech is dead! Torech is dead!" These were interspersed with shouts of "Hail, Sechiall, conqueror of Y'tor!" coming from picked men. The crowd quickly caught the cry and the celebration of victory quickly degenerated into adulation of Sechiall. Crowds poured out to line the street and cheers followed the army through the entire length of the town. As the last men of the army marched through the gates, the crowds gathered behind them and followed to the council square.

Sechiall rode into the square followed by the now deafening roar of the crowd funneling down the street, echoing off the rock walls of the buildings, and blasting across the square. Dajus and Subtur were seated in their black chairs, but rose when Sechiall dismounted before them. A soldier moved forward, received his spear, and stood stiffly holding the bridle. Sechiall looked straight ahead, well aware that he was the focus of attention; even the sun seemed to preferentially reflect his polished armor and golden hair. Keeping his back to the people, he casually bowed to the elders. Subtur made ready to speak, but the words died in his mouth as he realized that Sechiall was not finished.

Instead of standing at the foot of the dais to receive the blessing of the council, Sechiall stepped up even with Dajus and Subtur and stood in front of them facing the crowd. He gave an imperceptible nod to Oman and the troops formed ranks around the perimeter of the square. The leading men of the city found themselves inside a fence of spears, separated from the masses. Suddenly a roar went up from the army overwhelming the cheers of the townsfolk. "Hail, Sechiall; Sechiall, King!"

Louder and louder rose the cry. Those in the crowd who did not join in received warning looks from the nearest troops and meaningful gestures towards their weapons. Within minutes the square was an unending roar for King Sechiall. Cries of "Sechiall, King of Lamech and Y'tor" joined the others.

Subtur went pale and raised his hands, but none paid heed.

Finally Sechiall moved. He had seemed to stand half asleep as the cries washed over him. Now he awoke, and no man could fail to feel the pulse of power that flashed from his eyes, his stature, his hands. He raised one almost casually. The men of the army were immediately silent, and other cries faded into echoes. An unnatural stillness descended on the square. Sechiall was an imposing figure, head and shoulders above the two elders. He held one hand forward and in the quiet, he let his eyes range the square, holding men's eyes for a split second before moving on. Such was his power in those minutes that each man knew that his glance was only for him; each was stronger, more confident, and proud of it, and knew without doubt that his ruler stood before him.

Finally Sechiall spoke, but in a quiet voice that men had to strain to hear. "Citizens of Lamech, my friends," he began softly, "I am no king and Lamech is ruled by a council of wise elders. I am an orphan and you are my family. It is true that in these dangerous days the army must play a vital role in defending the city, and we have honored the trust that you have given us." With this, he received back his spear from his orderly and held aloft Torech's head. The cheering started again. He waited patiently for the people to express their adoration and then raised his hand again. Silence.

He started again, "My brothers, times are changing. Torech's evil murder of our beloved elder Lamech took from us the wisdom of our city, but it has shown us the path to greatness lies in strength. And our might has proven sufficient. Commander Jared saw this clearly before any of us, and was rebuked for his foresight!"

He began to raise his voice ever so slightly, "Jared gave his life for his city, and we will build a monument to him to preserve the memory of his service. But more enduring than stone will be the legacy of his wisdom." At this news, a groan went up from the assembled crowd; Jared had been well respected by all and this was the first word of his death that any save the elders had heard.

Sechiall bowed his head, reflecting the crowd's emotion, but then sighed audibly and pressed on. His voice took on a careful rhythm, emphasizing his points one by one. "The army of Lamech is more than a shield against its enemies. It is a sword that others will now rightly fear. It has gained us a colony and control of all the lands to the south—rich lands. It will force our overlords in Taspar to treat us with the respect due equals. So it is only reasonable that the army's increased responsibilities would lead to your desire for its more prominent role in our civic affairs."

His voice now assumed a familiar, convincing tone. "Torech was a tyrant and a failure. Our city is not Y'tor. It needs strong leadership, but tempered by wisdom and virtue. The Supreme Commander of the army of Lamech cannot be a king. Let us say instead that he will be a full member of the council, perhaps even the chief of the council, but by the council we have been ruled long and successfully. No great change is required, only the confirmation of what has existed in reality these past few years. But no change should be made without the consent of the leading men of our community. What say you?"

Like the first crash of a breaking wave upon a rocky shore, the army as a man shouted, "Aye!"

And like the lessened but more prolonged noise as the wave strives to gain its full reach inland, the remainder of the crowd echoed, "Aye!"

Sechiall spoke once more, "Men of Lamech! Continue in prosperity! We, your warriors, shall guard that prosperity and open doors to wealth beyond your imagination. As you wish, so we will serve. And with our esteemed elders, Dajus and Subtur, your council shall order all these affairs as they have for all these years. Return to your homes in full knowledge that we will strive for your benefit to bring all of this to pass."

Under the spell of his voice, the crowd dispersed quietly, though the warriors remained in solid rows around the square. Sechiall turned to the two men behind him and asked in a quite different voice, "Shall we convene?"

Subtur spluttered with anger, "What is the meaning of this? You did not refuse the calls for a crown; you only selected a facade to appease the ignorant. You are no different from Torech!"

Sechiall measured him with cold eyes, "Be careful of what you say, my fellow elder." Subtur shrank from the sneer in his voice. "I am not Torech. I am alive. I am strong. I stand before you. And I maintain a better mix of love and fear from my inferiors to keep order. I could be king now. And if I was, be assured that you would now be feeding the birds outside the walls!" He glanced around at the spears fencing the dais and Dajus and Subtur followed his eyes nervously.

Then he continued in a softer tone, "Come, let us be reasonable. You sought to use me to gain power over Methuselah, Lamech, and Noah. But you misjudged your tool, and find a blade facing you, not a hilt firmly grasped in your hands. But all is not lost. Apply your vaunted wisdom! Your choice is simple. I may not choose to be a king in name, but I have that power. You may aid or oppose me. If the latter is your choice, you see before you a thousand reasons why you will fail. If you aid me, then you will keep the trappings of power to which you are accustomed. Wealth will be yours in greater measure. And who knows? Perhaps you will earn the trust of your

Chief Elder, and actually come again into some measure of that power which you desired. It is really a very simple choice, especially for men like you!"

Dajus spoke quickly, "Subtur, my friend. Listen to Sechiall! Times are changing. Do not walk only part of the way down a new road. It is a good road, and there is no other choice. There is no way back. You will not regret this!"

Turning to Sechiall, he said, "I accept your terms. In truth, Lamech needs a strong leader, one who can command the love of its warriors, for days of war will be forced upon us no matter what we do. Better to fight to increase the power and glory of Lamech than to preserve that of Taspar. Lead us, Sechiall. Only remember that the men of this town are traders and merchants, not warriors. Treat them as they deserve and they will follow you gladly to great glory and wealth."

Subtur sat in thought for a minute. Finally he spoke with his head bowed. "I will walk with you Dajus, for the sake of our friendship and the sake of the good of the men of this city." Then he turned to Sechiall, grim acceptance showing in his eyes. "I will go with you Sechiall, for a time, and we will see where the path leads. If your words are true, then my service will remain true. If they are false, then I can have no part of them. However, I am no fool. Even without your men, I cannot stop you if you choose force as your strength. If I am not satisfied in one year, then I will leave Lamech forever. I will leave quietly and take all that is mine with me. That is my answer."

Sechiall nodded. "You speak well, as usual, Subtur. I want not what you fear. Stay your year in peace, and I think that you will never leave this town."

Subtur, being no fool, said no more and turned away, lest Sechiall read his thoughts. He knew that Sechiall's promise guaranteed only his death some dark night outside the city, and the time was probably much sooner than one year. As he turned away, he heard Sechiall say to Dajus. "For the present, I will live in the house of Jared. He was my only father, and I his only son."

"Very well," replied Dajus. "I can see no obstacle to your permanent possession of that which was Jared's. Go in peace and assurance of my loyalty to you."

Subtur with an effort controlled his face and resumed his place facing the crowd. The fence of spears that should have signaled a celebration instead sealed the end of all of Subtur's efforts. Sechiall stepped down and away from the elders. He dismissed his orderly with instructions to care for his horse, and waved Oman to him. Within hearing of Dajus and Subtur he said, "Choose one hundred of our most faithful men to serve under you. I want a guard of ten picked men near me at all times. Divide their duty as you see fit, but keep them in town and let them know that they must all be prepared to march in a few weeks."

Subtur cursed to himself. He had hoped that Sechiall would relax his guard and leave himself open to an untimely death. As Sechiall strode away from the square through the ranks of cheering soldiers and citizens, Subtur's mind wrestled with the problem before him.

The army was firmly under the control of Sechiall. He had cemented that alliance with the sack of Y'tor. His picked men would now control the army. Jared's death was a far greater catastrophe for the city than any would have guessed. His quiet demeanor had disguised the true power he possessed and his personal allegiance to the values of his fellow citizens had prevented them from guessing what might happen if someone without scruples assumed control of it. Even Subtur had not foreseen the full extent of the problem, for he had not suspected that Jared would not return, and even given that improbability, he assumed a period of negotiation between Sechiall and the remaining elders. Sechiall's bold and decisive takeover was a shock. He was not sure which stung more—the loss of his power or the fact that he had lost it by being outwitted by a barbarian boy. But as he looked on the faces of the soldiers around the square, he realized that neither were as painful as the personal humiliation, and he hung his head as he made his way back to his home.

Now Zered had built a large house near the northern wall of the city shortly after his accession to Supreme Commander. It was set on a large plot of ground, apart from the surrounding buildings. A low stone wall surrounded the property and many beautiful trees shaded its grounds. Pathways of brick wound though the trees, giving the feel of the forest within sight of the high white walls of Lamech. Jared had added onto the original structure, and now it formed a square, with a small garden as the central courtyard. Water played in the sunlight in a large fountain whose sound could be heard even inside the house itself.

With his marriage to Jeriah, a warmer, softer atmosphere could be found in the home. New plantings of flowers, new tapestries to warm the stone walls, and a new aura brought by the feminine energy that turns a house into a home had transformed the military mansion into a place of welcoming grace.

But on that day, the sound of water from the fountain echoed the tears of the mistress of the home. She sat inside the wooden-walled study, robed in black cloth with a veil over her face and ashes on her head. Shock, grief, and anger vied with each other for her heart. She had not heard of her husband's death until after the army had arrived this morning, and only then because one of Jared's old friends had left his cavalry unit without permission to come and tell her as much as possible in the few moments that he could safely spare. Jeriah was no fool; if Sechiall had not bothered to send an official envoy days ago with the news, then he had his reasons, and she could guess at what some of them might be. The distant roar from the town square supported some of her ideas and she imagined that events of the weeks ahead would confirm those and others. But the agony of her loss precluded political speculation for the present.

The emptiness of the room was a palpable thing, but was interrupted by a sound at the door. A servant's fearful face appeared at the open door and announced the coming of some delegation from the city center. Soldiers were present and they would be at the door any moment.

Jeriah arose and walked steadily to the front of the house. She opened the large front door and stepped out on the porch. She saw a group of soldiers with banners and spears waving over their heads as they walked up the path. At the front was the golden-haired giant who had been welcome here so many times before. But she noticed immediately that none were weeping; they were not even dressed for mourning. Instead they all seemed to be celebrating some great joy. Her anger at that slight temporarily overcame her sorrow.

As she watched them stride up the path toward her, a sense of unease seized her. She shuddered slightly as if some evil wind was blowing across her and into her home. The soldiers stopped a respectful distance away, but the blond leader swaggered up onto the porch. She could feel the heat off of his body and the leer on his face. She kept her eyes down and said, "Welcome to the house of Jared, Commander. How may I serve you?"

Sechiall pushed forward, towering over the woman. "Do not bandy pretty words with me, Jeriah. I know your mind and we will speak plainly with each other. This is no longer the house of Jared. I see that you have already learned the reason. You can put aside your mourning. He is dead. He left no one except me. This is my house, and you are my woman. That is not an occasion to mourn! All here is mine, just as are all in this town. Your choice is simple. Please me, and benefit from this change, or displease me and suffer. Nothing can shelter you from my desires, so think not of your father's house."

"Will you not even grant a time for grief?" she asked, appalled at his boldness. She felt disoriented at his nearness; his raw strength, now freed from Jared's years of restraint, washed over her as a palpable force. Desperately, she wished for time to think and act. But Sechiall pushed even closer.

"The dead are buried and have been avenged." He reached out suddenly and snatched the veil from her face. Her hair was pulled forward as it came away, and she instinctively reached up and pulled it back. Anger flashed into her eyes and in that anger she brought herself to her full height and challenged the lewd stare of the man before her. But she did so foolishly, and was caught and held by the power of Sechiall's flashing blue eyes. Always before there had been a hint of boldness, but in the presence of Jared, the fires of his eyes had remained banked. Now there was no restraint and she was not prepared for the raw power of his presence. Her protests died in her throat and she struggled for control. But she found herself foundering in the blue fire of the eyes before her.

She heard his voice now almost within her mind. "The tides of change sweep swiftly along now. It is time for decision. Move with the waters or be drowned in them."

Sechiall paused, and Jeriah again attempted to tear her eyes away from the deadly trap of his gaze. But her power did not equal her desire and even the desire began to fade with a scream inside her head. The controlling voice continued. "I will take what I want regardless of your choice, but your choice will be the difference between remaining my woman and living in comfort or begging your bread on the street."

"I may choose neither," returned Jeriah, finally tearing her eyes away and trying to find strength within to rally her spirit. The memory of Madrazi and her friendship entered her conscious thought and that gave her a measure of resistance. She faltered, but continued to speak. "I may choose to go to my friend, Madrazi. I will always have a place with her, just as she would with me."

Sechiall laughed wickedly, and a shudder ran through Jeriah. "Yes, by all means! You shall go to see Madrazi! You will accompany me when Noah and all that belong to him are destroyed. He has chosen to stand against the tide of my strength. It will overwhelm him. The only flood he will see is that of his house's blood which I will personally spill with my own sword! You are right! You must come with me and watch my final triumph. Then you will understand your own choice more clearly."

Jeriah paled and felt her limbs shake. Nothing could shield her from the flame of Sechiall's power and ambition. Jared was no more. She felt her spirit quail before him, but her love for her friend lent her strength to plead. "Please, Sechiall. Must you do this? Can you not leave them in peace? The town is yours. What concern can a little farm a day's march away have for you?"

"You fear for your friend?" sneered Sechiall. "Well, I will grant you one boon. Her life will be spared, if she is willing to join you. A powerful ruler requires more than one woman. Since you are such good friends, you can share me! If she is not willing, she can join Shem and the rest of them in death. Think well and long what words you can speak to sway her. For her life will be in your hands. She must make her choice and openly repudiate Shem before he dies. But even that opportunity depends on your immediate willingness to serve me in place of Jared."

Panic rose within her. Where was her old strength? It had been burned away before one much greater. Her only hope was her friend. She must escape and warn Madrazi, but how? She could not get past the town gate without Sechiall's knowledge, and he would never allow her to flee. Was her only chance to play for time and try to save Madrazi? But to what would she be saved? Was not death better than what Sechiall offered? Death would cheat Sechiall of his victory and salvage her own integrity. She was tempted momentarily.

Jeriah made one final effort to recover control. She felt in her heart that she was somehow facing the test of her life. Was she strong enough? Could she defy Sechiall even if it meant the choice of death not only for herself but also for her friend? It seemed the only alternative, and right now, a small voice in the back of her mind told her that it was the correct choice. She met Sechiall's eyes and strove to reassert her spirit. But his blue flame was beyond her and she felt that part of her soul shrivel. She did not want to die, and there was no other exit from his snare.

Foundering, she told herself that death was the end of hope. At least if she lived, she and Madrazi would still have each other. Sechiall was a bold man, and took many chances. Sooner or later those chances must lead to his destruction. Would there be any kind of life left to them if they waited patiently for that time? She could not foresee, but time was all that she had. She must preserve her life now for an opportunity to save Madrazi. She put aside the thought that there would be nothing worthwhile left of her life if ever she managed to escape Sechiall's grasp. She looked up again and her eyes were held again, shredding the tatters of her will.

"I will do whatever you ask," she replied haltingly.

"I know you will."

He shut the door behind them.

Chapter 32
SECOND CHANCE

Meshur had stood on the outskirts of the crowd in silence and watched the man he hated seize control of his town. He despised Sechiall and his warriors. He himself would have been a superb warrior, and had been tempted by Jared to enlist many years ago. Jared had been a good man, and one who Meshur could easily have followed. But his dream had always been the making of useful and beautiful things, not wreaking death and destruction. And in Ham, he had found a better master, one who could both see and share his dreams of shaping wood, stone, and metal.

But a small voice reminded him that he had made nothing beautiful for almost two years. Ever since that terrible choice had been made, he had felt no glimmer of the creative gift. Wine helped him forget his failure to be a man, but even now his guilt at betraying Ham's trust ate at him like a wound that would not heal. In between bouts of forgetfulness, he worked for a blacksmith doing work that required no thought and little skill. He earned enough to keep buying wine. He had lived with Pashtur for a few months, but the two had drifted apart. Pashtur began to blame Meshur for his brush with death, and Meshur returned the resentment for his own loss. The blacksmith allowed Meshur to live in a small room at the back of his shed, and the two cousins had not seen each other for many months.

A few weeks past, he had been given a more difficult job, and he had been drinking less and working harder. He began to recall with more clarity and less pain his days in the forest clearing, watching the giant ark take shape under the skill and strength of his hands. Although he had never really believed in the prophecy of Noah, the ark in its grand design and innovative construction contained a part of his soul. He knew Pashtur was wrong—Noah was a good man and Ham was easy and open in teaching like-minded men his priceless skill.

His mind returned to the scene before him. He rubbed a dirty hand against his torn tunic, and felt the hate within him swell with each shout of the soldiers for the new king of Lamech. Sechiall was the root of all of his troubles but he could never get close enough to kill him. What would hurt Sechiall? Noah was an elder. What if he challenged Sechiall's power publicly? If he could use the obvious fear of the other two elders, perhaps Sechiall could be banished and the army brought back under control.

Jared was dead, but how? Meshur was not a man easily satisfied when his curiosity was aroused. He did not want to talk to any of the soldiers, but only they had the information he wanted. With his size, he could easily scan the crowd. As it broke up, his dilemma was resolved when he saw Yur walking alone away from the groups of warriors. He could talk to Yur; they drank together occasionally, and Yur was not one of the young hotheads that followed Sechiall. And Yur had been appreciative enough of the skilled forging of a new sword to pay for wine for several nights.

The old soldier was headed for his favorite wine shop; one with which Meshur was intimately familiar. He set out as along the fringes of the dispersing crowd on a course to intersect the old soldier. Carefully, he avoided the larger groups of soldiers and came upon Yur as he had planned, in the alley that led to the shop. Approaching him, Meshur called out, "Old man! Can I buy a ewer for the victor?"

"There is nothing to celebrate, young fool, but reason to drink," returned Yur enigmatically.

"Then come with me," urged Meshur. "I have my own supply, and we can avoid the jackals."

They followed the alleys to the back of the deserted blacksmith shop, and within a few hours Meshur had learned all that he wanted to know. With the help of plentiful wine, Yur recounted the battle, its aftermath in Y'tor and the march home. By that time, the old soldier's distaste for the Supreme Commander had become clear and his conversation became less guarded as he realized that Meshur shared his hatred of Sechiall. He willingly shared the memories of his keen ears and observant eyes.

"King Sechiall, he called himself there," spat out the older man, finally. "That's what he wants here, no matter what honey comes from his tongue in front of the others. And he's got plenty of this young rabble that will be happy to have him. They don't understand the price that will come due later!"

"Everything seems to have been turned upside down since Lamech's death," agreed Meshur.

"Aye," said the older man after swallowing the remainder of his cup, "and with Methuselah gone, Noah would be better off a long ways from Lamech, or else he will soon join him." He laughed at his own joke, and held out his cup while Meshur poured the remainder of his wine in it. The big man had managed to drink very little, finding to his surprise that he no longer wanted it. There were many other things that he wanted to do now, but first he must find a way out of town. Surely the smaller gates that let out onto the fields would not be guarded yet.

So it was that Meshur found himself that night picking his way along the road to Noah's settlement, stopping and listening for patrols of soldiers and ever ready to slip into whatever cover was available. Getting out of town had proven as easy as he had hoped; the soldiers were probably sleeping or still celebrating their victories. But Meshur had remained cautious; he realized that the price of discovery would probably be his death. There was no mercy in Sechiall.

He did not care. Sechiall had taken everything from him; he would gladly risk his life to return the injury. Perhaps Noah could raise a force and sway the men of Lamech back to their old loyalties. Meshur imagined himself in the front ranks, beside Ham, marching to defeat and slay the usurper. But how could he? He had proven himself unfaithful; why should Ham or Noah trust him now? The shame of what he had done almost caused him to turn and retrace his steps. But what was a man unless he could admit his wrongs? He could at least explain and beg forgiveness from Noah and Ham. He stopped to consider that. Those thoughts almost drove out all desire for vengeance and blood. The next step was the hardest he had ever taken, but it was in the direction of Noah's home. A small spark of the past seemed to have ignited in his heart, and every step closer to Noah seemed to fan it to something greater.

The sun was rising as Meshur sat with water and bread set before him. Noah, Shem and Madrazi were with him in the great hall. In a few halting sentences, he summarized the past two years. He related the recent events in town, and was honest about his own failures.

"And now, Oh Master, I know that only you can challenge Sechiall. But if you do not act quickly, you and all that is yours cannot escape his wrath. You will not bend to his will as have Dajus and Subtur, and so he must destroy you."

Noah stared thoughtfully into the distance, seeming to consider the news. But then his eyes returned to the man before him. "Why did you come back, Meshur?" he asked quietly. His voice drew the big man's eyes and held them. Shem and Madrazi remained quiet and Madrazi sensed that Meshur's answer would hold much more for him than its mere words could express.

"I'm not sure, Master," he replied slowly with knitted brow. "I started out because I hate Sechiall and would see him destroyed. But as I walked, I realized that I wanted to explain to Ham what happened two years ago and ask his forgiveness. Then I think that I continued because I wanted to warn you of the danger you face. You are a good man and Sechiall is evil. Finally, in the darkest hour, there was nowhere else I wanted to go."

"Very well, Meshur," said Noah. "I choose to believe you. You did not sin in saving your cousin's life, but you should have come back much sooner. We would have protected you."

Tears of gratitude formed at the rim of the man's eyes, but he quickly wiped them away with his massive hand. Noah continued sternly, "I have abandoned Lamech because Lamech rejected the words of the Creator long ago. His judgment is sure and the ark is the only hope for my household or any other person. You know the prophecy, yet you chose with all the others to reject its truth."

Meshur bowed his head before the truth of those words, but Noah spoke on with gathering strength. "All is not lost. The day is near, and it no longer matters who rules Lamech. You have gained a final chance. There is no future in town or anywhere else on the face of the earth. You may accept the word of the Creator and come with us, or reject it and go where you will to your own destruction. Do you wish to save yourself?"

Meshur struggled to answer honestly. He had always let Pashtur guide his thinking about the tale of the ark. Finally he said. "I do not understand the prophecy or the Creator. But I know that you and your sons are good men, and are worthy of my trust. I will accept what you say, even if I do not understand." As he spoke these words, it seemed that a great weight was lifted from him. Although tears still rolled down his cheeks, his eyes took on light as a new sense of purpose shone forth. His eyes met Noah's and understanding seemed to pass between them.

When Meshur spoke again, it was with the strong, confident voice that Madrazi remembered. "I must return and bring my cousin back with me. I owe him that debt."

Noah nodded his acquiescence. "You have declared yourself, knowing that there is no middle ground. Go with care and bring your cousin. You may help us finish, and then accompany us in the day of judgment. Stay for a few hours; rest and eat, and then return to bring him here. You must go quickly, for the day is nearly upon us."

Shem looked at Noah. "With Jared gone, Sechiall out of control, and Dajus and Subtur openly participating in his treachery, we may not have those days. Now that he has tasted power, he will not hesitate to murder others to keep it. It is only a matter of time before he marches here. We must finish quickly."

The reminder of Jared's death pushed Madrazi's thoughts to her friend.

She paled at what might happen in the chaos of the following days. "What of Jeriah?" she interrupted. "What will become of her now?"

Shem hesitated, but Meshur spoke out. "Dajus announced that all that was Jared's now belonged to Sechiall. He will take her, too."

Madrazi's heart sank. "I must help her," she cried. "How can I?"

Meshur answered. "I have another cousin who is a servant for Jared, and has little love for Sechiall. If I could find him when I return for Pashtur, he could deliver a message to her."

"Would you try?" Madrazi asked, hope returning.

"Yes, Lady."

"Then tell her to come with you if she can. She will be welcome here."

Noah nodded, and led Meshur away to take some sleep before returning to town. Madrazi went out to the front porch, where she sat down and wept for Jeriah. Shem sat with her holding her until she could weep no more. She wondered at the tumbling of events in these past few years. Jeriah had achieved a life that Madrazi had once thought would be the pinnacle of satisfaction and contentment. Yet it had all been taken away from her by one thrust of a dagger. Now she was worse than a slave to a man ruled only by his own desires.

That thought suddenly struck Madrazi with the foolishness of her years of discontent. She had brought herself much misery by building a life of dreams that could not possibly come true. Shem's words of long ago returned to her; one's life could not be ruled by imagination. Why had she not learned from him? She saw her unhappiness in light of a refusal to face life on its own terms. The shock of insight overcame her sorrow for Jeriah with a much deeper sadness in her own heart—one that could not be erased by tears alone.

Later that day she found Meshur sitting on the porch staring off into the wilderness to the south. Approaching him with food and water, she sat down across the table from him. "I thought that you were going to sleep, Meshur," she said quietly, interrupting his reverie.

He looked back with a slight, bitter smile on his lips. "I have done much sleeping these past years, Lady," he replied, hesitating to meet her eyes. "It is no longer a time for sleeping, but a time for thought and planning and then action. I am a simple man. My cousin and I used to talk, but these past years I have not seen him and have no one to talk to."

Judging rightly that there was a request in his statement, Madrazi replied, "You may talk with me, if you will. I am just a woman, but I will listen."

A wider smile lit his face. "Lady, you have more of a mind than most men if what I hear is true, and I would count it a privilege to talk with you," he paused and looked down, "if your husband would permit it."

"Shem likes you, too," she said firmly. "He would be happy if I could help."

Gradually she drew out his story. He unburdened much in the lazy hours of the afternoon, and Madrazi found in him the simple trust of a friend. She was convinced that during those hours he came to see her as a person in her own right, apart from the wife of Shem, and somewhere during those hours they established a definite friendship that boded well for a future in Noah's new world. He told her of his youth in halting words, and then with increasing ease about how he came to work with Ham, and his love for the man and the things he had been taught over the years.

Meshur related his activities of the past years, and his anger at seeing the conquest of the city by Sechiall; a bloodless conquest by military might. He observed that it would not end as it had started, that blood would be required eventually. His account of the afternoon with Yur held her enthralled, for it filled in many of the pieces of the story that Juloch had not known. Madrazi in turn told him of Juloch's last days and his story. Meshur shook his massive head when he learned of Juloch's death.

"He was a better man as a servant than those that now command."

Madrazi had to agree with that. They sat for a few more minutes and then she left him as the sun began to sink in the early afternoon. She was not there to say farewell when he started back for town.

But his words haunted her. He had freely confessed his disbelief to Noah and Shem and she wondered if she could ever be that strong. For Madrazi knew in her heart that there was much to confess, but the old stubbornness was like a deep trail in her mind—she could not help but follow it. But each day brought hope. Jeriah was at the mercy of a traitor and murderer. But a man strong in both heart and arm was carrying a message of hope to her. She prayed that night that Noah's God would guard the man and the message.

Chapter 33
NEW ORDER

Jeriah lingered between sleep and waking. She was in her own bed and Jared was back from the wars. They would enjoy quiet days together. But why was the bed so hard? And why was her body so stiff and sore? The morning slowly seeped into her consciousness and with a shudder she realized that the night had held no nightmare, only a stark new reality. Her cheek was pressed against the cold, hard wood of her floor, and its unyielding firmness had stiffened her entire body. She felt its chill against her bare legs and instinctively pulled the thin blanket tighter about her.

Her fingers touched her swollen lips and awoke the pain there. A tear blurred her eye and began to find its cold track down her bruised cheek. Memory returned with its own pain, adding to her physical discomfort. Slowly, she tried to move. The hated laugh froze her into immobility.

"Beginning to learn your place yet, woman?" The evil undertones she had always detected in the voice were no longer masked. "You were not hard to break to my will, and even you must admit that after your pathetic resistance that you really did take pleasure last night. It only took a few blows and a few promises." He laughed again. "If I can break your will, Jeriah, just think what I can do to the sheep of this city."

Resistance flared. "The men of this city will not bow to you," she muttered. They will come to their senses and slay you. Your body will be thrown to the carrion outside the walls."

"Who?" mused the voice. The expected blow did not come, but she knew that it had been marked to her account. The hated voice continued with a sneer. "The men of this city are sheep. I am a lion. The army is mine. They learned their lesson at Y'tor. Obedience brings wealth and pleasure. Disobedience brings only death. Pleasure and peace are the two most valued assets of the men of your city. As long as I guarantee both and have the power to take them away at my whim, the men will flock to me and bless my name for generations."

Jeriah tried an argument, but she knew it was hollow. "The men of this city also value honor, truth, and civic virtue. They will see quickly through your shallow promises and threats and expel you."

Sechiall laughed again long and hard. "My woman! My woman! You amuse me! How little you understand men. Just because you were married to an exceptional man, you expect all others to be the same. You little fool. Jared is dead. Lamech is dead. Methuselah is dead. You see only what you wish. I am your new reality, and will be that of this city. As long as I can keep them rich, well-fed, and happy, they will do whatever I wish."

Sechiall paused, as if making up his mind. "Jared was right. Always attack," he said softly. Then louder, "You will come with me today and see for yourself. Remember. Power to give and take back pleasure and peace: once the sheep are convinced that it lies with me, then they will march into the sea at my command!"

Jeriah lay on the floor, closing her eyes and hoping that she would wake to another reality. Fully awake now, Sechiall sprang up. She watched, not daring to move, until he had thrown on his clothes and thrown open the door. Oman and another soldier stood guard in the front hall of the house. She watched them salute Sechiall as he emerged.

"There are eight others surrounding the house, Commander, as you ordered," said Oman. "All are loyal only to you."

"Good work, Oman," replied Sechiall. "It is good for a king to have men he can trust. Now I have another trust for you. Call on the houses of my fellow council members," he curled his lip in a sneer, "and tell them to meet me in the square at noon. Have one hundred troops armed and formed up in the square. Things are going to start changing in *our* town!"

Oman saluted and left quickly. Sechiall walked slowly away through his new house, obviously enjoying its décor and design. Jeriah pulled herself from the floor and splashed some water in a basin. She was bathing her tender face when a terrified servant entered the room and bowed down. "The Lord Sechiall commands that a meal be prepared and that you serve him in the garden." She faltered upon seeing Jeriah's face in the full light, but continued with a shake in her voice. "I will have food ready shortly." She stopped and tried to say something, but could not.

Jeriah dismissed her with a shake of her head and put on fresh clothes. Some of the stiffness was leaving, but the pain of the evening was still with her as she led the servant into the garden. It was fully surrounded by the house, but there were two soldiers standing guard at two corners. Sechiall gestured to them, "Walk a post along the street. I will not need you here."

They left with a bow, and hurried to obey. He sat on one of the benches and watched Jeriah lead the servant to a low table. She set the tray down and walked away as quickly as she could. Bright flowers distilled their color and aroma throughout the garden, but Jeriah hardly noticed.

Without looking up, she poured wine. This she brought to Sechiall and presented him with the cup. "You may have the first sip," he said, weighing whether or not she had the strength to try to poison him. Obviously not, as she lifted the cup to her mouth and then handed it to him.

"Stay and eat with me," he ordered. "Your life has changed. You might as well accept it and make the most of it. Before, you took many things for granted and were proud of your position. Now your very life hangs on my momentary desire. When you accept this fully, then you will be happy again. As long as you harbor thoughts of resistance, then you will be miserable and will be in danger of your life. For I love none but myself, and I would slay you as soon as kiss you. Think on that and live; forget it for a minute and die!"

"You are not the man that Jared was," replied Jeriah with a semblance of her old temper, "you are not a man at all, only a beast."

"Perhaps," sneered Sechiall, "but I am all that stands between you and death, so you must learn how to obey a beast. My teeth are strong and my claws, iron." Jeriah shrank before the power of those words, and wondered if she would ever find her own will again. Her mind was weak and her body, his.

At noon she watched from the shadows on the edge of the square as the men assembled as ordered, and a crowd gathered to see what would occur next. She kept the veil over her head and face to cover the bruises and shame. Dajus and Subtur were waiting in their accustomed seats as Sechiall strode into the square with his guard. She could see the apprehension on their faces that dominated the other visible emotions. She saw them tense as all of the soldiers saluted Sechiall and knew that they shared her fear of the man and his power.

As he came close to them he eyed each in turn and glaring at Subtur said quietly, "You will henceforth rise in my presence and bow to welcome me. You may sit after I have seated myself." His eyes burned and his hand hovered near the hilts of his sword. Subtur's face was contorted by a mixture of fear and hatred, but he reluctantly stood and bowed with Dajus.

Sechiall remained standing and faced the crowd, ignoring the two men behind him. "People of Lamech. We have won a great victory! Our enemies lie dead and the road to greatness is open. It is fitting that a celebration be held. The council proclaims a feast of five days, beginning on the morrow. All of the leading men who wish the favor of the council will contribute food and drink! Let entertainment be provided with music and dancing and games! Men of the army will demonstrate their skills with spear and bow. Let all join in!"

The crowd roared its approval. Sechiall held up his hand. "To provide an example for the men of Lamech, Dajus and Subtur, our beloved elders, will provide one hundred calves and sheep for the festival. Prepare yourselves for tomorrow! Gifts of gold and silver will be given to the winners of contests. Let the leading merchants compete to provide the richest prizes! Your own elders, Dajus and Subtur will provide prizes of one hundred pieces of gold each."

The two men paled at this announcement, but did not dare to contradict the announcement. The crowd roared its approval and the merchants were forced to join in by the presence of the soldiers.

And so a great festival was held for five days in Lamech. It was not the first festival in Lamech and certainly not a time of great joy as others had been. But never before had the people of the town given themselves over to their appetites for food, drink, and pleasure as they did in those five days. In hours, years of restraint, carefully engendered by men such as Methuselah and Lamech withered before the consuming will of Sechiall. The young rejoiced; older citizens felt a vague sense of regret, but bowed to the inevitable changes that seemed to overtake them.

By the end of the week, all had walked through the doors opened by Sechiall. Never had the people felt so free and most reveled in their newfound life. Although the richest merchants seethed at the extortion of their goods, and tried to hide as much as they could, they realized that their wealth was hostage to Sechiall and his warriors. For most of them, the realization that life was more precious than possessions came easily, a lesson reinforced by the disappearance of several who did not arrive at that conclusion fast enough.

On the last day of the festival, Sechiall ordered soldiers to tear loose four of the black chairs from the dais in the square. Dajus and Subtur stood appalled, but unable to protest. "The Chief Elder alone need sit in public judgment," explained Sechiall. "The other elders may sit before him in the square, but not on the same level." He ordered the chairs of Dajus and Subtur set at the base of the dais below Methuselah's, which he now claimed as his own.

Then silencing the mob, he raised his voice. "Lamech has enjoyed a council of five elders in the past. This is too many. It will lead to unnecessary debate and delay over simple matters. We will now have three!"

At his signal, six sturdy soldiers lifted a chair. "Lamech is dead," cried Sechiall. "His days of mourning, long past. We will carry his seat to the house of mourning and leave it there in his memory."

With a wave of his hand the soldiers picked it up and followed Sechiall across the square to the house of worship. Men followed behind, none daring to protest, and many agreeing in their hearts with the change. It was a fine gesture to Lamech. The soldiers entered the door of the temple and Sechiall led them to the altar under the high dome.

"Place the chair on top of the altar," he ordered. As the soldiers obeyed, Sechiall climbed easily onto the altar and stood beside the chair. "We offer this memorial to our beloved elder, Lamech. Let nothing ever again stain this altar." The men who had followed inside the doors nodded their agreement, though one or two of the older ones thought that Lamech would never have approved such an action. But they knew by now to keep such thoughts to themselves.

Sechiall made his way back to the dais in the square, and the crowds parted to make way for him, eager to see what would happen next. The six soldiers followed hard at his heels. When he regained his place he turned to the assembly.

"Men of Lamech!" he shouted, pointing at the remaining black stone in the middle of the dais. "Here stands another seat of judgment, but the one who should be in it abandoned our city decades ago. He deigns to return to us only at his will while pursuing his own pleasures far from town. He has threatened the men of this city with the sea. I say that we cast his chair into the sea and end forever our tolerance of his insults and neglect!"

Without waiting for an answer, Sechiall motioned, and six soldiers stepped forward and lifted the black chair to their shoulders. Sechiall led them through the square, then left and through the great gates, with the crowd pushing behind. Carefully the soldiers negotiated the steps and followed Sechiall out onto the stone quay. At the end of the quay they set it down and stepped back. The crowd hung back, gathering along the waterfront and on the great steps leading down from the gate. A sea of curious eyes focused on the scene at the end of the pier.

Sechiall stood alone at the end of the quay beside the black seat of judgment. He raised his hands to the crowd and shouted, "I am the new strength of Lamech!" With that he cast aside his robe and turned and bent over the heavy stone. A murmur of astonishment ran through the crowd. Sweat glistened from the corded muscles in the great shoulders and arms. Slowly the chair was raised. None were more amazed than the six soldiers, all young men and strong. They had felt the weight of the chair and knew that no two of them could have lifted it as Sechiall did now. But he did not stop. Holding it by the great arms, he stepped back with one foot and dropped almost to his knees, and with a mighty effort the chair rose above his head. Then with a great shout and supreme effort, he hurled it up and away. The black stone seemed to hang in the air for a moment and the sun caught the gold with a final flash as it fell down and disappeared in the green depths off the end of the pier. Dead silence descended on the crowd and the sound of splashing water came even to those on the top of the steps by the gate.

Sechiall turned to the mob, his muscles still red and prominent from the effort; sweat glistening in the sun. His smile was broad, and seemed to bring the light of the sun on all the men present. A great cry of admiration rang out and a way was made for the representative of the new order. Men agreed with their neighbors that a shrine to Sechiall outside the walls would be only fitting. Certainly women could be found to serve.

Later, inside the walls, the crowd gave themselves completely to enjoyment of the events, the food, the drink, and the abandonment of restraint. Excitement with no discernible origin ran through the people in waves that washed over in emotional peaks and then subsided into discontent and desire for more. "Who needs a group of old women to rule us when we have Sechiall, slayer of Torech?" asked soldiers of the crowd. No one disagreed and threats were no longer needed to secure assent.

Sechiall stood on the dais, surrounded by his guard, reveling in the chaotic adoration of the crowd. Wine flowed freely and the women no longer went about in veils. Subtur was slumped down in his chair, seemingly firmly in the grip of drink. Oman stood nearby. He stared for a moment at the lax form of Subtur, and then spoke quietly to Sechiall. "What of Noah, my lord? You have destroyed the symbol of his power. When will we finish that great work?"

Sechiall smiled indulgently. "I will wait five days to let things settle down here, and get the town back to work. Then we will attend to Noah. Do you have your hundred men selected yet?"

"Yes, O King!" replied Oman. "All are eager to stand with you and watch your sword devour the old fool and his sons."

"Good. They shall see it, and shall enjoy whatever is left of Noah's house when we finish. I want nothing for myself but blood!"

Subtur was not as drunk as he appeared; his posture reflected more his internal despair than inebriation. Content to dally around the edges of evil, he was appalled at the forces that he had helped unleash from its depths. No way of escape had seemed open. At Sechiall's words, however, his mind finally rebelled and began to think once more. He knew that his only hope was flight and that it must be soon. Death would be his payment for failure in that enterprise, but he understood now that death faced him regardless.

Sechiall had already proven his decisiveness along with his other traits. Once he decided to remove Subtur, the time between decision and execution would be short. He and his wife would have to leave with nothing more than they could carry. Then he would live out his life as a powerless outcast, always bearing the burden of having had power in his grasp and then losing it. Would that be worse than death? In that moment he was tempted to leap upon Sechiall and try to kill him. But that would be for nothing. An indolent older man would not overcome a man who could hurl one of the stone seats into the sea.

So he forced himself to loll in his chair, waiting until Sechiall tired of the morning and left. Then he signaled his servant, and allowed himself to be led back to his home. Anyone seeing him would think that he was far into his cups, enjoying the new freedoms with everyone else. He hoped so. He must alert his wife and begin to prepare for flight. In five days, Sechiall would leave with a hundred of his closest companions. It was an opportunity that would not be offered again soon. Subtur was certain that he must make his break then, or end up at the bottom of the harbor, food for the denizens of the deep.

Chapter 34
BLOOD DEBT

Meshur slipped like a great shadow along the darkened street. The festival had persisted far into the night, and although now it was over, soldiers still patrolled. He could wait no longer. His vigil in a deserted grain store that overlooked the street near Jared's house had been fruitless: he had not seen his cousin or anyone else that he could trust with the message to Jeriah. His night patrols had found no weakness in the guard around the house, either. Several times he had been ready to abandon his vigil, but the memory of Madrazi's tears drove him beyond prudence.

Soldiers were present all around the town, but most were not alert. However, Sechiall's guard was vigilant and competent. It would be suicide to attempt entry of the house or the grounds. Fortunately the week-long festival had provided cover to move and procure food and drink. People were walking the streets at all hours carrying food and wine. The second night, he had found a man drunk on the side of the street. Meshur had relieved him of a supply of bread, meat, and a wineskin. It was not much, but it had lasted the week, and he had not shown himself in any of his old haunts. He could not wait forever; perhaps his cousin no longer served Jared's wife since Sechiall had returned.

Reluctantly he realized that his time was slipping away: he must find Pashtur and convince him to flee to the ark. He had not seen his cousin since they had parted many months before, and he wondered what he had been doing. Pashtur's father had left him with some wealth; he would not have needed to work unless he wanted to. But Pashtur had apparently abandoned his old life. He was never in familiar places and Meshur had avoided his house. He could avoid it no longer. Once this task was finished, he would be free to leave the city. He hoped that sneaking out would be no more difficult than sneaking in.

Entering the city had been easier than he expected. He had not hurried back to town. He had been tired and knew that he could afford no mistakes once near Lamech. After approaching from the north, he had spent the rest of the night and most of the next day sleeping in a copse near the fields. Upon waking, he had made his way into the fields and mingled with a group of

laborers. He approached the gate as just another dirty field hand with two large
sacks of grain across his shoulders that hid most of his face. He did not think
that anyone would have any interest in him at all, but he took no chances. He
need not have worried; none of the guards paid the least attention.

He followed the men all the way to the warehouse where the grain was
stored, and then he kept to the middle of a large group that wandered off into
the heart of the city. Dusk fell and after a few blocks, Meshur felt confident
enough to slip away from the weary workers and find his way through familiar
back ways toward Jared's house.

Now he was on the move again. Meshur slid into a dark doorway as he
heard steps approaching down the alley. A man and a woman were hurrying
down the alley; the part of their vision not dimmed by wine was occupied with
each other and they passed Meshur without seeing him. Another turn and
another darkened stretch brought him to the familiar outlines of work buildings
just visible under the dim light of the moon. Meshur stopped for a moment in
the dark and looked upon the place where he had started his life's journey—his
uncle's workshop. He marveled at the twists and turns his life had taken, but
was now finally sure of his path. Gripping a tree limb, he pulled himself up
into the old tree and over the wall at the back of the yard. He made his way by
memory through the dark shadows of the outbuildings, and paused at the edge
of the workshop and looked up toward the back of the house.

A light burned in a window above him. He did not need to search his
memory; he would always know the window in Pashtur's bedroom. All seemed
quiet outside, but he did not want to make any noise or attract attention. For
all he knew, Sechiall might have a man watching the house, and the yard
between the workshop and the house was devoid of cover and well lit..
Thinking back to his youth, Meshur smiled. He remembered all the nights
when he had signaled his cousin with small rocks through his window. Then
the two boys would sneak out to whatever mischief tempted. Sometimes they
were caught, often not. Meshur hoped that his cousin remembered and tossed
a small pebble. The first one sailed through the window; Meshur grinned at his
remembered skill. A moment later, the light was extinguished, and Meshur
moved quietly across the yard to the door. It opened before him and the two
men moved without talking into the familiar inner room.

Pashtur lit a candle and turned to face his cousin. He was shocked at what
he saw. Instead of the unwashed broken hulk he expected to be begging for a
pitcher of wine, he saw the bright eyes and determined look that he had almost
forgotten. Silently wondering what had happened, he waited for Meshur to

speak. His excitement was clear on his face and in his voice.

"Cousin," he began. "I have come from the house of Noah."

Pashtur's face revealed his distaste. "Noah is a name which no longer has any meaning in this town. Sechiall is king now, no matter what he calls himself. He will take care of Noah in due time, and I don't think that it will be pleasant for the old man. It only took one sword to convince me of where the power lies in these days." He looked accusingly at Meshur as if he had been the one wielding the sword.

Meshur could only stare at his cousin. Pashtur's eyes were hard; nothing of the man he had grown up with seemed to remain. But Pashtur's life had been placed at risk two years ago because of his stubbornness, and he owed him the truth.

"I saw *King* Sechiall in the square, too," replied Meshur slowly, trying to feel his way with the man who suddenly seemed a stranger, "and I do not see any kind of life for either of us here. No decent man will want to live under Sechiall. Noah says that the day of his prophecy is near." He saw his cousin's face harden again at the mention of Noah's name, but he continued doggedly. "He has offered me a place on his ark, and for you, too. I returned to bring you with me. Come with me; we can make it out of town tonight and be away free tomorrow morning."

Pashtur's expression changed as he laughed, but the look in his eyes was not pleasant. "Come now, Meshur. We have had enough trouble with all the foolishness of that ark, and we both came close to losing our lives because of that old man and his madness. I want nothing more to do with him. If you know what's good for you, you will return to your wine and your ironwork and forget that you know Noah and that you know me. We obviously have nothing left to discuss."

Meshur recoiled as if struck. "But Pashtur, you are all the family that remains to me. You have always been my friend. We worked well together for many years."

"No!" snarled Pashtur. "You worked! I hung onto a place because of your skill and position with the son of Noah. I willingly followed your orders; foolishly seeking to please you in everything while your pride in your skill and strength took precedence over everything that should have been precious to you. I want that no more. I have new friends. To them, I mean something. I am important. And you are nothing. I do not have any reason to change. I have cast my lot with Sechiall. If you want to seal your death by following Noah—go ahead! I will not mourn you."

Meshur suppressed his surprise and sadness at his cousin. He felt no anger, only regret. "You are right in one thing, cousin. In my pride I did value my ability over my cousin, and in that I was wrong. I am sorry."

A flicker of doubt flashed across Pashtur's face. Meshur was right—he had no other family. Almost he wanted to hold out his hands to his cousin and accept his apology and regain what they had enjoyed during those years. He could see the sincerity in Meshur's eyes, and something else, too, that he could not quite understand. But he had made his choice more than a year before, and he could not give up what he had worked so hard to gain while Meshur had been swilling himself into forgetfulness. He would enjoy privilege in the new order, and he knew the price of failure that attended that privilege. His face hardened.

"I think that you had better leave cousin. Go your way, and do not come here again." Then another thought entered his heart. "Or, if you want, stay in the workshop tonight and leave in the morning. It is the least that I can do for you."

Meshur nodded and walked slowly outside and into the familiar confines of his uncle's workshop. He lit a candle and sat on a stool, looking around and remembering the years of his childhood. How could Pashtur have become so hard? In time he knew that he would mourn his cousin, apparently already dead to him. He gathered his thoughts. He needed to deliver the message to Jared's wife, but the late guard would be out and scouring the streets after the inns closed. He would be better to wait for a few hours until everyone was asleep. He could try one last time to deliver the message and leave by the old abandoned north tower. With a rope from the workshop—yes there was a suitable one—he could let himself down over the wall and make the fields before sunrise. Going north, he could circle around and make straight for the ark while avoiding the road. A few hours of rest would prepare him for the day ahead.

Meshur awoke confused at the lights and noise around him. Soldiers filled the workshop, Balech at their head. Pashtur stood behind him. Meshur heard him say, "I believe that this is the man you wanted, captain."

Realization hit him harder than any weapon could have, and he reeled back, still not wanting to believe. In that moment Meshur saw the whole scene clearly. Pashtur had entered with Balech behind three soldiers who had moved to flank the sleeping man, and now stood off to his right on the other side of a large workbench. Pashtur and Balech stood in front of him with two more soldiers between them and the door. More men were in the courtyard and one was standing blocking the door. Balech flashed an evil smile at Meshur but spoke to his cousin. "You have done well, and will be well paid. Sechiall will be pleased that we have caught and killed a spy from the house of Noah. And I will be pleased to do it," he sneered, turning his face back to Meshur.

Meshur ignored him as he slowly rose to his feet and brushed the straw from his tunic. The look of dull incomprehension and the slow movements of the large man removed any threat in the minds of the warriors, and they relaxed and waited for Balech to begin the evening's entertainment. But Meshur ignored the captain and looked at his cousin.

"What have you done, Pashtur?"

Pashtur averted his eyes and shuffled his feet. Meshur stared at him, and some power of will brought Pashtur's gaze up from the floor. Then he spoke defiantly. "I have done what I had to do. I made my choice and I will keep my commitments."

"What about the bond of blood, cousin?" asked Meshur quietly. "I gave up everything that I was for your life. Now you seal your treachery to evil men with my blood? What will it gain you? How long will it be before Balech decides that you are no longer useful? After all, you were a witness to his defeat at my hands."

Meshur saw that he had struck home with his last words. Balech stiffened and half turned to the smaller man as if to reassure him. But Pashtur saw the truth of Meshur's words in Balech's eyes. Slowly the realization of what he had become seeped into the remnant of his conscience.

Balech kept his eyes on Pashtur for that crucial moment, trying to decipher the puzzle of his face. And when some sixth sense warned him, Meshur was already a blur of motion. Although Balech had seen the big man's blinding speed before, time had robbed his memory. He was still half turned toward Pashtur. Meshur knew every stick of wood in that workshop, and there would be tools he could use as weapons. If he could kill Balech and a few of the soldiers, perhaps he could slip away in the confusion. Once about on the dark streets he could still make it over the wall before he was caught.

While still talking to Pashtur, he had glanced down to his right. A long, heavy iron rod lay in open brackets alongside the top of the table and near his right hand. It had been used in the past as an anchor to fasten wood for cutting or smoothing, but lay unused for years. Four cubits long, its weight and length would render it a lethal weapon in this confined space. At least Balech would atone for all of his sins. All of this had flashed through Meshur's mind in the instant of Pashtur's confusion. The soldiers remained distracted by the interplay between the little spy and their captain.

As Balech realized his danger and turned in alarm, the heavy pole was already arcing toward him with incredible speed and neither his bronze helmet nor his head slowed it very much. Balech dropped straight to the floor, his lantern bursting on the old straw, its oil spreading flame rapidly over the floor. Meshur had planned well, the blow that dropped Balech continued unchecked as he stepped forward, driving it on with his great strength, ignoring the fire that began to singe his legs. The blunt scythe crashed through the head of the next man, killing him also, then slammed into the shoulder of the man next to him as it lost its momentum. But its force shattered bones and that man fell back into the path of the others.

The three soldiers to his right had been caught unawares but seeing their dead captain, they began to react, spreading apart instinctively to gain room for their weapons. One had a short spear, and the others, swords. Meshur kept his grip on the iron rod with his left hand, and reached again for the table as he turned back to his right. He did not need to look and his hand closed around the familiar grip of his uncle's hammer. In the same move his arm came up and drove forward. As the warrior drew back his spear, he found the hammer slicing straight towards his face. He tried to duck and throw at the same time with predictable results. The spear flew high and stuck quivering in a post behind Meshur. The hammer missed its intended target, but was close enough, shattering the left side of the man's face. Hammer and soldier hit the floor together. Now the two swordsmen leaped over their comrade to swing around the workbench and close with Meshur. He brought the iron rod up and stepped back, but knew that he could not keep off two trained swordsmen for very long. Out of the corner of his eye he saw the confusion clearing at the door and two other soldiers fighting the flames to get through to their fallen commander.

Pashtur stood rooted in place staring at the fallen body of Balech. He was shocked by the intense joy that he felt seeing Balech's limp body at his feet. In a flash of insight he saw that his rage at his cousin was an outpouring of all he had been unable to express at his new masters. Shame flooded his heart; his treachery condemned him where he stood. Balech's blood was pooling underneath his broken head and spreading across the little man's sandal. He jerked his foot back, and saw not the stain on his foot, but the one on his hands—the blood of his own cousin. That realization brought his eyes and mind back to the present, and he saw at once that Meshur was charging a high price for his life. Pashtur saw the strength and quickness that he remembered plowing through Balech's men. As ever in his life, he belonged with Meshur, not these killers. Memory of all those times flooded his conscience, and thought preceded action by only an instant.

The two swordsmen had backed Meshur further into the workroom, and his side was turned to the men coming in the door. They did not want to run through the rapidly spreading flames, but the man in front held a spear and was trying to clear the doorway to hurl it. Before he could get set, Pashtur jumped over Balech, and dashed through the flame and around the table. Behind the nearest swordsman, he yanked the still quivering spear from its post. A quick glance over his shoulder told him that the soldier in the doorway was lining up a throw at Meshur, now bleeding from several cuts as he fought off the swordsmen. Pashtur swung the spear with all his strength and the butt struck the nearest man on his sword arm. He dropped the sword from his numbed hand and before his fellow realized that he was now alone, Meshur ducked and drove the butt of the rod into his throat.

Pashtur then whirled around and threw his spear at the same instant as the man in the door. In that moment he could have jumped out of the way, but he knew that Meshur was right behind him. Instinct spurred the act that thought would have rejected. Both spears found their targets, and Pashtur slumped over as the man in the door fell forward into the fire that now obscured the doorway. Meshur broke the other arm of the last man who clumsily tried to retrieve his sword left-handed. He fell back, awkwardly holding both arms close to his body. He tried to flee through the flames for the door, but slipped as he ran through the worst of the fire and did not get up again.

Meshur turned to his cousin. Smoke now clouded the room and flames drew near. But Meshur ignored both and knelt beside his cousin. Pashtur was still conscious, half sitting against the post, but blood trickled from his mouth and his face was white. When Meshur looked into his eyes, the man he knew as his cousin had returned. Pashtur gripped his hand. "My blood for yours, cousin," he choked. "Heed the words of Noah and save yourself. Carry my memory unstained into your new world."

Meshur hesitated, not feeling the tears on his cheeks. "We should have gone together, cousin. I will always love you."

Pashtur nodded once before his eyes saw Meshur no more.

Meshur looked up. Only a few moments had passed since Balech had paid for his evil deeds, but the fire that blocked the front door was already impassable. He could hear soldiers milling around in the yard. Snatching up a fallen sword, Meshur swung into the loft, searching for the escape route of his youth. The smoke there was thick, but Meshur held his breath and trusted his memory for the path. Halfway to the back, a trapdoor opened onto the roof of the workshop. Meshur was through in moments, gratefully filling his lungs with fresh air. The interplay of fire and night kept him in shadow as he moved back along the roof toward the back fence.

Still clutching the sword, Meshur dashed lightly across the dark roof and leaped into the air with his arms outspread. The branches of the waiting tree caught him across the chest and arms as he frantically struggled to hang on to both tree and sword. He thought for a moment that the limbs would not hold his adult weight, but thankfully the tree had grown, too, and the branches swayed but did not give. Slipping down one branch to the trunk and then out another, he dropped over the back wall and into the dark alley, free of the chaos behind him.

Seeing no one, he stopped for a moment and listened. Men were shouting to be heard over the increasing roar of the fire, but it seemed that no one had seen his escape. But he knew the hunt would be up soon. He and Pashtur had killed five men and wounded two others, and their comrades would soon be fanning out to search for him. He would have to clear the wall very soon to have any chance of escape. But even an hour's start outside the wall in the dark would enable him to elude pursuit and make the Great Forest by morning. There was no possibility of passing the message to Jared's wife now, and he hoped that Madrazi would understand. Gathering his wits, he ran instinctively toward the north wall, keeping to the dark alleys, hoping that no one saw him.

Pulling up softly, he swore to himself. He had forgotten the rope in the confusion! He could not survive the drop from the tower uninjured without it. Looking at the sword in his hand, he realized that he would have to try to overwhelm the guard at one of the smaller gates. That would give his position away within minutes, for a mounted patrol checked the gates at regular intervals, and he would have to run hard into the fields to put distance between himself and his pursuers. His chances of escape would be reduced, and he would need more than his share of luck. He started off, his legs reacting faster than his mind. If the warning went out before he was outside the walls, the guards would be alert at every gate, and he would have no chance at all.

Down a few dark streets was the wine gate, named for the vineyard that encroached upon the walls outside. It was just a small door and there was a chance that the guard was asleep. Maybe he could get through without any more killing. Coming to the end of the alley, he saw that the main road that ran along the inside of the wall was deserted. However, there was no cover between him and the gate. There was only one guard visible, but he was awake and facing in.

Meshur's eyes scanned along the wall to see if any other men were present. The area was quiet and deserted, but there might be a patrol outside the wall. If they caught him before he made the fields, he could neither outrun them nor outfight them. But none of that mattered if he could not get through the gate. That would be challenge enough. Meshur pondered whether to walk along the road and try to surprise the man when he was stopped, or just rush the man from here. It would not take long, and if the man's reflexes were slow, maybe he could overwhelm him quickly.

Just as he had decided to feign drunkenness and try to get in close, he heard hoof beats away up the main road. What if it was a rider alerting the guard? He froze for a second, but then his mind forced action. Now, he must move, and rush the man. The horseman had distracted the guard, and he had walked a few steps down the road. Listening for the horse, he did not hear Meshur; only the swish of the sword's hilt that caught him full behind the ear. Meshur caught the unconscious man in one strong arm and gently lowered him to the ground to avoid noise. Pulling him into the small shadow under the arch, he ripped at the bar and fumbled back the lock. Any instant he expected to hear the clattering of hooves and a loud challenge. But the improbable silence held. A deeper shadow appeared as the gate opened enough to accommodate the bulk of Meshur; he slipped through, and then quietly closed it behind him. The moon was low in the sky and Meshur stood still against the dark gate surveying the ground ahead.

He saw nothing in his first look around, but before he could look again, he heard the horse coming toward the wine gate. There was no time. He rushed down through a gap in the hedge and into the tangled rows of the vineyard. Tendrils clutched at him as he ran between two rows of ripening grapes. He cut across, down another row; then to the far hedge. He could not find a break, so he made one. He tore through, dropping the sword to use both hands.

A trumpet blared behind him. The unconscious guard had been found and the hunt was up. A stretch of open ground lay before him; a pale desert littered with strange shadows dancing in the moon. Beyond it, an oasis of dark trees marked the edge of escape among the maze of fields, thick and high with growth awaiting the upcoming harvest. Once among the crops in the dark, he could elude the entire army.

Drawing a breath, he began to hope again as he started across the open ground. But out in the open, too late to pull back and with still too far to go, he heard another trumpet answer to his right, and horsemen galloped behind its notes. Could he make it across? Feet churning, he chanced a look over his shoulder. The trees were a few paces, the riders much farther. A wave of exultation swept over him. Escape beckoned—the temporary sanctuary of the dark fields; the permanent refuge of the ark. Another step remained to the verge of the trees; their shelter loomed dark and tall into the night. Not looking back, he leapt into their shelter. As he did, he felt a sting, then a sudden numbness in his back. Beyond the first line of trees, Meshur glanced down in surprise and saw a dark iron point extending a finger's width out of his tunic on his left side. But he did not stumble and was lost among the trees before any of the soldiers could come close.

Ducking into the field ahead, he pounded down a row of barley and crossed over into the next field. He was suddenly very tired; the excitement of the night had left him, and his legs were trembling. He looked down again at the arrow's point and did not see much blood; there would be little on the ground to leave a trail. His breath was short, but relief flooded him. Perhaps it was not too bad. He could make his way to Noah and they could cut it out and treat it.

But his legs continued to weaken and he heard the first sounds of dismounted soldiers blundering behind him off to the left. At the end of this field was a thick hedge, apparently impenetrable. But Meshur was on the paths of his boyhood, and knew of a hidden tunnel cut through it. He took his bearings and pulled back the branches that granted access. Crawling in, he realized how tired he was. The soldiers behind were moving in this direction. Better to lie still in silence, let them finish their search here and then make his escape. He twisted carefully to keep the shaft of the arrow from catching on a branch.

As he lay still, the numbness was gradually replaced by a fire that began to burn hotter with each beat of his heart. The circle of pain began to spread outward from the arrow across his great chest. He knew it would help if he could break off the back of the arrow, but there was no way to reach it. Quietly he eased himself onto his side. He waited. Heavy with weariness, he heard the soldiers blundering nearby, and he began to fade in and out of sleep. For some reason the pain seemed to fade, too.

Strange dreams flickered through his mind. He saw the faces of Noah and Ham as they walked with him through the vast ark, admiring the workmanship of the feed storage bins and the rooms in the upper deck. Ham was showing his father a line of paper-smooth joinery. Meshur glowed with pride; he had done that work three times before being satisfied with the result. Suddenly, they were standing together at the great door at the middle deck. Meshur looked over Noah's shoulder to the forest and saw lines of golden light converging on them from all directions. Light surrounded the ark and began to stream in, swirling around Noah in an intricate dance. He was standing right beside the old man, but the light carefully avoided him as it playfully wrapped itself in intricate patterns in and around Noah. It took a moment to realize that light was moving with a wild joy both into and out of Noah. Meshur felt a desire in the light to join with him, but he must call to it. What could he say?

What was that about the prophecy...?

He did not understand. He wanted to. Was that that...? Desire? Acceptance? He could believe...he should decide...he would accept. Now he understood.

For a moment, he thought he saw a dark body huddled under a hedge, with vague shadows moving about in the larger darkness. But the light beckoned, and he was free to go.

****

The old woman leaned back as the first rays of the sun trickled light into the dim room. Red coals still simmered in the fireplace, but no longer lit the room. She looked into the changing light, seeing things beyond the coals. She saw the faces of two good men who had been betrayed and murdered. Would she see them again? Perhaps. Their betrayal had been avenged alongside the universal betrayal. The Creator was a subtle being, intervening unexpectedly and often from a direction no one anticipated. But however shrewd the interventions, they never lacked power. To see that power, to feel that power, to be caught up in that power was awesome: to be taken unawares by it was something else indeed.

Chapter 35
MIGRATION

It had been eight days since Meshur had left for Lamech. They all waited anxiously for his return, but none more than Madrazi. Each hour seemed a year. Ham had rejoiced in the news of Meshur's return, and was as anxious as Madrazi to see him again. After the fifth day, hope began to wane and Madrazi and Ham both sank into gloom. Ham was convinced that Meshur had been caught and killed, and asked Noah for permission to confirm his suspicions. Noah refused. Madrazi took to waking early and standing by the gate on the road for hours on end, hoping to see Meshur and Jeriah come over the top of the hill. But the road remained as empty as her hope. As the days crawled by, she grew restless and irritable.

On the eighth morning, Yaran intercepted her on the way to the gate. All the family had gathered in the great hall at Noah's insistence. Yaran and Madrazi were the last to enter and as they quietly made their way to sit with their husbands, Noah stood and gazed upon them. Madrazi sat up straighter. His usually gentle face was hard and decisive. She had always perceived an inner strength, hidden to most and rarely displayed. But this morning, power played around his every word and gesture. He called for their attention and then paused for a moment. The room became deathly quiet.

Then he held up his arms and spoke in a voice that Madrazi had not heard before. It seemed to echo inside her mind. "We have all heard of the news from Lamech. Evil has triumphed, and we rightly fear for Meshur and his messages. If our fears prove true, then we must also take thought for ourselves. Sechiall has proven to be a child of the serpent, and evil drips from his hands. If we depended on our own strength and prowess to save ourselves, then our case would be desperate. But we do not trust in sword or shield; we trust in the Judge of all the Earth. And that faith is not vain—He has appeared to me again!"

Those words exploded in the room: everyone's attention was riveted on Noah. Shem sat forward, expectantly; Madrazi felt her stomach tighten in nervous fear. Noah could have said nothing to confound her more completely. Silence hung in the air during those few seconds, and Madrazi shivered as goose bumps appeared on her arms, mirroring those she felt creep along the back of her neck. She felt disoriented and dizzy. How could this man that she had known for many years, good as he was, possess the very words of the Creator?

But as he began to speak, even Madrazi felt the supernatural power that wrapped itself around each words. Each syllable resonated throughout the room, and no one in that room ever forgot them.

"Last night a vision came to me in Methuselah's grove and the same voice I heard in the forest long ago spoke new words to me. 'Go into the ark,' He said to me, 'you and your whole family, because I have found you righteous in this generation. Take with you seven of every kind of clean animal, a male and its mate, and two of every kind of unclean animal, a male and its mate, and also seven of every kind of bird, male and female, to keep their various kinds alive throughout the earth. Seven days from now I will send rain on the earth for forty days and forty nights, and I will wipe from the face of the earth every living creature I have made.'"

For several minutes silence ruled in that room as each heart tried to grasp the words. Ham was the first to speak. "Father, the ark is complete and Japheth has loaded all the food and stores that we need. We can go aboard the ark today. But please tell me how we are to take the animals into the ark. Have not you and Shem planned for the ark to carry fifteen thousands of animals? True, we have some here, and I do not doubt that in seven days we might be able to move many of them through the forest, into the ark, and into their cages. But what we have is less than a tithe of all that need to come to fulfill the commandment. Where will the others come from? How can we bring animals into the ark that would prefer to turn and devour us or run from us faster than we can pursue?"

Noah held up his hand. Madrazi was almost nodding her agreement, for Ham's logical arguments paralleled her thoughts exactly. They also helped to anchor her mind against the impossibility of Noah's words. At best all the people of the household could move a few hundreds of animals to the ark in the seven days. Not all of the animals would be content to mix together on the trail to the clearing, and great care would be needed to keep those separated that were natural enemies. And, like Ham, Madrazi had no stomach for attempting to shepherd poisonous serpents or large predators into some pen aboard the ark.

But once more Noah's words rang out in the hall, this time with an even greater authority. All quailed before his words. Seldom had they seen the iron will that lay hidden beneath his gentle demeanor, but now it bent each of them to it. His face was hard and Ham visibly recoiled from its intensity.

"For one hundred and twenty years have we labored to obey the prophecy that came to me in the forest. We have built the ark. We have filled it with food for many people and animals. We have testified to the truth and righteousness of God before all the people around us, and word of our acts have spread across the face of the earth. When I set out to accomplish this, none of it seemed possible at that time, yet God has provided each and every day for our needs. We found good land to settle and a protected place to labor. We found gold to pay for what we needed. I found shipwrights who taught me how to fashion the ark. God provided three strong sons to help in the endeavor. Do any of you think that the talents that you have are not a gift of God, fit for the occasion?"

He looked at Ham who dropped his eyes and said no more. Noah continued, more softly, "You say that we cannot take the animals into the ark. One hundred years ago I would have said that it was impossible even to know which animals were to come, and how we could feed and care for them. But God has opened our minds and supplied knowledge of each kind of living thing. I am rightly held in many lands to have knowledge of created things greater than any other man. This knowledge too is a gift from God—a heritage of Adam granted in our need.

"Do you think that God would command what we cannot do? How could we then call Him just and righteous? What God has commanded, we will perform by trusting Him. Now hear my words. Come and see what God will do with your own eyes and have done with doubt!"

Madrazi had an uncomfortable feeling that his eyes flickered past hers purposefully as he said these last words.

Without a glance Noah wrapped his cloak about him, and strode out of the room. Such was the power of his speech that all of the family rose and followed him as one. He strode ahead, Wen-Tehrom hurrying to catch up to him. Japheth and Yaran followed close behind and then Ham and Debseda. Shem stayed with Madrazi, who found her feet heavy but the pull of her father irresistible. They passed the grove, the barns, and as Noah arrived at the animal enclosures, he began to throw open the gates and doors. Moved by his will and spirit, all imitated his actions and within a short time freedom beckoned all of the animals. Not stopping, Noah strode towards the forest path. He stopped only to cut the ropes that held the great nets of the aviary in place. Shem ran around to the other side and did the same, and the nets collapsed and folded to the ground. But as Madrazi watched, the birds did not immediately take wing.

Noah did not hesitate. With Wen-Tehrom at his side and the rest close behind, he set off up the trail to the clearing. Turning her head, Madrazi saw a sight that remained with her the rest of her days. The entrance to the forest path was higher than the ground behind, and standing there among the first trees, one could look back and see the entire area between the house and the trees. Animals were streaming out of the barns, pens, and enclosures. They began to mill in confusion, a whirling maelstrom of life in the middle of the great yard. Out of that mass, individual animals flung themselves to freedom, seemingly thrown off as from a great wind and fleeing away in all different directions. But from the core of chaos emerged a steady line of animals following the steps of Noah in groups of seven or by pairs. Even the morning sun could not obscure the golden aura around each of these animals—the same light Madrazi had seen in Methuselah's face at his death.

In perfect order and at the exact pace set by Noah, humans and animals moved up the trail. The string of animals stayed each in their place and paid no attention to those around them. As they came together from the large yard onto the trail, the golden light coalesced around the entire line and streamed back from Noah like the tail of some great comet in the heavens. Madrazi recognized many of the individual animals that followed; horses, dogs, sheep, goats, cattle, peacocks, chickens, hares, all the domesticated kinds that had been a part of the settlement. She saw, too, that most of them were young, and all were strong, healthy representatives of their kinds. With them came pairs of many of the wild animals that Noah had kept in captivity; badgers, wildcats, great lizards—even a pair of antelope. Birds, great and small, patrolled above the cavalcade, creating patterns of golden light in the sky above.

Madrazi walked on, drawn as irresistibly as the animals in Noah's wake. Even then her mind was still trying to say that this could not be; but she could no longer deny what her eyes saw. For too many years, she had trusted her senses and her mind to comprehend the world about her: now the faculties that had suppressed the sense of the supernatural down deep in her soul were leaving her without any excuse. Her carefully constructed world was falling apart, and she could strive no longer against what she had known in her heart since arriving at this place. It was not her husband or father who lived in a world of delusion. It was she who had spent years denying what should have been obvious. The Creator was present all around. The Creator was at work in the world; perhaps brushing against her very soul as it hurried blindly through time. The Creator saw and heard. It was not a question of her knowing or not knowing; it was more a matter of accepting or denying deep within. Walking beside her, Shem's face showed his rapture and delight; Madrazi tried to hide her terror.

Although fear dominated, part of her was attracted to the light. Its soft color caught at something within, and she recalled the peace that had been hers during Methuselah's last days. She remembered suddenly the vision of her wedding day. During the walk down the path, the haunting strains of music had pulled her soul toward the world that she now saw. Then, she had not been ready to step through that door. Nor was she now, but neither could she retreat any longer from this new reality. With a flash of insight she saw that for twenty years she had stood on the threshold—unable to retreat or advance and unable to find peace on either side.

Shame also troubled her heart; her thoughts and words of skeptical condescension toward Noah and his family beat hollow within, accusing her with every step. Her deceit was unmasked in her mind as she remembered her selfish and arrogant plans for a future suited to her own whims.

In that potent cauldron of emotion, fear and awe permeated her soul. If the Creator could select and draw hundreds of individual animals to follow Noah up this path, then He could certainly bring destruction upon the earth. Moreover, if His word to Noah was true today, then His words to Noah years ago were also true. Madrazi could no longer deny the reality of the prophecy and she finally glimpsed the life-or-death drive that had sustained the labor of Noah and his sons.

Understanding came with a burden of fear and guilt that crushed her. She faltered, and could not go on; she did not deserve to stay in the company of these men. She must escape the light and flee into the darkness of the forest with the other animals that did not enjoy the Creator's favor. She feared that darkness, but the mirroring darkness of her heart seemed to justly condemn her and drew her away from the light. Just as she was ready to turn aside, Shem reached out his hand and grasped hers. His strength flowed into her and she saw his love in his eyes. Madrazi was drawn back to him and her desire to flee was overcome. He would not allow it, and she accepted that unspoken compulsion with silent relief and thanks.

Looking outward again, she saw that more animals, carried along by the same light, were joining the march. Like tributaries of a mighty river, thin lines of light came together out of the depths of the forest and these animals took their place behind those from the settlement. Overhead, strange but beautiful patterns traced by the birds mirrored those on the ground as they, too, followed Noah. Two young bears emerged from the forest behind a pair of sheep. Madrazi wanted to run back and protect them, but was stopped short by the sight of the bears placidly shuffling along with no apparent desire for the easy meal in front of them.

And so they came. The serpents that she feared, sliding along in their places; the boar and sow behind them keeping their place, not treading them under foot. Two of the great lizards, young, but already as tall as a man, walked upright, balancing on their long tails; their short forelegs reaching ahead as if to grasp the light flowing around them. The line now extended back farther than one could see, and still they came.

Up ahead, Noah continued at a faster pace up the trail. Madrazi did not remember hunger, thirst, or fatigue that day. The light seemed to lift her feet and carry them on. Even if she turned and tried to run, the light would have carried her forward beside Shem. But he took no chance. He had seen her fear earlier, understood it better than she did, and did not let go of her hand the entire way. Its warmth reassured her and his touch steadied each step.

The hours passed as in a dream. No one stopped and no one spoke. Words would have only intruded. They climbed the steep trail of the last hill with no more effort than was required when they had started on the path on level ground. Mounting the summit, Madrazi saw something that thrilled her anew. In the clearing, other lines of light stretched out in all directions through the forest, converging like arrows upon the ark. She wanted to stop and watch, but Noah continued on and led them down, across the clearing, and up the ramp that entered the huge door in the side of the ark.

The animals behind them streamed out of the forest as other lines of light converged on the clearing from many directions. Animals and people simply crossed the grass and climbed the ramp of the ark. Despite the apparent chaos of converging lines, the animals found their place up the ramp with no jostling or confusion. As each pair or group entered the door, they turned aside in the correct direction, and began to move toward the section of the ark allotted them. Madrazi followed Shem forward on the middle deck and without a word imitated his example as he began to open the doors and gates of the pens, cages, and enclosures. They walked the length of the deck, throwing open each door and gate as they went. Behind, the animals waiting patiently in the walkways simply climbed, walked, lumbered, slid, or crawled into their respective new homes. Some needed help and submitted without fear to human hands. Madrazi did not know which enclosures were for which animals, but the infallible light guided each creature straight to their proper place.

Shem and Madrazi worked their way to the front of the deck, opening doors to their right and left and then back again, closing the entrances behind the animals that had settled down in their cages. It took several trips back and forth to cover the width of the great vessel, but the work was easy and there was no wasted effort. All the animals were content and tame, and none offered any resistance or threat. Her earlier fear of them dissolved, and she remembered Methuselah's tales of the great garden and the time when Adam was said to have lived in perfect harmony with all animals. She had not believed it then, but was experiencing it now, and somehow, it seemed much more natural than the hostility, fear, and suspicion that existed outside in the darkness.

As Shem and Madrazi worked their way back for the last time, they saw Noah framed in the doorway, smiling as the lines of light streamed in around him. He seemed to partake of the light and reflect it back to the animals. Methuselah's story of Adam receiving dominion over the animals of the earth from the Creator was being repeated in the person of Noah. Shem looked at his father questioningly and Noah waved with a smile to the upper deck. They followed the light up that ramp, watching for the smaller animals, and repeated the process of ushering the creatures into their new homes. By then many of them were lined up and waiting outside their respective cages, and Madrazi had to be careful where she placed her feet. Shem glided among the crowded decks with his usual grace and completed most of the work.

The upper deck held quarters for people along with their food and water. There were fewer enclosures for animals here, and they finished more quickly than they had below. Madrazi had not noticed the passing of hours, but arriving back at the great door, saw that the sun was westering in the late afternoon sky.

The rest of the family joined them at the door. Breaking the silence of the day, Noah questioned everyone, and found that all of the animals and birds were caged. Japheth had engaged the mechanisms that delivered food and water to the pens, and so the humans left the creatures in the embrace of the ark, walking down the ramp to the living quarters at the edge of the clearing. Wen-Tehrom had been busy cooking, and the smells of food awakened Madrazi to the hunger and thirst that came suddenly as the spell of the day broke.

For the first time in hours, Madrazi's feet followed her conscious will as she walked quietly beside Shem toward the aroma of dinner. Her mind was just beginning to recover from the numbness engendered by the day's events, when with a startling clarity she recalled the words of Methuselah.

Child, your choice has never been faith in the words of Noah. You will see the deliverance with your eyes, and go into the ark and survive the judgment of God by the choice of others; Methuselah, Noah, Shem. Your true choice will come after you see the truth of the prophecy.

It had happened just as he had said, and she felt that even in death

Methuselah was calling her to trust him as she had done so many years before. She had seen—was seeing—with her own eyes that which she never would have believed. Even now, she was not sure if she could trust what she saw. If her mind had deceived her before, why could not her senses now? But if she followed that road, there would be no foundation at all, no footing on which to integrate her life. That way led to madness. Looking back at the ark, she saw even now a faint golden glow around it, fading, but unmistakably present. She must trust her eyes and her mind until she could find the key to reconcile today with what a lifetime of experience had taught her.

As they walked across the grass, Madrazi remembered too, her foolishness that morning; the practical objections of her limited mind to the task they had faced. All of these had been met in the directing control of the Creator over his creatures. Her mistake had been to think of Him as unable or unwilling to accomplish anything of substance. Was the Creator the key she sought? If so, then she must reassess just who and what the Creator was. Could she do so, knowing that it would require another reassessment—of her own soul? The path beckoned through the door; but Madrazi still hesitated. It would be a painful journey, but she now understood that if she faltered now, that peace would forever elude her.

Chapter 36
NEW PATH

That evening, Madrazi slept deeply without dreams, but when she awoke, she was still unsettled. The memory of the march to the ark remained sharp, a weight upon her mind. Desiring solitude, she walked outside before breakfast, along the edge of the trees. She noticed immediately that the clearing seemed strangely still and deserted. The air hung heavy and damp and it seemed unusually warm. No breeze stirred the grass, no crickets chirped, no birds sang. The sun was still below the trees to the east, and in the early morning mist she could still perceive a faint golden glow around the ark: whether it was the remnant of yesterday or merely a trick of her imagination, she could not tell. The forest seemed to be holding its breath and she found her own breathing slow and forced.

Her gaze was drawn back to the ark. Surprisingly, the instinctive fear that she had always harbored of that great ship was gone: no premonition of death lurked in its imposing bulk, no hint of her nightmare was mirrored in its dark wood. She could not say that she was attracted to it, but at least she felt ambivalent. It was a beginning. For some reason that made the burden of yesterday easier to bear and she turned back, ready for companionship.

She slipped in the door just as the others were gathering at the table. Wen-Tehrom motioned for her to sit and she slid in beside Shem. He smiled at her, but she sensed worry behind it. It was just the eight of them; none of the servants had followed the train of animals.

Shem spoke after they had begun eating. "Father, our household did not come with us. They have remained faithful and we must not break that trust. Please allow me to return with the news of yesterday and prepare them to come to the ark."

Noah nodded his agreement. "You speak well, my son. We cannot abandon those that have served us long and well, although my heart is troubled that they did not follow."

He frowned and looked down at his food. "None of us can travel as swift and there is need of speed. Return quickly and tell them to make haste. They need bring nothing, but I suspect that they will want some of their keepsakes." He looked up at Shem and spoke more sharply. "Tell them that the day will not wait; they must come quickly. The rest of us will finish preparations here. I will complete packing our tools and your brothers can complete the water supply."

Madrazi recognized the need for her husband to go, but felt a strange misgiving. Forcing it down, she finished eating and then moved to help Yaran and Wen-Tehrom clean up. But the older woman stopped her with a smile. "Yaran and I will provide meals and keep the quarters clean," she announced. "Madrazi and Debseda can lend their strength to help the men with their work."

Madrazi walked outside, clinging to Shem. Ham and Japheth veered off to the ark to fetch oxen. Noah took Debseda with him to the far barn, leaving Shem and Madrazi alone at the head of the path behind the house.

"It is early," he said, glancing at the sun. "I will return tonight after I have instructed the household to pack their belongings and come." He embraced her, and as he let go, a tremor of apprehension ran through her. Her eyes followed his easy lope to the top of the summit, and she remained watching the break in the trees for some time. She could not dispel the feeling of danger. It was simply emotion, she told herself, and not of her mind. The events of the previous day had unsettled her. She tried to put it away and went to help Noah.

But the day passed slowly. Although only six days remained until the judgment, she could not begin to grasp the extent of the events that awaited them, and the slow hours of the first day suggested that all six were destined to pass in an endless, winding stream of time. Madrazi fumbled about the barn for a time, her mind refusing to help her hands. She guessed that Noah was similarly preoccupied, but at his age, tasks were done cleanly without the need for conscious thought. Finally, she turned away in frustration and checked the sun. It was still in low in the eastern sky. With Shem gone, the clearing seemed larger and emptier than usual. Unable to concentrate on packing tools, she walked to the far side of the clearing to help the brothers. Wrestling a heavy barrel up the bank of the stream onto the small cart, they told her with some annoyance that they needed no help. So she wandered back, slowly contemplating the events of the day before. She knelt and touched the grass. It seemed the same; there was no evidence of the tapestry of light that had been woven across it. In the sunlight, there was now no visible gleam from the ark. Yet she had seen what she had seen, and it remained beyond her understanding.

Finding that her steps had taken her near the stone altar, Madrazi sat in the grass, determined to resolve her conflict. She did not see Noah gaze in her direction and warn Debseda not to disturb her. With her head bowed, Madrazi sat for hours, turning over and over again the happenings of yesterday and the conflict between what she had long wanted to be true and what she had seen. She could no longer deny or ignore the presence of the Creator, or pretend that her life was unimportant to Him. She was the daughter of a prophet, of a man whose years of planning and preparing accused every other, and a man whose entry into the ark would condemn them to death. She must accept Noah's words and Shem's beliefs as true, but her heart still rebelled, and she felt no inclination to simply submit without some deeper understanding.

"I want to talk to you," she said softly to the stones before her, "but I do not know what to say." The surrounding silence amplified her voice and startled her, but there was nothing but silence in return.

"Why don't you reply?" she asked, but as soon as the words left her lips, she regretted them, because she knew the answer. There was little reason for the Creator to speak to her. A vivid impression of twenty years of selfishness and deceit welled up in her mind. She had stubbornly refused to submit to the Creator, to his prophet, and even to her husband. Past thoughts echoed in her mind, simultaneously accusing and condemning. It was a hard hour for Madrazi and she was glad that she was alone; none saw the bitter tears that accompanied the upheaval of her spirit. She wished to escape, but a lifetime habit of shouldering responsibility left her no choice. In a moment of quiet, she resolved to seek the forgiveness of Shem, then Noah. Her hands were damp at the thought of confessing the extent of her wrongdoing. Even the comforting words of Methuselah seemed muted and she knew that there would be no peace in her mind until her conscience was clear.

When she had reached this unsatisfying conclusion, she began to look for something to distract herself. It was not hard. There was still work to be done, and she threw herself into it with a will, seeking in physical action a surcease from internal struggle. The previous night, Noah had assigned each son to the oversight of the animals on one deck. Shem's lot fell to the upper deck, Japheth's to the middle deck, and Ham's the lower. Since all of the others were busy, Madrazi spent the rest of the day walking through the ark and making sure that the animals had food and water. She expected them to be unsettled at this change in their habits, but to her surprise they seemed to be content with their new home. Caring for their needs kept her mind off of her own troubles and the remaining hours sped by.

By the time she was well into her work, she was able to set aside her guilty conscience and her fears of unburdening it, but her earlier apprehension for Shem returned with some force. It would not abate and the calm of the animals contrasted sharply with her growing tension. There was no reason for it. It defied logic. He was able to take care of himself in the forest, and he was simply going back to the house to ready the others, yet she could not shake a feeling of dread. In a moment of weakness, her mind cried out to him to come back. Taking a few deep breaths, she told herself she was acting like a foolish little girl, but self-ridicule did not change her heart.

When she had completed all of the upper deck and helped with a good part of the middle, the encroaching darkness of early evening forced her to stop. She walked to the great ramp, standing in the open door to face the remains of the daylight. The dim stillness of the ark behind her was haunting, but no more than the stillness in the clearing. The sky was tinged with red as the sun sank behind the hill, and in the silence Madrazi fancied that there was no life outside the ark: she had seen no other animals or even heard any birds in the clearing that whole day—indeed she would not for the rest of that week. Inside the ark, the animals were placid and quiet and it all made her feel strangely alone.

Worrying about Shem turned her thoughts to Jeriah and Meshur. Shem had reassured her that he would bring them to the ark if they were at the house, and Madrazi tried to convince herself that they were even now coming back up the path with him. As the evening dragged along, her apprehension increased. Not hungry, she left the supper table and paced the area behind the quarters and barns, expecting to hear her husband's reassuring voice any minute. But as the darkness settled heavily, she finally admitted that he was late. Finally, she went to bed, to a sleepless night spent wondering what evil had befallen him. Her imagination admitted any dire possibility, and before the sun rose she realized that sleep would not come and she rose and went outside.

Waiting for the sun to rise, she resolved to go search the path herself. She would have to leave quietly; the others would never let her go. Remembering all that Shem had taught her, she made her way silently out of the cabin, then relaxed as she approached the top of the hill. There she paused, watching the orange rays of the sun shoot across the landscape and light the tops of the trees. It was a beautiful sunrise and she leaned against a tree to feel it before she plunged on.

"I love the way the light and shadow mix at sunrise."

Madrazi smothered a scream, but jumped away from the tree. Shem stepped from behind it, a satisfied smile on his face. He braced himself for the expected rebuke, but it did not come. Instead, his wife simply stared at him and then began weeping. Now it was Shem's turn to be taken aback. Madrazi seldom wept and never at something as trivial as being startled in the woods. It did not last; she flung herself into his arms with inarticulate cries and tears.

After holding him tightly for a few moments, she looked up through her wet eyes to see a quizzical smile playing on his lips. Sleeplessness, anxiety, relief, and frustration mingled and kept her emotions high.

"What is troubling you?" he asked. "Is anything wrong?"

"I expected you back yestereve," she said, words rushing out between tears. "I was frightened for you all day and when you did not come I could not sleep; I could only think of some terrible fate preventing your return. I cannot go on without you."

Those last words surprised them both, but Madrazi immediately realized that her heart had spoken. Even as she said the words, her memory returned to his touch that had drawn her back to the light the day before.

He seemed to understand. "I am here, and you do not need to fear," he said simply. The warmth in his voice and embrace brought calm; her emotions gradually subsided and her mind regained a semblance of control. He released her but she would not release his hand as they walked slowly down the path and along the edge of the clearing, she held herself close to his side.

Not sure what to say or how to react to her unusual behavior, Shem did not question her further, but instead gave an account of his trip. "I found our household like sheep without a shepherd," he explained. "They did not know what had become of us and were afraid when they found the empty cages and barns. None had been near when we started out, although many saw flashes of light at the edge of the forest and the fleeing animals that did not come with us. I gathered them into the house and calmed them, then related the wonder that we had experienced. They seemed astonished that the day was upon us; it has been approaching for so long that I suspect familiarity has caused them to neglect its import. Most wanted to pack their belongings, and several of the children are ill. The men asked if they could put everything in order and come in a few days."

He shook his head at this. "I felt in my heart an urgency that they did not and perceived that if I left, they would revert to fear and paralysis. So I resolved to stay with them, order their affairs, and bring them with me as quickly as I could. I knew that you would miss me, but I did not think that it would be an occasion for such fear. I am sorry." He paused, waiting for his wife to speak.

"I am the one who should be sorry," she replied. "I acted like a silly young girl, but the fear was nonetheless real. Once again I have much to say to you and much to hear, and once again, circumstances intervene. But I will say this."

She stopped and turned to face him, a look of intense determination in her eyes. "Now I am happy for yesterday's fear, for it has shown me my heart—at least in regard to you, my love. I would not have been so afraid if I were not sure that whatever happens to you happens to me. Your life is mine and without you there is no life worth living."

Shem smiled and entwined his fingers in hers. "It is strange to hear your tale," he said as they resumed walking. "It is you that brought me back. After I had resolved to stay, I began to organize the servants and prepare them. But all through the day the thought of you was nagging at my heart. I grew uneasy. My life in the forest has taught me the value of attending to these types of feelings, for I believe that they are a hidden part of our minds that speaks in a way other than clear thought. By late afternoon, I resolved to return to you, so I gave final instructions to the men and left when the moon was high. I stopped briefly at our spring, but then hurried on."

"You made the journey quickly, all the same."

Shem shrugged his shoulders. "I ran most of the way."

Those simple words uprooted the last foundations of the walls surrounding Madrazi's heart. In them she finally understood the core of the man beside her: what she had missed for twenty long years. Since they were still beneath the trees above the clearing, she drew him to herself with a strength that surprised both. She clung to the folds of his robe with tight-clenched fists and locked her eyes upon his, searching for his soul.

"Wherever you go," she declared with a shaking voice, fighting back tears, "I will go of my own free will and with all my heart."

Shem did not understand all that lay behind those words, for he did not know the secret places of her heart that had been kept closed to him since their wedding, but Madrazi swore to herself that he would know soon, regardless of the shame it might cost. But that moment was not one for words, and as he kissed away her tears, they felt a unity of heart and soul beyond any they ever had before, and it was in that hour that she realized what her marriage was truly meant to be.

Madrazi later wondered if her understanding of marriage would have changed had it not been for the internal vertigo brought on by recent days. Certainly her world had been turned upside down: the changes in Lamech and the destruction of Jeriah's life, the loss of her own dreams of a similar one, the painful loss of Juloch and Jared, and the startling awareness of the Creator's power, presence, and protection of Noah and his family. It was not hard to accept a new vision of marriage with the crumbling of so many other misconceptions.

She suddenly understood that what had been passed on by her parents was easily reinforced by years of compatibility with her selfish desires. She had always thought marriage was two individuals sharing a carefully defined part of themselves—a life together that was a constant balance of giving and taking that might somehow trap an illusion of happiness. This could no longer be. If satisfaction was defined outside the bounds of what was shared, it must always be an illusion, for selfishness could not bring true happiness.

Then and there, under the trees, she saw in a flash of insight that her love for Shem must be nothing less than a complete surrender of all of herself in return for nothing but a trust in his love. In spite of her vows years earlier, she had never given herself to him in that fashion—as Noah had so astutely perceived. His words were but one of the memories that haunted her. *But neither Shem nor I command your heart, I think. You give or withhold that by your own choice.*

Hard on the heels of that conviction came the disturbing realization that Shem had loved her for all those years anyway, knowing that she did not return or even understand it. She pressed herself to him, marveling that his love had not soured to contempt or hatred and wondering what secret he possessed that kept his heart pure. But now was not a time to question or debate such things; that would come later. In that moment, she set all thought aside and abandoned herself to the pure enjoyment of love's beauty—a splendor that flowed from him in their embrace and filled her, carrying away fear and doubt.

That moment would define the rest of the week for Madrazi. Thoughts of the impending doom, of her losses of Methuselah, her father, Jared and Meshur, and even Jeriah, all faded. Nothing remained as bright and solid in her memory as the discovery of her unconditional love for Shem and the happiness that it unlocked for both. She saw him so differently now; his inner majesty shining through every physical feature in a mosaic that took her breath away each time she looked into his eyes. For she now saw his soul and knew that her own was open to him. She would have to help him explore and expunge the dark corners over the following days, but she determined that he would have all of her and that she would have all of him. Nothing less would suffice.

Madrazi initially thought her feelings an internal issue until they came down off the hill and entered the building for breakfast. But some things cannot be hidden, and Noah and Wen-Tehrom saw immediately, and the others understood almost as quickly. Madrazi was discomfited for a moment at the broad smiles that lit each face, but soon realized that she was smiling, too. Yaran hugged her without speaking and Japheth embraced his brother. Even the reticent Debseda took her turn embracing the couple, while a rare grin lit Ham's face. In the midst of the internal and physical tensions building in that small clearing, all were heartened by their happiness. For the remainder of that day, Shem and Madrazi spent every minute together, reveling in the new reality that was their love.

Chapter 37
FINAL PARTING

Gray fog merged into the gray half-light of pre-dawn stillness. Madrazi stood at the top of the hill on the west side of the clearing, waiting for the bright rays of the first sunlight to burn through the surrounding absence of color. It was the morning of the sixth day and Madrazi had hiked up the road each day since Shem's return to welcome a new morning and to mark the last days of a world she would leave behind forever. Within minutes, waiting in silence, she saw the first beam of light stretch from the far horizon, across the tops of the dark trees and through the now-dissipating fog to warm her face. The ark was still a shadow in the gray clearing below, wrapped in the fine gray mist.

A smaller gray figure appeared toiling up the hill. Its movements were not Shem's, and in a moment she was able to discern the welcoming smile of Noah and return it in full. "It is always a pleasure to welcome a new day, my daughter," he said lightly, "but even more to see it start with the first light of the morning illuminating the happiness and beauty of your face."

"I owe you much for many trying years, my father," she replied more seriously, "and if I can lighten one morning, then so much the better for us both."

"Many things are coming to an end, daughter," he said with a sigh, echoing her thoughts, "and it will be a great burden for us to see it happen. But there are some things that we are all glad to leave behind, and this week has been easier for having seen and shared the joy that you and my son have discovered. There is much that I would say to you and hear from you, but I must be patient, for great things are at hand."

There is a time to speak and a time for silence, and so both stood quietly watching the sunlight burn the mist away, revealing the stark outlines of the dark shape that dominated the clearing. Madrazi still felt a measure of awe at its dark bulk, but since witnessing the coming of the animals, the old, unthinking fear that had oppressed her for so many years had vanished completely.

They were both startled to hear a call behind them. "Hail, Noah!" cried a familiar voice, subdued and obviously not sharing in the joy of the morning.

As they turned, Madrazi saw the elder, Subtur, and heard a sharp intake of breath from Noah before he composed his face and replied, "What am I to you, Subtur?"

Subtur bowed his head at that reply but continued his slow, heavy steps. A servant walked behind him with bowed head and stopped a short distance away. No one spoke until Subtur halted and lifted his head. Madrazi had always before seen Subtur in the exercise of his public office and always with the bright eyes and chiseled features that conveyed power and honor. But that man was not this one; his face was haggard and his beard and hair lank and disheveled. But his eyes were dark and intense, and Madrazi saw raw emotion in his face: anger, mixed with fear, sorrow, and regret. He ignored Madrazi and fixed his gaze upon Noah.

"What are you to me, my brother?" he asked half-mocking and paused. Finally he laughed a bitter laugh and replied, "We are more to each other than you realize. We are both displaced from high and honorable office. We have both deserted a home that consumed much of our lives and strength. We have both been deserted by a people so fickle in their affections that my mind is still numb from their treachery." He paused and glanced at Noah with a calculating look, but Noah's face was set and hard. So he continued, more softly. "We are both now in danger of our lives and property and we are both fleeing that danger, each in his own way. But your way is sure death; only I will escape the wrath chasing hard after us!"

Noah remained still, waiting, not speaking a word. His silence seemed to exasperate Subtur. He gestured vaguely with his hand back towards the west. "Do you not even care to know what has happened?" he asked.

Noah stirred and finally spoke. "I know what has happened. One hundred and twenty years ago the men of Lamech rejected the word of the Creator. For daring to speak it, I was ostracized, ridiculed, and betrayed by those for whom I gave so much for so long. Death is coming and danger is at hand, but you look, as ever, in the wrong direction. We have heard of Sechiall's triumph and I can guess that is the source of your current concern, but his small anger is nothing compared to the Creator's wrath that is almost upon us." He paused and spoke more gently, "But even now, it is not too late to turn."

Subtur could not meet Noah's eyes and averted his gaze. Madrazi followed the exchange with interest, but kept still and silent. The sun had now risen above the trees and its rays illuminated the clearing. Subtur's glance was drawn there, and Madrazi saw his face pass through incredulity, awe, and fear—emotions that she remembered well from the first time that she had seen the ark. In a flash of insight, she realized that in all his years as Noah's peer and supposed friend, Subtur had never once bothered to come and see the ark for himself. He slowly forced his eyes back to Noah, looking for something in his face, but it was not there. Finally he dropped his eyes and began to weep silently.

Seemingly aware of Madrazi for the first time, he stifled his tears and turned again to Noah with a softer voice. "No, my old comrade," he said shortly, "there are many reasons why that is not possible. Some you know, some you surmise, and others are yet hidden from you. I came here not for an invitation onto your ship, but for a few words which my conscience and honor demand me to speak. Some are to my shame and perhaps to your anger—and that rightly so—but others to warn you of imminent danger. Please hear me out, and then say what you must. I will hear you, too, but then I must rejoin my wife on the road. We are fleeing to Taspar, where I hope to find refuge from the storm that has unleashed itself on Lamech."

Having heard the story of Sechiall's victory and triumphant return, neither Noah nor Madrazi was surprised to hear Subtur's words. But Madrazi was intensely curious about what had happened in town and could barely refrain from blurting out her questions about Jeriah. But she knew that this was a time for speech between the two men and kept silent. Noah seemed to understand her desire and made no move to dismiss her. Subtur seemed beyond caring.

"I never saw myself as a homeless wanderer," continued the elder, finally. "And yet such are the vagaries of fate. To my shame I must confess that I schemed together with Dajus, Zered, and Zered's son to reorder the council away from the majority that your family enjoyed for so many years."

"So Zered confessed to us upon his deathbed, more than twenty years past."

Subtur stood amazed, and stammered, "But you said nothing; you did nothing."

"Yes, and in that I erred. Lamech was no longer my home. What mattered who held power for a few short years in a town that would soon perish completely? But had I thought that any of your petty plans would lead to the murder of my own father, then we would have stopped them stillborn."

"I knew nothing about that until it was too late," returned Subtur with some heat.

"But still you pressed forward, not punishing the guilty or protecting the innocent."

Subtur bowed his head at that. He began again, "Events moved rapidly beyond what I had envisioned. What began as a desire for the betterment of Lamech became more than I can bear to tell you, but I feel the need to ask you and the souls of your fathers for their forgiveness."

Noah was silent and Subtur continued doggedly. "As you may know, Sechiall returned triumphant from battle with Y'tor. Jared was slain and the army that returned was not the one that left. The spirit of that demon has inflamed them all and they returned to master the town, not to serve it. Sechiall sees himself as the king of a people who should have no use for kings. He humiliated Dajus and me before the men of the city. Dajus accepted humiliation as the price of his wealth. I could not! I determined to leave, but to do so alive was no small feat; Sechiall had all but threatened my death for the slightest betrayal."

"But treachery comes easier with practice, does it not?"

Subtur reddened, whether with shame or anger, even he did not appear to know, but with an effort he restrained his emotion and continued. "Sechiall left town quietly yesterday with the worst of his killers. Once he was gone, I knew that I must take advantage of his absence and flee for my life. My wife and I left by separate gates at separate times. Even I, an elder of the town, had to justify my exit to the guard! But he accepted my story that I was inspecting my fields and let me go. Riders followed me at a distance and made sure that I went to my farmhouse on the north side of the fields. There I met my wife. We gathered what small wealth I could carry and with two faithful servants we slipped away late last night. We are fleeing certain death. Yet I could not go without seeing you. No matter what has happened, we were once as brothers. I may have betrayed you once, but I admit now that I was wrong and cannot stand by and see you and your family slaughtered by Sechiall. All that I have is gone; years of labor wasted. No home. No town. No respect. No return." He fell silent.

"You have spoken wisely as far as you go," answered Noah. "You see part of the vanity of your life and the destruction of those vanities. Look further! You still have your wife, servants, more wealth than most men, and your life. While life exists there is always a chance to turn completely away from the present and accept my warning. Today is the day. There will be no tomorrow! You had some part in the death of Lamech and the destruction of all that Methuselah built. You say that it was unforeseen. In this you admit your lack of foresight. Humble yourself now and do not exercise that same faulty wisdom in rejecting my offer!"

Subtur protested, "But I did not draw the sword that struck Lamech!"

"The hands of him who watches without pity are as red as those of him who steals the blood of life!" exclaimed Noah, drawing himself erect. Subtur visibly shrank before him, and Madrazi saw once again the strength of Noah revealed. Against it, Subtur seemed smaller than she remembered. She half expected Noah to strike Subtur. But instead he reached a hand towards the shaken man and spoke in a gentle voice. "Even so, if I can receive mercy, then I can extend mercy. Come with us, Subtur. It is your only chance."

For a moment he wavered. The dark eyes looked up at Noah as if seeing him for the first time. Amazement was on his face, but at that moment he looked past Noah and saw the dark mass of the ark. His face hardened. "No," he replied. "I cannot come with you. Come with me. Taspar will supply refuge. Even if Sechiall dared to strike within its walls, he could not. Come with me, Noah! We were great in Lamech. We can be great in Taspar. Are not two better than one?"

Noah glanced at Madrazi and signaled her away with his eyes. She quietly walked over to Subtur's servant and led him further away to give the two men their privacy.

As they walked she caught at his sleeve. "Please, sir," she begged, "grant me the grace of two questions before you go."

Surprised by her boldness, he could only nod his acquiescence.

"Please, sir," she repeated, "what can you tell me of Jeriah, the widow of Jared. Is she alive?"

He looked down. "I do not know much, but I have heard that she is the willing woman of Sechiall. Dajus granted him the belongings of Jared on his return. I have heard that Jared's widow has taken him into her home, but I have not seen her in all the days since the army returned from Y'tor."

Madrazi shuddered, knowing that Jeriah would never willingly give herself to Sechiall. She wondered what threat he had used to force her compliance. Had her message arrived?

Steeling herself, she asked her second question, "Have you any word of the man, Meshur?"

At this question, his faced showed clear surprise. "Yes," he said, "everyone is talking about it. He was slain outside the town six nights ago. There was a great fight at the house of his cousin, Pashtur—a spy in the service of Sechiall. He led Captain Balech and his men to Meshur, but there was a fight and Balech, Pashtur, and many soldiers were slain. Meshur escaped in the confusion, but a patrol saw him run from the walls towards the fields. They shot him. He ran into the fields and it took them all day to find his body."

Madrazi felt faint with despair. Meshur was lost—betrayed by the cousin he had sought to save. She knew then that no message had reached Jeriah. Her knees were weak and she felt the servant's hand upon her arm, steadying her. As her vision cleared, Noah and Subtur walked to them; concern on

Noah's face, regret upon Subtur's.

"I am well," she said quietly to Noah, but leaned heavily on his strong arm.

Noah turned to Subtur and said, "I beg you one last time, Subtur, come with us. Your only hope is the ark."

Subtur did not even turn back but walked away with bent head and a slow step.

As they watched them go, Madrazi told him dully of the news of Meshur. Noah sighed. "He was a good man; confused and easily led astray by those he trusted. We will miss him. Please let me tell Ham. He has been eager to see him and have him beside us. This will be a sore blow to him."

"May I tell Shem?" she asked.

"Yes, but warn him to keep it to himself until I have talked to Ham."

The early glory of the morning was gone. As they walked down the hill, the dull stuffiness of the week seemed to enfold them and Madrazi noticed its weight for the first time in several days. Shem met them coming down the hill and as soon as he saw their faces, his smile disappeared and Madrazi saw her own worry reflected on his face. Blankly he stared from his wife to his father. Then Noah described Subtur's presence and the news from town in terse sentences. Madrazi only half listened; sunk in her own worries and not listening to their discussion.

At the bottom of the hill, Noah directed his steps away and Shem loitered with Madrazi across the clearing toward the far side. As they walked, she related the words of Subtur's servant about the fates of Jeriah and Meshur. Tears stained her face as she freely shared her fears—something that she could not have done even a few weeks before. But much had changed in just a few days, though it still surprised her how easy it was to talk to him now.

They walked on and Shem was silent with his head bowed. Madrazi sensed that he, too, had some inner turmoil to share. Finally he stopped and began to speak. "My love," he began, "my heart also warns me of evil—our servants have not yet come. They should have arrived yesterday, or even earlier. Your news increases my fear—if Sechiall truly has evil designs against Father, then he will go there first. I must go back."

Madrazi nodded, though she wished she could prevent him from that duty. She frowned: the wonderful spell of the last few days was broken. It was a time to treasure; a time to remember; but now a time that must take its rightful place in the past. It would be the foundation of many good years, but they would come later. Madrazi wanted Shem to stay, but knew he was right. As she reached that conclusion, she realized, too, that the fear that had overwhelmed her just a few days ago was gone forever.

"I will be waiting for you, my love," she said, pulling him close. They enjoyed a brief moment, and then he was gone; the warmth of his body against her dissipating in the cool morning air. She lost sight of him under the trees, slipping back into the forest he loved.

Walking back around the ark, Madrazi found Noah deep in conversation with Japheth and Ham. She stopped short, a respectful distance away, but Noah immediately beckoned her forward. "Shem has returned to the house," she said, realizing that she could no longer call it a home. "He will return with the servants as soon as he can." Noah nodded his agreement, but Madrazi's worry was reflected in his face.

The remainder of that day passed quickly. She helped wherever her hands could find something to do, and everyone was busy. She did not notice the passage of time until she found herself at the foot of the ramp, resting for the first time that day. The red glow of the sun hovered over the western hill and the family had gathered for an evening meal, but Ham was still hard at work. Noah had told him earlier of the fate of Meshur, and Ham had taken the news hard. He went into the ark immediately by himself and began working. Throughout the rest of the day he would not stop, eat, or drink. It seemed to Madrazi that he was searching for the memory of his friend in the planks and beams of the giant ship. The family had left him to his grief all day, but Madrazi understood his loss better than the others and determined to provide company, even if she could comfort him in no other way.

Seeing an opportune time, she found a skin of water and some bread and went up the ramp. She stopped and listened, then followed the faint noise of a hammer to the forward area of the middle deck where Ham was assembling a storage bin. With some trepidation she approached. If he heard, he gave no sign, but she would not be put off by his resolutely turned back.

"My brother," she started, "I do not know your sorrow, but I know what it is to lose those close to you. Please accept my sympathy. He was my friend, too."

Ham turned at that and looked at Madrazi with his hollow, dark eyes. She had not noticed before how the past few years had worn him down. "Yes," he agreed slowly. "Meshur liked you. He told me once that you were the only woman that ever made him feel easy in conversation."

Silently she handed him the water and bread. He shook his head but Madrazi would not be put off and stood there with the skin and loaf extended, with as stubborn a look on her face as was upon his own. Finally, with a snort, he took the water and poured it over his head, wiping away the dust of the day on his cloak. Taking a bite of bread, he turned back to his work.

"The hour is late, Madrazi," he said after realizing that she had not left, "and the others are gathering for the evening meal. I am loading the last of my tools and have only a few hours of work remaining. Go to the others."

"Many things might have changed with me this week, brother," she replied with spirit, "but my renowned stubbornness remains as it always was. I will help you until we are finished, and then if they have finished the meal, I will make you another." Ham saw that he had no choice, and so he accepted her offer with a shrug.

True to her word, she worked with him for more than an hour, until the light was failing, but they finished the bin and loaded his tools in their proper places. As they worked, Madrazi continued to talk, forcing him to respond. Ordinarily preoccupied and aloof, Ham found speech easy that evening.

"I am always amazed at the workmanship and design of the ark," she said as they finished, "although it frightens me at times. It is truly a wonder and you should be proud."

Ham straightened from the chest where he had carefully stacked the load of tools and gratefully accepted another swallow of water. "There are times when I wonder how we ever accomplished it," he admitted. "At times my own heart swells with pride over the perfection of some joint or mechanism—for things built well have always given me pleasure—but after seeing the animals brought on board, I have begun to realize what an insignificant thing we have done. I wonder why the Creator did not make the ark Himself, and present it to Noah with the prophecy."

"One hundred and twenty years is a long time," Madrazi thought aloud. "It is almost like Noah has been subjected to some test of endurance, or stubbornness…"

"Or faith," concluded Ham. "We should be grateful. If the time of judgment had been one hundred and twenty years ago, neither of us would have been here nor seen the marvels we beheld. If that is the Creator's power to prepare for judgment, I wonder what His power displayed in judgment will be?"

"Terrifying," she returned, saying the first thing that came into her mind. Although the vision had not haunted her since the death of Lamech, she had been thinking anew about it over the past days and pondering its relationship to Noah's prophecy.

Ham looked at her eyes for a moment and nodded at what he saw. "Yes, you have clearer sight than I in understanding the coming wrath."

Chapter 38
SECHIALL STRIKES

Jeriah lay uncomfortably behind the trees bordering the field, but dared not move. Oman lay beside her and scanned the area before them. Jeriah shuddered. She hated Sechiall and was ashamed of her new status as his casual slave, and it particularly galled her that men who had once deferred to her because of Jared now openly mistreated her and laughed about it to her face as well as behind her back. Jeriah repressed a moan, but the wet trail of a tear found its way down her dirty cheek. But she lay still and said nothing. Oman was brutal and cruel. He would not hesitate to strike her, and Sechiall would not object. Fortunately, Oman was not paying any attention to her. She could see from his expression that something was wrong, and she rejoiced inwardly at whatever it was.

But those feelings were soon forgotten as she stared over the expanse of the cultivated fields. In a very few minutes, her only remaining friend would lie dead or at the feet of Sechiall, having betrayed her husband and father. Jeriah had made her choice, but did not know what Madrazi would do. Jeriah was torn; if Madrazi chose death, then she would be alone, if life, then she would be subject to the same indignities and pain that had marked her recent days.

The sun was high in the sky and its warmth made her drowsy. The fields were exceptionally quiet and few people could be seen. She knew that men should be busy in the fields and around the buildings. Even the pens and barns were quiet. Oman waited patiently, memorizing the ground in front of them, counting the people, and scanning likely places for ambush, as Jared had taught him.

Finally Oman finished his reconnaissance. Seizing Jeriah's arm, he pulled her to her feet and dragged her back to where the main body of men waited among the trees.

"There are less than twenty men visible, Commander," he reported. "There are also some women and a few children, but I did not see Noah or his family. Perhaps they remain in the house. Perhaps he has a spy in town and they have fled into the forest. But it is too quiet, and I believe that something is wrong. The woman did not recognize anyone."

Sechiall paused, obviously considering his words. Jeriah knew that he trusted Oman. Whatever else he was, he was a good soldier with good instincts.

"Very well," Sechiall said finally, "we will attend to whoever is here first and then pursue the others wherever they may be. Divide the men into three companies. Take one around the back and approach through the forest. Gatar shall take another and approach from the road. I will keep the third and go straight in from here. Kill everything that you find; men, women, children, animals, everything! Spare only the lives of Noah and his family. Their blood is mine!"

Jeriah caught her breath, but the words never came. Sechiall grinned, looked at Jeriah, who quailed, and nodded. "You will have your chance. I have said it." Looking back to his men, he continued, "I will give you one hour to get into position and then we attack."

Oman and Gatar saluted. Quickly they selected their men and hurried off. Oman led his men wide into the forest to have the cover of the trees and Gatar led his around the other side of the Great East Road. Sechiall turned to Kenah. "Keep a good watch on my woman," he sneered. "I would not want to see her become separated from us and killed accidentally."

Kenah saluted and motioned to Jeriah to follow him. She nodded sullenly, her head down. The men waited at the edge of the trees behind Sechiall. The time passed slowly, but Sechiall appeared strangely patient. Jeriah was bored by the silence and time dragged. "What are you thinking," she asked him.

Sechiall was surprised at the question. Jeriah saw it flicker across his eyes, but then he laughed low and long. "So, you are finally beginning to accept your place."

Jeriah paled. She had only asked an innocent question to pass the time, but she realized with a shock that it was not a question based in rebellion. She hung her head.

Sechiall looked at her and nodded to himself. "I will tell you woman," he said softly. "I am only a few hours from completing the task that I set myself to so many years ago. I would never have imagined that it would be so easy. And this will be the easiest part of all: nothing stands in my way now but an old man, three sons who know nothing of battle, and a few frightened servants." He laughed again.

When the allotted hour had passed, Sechiall stood and waved to his men. "Come, let's finish this traitor, and Lamech will be ours and our sons forever!"

The men cheered and began to run behind him. Kenah stayed towards the rear and prodded Jeriah to keep up. As a solid wall of bronze and iron, Sechiall and his killers burst through the hedges and into the fields, the long yellow hair of their leader floating before them and leading them on to blood and destruction. The few servants in the outer fields were without weapons and began to flee the advancing line of death. Despite the weight of their armor, the soldiers caught them and quickly dispatched them, with a cold efficiency that repelled Jeriah. She struggled to keep up and not fall as Kenah prodded her.

The line burst around the first of the barns and outbuildings, and Jeriah saw four more men loading packs upon donkeys beside the largest barn. The men saw them and began to run toward the house, but the soldiers were on them within seconds, and all four were slain before they had gone more than a few paces. Jeriah stared in horror at the bloody shapes that littered the ground as Kenah dragged her past.

Sechiall was a good commander, even when inflamed by the blood lust. He sent several men into each of the outbuildings and kept his unit together as they methodically swept the grounds. When the men reported that a building was deserted or cleared, Sechiall ordered them to fire it and continue on. As they moved towards the main house, smoke and flame sprung up behind them.

Now they began to see more people. A few women and children were running from the house to see what was happening, and soldiers advancing down from the forest path cut them down without mercy. Others came running towards them, looking back in fear at Gatar's men following them with bloody swords. They pulled up in surprise at the line of grim men before them and soon all were dead. Jeriah strove to contain her fear and revulsion, but she could not restrain her tears for the dead children lying under the open sky. Oman and his men soon appeared through a grove of trees to their left and Oman quickly came up to Sechiall.

"We have killed everyone inside the house," he reported. "There is no sign of Noah or his family and even the animals are gone."

Sechiall ground his teeth in frustration. "Find me someone still alive who can talk," he commanded. Within minutes a warrior dragged a bleeding woman up to him.

Sechiall reached down and yanked her to her feet with his dagger to her breast. "Where is your master? Tell me what I wish to know or die!"

Whether it was the threat of death or the power of Sechiall's eyes, the woman wilted. "All have fled to the ark," she gasped. "We were to have gone today."

She looked hopefully up to Sechiall as she spoke, but when she had finished, she saw only anger in his eyes and tried to jerk away. In a flash, the dagger slid through her tunic and was buried deep in her chest. Then she relaxed and looked at Sechiall once more, "They alone will escape the wrath," she choked. "You are a dead man."

Sechiall held the body long enough to withdraw his dagger and wipe it clean in her hair. Then he casually released his iron grip and she slumped to the ground. Sechiall laughed. "So, they flee into the forest to hide in this ark that the madman has built. I have always wanted to see it. Now we will herd them into it and watch it become a funeral pyre for Noah and his sons."

Turning to his men, he ordered, "Destroy everything save the house. Search it out and make certain that no one is left alive inside. Tonight we will sleep there, and tomorrow morning we will burn it to the ground and march into the forest to finish this task. Then we return to Lamech and celebrate our complete victory!"

The men spread out in small groups of three and four. Some lit torches and completed the burning of barns and outbuildings. Others set fire to the fields and vineyards. Still others ransacked the large house and brought out food and wine, and any riches that they could find. Fire soon covered the grounds with a thick pall of smoke. Bodies were dragged indiscriminately across the yard and thrown into the burning buildings.

Jeriah shuddered at the callous ruthlessness of the men as they casually burned the dead and then joked about their share of the goods being piled up in the yard. She hung her head as she considered the last few days. They had passed as a nightmare, one bringing new horror just when she thought that her life could hold no more. Sechiall was brutal and uncaring; the opposite of everything that she had enjoyed with Jared. She wept at night for her lost husband; some tears for him, but most for herself at the disaster his loss had brought on her.

But even after the tears had been exhausted, her nights brought no peace, even at those times when she was not forced to satisfy the depraved lusts of her new master. Far worse than his attentions was the dark dream that came to her almost every night, now. Behind the terror, she sensed warning, but she had not heeded the warning of her conscience before, and she felt stained beyond recovery. After declining to embrace death rather than Sechiall, she was convinced that there was no profit in any warning for herself—she was already lost. Her only hope was that Madrazi would somehow escape the horror that defined her days and nights since the loss of her soul to Sechiall.

She stood, listless, watching the evil deeds, but dulled to their meaning. She watched Sechiall destroy even the simple enjoyment that the men took in plunder. He halted them with a sharp order. Guards were selected and sent to watch the road and trail into the forest.

"You will be relieved later," Sechiall told them. "Then you can enjoy food and drink. But now keep watch."

He turned on her and gestured. She obeyed and stood before him with her head down. Sechiall put a rough hand under her chin and pulled her face up to his. She quailed again before his gaze and felt anew the pain of her despair. But she no longer desired an escape in death; it was too late. She had already chosen life and even taken pleasure with Sechiall. She was bound to him and they both knew it.

"One more battle, woman, one more victory! Then I will be supreme in Lamech and over all the surrounding regions. Eventually, I will be the king of a great kingdom—I am young and the blood of my fathers runs true in me. You will see me achieve glory and wealth beyond the imagination of those fat fools in Lamech. It will become a great capital, not some insignificant port. No longer will its potential be denied by doddering old fools that resist the winds of the world."

"At least we were happy with the old fools," returned Jeriah in a fit of anger.

"You don't know what happiness is," sneered Sechiall. "After all, you say that you were happy with Jared, but you take pleasure with me easily enough, now. What is happiness, but some fleeting illusion? I have found happiness. It is the power to take whatever you want!"

"Then perhaps someday I will be visited with Jared's strength and skill while I am alone with you with a sword in my hand," replied Jeriah with a spark of her old spirit. "Then I will be happy!"

"We will see," laughed Sechiall, "later."

"Kenah!" he called, "Take her into the house and see that she is clean. Then she can prepare food for me."

Jeriah was surprised that she had not been struck, but she knew that Sechiall would not let even a small sign of rebellion pass. It would come.

But it appeared that she was wrong. She had found the warm baths that Madrazi had described to her long ago, and felt the simple joy of being relaxed and clean. When she took food to Sechiall, he spoke with a rough kindness and insisted that she eat with him. Later that night Sechiall came to her. But in stark contrast to her past treatment, he was surprisingly tender; she found only kind words and a soft hand. Later, as they lay silent in the dark, she knew a fleeting memory of peace and comfort in the past days. She was warm, well-fed, and clean. She even wondered in that moment if she could ever feel anything for this man. At that instant, Sechiall leaned over her and softly whispered, "I killed Jared."

Jeriah's ears heard the words, but for a moment her mind did not. Then they struck, and she froze in shock. As they penetrated her consciousness, she screamed like a wounded animal and hurled herself from the bed. Curled up in a corner of the room, she sobbed out her grief and anger—at herself and him. From a distance she heard his soft chuckle.

The vision returned that night.

Chapter 39
CONVERGENCE

Madrazi stared blankly at the opposite wall, barely aware of the aroma of hot tea steaming in front of her. Today was the seventh day and the events of the past week had erased many doubts that she had harbored before. She had seen the animals come, brought by the hand of the Creator. She had felt the same compulsion pulling her on, too, and still pondered the mixed desires that it caused. She had the words of Methuselah, and she had a taste of love freely given and returned with Shem. Somewhere in the depths of this forest, her old self had been left behind; in a sense, the past seventy years seemed an insubstantial shadow. Her reality was the future; not those wasted years. Though not yet living in a new world, she was no longer chained to the old.

But the ambivalence did not concern her. Her immediate reality was love—love as it really should be—love as she had never before imagined. Each day of the past week had brought her new insights into her husband and into her own heart. A man had given himself to her knowing that it was not returned. He had remained constant for years, patiently waiting for that love to penetrate her stubborn heart. In spite of misunderstanding, coldness, deceit and unbelief, he still loved her. Madrazi vowed again that all of her remaining years would be given to him as freely. She could not atone for the past, but she could live a different future.

That new life would not be one merely of duty or oath-keeping, because heartfelt convictions cut much deeper than words. Love's beauty lay in Shem receiving within her inadequate words all that could not be said. Her life would know true happiness; a giving of self, receiving the same in return, but never the one just to get the other. Instead, she had discovered happiness in the giving, a seed that having finally germinated, would now bring happiness from within, protected from the storms of circumstance.

Her insights into the nature of that kind of love revived a dimension of her life that had lain dormant since her mother's death. In her single-minded emulation of Pomorolac, she had ignored the depths of her own soul. She had spent the past fifty-five years sailing aimlessly over an ocean of ignorance. Now she would sail across another ocean—one of destruction—to a new world. Would that voyage bring insight? With a shudder, she remembered that today would bring an end to all speculation. Today would bring the final reality that Methuselah foretold.

She missed Shem as she rose and dressed. Although he could find his way through the forest on even the darkest night, she still felt his absence. There would not much time remaining and yet she knew that he would never forsake his family's debt to their household. But she feared the portents of the day. Last night, the moon had been a strange yellow color, and even the stars seemed dim.

It was still early when she went into the kitchen and lit a lamp. She knelt and gently blew away the ashes that banked last night's fire. Gratified to see the bright red of a few hot coals, she fed them with straw and kindling. Soon the morning fire was blazing, adding its light to the room. As she drew a pot of water from the barrel outside the door, she saw six dim figures making their way towards her. Most of the family had settled in the ark during the week, but Shem and Madrazi had remained in their old quarters, enjoying the privacy that they offered. However, everyone still took their meals here; there was a large store of food remaining, and Noah thought it wasteful to begin consuming their stores on the ark when there was no need. But this meal would be the last, for Noah insisted that all must be in the ark this morning.

Over their simple breakfast, Noah said that he had one last labor to perform. "For many years I have collected the knowledge of men on scrolls to bring into the new world. All that I could gather over the years, I have recorded. Everything from histories of our families to farming techniques: from our knowledge of minerals and metals to our laws and customs. I have sealed the scrolls in clay jars in the barn. Who can help me carry them aboard the ark?"

Japheth spoke up, "Ham and I must feed and water the animals this morning. If the judgment is violent, this may be the last chance for several days. Are the jars light enough for women to carry?"

"Yes," returned Noah. "They are not heavy, but there are almost fifty."

Wen-Tehrom interrupted. "Debseda, Yaran, and I have tasks to finish aboard." She paused, glancing at Madrazi, who smiled back and agreed to help Noah.

As the others returned to the ark, the old man and young woman walked to the barn and began carrying the jars to the foot of the ramp. Madrazi could carry them easily enough and was grateful that the task would soon be finished. After carrying several dozen out, Noah gestured her to rest for a moment. They sat together on the back of an old cart staring around at the empty barn. She sensed that he wanted to talk and sat quietly waiting.

"You have given me much joy this week, my daughter, and for that I offer my thanks. We are setting forth on a voyage to an unknown future, leaving all behind. You have begun your own journey, shedding enough of the old to begin seeing the new that lies inside. You have found a few answers, and more importantly, you have found questions. Most importantly, you have plumbed the font of love that we glimpsed in your relationship with Methuselah. Shem has been patient, and you have begun to reward his endurance. Do not allow the coming events to distract you from your own journey. Follow your soul and you will find your path."

Madrazi reached over and hugged the old man. "Methuselah is gone. He said that he would be waiting for me. But until then, I have only one father."

She felt his arms tighten around her and looked up to see his eyes grow damp. Quickly he released her and stepped down. "Thank you," he said simply and turned to pick up another jar. Madrazi smiled to herself and jumped down to help.

Jeriah awoke slowly and reluctantly to the smell of smoke and the stench of destruction that Sechiall had wrought yesterday. At least in sleep she could find forgetfulness and the memory of her fleeting years with Jared. Last night the storm of emotion had seared her soul. She felt only a dull self-loathing; Sechiall had effectively crushed her spirit in a way that she would not have thought possible. Her strength was nothing. She was nothing: merely a thing to suit her master. She stared dully over at the bed. Sechiall reclined, watching her. He was wide awake, his eyes gloating.

"Today, it will be done," he said. "The final obstacle removed. Methuselah is dead. Lamech is no more; Dajus and Subtur have sold themselves to my service. And now," he paused and smiled a smile of great contentment, "now, all the spawn of Methuselah will be crushed. They will burn alive inside the symbol of their degenerate folly. I am the new power. I will rule."

Jeriah moaned. He was right, of course, but she did not rejoice with him. Stiffly, she flexed her legs. "Get up, woman," he said roughly. "Today you must march again with men so that you can behold the death of Noah and the beginning of Sechiall's reign."

His words stirred a spark of feeling within. "The reign of a butcher, the brave slayer of women and children, and a murderer of his own," returned Jeriah with new tears of anger blinding her red eyes.

Sechiall laughed, "I won't even strike you for that, woman. You must have both eyes intact to watch the blood flow from Noah and his family—including

their women.   A great day," he continued, "death to my enemies and
destruction of their works."

"There will come a day of your own death and destruction of your evil!"
replied Jeriah, feeling strangely defiant. "I only hope that I am alive to see it!"

"I doubt that you will be," returned Sechiall with an undertone of promise.

He caught her up and forced her to eyes to his. "Jared is dead. There is
none who could stand before me with spear, sword, knife, or bare hands,"
boasted Sechiall, "least of all that doddering fool or his three sons. They are
not warriors. Why, your friend, Madrazi, will probably put up a better fight
than her men! When they are dead then who will fulfill your desire?"

Jeriah quailed again before him. The mention of Madrazi and the fear that
she would become a slave like herself drowned the feeble resistance of the
moment before. "Please spare her life," she begged. "I agreed to your terms
before and will serve you freely if you will only let her go."

Sechiall's blue eyes burned with an inner fire. They held Jeriah's for a few
seconds and her head bowed. "You will serve me regardless—as will she. Not
only will I grant her life, but I may also give her the privilege of being one of
my wives if she will renounce Shem and his family. Come, now, we leave in
less than an hour."

The morning sun shone with an odd redness on the smoldering wreckage
of Noah's settlement.   Smoke still curled from the charred remnants of
buildings and animal pens. Sechiall's guard had piled the booty from the
plantation before the house. Sechiall detailed ten men to stay with it. "Only
make sure that it is all here when I return," he warned.

The fear in their faces assured him that his trust was not vain.   Jeriah
looked away in disgust. Without Jared's control, the army had turned into a
mob of killers, and Sechiall ruled it by fear, not love and respect. She stifled
her tears as she thought of Jared; she missed him with an intensity of passion
that she had not even known in her marriage. The guilt of her surrender to
Sechiall was more than she could bear. Dully, she looked around at the carnage
of his slaughter.

A few cold bodies still lay in dried pools of their own blood, victims of the
orgy of violence yesterday. Jeriah shuddered as she saw the small bodies of two
children together in a corner with a dead woman—probably the mother—in
front of them. Jeriah felt bile rise in her throat and turned away quickly, but
Sechiall viewed the scene with approval.

"None escaped. The brave Noah and his sons and their women fled, but
his home is burnt, his servants are dead, and we will root him out of his hole in
the middle of the forest before the sun goes down tonight."

He turned to Kenah. "Have the men form up ready to march in fifteen minutes. We need to move quickly and bottle them up in that ark. Noah knows this forest better than we and I don't want him to slip away. There are enough fools back in town that might listen to him if he had a chance to speak."

"It will be done, Supreme Commander," returned Kenah with a salute. He hurried off and began getting the men in order for the march.

Shem had left the clearing the previous day with a sense of impending dread. The feeling had intruded on his newfound happiness, growing until he could no longer ignore it. The final words of Noah still rang in his ears. "*Very well, my son,*" he had replied. "*I know that the appointed time is very near, and we cannot abandon those who have remained faithful to our house. Go with my blessing, but be wary and tell them to hurry. There is sufficient store for us all, they can leave all and come as they are. The anger of God is going to burst upon the earth tomorrow. Do not delay!*"

With that warning uppermost in his thoughts, Shem sped through the forest. He could run at a lope for hours on end but long experience in the forest taught him that now was the time to move unseen and unheard. He doubted that Sechiall's band was in the forest, but he must assume the worst. So it was that he did not near the end of his path until twilight. He rested at a spring until the moon rose and then crept along under its light. The minutes slid by until he found himself at the edge of the forest. The smell of smoke was now quite noticeable to his keen senses, and fear began to mount in his breast. Slipping quietly off the path, he advanced slowly from tree to tree, drawing near to what was left of the aviary. There he saw a fire and two men carrying spears and wearing the armor of Lamech walking guard along the verge of the trees. They were talking together, and Shem crept closer to hear.

"… all burned up. We should have saved some of the outbuildings so that we wouldn't have to sleep on the ground tonight. At least there is plenty of food."

His companion replied, "Tomorrow will be an easy march, and Sechiall...."

"King Sechiall, he likes to be called now," interrupted the other.

"Fine!" replied the other. "*King* Sechiall, then, he wants to kill the old man and his sons with his own hand, so there won't be much for us to do; a little burning and looting."

"Yes," said his friend looking around, "but we'll get a sack of gold out of it, and the appreciation of *King* Sechiall. If things are going to change in town, we might as well be on the right side!"

As they strode off, Shem stood taut against a tree, not wanting to have heard those words. What of the servants? All dead? He hoped not, but he feared it true. With Jared dead, there was nothing to restrain the evil of Sechiall. But he owed it to those faithful to his father to make sure. There still might be a few hidden or even prisoners that he could spirit into the forest. He saw other soldiers patrolling the grounds. Prudence won over impatience and he waited silently for the moon to wane. He would have less time, but more darkness and the guards would be less alert in the early morning hours. If they marched tomorrow, they would surely stop at the big spring up the trail for drink and rest. If he could be there, then he could listen to their speech from the thick ferns on the far side of the spring, and still have time to run back to the ark well ahead of the soldiers.

Finally, Shem moved. He evaded the outer guards easily enough, having marked the other fires of the outposts. He accepted the risk of quiet guards walking at random, but the speech of those two suggested that most of the men would be eating, drinking, or sleeping. He slipped quietly from cover to cover and made his way around the edges of the fields and the burnt shells of the barns and outbuildings. When near a group of sleeping men, he would move carefully, sometimes pausing minutes between steps. But most of the time he could slide quickly through the shadows, making no more sound than a falling leaf. No living thing stirred, but the weak moonlight illuminated the remaining dead bodies strewn around the grounds. The stench from the smoldering ruins told the fate of others.

With difficulty, Shem controlled the anger he felt rising with each step. Most of the bodies had been burned in the still-smoking outbuildings, but a few lay scattered on the grounds. Were any still alive? Like a shadow, he noiselessly slid between groups of sleeping men around the main house, but found no evidence of life. After a complete circuit of the grounds he was forced to the realization that all their servants had been murdered. Anger surged within him and had he not been sure of their destruction the next day, he would have slain many of the killers in those dark hours.

Dawn was only an hour away when he finally reached the edge of the Great Forest. He wanted to hear more of Sechiall's plans. He would do as he intended last night and beat them to the spring. There, he might hear more. It was the first good rest on the way to the clearing and the soldiers would probably be in need of rest and water after their debauch that night. He waited a little longer to see if he could glean any more conversation from the pickets, but by this time of night they only grunted or nodded to each other as they walked their beats.

Finally, just at first light, Shem melted back into the woods away from the path, and looped around to the spring. Silently, he came into the clearing opposite the path, and crawled into the thick ferns that grew in profusion at the west end of the spring. Even then his instincts did not leave him; he carefully pushed each stalk aside to avoid leaving any sign of his passage, and lay down in the thickest part of the patch. The ferns closed around him, and he lay controlling his breathing. His anger had dissipated, replaced by a great sorrow. As his body relaxed, weariness settled over him. He had to force himself to stay awake. Sechiall would be making for the ark, but Shem knew little of military tactics and wanted to learn more.

As he lay, Shem could not help but remember the moonlit statues of the dead scattered around the grounds of a place they all thought a refuge. Thinking of the dead brought an icy touch of fear. Their faint voices seemed to speak warning to him. Death would be inevitable if he was caught. Sechiall would not hesitate. Almost he began to slide back to the shelter of the trees. No man in the army could catch him in the woods. His thoughts turned again to Jared and he stayed. There had been too many murders already. He must do whatever he could to stop more and that meant gaining information.

Then another thought struck him like a blow. He had first intended to stay with the servants and lead them to the ark. Only a premonition spurring his return to Madrazi had taken him from the house! Had he stayed... he shivered in wonder. He owed his life to her. He thanked God again for Madrazi and the changes that were beginning to occur. His woman was finally becoming a wife. She had not yet come into the light, but his confidence in Methuselah's wisdom was being vindicated: she would come in time, and then their hearts could be truly one.

What a strange week it had been—the world was awaiting its destruction, but he and Madrazi were beginning to build a lasting and beautiful marriage. For years he had persevered in hope and faith, but with little else. He had always fought a tendency toward pride for his patience; but in that moment of insight his pride was permanently shattered with the realization that only the power of his wife's love drawing him back to the ark had saved his life. Methuselah had always told him that God's ways were unfathomable to men. Now he had seen it. It was something to ponder while he waited.

He had to remain still for two long hours, but the ways of the forest had taught him patience and the need to be still for long periods. Finally he heard the noise of the advancing column and a few minutes later saw the warriors wind into the clearing. From his vantage, Shem could see their faces, and saw with despair that the men were those of Sechiall's own guard; the sweepings of the army, vicious killers governed by fear and greed. For a moment, he wished for his bow, but this was not a time for killing—he must listen and learn.

Shem watched them file into the clearing. Then his attention was drawn to the hooded figure following Sechiall. The figure sat with obvious weariness and pulled back the hood. Shem almost leaped to his feet when he saw the face of Jeriah. He forced himself to stay still, but his anger surged against his patience. Her appearance and manner told him clearly enough what she had undergone at Sechiall's hand. Once again he wished for his bow and one arrow. Sechiall was close and his throat exposed. But caution learned over many years kept him still and silent.

Jeriah sagged limply to the ground and Sechiall raised his hand. "Fifteen minutes," he shouted, and the column dispersed around the clearing. Sechiall dragged Jeriah over to the spring. "Drink, woman," he commanded. "Enjoy the water. I want none," he said to a man who offered him a cup, "I am saving my thirst for the blood of Noah and his sons. You men can enjoy the women."

Jeriah was tired, but still had some spirit. "Are you not sated on the blood you spilled, yesterday? Was not that of the women and children especially filling? And what of the ark? Madrazi has told me that it is large and strong. What if they retreat behind its walls?"

Sechiall could not rest. He was striding back and forth in front of her. At her words he turned on her with fury. "We burned his settlement yesterday and slew everyone there."

Shem bowed his head. His worst fears were confirmed. He and his family would be alone on the ark—if they survived. Sechiall's goal was clear and he must warn his family quickly.

Sechiall continued, "Although Noah and his family escaped my wrath, they have only postponed their judgment at my hands by one day. If they scamper into their ark, then it will become their pyre! I will put the torch to everything that I find there. By this time tomorrow I swear on my own head that nothing will remain of Noah but ashes! We will see whether his god is more powerful than mine."

He turned and eyes flashing, he shouted, "Who among you is satisfied? Who wants more blood? Who wants Sechiall as the King of Lamech? Who wants to join me as I conquer all the lands about us?"

The men as one jumped to their feet, shouting, "King Sechiall, King Sechiall," as they clashed spears against shields and stamped their feet on the ground in a frenzy.

He waved his arms to the men and the volume of their roar matched the motion of his arms up and down. There was no will in that clearing except that of Sechiall and Shem was awed by the sight of his naked power over the hearts of his men. He hung his head. How could they hold off more than four score of bloodthirsty warriors led by such as Sechiall? His heart faltered.

Then amid the din, the quiet of his own mind brought him the voice of Methuselah from long years ago by that very spring. *Who is like unto our God, young Shem? It was He who spread the heavens by His word and set boundaries for the sea. He raised the mountains with his hand and calls each living thing by name. What can He not do for those who love Him with all their heart and strength?* His anxiety pacified, Shem watched the back of the column start up the path. While he waited for them to move down the trail, he gathered his thoughts. If he ran straight through the forest, he could arrive at the ark maybe an hour before Sechiall's men—at least an hour if they stopped again.

He leapt to his feet and prayed as he ran, "Oh God, you who knows us each by name, strengthen my feet and slow my enemies." With that, he gave himself to the race; his heart beat strongly and hot blood carried new strength through his body. Without thought, eyes and feet cooperated to carry him swiftly and silently among the trees. He saw the path ahead in his mind and thanked his curiosity and love of the forest for that knowledge. Ham or Japheth could not have covered the distance in near the time he could; they had never bothered to learn the forest ways. Like an arrow released by a strong man, he flew straight for his goal, leaping small streams, running up and down hills with the surefooted speed of a deer. His body felt strong in the strength of his youth, and he knew that he would easily outdistance the soldiers. But to what end?

Chapter 40

JERIAH'S CHOICE

Noah walked carefully in front of Madrazi with a clay jar in each arm. Without looking back, he warned her of broken ground by the ramp. The one jar that she carried was not heavy, but its shape obscured her vision and she thanked him for the courtesy.

"Carefully," he said turning around, "set it down here beside mine. The scrolls inside contain the work of three generations, and will preserve much of our wisdom in the coming years."

Madrazi tried to lighten the mood by saying, "So it was the jar you were worried about, not your daughter." Noah smiled at her effort, but words could not dispel the tension they both felt.

Some of the jars were already stored in the ark, but there were still many to go aboard. Madrazi set hers down beside the others and turned to go back for another. Once they had them all at the ramp, they would carry them into the cavernous main deck. As they turned back for the remaining few, Shem burst from the forest, not on the path, but from the corner of the clearing. He was running at full speed, gliding across the ground like a frightened stag. Noah and Madrazi stopped to stare. His eyes were fire and his body tense even after he stopped.

"Father, gather everyone at once!" he panted as he stopped, bending over to rest his hands upon his thighs. Madrazi went to him and placed her arm around his hot shoulder.

"What is it, my son?"

In spite of his obvious distress, Shem regained control and spoke as clearly as his labored breathing allowed. "Sechiall is on the way here with many men. They have destroyed the farm and killed all of our people. We are the only ones left! He will do the same to us and I heard him speak of burning the ark. We have little time."

Noah immediately took charge. "Madrazi, go now and gather up everyone into the ark. Tell them to stop whatever they are doing and get aboard without delay." She had never heard that tone of voice before from him. It reminded her of Pomorolac during some crisis at sea and she reacted instinctively to the well-remembered tone of command.

Running back past the ark to the storage barns, she met Ham and Japheth, who were attempting to finish dismantling a grain press. They wanted to try to bring it aboard for use in the new world. They insisted that it was important, though Madrazi thought that they were simply trying to pass the time.

Stopping and gathering her breath, she blurted out, "Where are the women? We must go into the ark immediately. Soldiers are coming to kill us. Noah wants everyone on board!"

Japheth responded calmly, settling Madrazi somewhat. "All three women are already there. Go, Madrazi, and join them. We will tell father." Even in the face of disaster, Japheth had not lost his head or his ready smile. Encouraged, she nodded and walked back along the dark mass of the ark and up the great ramp onto the main deck. Wen-Tehrom, Debseda, and Yaran were all there just inside the door.

"Child," asked Wen-Tehrom. "What is wrong?"

"Men are coming against us, Mother," Madrazi replied and paused for a moment. They looked at each other in surprise for Madrazi had never used that term before, and Wen-Tehrom knew of her feelings for her dead mother. She laid her hand warmly on Madrazi's arm in understanding. "God will protect us, daughter. He would not let us come to this point only to be slain by evil men."

"Noah wants us all in the ark," Madrazi continued. She turned and looked out of the great door. Noah and his three sons were talking, standing in the clearing. Noah looked back and she waved to him from the door, indicating that all the women were in the ark. He waved back in acknowledgement.

As she stood leaning on the frame of the giant door, Madrazi watched Shem point back up the hill and then gesture towards the ark. She was suddenly filled with pride for her husband, and realized that she had underestimated him again. It was not hard to imagine what he must have done to obtain the information, but he had returned swiftly and without fear. His demeanor reminded her of the confident determination she had seen on his face the day before he set out to kill the giant lizard when it threatened his men. He had never set himself forth as a man of great deeds, and thus few recognized that he was.

But in the last day he had twice run a half-day's journey. He had come upon a strong force unawares. He had hidden himself, gathered needed information, and returned in time to warn his family. He had the strength and determination of Lamech, yet a quiet way that hid it well. With his strength was a gentleness and compassion that she remembered from the day she learned of her father's drowning. Her strength and love were as shallow as his were deep.

She was grateful to belong to such a man, and even more thankful that she had glimpsed his hidden depths, even if death were just minutes away.

"Father," Ham was saying, "death is upon us. We must prepare to fight or flee into the forest. We know its ways and Sechiall does not. Let us go to the mountains and hide."

"My sons," Noah said, looking at each in turn, "we trusted God when He warned me of the destruction to come and instructed me to build and fill this ark. It is built. We trusted God for wisdom to overcome all the problems that arose. He has not brought us to this point to see everything fail under the hands of evil men! Put your trust in God and do not fear Sechiall. We will obey the word of the Creator and go into the ark. That is my command."

Without another word, he turned his back to the forest and walked resolutely to the ramp. Shem and Japheth nodded to each other and followed Noah. Ham hesitated, but then ran to catch up with his brothers.

"We must at least raise the ramp and secure it on the deck," Ham said, when he had reached the top. "It is well that we devised the means for doing so from inside."

The brothers motioned the women back. Ham unfastened the pegs locking the ramp into its extended position. Then all four men slid stout poles into the holes of a windlass on the far side of the deck, opposite the door. Ropes tightened against the multiple sets of pulleys and the ramp slowly slid upward into the ark. Madrazi watched the ropes carefully, but they took the strain easily. The ramp continued up into the ark. As the top edge came close the underside of the upper deck, the angle began to change and the men slowed their turning and Ham set a brake on the windlass. Letting it up one notch at a time, he maintained control over the great weight. Gradually the ramp settled, pivoting on the edge of the doorway and coming to rest onto the floor as it continued moving inboard.

Before long, the ramp lay on the floor of the deck completely clear of the doorway. Ham locked fastening pegs around its edges, securing it firmly to the deck, while Shem and Japheth disconnected the ropes and stowed them in their bin behind the windlass. Then they joined Noah and the women at the doorway, looking out across the world that they would soon leave behind forever.

Madrazi was as curious as the others. She stepped onto the ramp just behind Noah and peered out the door to the top of the hill. She let out an involuntary cry, for she could see the glint of bronze among the thin trees at the hill's peak. The sun was strange, though high in the sky, it was blood red and the day was darkening as though evening was coming. There were other flashes of light in the heavens, and some extended into lines of fire moving toward the earth. The reflected sunlight from the helmets of the warriors under the twilight of the trees was like a line of torches coming down the path. Beyond the edge of the hill the sky was turning dark, like a veil of evil following the line of their march.

As they watched them come, Shem pulled her aside. "My wife, I have bad news for you. Jeriah is with them. She accompanies Sechiall under duress. I fear the worst." Madrazi felt the blood leave her face as tears welled in her eyes.

Shem put both of his arms around her and looked at her, wincing at the anguish in her face. The he loosed his embrace and brushed away her tears with a gentle hand and spoke. "If she is willing, she can still come with us on the ark. Her destruction is sure, whether at the hand of Sechiall or the hand of God, if she does not."

Hope leapt in her eyes as Madrazi embraced him tightly. "Thank you, Shem. Great-grandfather was right about you. I am sorry that I have not been what he expected of me."

Shem started to speak, but was interrupted by Ham's shout. "Here they come!"

They turned back to the door and saw Sechiall emerge from the dark wall of the forest. His height and long yellow hair stood out from the dark group following. He was giving orders to his men that were inaudible from the ark, but they soon became clear as more than half ran to surround the ark in a loose circle, while others kindled torches and advanced upon the buildings. Sechiall and the remaining band advanced to the line in the dirt that had marked the base of the ramp. Noah's jars of scrolls stood there, deserted in the dust. Sechiall contemptuously kicked one out of his way.

"Hail old man, last of my enemies!" he called in a derisive voice. "Methuselah has finally gone into a well-deserved oblivion, I personally sent Lamech to precede him, and now it is time for you and your sons. When you have all mingled your blood with the ashes of this oversize coffin, I will return in triumph to Lamech to be crowned king. You thwarted Jared for years—but he was too weak to take the necessary steps to achieve his end. I am not so limited. I am Nephilim. I am a god!"

Sechiall's eyes blazed and his body shook with raw passion. Like a great snake, he appeared to be drawing that passion into a tight coil so that he could release the venom of his hate in one fell stroke. He exuded a physical presence that was unmistakable even across the distance between them. His eyes flashed blue fire. Madrazi quailed before it, sure in a moment of weakness that he was right and they were on the verge of destruction. How could anyone stand before his wrath? No man could face him.

But at Shem's touch on her shoulder, Madrazi dragged her eyes away from Sechiall and saw that Noah was no shivering prey awaiting his inevitable destruction. He stood tall and strong, facing his enemy, like a seaside cliff, battered by many storms, but still standing high and proud. Noah could not have faced Sechiall with a sword, but she could see that the battle between them was not one of swords or spears. She could sense the air between them crackling with an energy that was not of the world. While Sechiall burned with a bright fire, she fancied that Noah glowed with the golden light that a thousand Sechiall's could never withstand. She had seen it unmasked as the animals had followed him into the ark; now it stood forth as a shield, turning Sechiall's malevolence away from all inside the door.

In a voice of contrasting calm, but that still echoed across the clearing, Noah broke the strained silence and replied. "We have learned of your foul murder of Lamech, although we had not the proof to bring you before the council. We have learned of your murder of Jared, and many more. Your nature has also been clear to me for some time—you are of your father, the Serpent, and like him you are a liar and a murderer by nature. But God has promised to bruise the head of your line, and you are too late to work your evil in this place."

"Behold!" He raised his right hand and pointed to the sky behind the soldiers. "The day of destruction is at hand, but it is not your design, but the doom of everyone outside this ark. For long years I prophesied truly in God's name of this day, and none chose to believe me. Only these of my own family have been destined to enter this vessel of salvation with me. You call it a coffin, yet I tell you that all outside of this ark that possess the breath of life will be buried beneath the waters that bear it up! Your strength and savagery are useless against the Judge of all the Earth. Look!" he said pointing again behind Sechiall to the horizon, "The hour is at hand!"

No one present could resist the power of Noah's voice and even Sechiall turned to see. The darkness that had been imagined as much as seen had now gathered itself and had obscured large parts of the sky. The sun was as red as blood and there was a sudden chill in the air. As Noah pointed, another bright line of light was seen in the sky, pointing like a divine arrow at the earth. As all looked in amazement, the ground shook, and many of Sechiall's men were thrown to their knees by the violence of the tremor. Even cushioned by the vast bulk of the ark, Madrazi stumbled and was only kept from falling from the doorway by the strong arm of Shem. Clinging to him, she wrenched her gaze away from the angry sky and searched for Jeriah.

As the tremor ended, there was an eerie moment of almost complete silence, as though the earth was holding its breath. Madrazi seized the opportunity to call to her friend. "Jeriah, Jeriah," her voice sounding small in the oppressive air. "Come and join us now. Escape the doom upon you. Remember my dream!"

Jeriah's spirit had been all but crushed by the cruel rampage the previous day. Sechiall had virtually completed that task with his admission to Jared's murder. There had been little sleep the night before and what little there was had brought the terror of her nightmare. Then her tired body was forced to march a half-day's walk through the forest only to stand before the dark symbol of death. Sechiall had dragged her with him, but she did not care. Once her feet stopped moving, she simply let herself slip into a numb apathy, seemingly unaware of her surroundings. But Madrazi's weak call penetrated her consciousness and as if waking, she slowly turned her eyes to her friend. She stumbled up from the ground to her knees and Madrazi could see a spark of hope in her face, as she stretched out a hand toward the ark.

Japheth had been next to Madrazi and saw what was happening. He sprang back into the ark and seized a rope. He returned and touched her on the arm to let her know he was ready. She smiled thankfully, but kept her eye full on the face of Jeriah. She started to get up, but then paused and looked back at Sechiall.

Madrazi remained convinced for the rest of her days that if Jeriah had kept her eyes on the ark, she would have come. But Sechiall's power could not be denied. He was erect and turned from his anger at Noah to her in contempt. Even from where Madrazi stood, she could feel the intensity of his gaze and power. "Get up and go to these doomed fools," he mocked. "Make your choice. Die now with them, or live on with me. Who knows," he laughed, "I might even marry you in time. They are weak, but I am strong. You have chosen wisely so far. This is your last test."

Madrazi saw her waver under the proximity of his raw personality. "Jeriah," she called again, trying unsuccessfully to project the calm power of Noah that she did not have. "I know that I did not believe before, but it's true. Please come with us. Sechiall lies—if you don't come with me, you will die today. Please come to me, my sister."

Jeriah heard. Rising, she staggered one step forward. But Sechiall turned on her. Seizing her shoulders, he forced his gaze upon her. He said nothing, but held her eyes as time seemed to stand still. Then he contemptuously let her go. She turned to Madrazi again, but with a look of regret, the hope gone from her dull eyes. "I'm sorry for you, Madrazi," she said, "but I must stay. My place is now with him."

Whatever else she might have said was interrupted by another tremor. Beyond the trees, black smoke mixed with brown dust in the churning winds, blotting out the horizon. Smaller lines of light flashed through the sky toward the earth. Sechiall's warriors shouted with anger and alarm as they staggered at the shuddering of the ground, grotesquely waving their spears to maintain their balance. Sechiall, struggling against the tremors, fell to one knee.

His face contorted with rage, he swiftly regained his feet. Eyes blazing, he put forth all his strength and hurled his spear at Noah. It sliced through the air towards the older man, but guided by a sudden gust of air, it wavered and stuck quivering in the doorframe of the ark beside him. Noah had not moved or flinched; Madrazi wondered if he even saw Sechiall any longer. If he did, he was ignoring him, standing firm and upright, his eyes fixed on the sky.

Sechiall shook his fist and began to curse, but was struck suddenly silent with alarm and fear as the giant door creaked loudly and began to slowly swing to without any visible sign of motive force. All the warriors stood still and stared and some cried out in fear and amazement. The chaos outside the door swirled in Madrazi's vision but there seemed to be a tunnel of calm between her and Jeriah. They stood for a short time, oblivious to everything around and their eyes locked.

The door was not yet shut. It had caught the end of Sechiall's spear and stopped. There was still time. Madrazi heard herself scream as she desperately waved Jeriah toward the dark safety of the ark. Jeriah started forward, but then looked at her friend with regret shook her head, and turned back to Sechiall. The she turned one last time, with resignation in her face, and looked back at Madrazi, mouthing the word, "farewell."

Smoke and darkness seemed to fill Jeriah's eyes. All around her was dim. She could not turn away from her friend. She swung around again and saw the golden light from her vision emanating from inside the ark. But the door continued to press closed and shattered Sechiall's spear. Now it was almost shut, and all was dark outside. Looking up, her eyes held Madrazi's for the last time, until the door swung shut, merging with the black side of the ark and sealing the light inside.

As the door boomed against the beams of the ark, Madrazi's vision failed, her eyes blurred with tears, and for a few moments she was even unaware of Shem's arms around her.

Jeriah turned away for the last time and Sechiall grabbed her arm and shook her. "Come," he said. "The gods are fighting for Noah today. They have escaped into their ark, but I will burn it and let its ashes lie here for all time.

Gathering his men, Sechiall ordered them to bring wood.

"Oh great king," cried one, "Let us return to Lamech! We can destroy them another day!"

Sechiall turned on the men crowding around, searching for the author of those words. "Are you not men?" he snarled, "Are you not my men? Obey me, now!"

Cowed, most turned and began to search for wood. But even as they did, a new tremor struck, and knocked Jeriah off her feet once more. As she struggled to rise, a drop of water struck her cheek; then another; then several more. Soon drops of water could be seen falling from the sky all around the clearing.

At this manifestation of divine displeasure, the men turned and fled back up the road. One called to another, "Water from the sky! Impossible! What have we brought on ourselves?"

His comrade replied, "Noah called on the earth to shake, and it shook! Now he calls water from the sky making fire impossible. Let us flee while there is yet time!"

Sechiall continued to shout incoherently, spittle running into his beard. His eyes were aflame, but his power had been broken and none listened. Seizing Jeriah, he pulled her to her feet and started after the men. "Perhaps the gods are against us today," he said, "but we will return to Lamech and sacrifice until the earth is stilled and then we will return."

Jeriah heard his words at a distance. The ground continued to shake. As in a dream she staggered blindly behind the men up the road to Lamech. As she mounted the hill, she felt as though she was slowly waking from a nightmare: she realized that Sechiall's power over her was no more. That of Noah's God was greater. She felt a return of thought and will. Shaking herself free of the black nightmare, she began to take notice of her surroundings. The water was falling more heavily now and as she reached the crest of the hill, a gust of wind carried a sheet of rain into her face, battering her back. Then the wind subsided, the water relented somewhat and sight returned. Black smoke rose to the north and east. A red tinge was on every horizon.

Jeriah felt a strange lassitude descend upon her. She quit following Sechiall and turned back to look into the clearing. More water was beginning to fall from the sky, slowly at first, but increasing. Through the mist of water, the ark stood, black and indomitable in the forest hollow below. "You were right, Madrazi," she breathed to herself. "The vision was true. You will live and I refused the light. Take at least my memory into the new world."

As she stood there, she heard Sechiall shouting, but she no longer paid any attention. Sechiall's strength and hatred had proved of little consequence against Noah's confidence in the Creator. She sat down in the mud at the crest of the hill, heedless of the water sluicing down from the sky, drawing a curtain across her view of the dark, impenetrable walls of the ark. Against that backdrop she saw again the face of Madrazi vanishing into the failing light. "I am here and you are safe from the coming destruction," she mused. "Why? We were closer than sisters. What choice did you make that I missed? Perhaps you made your choice long ago, before I even knew you. Perhaps I did, too."

The waters increased in force as they poured down upon the earth, and the gusting wind tore through the falling curtain. Still sitting in the mud of the road, she heard a rumble far away from the sea, heralding the overthrow of Lamech, and much more. Standing and looking back across the trees and the plain of Lamech, Jeriah could see only blackness swallowing the horizon. For a moment she fancied that she saw Lamech gleaming white against the consuming blackness. But water was coming down harder from the sky now, and the line between sea and sky blurred and merged.

She turned back and watched the rain beat against the ark. Her memory returned to the day when she held Madrazi in her arms and saw in her eyes and words the hideous nightmare that had haunted her life. Madrazi's fear had touched her sympathy, but it was an emotional response to a friend in need, without understanding. But then the nightmare had invaded her own mind, giving her deeper insight and empathy; she had truly learned why Madrazi had been shaking in her arms. But emotion and empathy had not plumbed the depths of truth. The water and wind in her face, the shaking of the ground, the dull red darkness of the daytime sky; these were no vision—there would be no waking from this. She had refused the heaven-sent warning to turn to Noah the night after Jared's death. Shivering now, she recalled with shame her laughter at the idea of seeking shelter with the "prophet." Why had she not listened to that inner voice? And then she had taken into her bed the murderer of her husband. Why had she not chosen death and defiance and joined Jared? Sechiall's way had led to destruction and defilement. Why had she not heeded Madrazi's call at the end? Why had she chosen to give her soul to evil, instead?

Jeriah looked around again. The water was coming down harder and she could hardly see the ark. The earth convulsed and shook again, throwing her to the ground. Mud plastered her hair and face. She turned upward to let the rain wash her clean. A sullen roar rolled across the plain from Lamech, audible over the beating rain. The sea had been gathered into the heavens and would crush all beneath it. The only sure shelter, the ark, was sealed against penitence, regret, or desperation.

As the drops of water stung her face, she rose and began to walk, no longer sure of her direction in the gathering gloom and falling water. No longer caring, she just continued to wander letting her feet take her where they would. What did it matter? She was here by her own choice; her surrender to Sechiall when Madrazi had called for her to come into the ark had sealed her destruction. Why should she not be destroyed? She had taken the murderer of her husband into her bed because she valued her life, comfort, and affluence. The thought of Jared brought new agony. She had been warned in so many ways so many times. But each time a way of escape had presented itself, she had turned away. Her decisions were her doom and that thought consumed her mind as she staggered alone toward the advancing sea.

****

The young woman stirred and opened her eyes. Her neck was stiff, but it would loosen easily enough with activity. She felt refreshed; not in many days had she slept that soundly or that long. Her eyes automatically moved to the old woman. For a moment, she caught her breath at the stiff, frozen features before her, but then she saw the shallow breathing and knew that another day of life remained. She would continue here and perform her duty to the old woman to the end of that fragile life; then she would complete it by returning south. She had been driven out because of her questions; she would return with the answers they feared in the scrolls. What fire would that ignite?

She wondered anew what the old one saw in the dying embers of the fire. But catching the line of tears in the early morning light, she decided again that she did not desire the pain of that knowledge.

Want to keep reading about
Lost Worlds?

Look for the continuing story in:

Book II
Mabbul
&
Book III
Mystery of
Lawlessness

Coming soon from

Word Ministries'

About Word Ministries

Word Ministries, Inc. is a non-profit charitable organization that exists to teach others about the Gospel of Jesus Christ and to present His will for their lives as revealed by the Holy Scriptures. It is governed by a board of directors, and sends emissaries supported by local churches or presbyteries. Word currently includes the outreach, speaking, and writing ministry of Dr. Gordon K. Reed, and the research, writing, and speaking ministry of Dr. John K. Reed. Mabbul Publishing produces books for Word Ministries. For additional information, please contact:

WORD MINISTRIES
P.O. Box 2717
Evans, GA 30809
<www.wordmin.org>

Other Books from Word Ministries

Books by Dr. Gordon K. Reed
Plain Talk about Christian Doctrine
A pastor's perspective on the Westminster Shorter Catechism, with the systematic teaching of that great document interwoven with practical lessons from decades of Christian ministry.

Living Life by God's Law
Dr. Reed explains how the unchanging wisdom of God's Ten Commandments can enrich the life of the most modern Christian.

The Ministry: Career or Calling?
Is Christian ministry just another white-collar profession, or is it a unique calling from God? This modern parable illustrates the modern errors of the "professional" approach.

Christmas: Triumph over Tragedy
Developed from a series of Christmas sermons, this short book takes an in-depth look at the central characters of the incarnation, showing modern believers how they, too, can become a part of God's great kingdom.

Books by Dr. John K. Reed
Crucial Questions about Creation
Laymen interested in origins issues will find a refreshing theological examination of creation, with an emphasis on seeing that *why* God created bounds scientific issues addressing evolution and the age of the earth.

Plain Talk about Genesis
Using the Presbyterian Church in America as an example, Dr. Reed explains for Christian laymen the origins debate and what is at stake in those discussions.

Natural History in the Christian Worldview
Interpretations about natural history rest on worldviews. Any Christian thinker can discern truth from falsehood in this area by comparing those worldviews (Published by the Creation Research Society).

Plate Tectonics: A Different View (editor)
Technical critique of the dominant paradigm of modern geology from a biblical perspective (Published by the Creation Research Society).

The North American Midcontinent Rift System: An Interpretation within the Biblical Worldview
Technical description and interpretation of one of the largest geological features in North America (Published by the Creation Research Society).